Jennifer Blake is a *New York Times* bestselling author who writes contemporary as well as historical novels. She draws upon her experience of the American Deep South where she was born and raised. Jennifer Blake and her husband live in Louisiana in a house styled after an old Southern planter's cottage.

Also by **JENNIFER BLAKE**

The Masters at Arms series

DAWN ENCOUNTER
CHALLENGE TO HONOUR

The Louisiana Gentlemen series

KANE
LUKE
ROAN
CLAY
WADE

GARDEN OF SCANDAL

ROGUE'S SALUTE

Jennifer Blake

*First published in Great Britain 2007
by Harlequin Mills & Boon Limited,
Eton House, 18-24 Paradise Road, Richmond, Surrey TW9 1SR*

© Patricia Maxwell 2007

ISBN: 978 0 263 85536 4

37-0607

*Printed and bound in Spain
by Litografia Rosés S.A., Barcelona*

For Sandra Gourrier, with thanks for strolling with me through the streets of the French Quarter and helping search out great New Orleans food.

You always turn work into fun!

ACKNOWLEDGEMENTS

This book would have been much less colourful or complete without the resources available for writers at the Williams Research Centre, a division of the historic New Orleans Collection, on Chartres Street in the heart of the French Quarter. The meticulously kept records found there, including long-out-of-print histories, obscure journals and microfilm copies of Victorian-era newspapers such as *L'Abeille,* have been invaluable for *Rogue's Salute* in particular and the MASTERS AT ARMS series in general. Publications sponsored by the collection, particularly the architectural survey known as the Vieux Carré Survey, have added greatly to the authenticity of the backgrounds for the books. I'm immensely grateful to the Centre's staff for making access to this material both easy and pleasant.

Sincere appreciation also goes to Faulkner House Books, Pirate's Alley, New Orleans, for their prompt ordering and shipment of reprints of famous Louisiana histories and guidebooks. My private research collection is much richer for their aid.

1

New Orleans, Louisiana
January 1842

"Send a husband for me, I pray, most Holy Mother. Intercede in this matter, if it be thy will, for I have desperate need."

Juliette Armant gripped her fingers tightly together as she stared up at the benign carved face of the statue of Our Lady before her. The prayer bench's hand rail, polished by countless hands over endless years, felt cold under her wrists, and the chill of the knee rest penetrated her thick skirts of gray *cord du roi*. The emptiness of the cathedral echoed around her while the scents of ancient dust, incense and smoke from the prayer candles burning on their wrought-iron stand nearby wafted about her face. The fluttering of the flames on their wicks was loud in the stillness. She had knelt here a thousand times before, yet everything seemed strange this morning.

"I don't ask this boon for myself," she went on with a brief but decided shake of her head. "You know well that I never expected to marry. To be dedicated to the church at birth was my fate and I accepted it in all humility, truly I did. But now all is changed. I lack the beauty or skill at flirtation to attract a husband and there is no one to arrange a match for me. My mother has not the will—but you know her trials. I must wed without delay or all will be lost."

Was she doing the right thing? Juliette wondered. She had tried diligently to find another way out of her peculiar dilemma, but nothing that sprang to mind seemed likely to be of use. How had it come down to this when everything should have been so different?

"Oh, Holy Mother, make this husband you will send kind, if it pleases you, yet not too gentle of spirit. He must have strength and a will of steel for he will surely need them. Intelligence would be useful, and diplomacy as well. I don't ask that he be attractive, still it would not upset me if he were pleasant to look upon for the sake of our future children." She closed her eyes with a small moan and went on hurriedly, "No, no, forget I said that. You who know all things must surely understand what is required. Only send a man to me soon, I beg, as quickly as may be possible."

Juliette crossed herself, touched her fist to her

lips and heart in quick succession, then pushed to her feet. She could not linger here in the sacred quiet. They would miss her at home, and she had no desire to explain where she had been or why she had left the house without even a maid as chaperone. She might perhaps fob off her mother and twin sister with some tale, but prevarication was not something that came easily after all her years with the nuns.

To leave the cathedral, she had to pass the bank of prayer candles glimmering on their stand near the heavy front doors. The draft of her passage seemed to make them flare up, for she caught a sudden light from the corner of her eye. As she turned her head in that direction, her gaze caught the bright flame from the taper she had set burning just before she knelt to pray. It sprang tall and strong on its wick, many times more brilliant than the rest. Dazzling in its intensity, it bloomed and danced before her like a stalwart golden star.

Juliette came to a halt with her breath trapped in her throat. She was not so superstitious as her mother, who had a thousand beliefs, prohibitions and proverbs that ruled her life—still she could not prevent the *frisson* that moved over her from the top of her head to the tips of her toes.

Was this an omen? Could it mean her prayer would be answered?

She closed her eyes tightly, crossing herself again. Then she moved on. As she quitted the church her steps were lighter and hope burned as bright in her heart as the candle set aflame for her prayer.

Pausing on the stone paving outside, Juliette took out the gloves from where she had tucked them away inside her sleeve before searching out a coin for her candle. She had almost forgotten them. How aghast her mother and Paulette would be if she were to be seen on the street with bare hands. Such things had not mattered only two weeks ago. At the convent it had been more important to have willing hands rather than perfectly kept ones. A wry smile touched Juliette's lips before she sighed and began to tug on the gloves of lavender kid borrowed from her sister.

The day promised to be fine. Already, the rays of the rising sun poked shining fingers through the river fog beyond the levee, and the air was soft, almost warm. The steam whistle from a departing river packet moaned, setting off the screaming of monkeys and squawking of parrots from the shop of the birdman down the street. A light breeze brought the odors of mud flats, fish, fermenting molasses and overripe bananas from the dock area, along with the stench of refuse in the gutter that centered the alley beside the cathedral. It also wafted the scent of roasting coffee from the market where vendors were opening their stalls, making ready for the morning shoppers who would soon amble forth with baskets on their arms in search of fresh bread, brioche and croissants. Juliette's stomach rumbled slightly at the thought, and she wished she dared purchase a few of the goods she could smell from the nearby bakery. That would not do, of course, since it would give away her early-morning outing.

Just then, a high-pitched shriek ripped through the morning air. Shrill, desperate, it came from no parrot or monkey, but from a living child somewhere behind her.

Juliette swung in a swirl of heavy skirts. She was just in time to see a young boy fling around the corner of the cathedral, running flat out. Hardly more than three years of age, he was slight of body, with a mop of black curls and black eyes blared wide with terror. His short legs churned, his arms pumped and his mouth was wide open as he wailed.

Booted feet thudded on the ballast stone pavement behind the child. A man burst into view then, racing after him. Of superior height and width of shoulder, his long legs covered the ground with great strides. His face was grim with determination as he gained on his quarry, stretching out a hand to snatch at the back of the boy's ragged, flapping shirt.

The child swerved, evading capture by a hairsbreadth. His new path took him straight toward Juliette. Dodging to one side, he caught a handful of her full skirts as he sped past, spinning her halfway around before taking refuge behind their crinoline-supported width.

The gentleman skidded to a halt then lunged to the left around Juliette as she struggled to face him. The boy jumped back the other way, jerking her nearly off her feet. His pursuer feinted to the opposite side. The boy dodged back again.

"Stop it! Cease this at once," Juliette cried, grasping her skirts to keep from being hauled around yet again. "Stop it, do you hear?"

It was the voice she used to quell young female pupils at the convent school. The effect was gratifying. The child stood still, his narrow chest heaving. The gentleman paused, then straightened to his full height. For an instant, the three of them were silent, sizing up each other with wary regard.

The boy's pursuer recovered first. Sweeping off his beaver hat, he executed a bow of consummate grace. "Your pardon, mademoiselle. I only require to lay hands on that imp of Satan behind you."

His voice—deep, rich and almost musical in its cadences—affected Juliette in the oddest way. She could almost feel it wrapping around her, invading her senses, vibrating deep inside her chest. A slow and disturbing heat bloomed in her midsection and spread throughout her body. It was a most peculiar sensation, one she had never before encountered. She stood quite still for a bemused instant, her gaze on the gentleman before her.

That he was masculine beauty personified was

without question. Lustrous black hair, rakishly disheveled from his pursuit of the runaway, covered his head in dense waves that dipped forward onto his brow in an errant curl. His eyes were richly black and edged with thick lashes, which curled at the tips. Dark eyebrows with satanic arches, straight Roman nose and mouth almost sinful in its full and perfect contours formed such a perfect collection of features that Juliette was strongly reminded of engravings she had seen of fallen angels done by Italian masters.

She should know him, she thought in distraction, though she was sure they had never been introduced in a formal way. She went about so little on her rare visits home from the convent, mainly to the entertainments given by the family or their friends, that her circle of acquaintance was small. Still some dim memory teased her.

The gentleman returned her gaze, his own darkly appraising as he allowed it to drift over her face, then flick downward over the curves of her shoulders and breasts under their dull covering. It was done so quickly that she might not have been aware of it if she had not been so intent upon him. Still, she felt it like a tingling caress, felt the peaks of her breasts tighten as if with chill, though she was sure the effect was merely the unusual nature of that regard. Most men of her acquaintance would have been well aware of how inappropriate such a thing was where she was concerned. Or that it had been until recent events, she reminded herself.

Noting, perhaps, the fresh wave of hot color across her cheekbones, the gentleman turned his attention back to the boy who still clung to her, taking a step toward him.

"*Non, mais, non,*" the little one cried out, dragging her from her reverie with his lisping protest. "I not go wit' you!"

"You will if you know what's good for you," the gentleman said grimly as he resettled his hat on his head.

"*Non, non, non!*"

"I'll give you a bonbon—"

"You gi' a baf'. I no want baf'!" The boy's voice rose to a hysterical edge.

The gentleman feinted to one side of Juliette, then plunged to the other with a lithe twist of his body. He grabbed for the boy's thin arm, and would surely have had him if he had not shrieked and plunged backward, falling on his small bottom.

"Monsieur," Juliette said with force as she stepped in front of the child, "it will be very much better if you try the effects of reason instead of frightening your son."

"What will be better is if you step aside." The gentleman barely glanced at her as he bent down, snatching at the boy's legs as he scooted backward.

"Don't let 'im get me, don't, don't, don't..."

moaned the small boy, scraping his skinny backside over the rough stones that fronted the cathedral, scuttling out of reach.

"Monsieur!' Juliette darted forward as the boy's cries and pitiful smallness wrung her heartstrings.

Features grim, the father ignored her, bending over, reaching for the struggling child. Juliette thrust out a hand to stop him. Her grasp closed forcefully on the rolled velvet collar of his tobacco-brown frock coat. There came a dull, ripping sound.

The gentleman froze in position for long seconds. Then he came upright with slow precision until he towered over her. A frown drew the slashes of his arched eyebrows together, giving him a look of demonic anger.

"Mademoiselle," he began in ominous tones.

Juliette released her grip while heat burned its way to her hairline. Her gaze on the torn fabric where the collar had been pulled away from the lapel, she spoke in stiff tones. "I am sorry for the mishap, but it is your own fault entirely. I cannot permit you to manhandle the boy. It's cruel and—"

"Cruel?" the man who faced her demanded in indignation. "You mistake the matter, I promise you. The brat is making a to-do over nothing and less than nothing. If you had any idea what he is capable of…"

There was more, but Juliette was no longer listening. Suddenly, the identity of this gentleman was distressingly clear. If she had been more worldly, had spent less time behind convent walls, she might have recognized him at once. News of his exploits had penetrated even those barriers, however, whispered by young girls who should know nothing of such things. He had been pointed out to her on the street by Paulette on one of her family visits during the winter season of the year before. Now her heart thudded against her ribs so hard she could barely draw breath into her lungs.

La Roche.

The man before her was the notorious sword master Nicholas Pasquale, called The Rock, *La Roche*, for his immovable fighting stance on the fencing strip and the stonelike tone of his body. He had never been touched on the dueling field, so it was said, seldom allowed a touch during the fencing lessons he imparted, was certainly never touched by the more tender emotions. The best swordsman in the city according to those who should know, he fought in the position sinister, or left-handed, which made him a formidable and rather bizarre foe. Young men aped his manners and sartorial perfection. Older men blanched at his name and tried to ingratiate themselves with him. It was whispered that he had killed a half-dozen men in affairs of honor, one the husband of a woman discovered half-dressed in the private rooms of his atelier. More than that, he had Lucifer's own luck, for he had just turned in the winning ticket for the state lottery, gaining a fortune worth an unheard-of sum.

He was the most dangerous and the most feared man in all of New Orleans, one known for his dedication to and taste in matters of dress. And she, Juliette Armant, had not only laid hands on him, but torn his coat.

The small boy, perhaps sensing an ally, scuttled behind Juliette once more. La Roche bent down again as if to seize him. Quick as a kitchen mouse, the child snatched up a handful of Juliette's ash gray *cord du roi* skirts and their petticoats and dived underneath. The heavy layers of fabric settled over him, covering him so completely that he vanished beneath their copious folds.

For an instant, Juliette stood in paralyzed chagrin. She could not breathe, could not speak. Dismay and admiration for the boy's daring, fear and wariness jarred each other inside her while she stared into the coffee-black eyes of Nicholas Pasquale.

The sword master whispered an imprecation, then flung away a few steps to stand with his back to her. He raked a hand through his hair, clasped the back of his neck while his chest swelled with the deep breaths that he drew in and out of his lungs. It was clear that he was attempting to control his temper. Juliette thought it best not to interfere with the process.

As she stared at the sword master's broad shoulders that tapered to the waist of his frock coat, she was aware of the child squirming closer against her legs. She could feel the warmth of his small body with its lightweight, bony angles as he leaned against her ankles and shins. Her heart melted, flooding her with an odd yet fierce urge to protect him at all costs. Yes, and against all enemies, no matter how dangerous.

Compressing her lips, she drew a fortifying breath through her nose. "Monsieur," she began in as firm a tone as she could manage, "I suggest—"

"You suggest what, mademoiselle?" Nicholas Pasquale demanded, cutting across her words as he turned on her. "You had no right to interfere. Now look where it has landed us. The only saving grace I see is that we haven't collected an audience. At least, not yet."

It was true enough, Juliette saw as she glanced around the cathedral entranceway and the Place d'Armes that lay before it. The few people out and about paid them no heed. Such circumstances could not last, and she frowned a little as she considered it.

Seeing her hesitation, the sword master pressed his advantage. "If you are to be rid of…of your intruder without embarrassment, then it should be at once, don't you think?"

She gave him a cool look. "I don't know that I wish to be rid of him."

"Come, mademoiselle, be reasonable. I mean no harm to the boy beyond ridding him of his dirt and assorted vermin. All you need do is turn your back and bring him out. I'll take it from there."

"I'm sure you think—"

She stopped abruptly in midsentence. Her lips parted as she drew a sharp breath of surprise.

"Mademoiselle?"

The boy under Juliette's shirts had put a hand on the back of her knee. That would have mattered little, except that he seemed to be testing the silk of her stocking, sliding his hand downward over her calf to her ankle in slow, tactile exploration.

Juliette closed her mouth with a snap. Patting her skirt, locating the boy's head beneath them, she gave him a quick tap. "Unhand me, *mon petit*," she commanded. "Stop that at once."

Nicholas Pasquale's black gaze narrowed a little as he took in her predicament. Then a slow smile of devastating attraction curved his lips. In deep tones that were rich with suggestion, he said, "You have a problem, mademoiselle?"

She refused to answer. The young miscreant had cupped a hand on either side of her lower leg and was brushing up and down as if fascinated by the silken glide of the fabric.

"His name, in case of need, is Gabriel." Pasquale crossed his arms over his chest as he surveyed her.

"Thank you," she said stiffly. "I somehow doubt

that I can extract him, as you said, without a struggle. Perhaps you—"

"Oh, I don't know. It might be cruel to interrupt his play. Poor, mistreated mite that he is, he has scant opportunity for pleasure. I'm sure you can find nothing to fault in whatever he may be doing under there."

Juliette's face burned and she turned her head so the side of her bonnet would conceal it from him. "He is only a child, so naturally curious. I attach no importance to it, I assure you. Still you must see that it's awkward to have him—"

"To have him exploring under your skirts where no male has dared venture, or so I would guess. I could almost envy him." The sword master's smile had a molten edge.

"His invasion is entirely innocent!"

"As mine most certainly would not be, or so you mean to imply, and yet you invited me to venture there."

"I did nothing of the kind!"

"You were about to suggest I reach under and remove our Gabriel, I think. Tell me that wasn't in your mind before you thought better of the idea."

"I can do no such thing—what I mean to say is…" She shifted a step, her skirts swaying as she attempted to discourage the boy's assiduous attention. He only moved with her, shuffling on his knees so his head bobbed along under her skirts in a most embarrassing manner.

"I know exactly what you mean," Pasquale said with spurious sympathy, making a clicking sound with his tongue before he went on. "*Mon Dieu.* Such a Casanova as the imp is turning out to be, and at his age, too."

"I'm sure he came by the skill quite naturally," she snapped.

Laughter flared in the sword master's eyes. "Skill? Ah, yes. Like father, like son, you mean to say. I should be gratified by the compliment, though I should tell you that his touch cannot be…quite… like that of his model."

The heated promise behind the amusement in his black, black eyes took Juliette's breath. Suddenly, her whalebone stays felt too constricting around her ribs and the prim neckline of her day gown much too close around her throat. Her gaze was drawn to his hands, with their long, graceful fingers. It seemed she could almost feel them, strong and sure, playing around her garters as young Gabriel was doing now. Fiery heaviness invaded her lower body and she swayed a little where she stood.

"What a pity," the swordsman added softly, "that we can never know for sure."

He was engaging in flirtation with her, this sword master, the most notorious in New Orleans, Juliette thought in dazed wonder. She had watched as her twin countered extravagant praise and delicately suggestive innuendo from her suitors at soirees or the opera, but never practiced the art herself, particularly with such an opponent. How very heady it was. Yes, and how disturbing, for she was aware the gentleman's comments should not be quite so personal. She was also fairly certain that he meant not a single word of them.

In a supreme effort to gain control of her senses, she forced herself to look away. "Enough, monsieur. I feel sure that Gabriel will obey you if you speak to him firmly and without threat."

"Do you indeed?"

"Why should he not? He must be used to it."

"By no means. He is the devil's own spawn, if you must know. He bites and scratches like a feral cat and bends to no will other than his own."

"Good heavens, has he no mother to teach him trust and obedience?"

"She has not been seen for at least a month, and maybe longer."

His voice carried minimal concern and less responsibility. A love child then. She could not be surprised since she had heard no mention of a permanent female, much less a wife, in the life of La Roche. Poor little Gabriel.

"It's good of you to take charge of the boy, I suppose, but you obviously have not been bringing him up properly."

Nicholas Pasquale gave her an arrogant look. "And what concern might it be of yours?"

"None except normal compassion."

"Yet you would interfere."

"It's the duty of anyone who sees a child being mistreated," she said with a lift of her chin.

"I am not," he said with hard emphasis, "mistreating the little bugger."

"From what I can see, you aren't endearing yourself to him, either."

"But you would?"

"Any woman might," she answered in exasperation. "It's clear to me that what your son needs is a mother."

"A mother."

"Precisely."

He stared at her a long instant, then a grim smile tilted the corners of his mouth. "Marry me, then, and become his loving *maman*."

"Marry you! Why of all the…"

Juliette stopped short in the midst of her wrathful spate. She could not have spoken another word in that instant if her soul's salvation had depended on it.

Marry him.

He was standing there, staring at her with his hands on his hips as if waiting for an answer. But he could not mean it. Could he?

Marry him.

The words of her prayer came back to her as in a dream. Strong. Will of stone. Attractive…or, no, make that outrageously handsome with his shoulders and chest molded with muscle gained on the fencing strips and flashing eyes that spoke of bedroom delights. Intelligent, for he spoke well and understood without the need for tedious explanation or, indeed, any words at all.

Yes, but was he, could he ever be, kind?

She had prayed for a husband and one had appeared. The omen of the candle had been real. Here he was before her, the man sent in answer to her plea.

Marry him.

Was this really the man sent by Our Lady to be her husband? If so, then the most Holy Mother could not have been paying attention!

"You are a sword master," Juliette said a little desperately.

"Not for long. I expect to set up a household and become a decent citizen."

"For your son, I see," she said, doing her best to ignore the heavy sarcasm that colored his tone. "You don't really wish to be wed."

"I had not considered it until this moment, but the merit in the idea grows clearer with every second."

He smiled, and his face shifted into a pattern of such open charm, with radiating laugh lines at the corners of his eyes, that her heart jarred in her chest. "I don't know you, and you most assuredly don't know me."

"A problem time will remedy. It's also a situation often encountered in convenient alliances of this sort." He tilted his head. "You would really consider this as a proposed union?"

"I must, that is…"

"Must?"

His voice was even, his expression nothing more than mildly inquiring, much to Juliette's amazement. Most men would have not have taken the oblique suggestion that she might be with child in such good grace. "Not for the reason you may suppose. I am not…that is, nothing of a physical nature compels marriage for me. I am quite…quite…"

"Untouched, yes. It's gratifying to know my first impression was correct."

"*Mon Dieu*, will you not allow me to explain?" she cried in vexation.

"Are you sure you really wish it? I thought to save you the discomfort."

And so he had, she realized with a small sense of wonder. "Thank you, I'm sure. But what of you?"

"I promise you that I am not with child," he answered, his voice grave.

She closed her eyes, wondering if her face could flame any hotter. "I realize, not being a simpleton. What I mean to ask is if you truly wish to marry."

He gave a decided nod. "Mad, is it not? And yet I make decisions of greater moment every time I take the dueling field. Where is the difference between this and deciding on life or death for another human being? You were quite right, I do require a wife. I would be pleased to have you accept that role."

"Pleased."

His smile turned ironic and a shade caressing. "You would prefer more a more passionate wooing? I could promise it for afterward, if you like."

"That would be unnecessary, I promise you!" she said at once. "I am not so foolish as to think that you may ever have feelings for me."

"Now you intrigue me. I am to understand, I suppose, that you expect to have none for me, either."

Could this possibly become more incredible or more embarrassing, Juliette wondered. "We are strangers speaking of a convenient arrangement," she answered in tones of stiff reason. "It seems unlikely."

"But you will marry me, nonetheless."

It was madness, just as he had said. It was also a thing of faith and miracles. The question was how strong her faith in the miraculous might be.

If she had thought in physical terms of the husband who might be sent to her, she would surely have pictured an older man of substance, someone who would pacify her mother and her sister and make everything right with the weight of his unassailable respectability. Never had she expected a

maître d'armes with a skinny urchin in tow and a reputation for being dangerous to know for both men
and women. What need had she for a husband who
could best other men with a sword? What would she
do with him when her problem was solved and life
returned to the way it was before?

She should be shut up in the parish prison with
the other lunatics for even considering marriage to
this man. Or she should take to her heels, now,
before it was too late. Instead, she stood perfectly
still.

"Yes," she said in quiet resolve, "I will marry you."

She was so serious, this bride-to-be of his,
Nicholas thought. He liked that. She was clear in
her opinions and forthright in voicing them. She
didn't simper or flutter her lashes or pretend to
shyness she didn't feel, but looked him in the eyes
as if she could penetrate his very soul. The clothes
she wore were of good quality but serviceable rather
than stylish, and in a somber color more suited to
demimourning. Her hair that barely peeped from
the edges of her bonnet was an unassuming brown,
and her eyes, though large and liquid, were that
mixture of colors known as hazel. She was neither
short nor tall, thin nor plump, but had a neat form
that still managed to exert extraordinary presence.
Her best feature was her mouth. Her lower lip had
such enticingly lush fullness that he could hardly

tear his gaze from it, and his mouth felt dry with the need to taste its soft generosity. She would be as sweet on his tongue as some perfectly prepared blancmange, he thought, and as imminently satisfying in rich, wholesome goodness.

"It might be helpful," he said, clearing his throat, "if you were to tell me your name."

She gave it, the syllables quiet, almost a whisper in the morning air.

Juliette Armant…

Fatalistic acceptance rolled over Nicholas. Juliette Armant, of course. He had seen her sister at Tivoli Gardens only last week. She had been chattering to her friends about some hysterical obsession of her mother's concerning her twin sister, who had recently returned home after more than a year's absence. Yes, and from whence had she returned? From the Ursuline convent, that was where.

Nicholas closed his eyes. He had proposed marriage to a nun. Worse, he had accused her of impure thoughts, imaged touching her under her skirts, lusted to sweep his tongue across her lower lip and, in all truth, other places less accessible. He was surely damned to hell, though there was small wonder in that. He had been bound for those nether regions any time these past thirty-odd years and more.

Snatching off his hat, he tucked it under his arm and bowed his head. "Forgive me. I meant no insult,

I swear it. If I had known, if the circumstances had not been so curious, I would never have ventured to speak to you in such a way."

"You would never have suggested a marriage between us."

Odd, but she didn't sound insulted. "Certainly not."

"You know who I am and something of my…let us say my history."

He risked a quick glance. "As it happens."

"But you do not know, I think, that I have left the good sisters of St. Ursuline and will not be returning."

He straightened, allowing his gaze to rest on her face that was so serious, so still. "You have given up the veil?"

"It was never taken, though I was a novice mere weeks away from the final commitment. My presence was required at home and…and I am not so certain I had a true vocation in any case. Therefore there can be no objection to a marriage between us. That is, if you still wish it."

Nicholas was not particularly devout but had learned his catechism beginning when hardly older than Gabriel, had learned also how to revere the priests and nuns who sought to save nameless devil's spawn as he had been. He had not forgotten. "Such a thing is barely permissible," he said with a wan edge to his smile. "It would be a union of the sacred and the profane."

She frowned at him, her brow pleating, almost meeting above her small, straight nose. "I don't understand."

"You are so very innocent," he said spreading his hands before her, "and I am the opposite. You have been taught kindness, and I have little enough in me. You seek to protect life, as witness your hiding young Gabriel, and I have blood on my hands. I am hardly fit to stand in your shadow, much less take you to wife."

Color rose in her face, a delicate bloom that spread across her cheekbones. "I fail to see it. More, I will tell you plainly that I have need of all the qualities that you deem faults. I require a husband, but not just any man will do. I must have one who will stand beside me regardless of the consequences, one who will not turn away from a challenge or shrink from confrontation."

"I could do those things without the tie of marriage," he suggested, his voice even.

Emotions passed swiftly over her face—wonder, gratitude and distress, with anger hard on their heels. Clasping her hands in front of her, she said, "You don't wish to marry me after all."

"It isn't that, I swear it. My fear is that you will regret the union. I have no honored name to give you, no family connections and no position other than that which a lucky and undeserved fortune may achieve. If you were the retiring lady from the edges of society that you first appeared, it might be enough. As it is…" He shrugged.

"Who and what I am matters little. I must be married."

His gaze narrowed. "No doubt there is good reason for such a statement."

"I will tell you about it if you will promise not to draw back from your proposal."

Her eyes were huge in her heart-shaped face, the skin underneath smudged with shadows and tight with worry, Nicholas saw as he studied her closely. It was obvious that she was under some kind of strain. The urge to take it away, to make her smile or even laugh, rose inside him.

She needed him; she had said so. It was a novel thing for him, to have a woman's need stated so simply yet without a particle of salaciousness in it.

Well, he had need of her as well. The recent turn in his life had left him floundering, uncertain how to achieve the stable home he craved. His instincts said this woman would be perfect for his purpose. They had not failed him thus far.

"Mademoiselle Armant," he said quietly as he placed his hand over his heart and inclined his head. "You have that pledge, this I swear, and I will honor it all my life long."

2

An awkward pause fell. Nicholas might have filled it, but his attention was caught by a movement at the back of Juliette Armant's skirts. The lower hem of her gray gown was lifting. An instant later, a small head appeared. Then Gabriel scrambled from his hiding place in a froth of petticoats, leaped to his feet and sprinted away.

The lady gave a small cry, twisting away from him as she leaned to slap her skirts into place behind her. Nicholas caught a brief flutter of lace and white embroidered linen, and an amazingly stirring glimpse of trim ankles and gray leather slippers.

"Aren't you going after him?" Juliette asked as she swung back to face him, flushed but valiantly composed once more.

"I believe the delay of another hour or two before his dreaded bath will make little difference. He will be brought to heel in good time."

"If you say so."

She frowned as she spoke, Nicholas saw, apparently dubious of his cavalier attitude. That was a good sign for the future. "My duty is here with you now. I can hardly allow my betrothed to wander about the streets unescorted."

"That is gallant of you, but I live only a short distance away."

"Even so, you have no family member or servant to safeguard you that I can see. It would be remiss of me not to supply the lack."

"You are suggesting that I should have brought someone with me. Truly, Monsieur Pasquale, I am not the kind of female to incite improper advances."

"Any woman is open to insult, mademoiselle, whether she incites it or not," he said gravely as he took out and donned the gloves he had removed for cleanliness sake while chasing Gabriel, then held out his arm. "If you will accept my escort?"

She wanted to refuse; the struggle as she sought for a reasonable excuse was plain to see. It amused Nicholas to note it, for he was not used to women who were so obviously reluctant to touch him. Of course, he was not used to escorting innocent young females of any kind, particularly those fresh from a nunnery.

"Very well," she said finally, then stepped nearer to lay her gloved hand on his sleeve.

It felt like a victory. It also felt peculiarly right, as if he were meant to support this woman. The muscles of his arm contracted involuntarily at the tingling heat of her touch, though whether to impress the lady or in instinctive, age-old preparation for protecting her he had no idea.

"You live on the rue Chartres?" he asked when they had traveled two or three stiff steps along the street which fronted the cathedral.

"Just off it, on rue St. Louis between Chartres and Royale but closer to the latter."

Her voice was so low that Nicholas had to bend his head to hear. "Excellent," he said, and turned toward the alleyway to the right of the cathedral and between it and the *Cabildo*—or city hall from the days of the Spanish regime—that would take them to Royale. The address was only a few steps on the river side of the St. Louis Hotel and Stock Exchange, so not far at all from his atelier on the Passage de la Bourse.

She held back a little, and who could blame her? The alley was dank, moss-grown and littered with refuse. The buildings looming up on either side closed out the morning light. He was a stranger to her and had not been entirely respectful in his first approach, something for which he winced yet again as he thought about it. It behooved him to put her at ease, but he could not quite think how, particularly with the clean soap scent of her wafting to his brain like the finest perfume and her skirts brushing his booted ankles, clinging to them with every step.

He couldn't see her face for her prim, black-trimmed gray bonnet. The urge to stop and persuade her to look at him, to smile, to open her lips to him while he tasted their smooth ripeness, was an ache inside him. The muscles in his arm tightened again, and so did that most unruly organ of his body hidden by his pantaloons. It was uncalled for, uncomfortable, even depraved. He had thought he possessed better control.

"You have a sister, I believe," he said, his voice more abrupt than he intended as he sought distraction.

"Paulette, yes. She is my twin, to be precise. You've met her?"

"Not formally," he said, his voice dry in acknowledgment of the fact that such protected flowers were not introduced to sword masters like himself, at least not without protest. "But who else is at home with the two of you?"

"You are asking about my circumstances, I suppose." Her brief glance gave him a flash of wide, green-shaded brown eyes. "Certainly, you have a right to know them. My mother is alive, but my father is…is not. He died a few seasons ago. We are an all-female household at present, though my sister is as good as promised to Monsieur Jean Daspit."

Nicholas lifted an eyebrow. He had met Daspit on several occasions, none of them especially congenial. "No brothers, no other sisters?"

"None who survived childhood."

He understood the answer well enough. The climate of New Orleans, so he had discovered during his two years in residence, was not always kind to children. The typical diseases of childhood could be virulent, emptying a nursery in a matter of days. "Uncles? Cousins?"

"Many." She turned her head again to give him an inquiring look.

"I only wondered that there was no one to secure a husband for you."

"None who cared to take on the responsibility. But then, it proved unnecessary."

"Meaning?"

"You were sent to me without that intervention," she said, then set her teeth on her lip as she looked away.

"Sent?" When she made no answer, he went on with the threat of laughter in his voice. "Come, you can't leave it at that. If I am under some compulsion, then I should at least know what it might be."

"You'll think it foolish."

"If so I promise not to tease you with it for the rest of our days."

"I confess it seems a little foolish to me now. Yet for a moment back there, I was so certain."

An odd sensation crept up the back of his neck and ran across his shoulders to prickle down his arms in goose bumps. "You had just come from the church."

She nodded.

"And you had prayed for—what?"

"A husband, of course."

He stopped. There were half a dozen possible responses he could make to that. They tumbled in his head, from a shout of mirthful scorn to the stern refusal to take another step along the path where she led. None of them passed his lips. Instead, a slow smile widened his mouth, one he could not have stopped if he tried. "Fascinating," he said in quiet amazement. "Never before have I been the answer to a maiden's prayer."

"If you think you appear in that guise to me I'm sorry, but you are mistaken," she said with a frown wrinkling her pale brow. "My need for a husband is purely…"

"Unselfish," he supplied as she paused. He thought he kept his affront at her instant rejection hidden behind a look of polite interest, but could not be sure.

"Not exactly, because that sounds as if I expect to martyr myself with this marriage and that isn't the case. It's simply that I must be married or a special legacy that has been in the family for generations will fall into the wrong hands."

"It's about money." His voice was flat. He had somehow expected better.

"Not at all," she said, flinging him a look of exasperation. "If you must know, it's about an old chest, a family heirloom. It was given to my mother when she married, and to my grandmother on her wedding day before that, and my great-grandmother before that all the way back to an ancestress who came to New Orleans as a casket girl."

"Casket girl?"

"One of forty or fifty young women sent here some hundred and twenty years ago by the French crown as brides for the colonists. Most of them left no family behind them, had nothing at all in this world except the chest, or casket, containing the dowry that was allotted to them."

"So the chest is this casket?"

"Not exactly. My ancestress, Marie Therese, had a chest of her own made of some exotic wood and inlaid with ivory. Since she refused to part with it, the linens and clothing and other dowry items were put into it."

"Linens and clothing."

"Oh, they are long since gone and no longer matter. What is important is that my mother is making herself sick with worry over the chest because of a family legend which says that disaster will strike if the wrong person receives it."

"She believes that?"

"Indeed she does, since she was brought up by a nurse who filled her head with hundreds of superstitions and bits of voodoo magic. You can't imagine the things she believes—though I should not speak so of her to you. I thought all my life that this thing of the chest would not matter to me. I thought Paulette would be the bride to have it in our generation because she was supposed to be the elder by some few minutes. But now our nursemaid swears the two of us were confused in our cradles and I am the older of the two."

"That makes a difference?"

"It's the oldest girl in each family who safeguards the chest, you see. She receives it on her wedding day and only passes it on when her oldest daughter marries."

"So you are going to the altar because of this chest that has no value."

"I didn't say it has no value," she protested. "Some call it a treasure chest."

"What kind of treasure?"

"No one knows, at least none except the bride who receives it. She may open it and add something she prizes to it, but must never take anything from it and never tell anyone, not even her husband, what it holds." She put a hand to her mouth. "Oh, I should not have said that! Now you will be like Monsieur Daspit, eager to reach the altar to share in the legacy."

Nicholas lifted his head. "What can I have done," he said in tones of exquisite softness, "to give you such an opinion of me?"

She looked at him fully then. Her eyes were

enormous, the pupils so huge they made the mingled colors there appear like dark green velvet edged in gold lace. He thought she searched his soul, invading some fastness of his being that had never been breached. And he waited, breath stopped in his lungs, heart thundering in his ears, for her to find the blackness hidden there and reject him once and for all.

"Nothing," she whispered. "You have done nothing. Forgive me if I seemed to suggest it."

An odd feeling crept over Nicholas, one that was very like reverence. It was not his usual response to a female. He liked women, their company, the way their minds worked, their smiles and open conversation. Admiration for the small and large sacrifices they made for those around them, particularly their children, ran deep inside him. He was comfortable in their presence in a way that few other men of his acquaintance seemed to manage. That he could let down his guard around them, the eternal swordsman's guard against saying or doing something that could mean another trip, however inadvertent, to the dueling field, was beyond gratification. He loved their bodies as well, so different from his own with their round limbs and infinite softness, infinite capacity for sensual delight. To lose himself in the moist and yielding heat of a woman, to give and receive pleasure in a slow and deliberate duet of love, was his idea of earthly paradise.

In truth, his appreciation for women went beyond mere liking to something near adoration. And yet, his slow-growing sentiment for the lady who walked at his side seemed on an even higher plane, one so far removed as to be almost unreachable.

It was a moment before he could speak, and then his voice was hoarse in his throat. "Never mind. We have much to discuss, I think, and this is not the place." He reached to take her hand and return it to his sleeve where he held it captive. "Perhaps you will invite me inside when we reach your home. I should meet your mother, don't you think? It would be only polite to ask her blessing on our marriage, if not her permission for it."

If the lady who was to be his wife answered, the words were too low for Nicholas to hear. Still, she made no effort to release herself from his grasp but walked sedately at his side until they reached their destination.

The Armant town house was three stories tall but only two rooms wide on the street front, a graceful row house that used the adjoining buildings for its end walls. Of brick covered with stucco, it was painted an elegant cream-gold with narrow balconies of ironwork in the traditional dark blue-green. The ground floor housed an apothecary shop in the typical Parisian-inspired arrangement for gaining income from space considered too noisy, dirty and dangerous for comfortable living. French doors opened from the main rooms on the second floor for air, and casement windows marked the third floor garret that was usually given over to servant quarters.

Juliette used a large key taken from a chatelaine at her waist to open the heavy, brass-studded entrance set in its archway next to the apothecary. Passing under the second floor, they made their way down a cool, vaulted corridor to emerge in a narrow courtyard. On the left, against the brick wall of the dwelling next door, was a low brick parapet that formed a bed where grew banana trees and ginger, myrtle and a vine with small, narrow leaves that made a green lace tracery as it swarmed upward toward the light. Chairs and a table sat on the stone paving with doves stalking around beneath them looking hopefully for crumbs. On the other side, under wide stuccoed arches, was a *garçonnière* wing set at a right angle to the front section, one which housed the kitchen and laundry on the lower floor. Above these, overlooking the quiet courtyard and set back under a railed gallery that also ran along the front rooms, would doubtless be the family bedchambers. A curved staircase with a mahogany rail mounted to this gallery on the immediate right while a cruder servant's stair led upward at the far end. Activity was minimal in the work area under the *garçonnière* indicating a small number of servants for the household, probably no more than a cook and maid or two of all work.

"This way," Juliette said, moving ahead of Nicholas toward the curved stair. She had hardly set foot on the bottom step, however, when a door opened somewhere above them and swift footsteps sounded on the upper gallery.

"There you are at last," a clear voice, sharp with annoyance, called down. "Where have you been, *chère? Maman* has been driving me mad and I— monsieur?"

Nicholas looked up to see the lady who appeared at the head of the staircase. She was *en déshabillé*, in a common Gabrielle wrapper of printed muslin with her front hair *en papillote*, twisted in curl papers, and the back falling over her shoulder in waves as luxuriant and glossy as a mink's pelt. The costume displayed skin pale and fine as milk at her neck and shoulders and voluptuous yet graceful curves. Her features were not quite so refined as Juliette's and her mouth a shade thinner, but it was like seeing a double of his future bride.

It also gave him a moment's pause to realize that there might be more to his newly promised lady, hidden beneath her drab bonnet and day gown, than he had first imagined.

Sweeping off his hat, he made his best bow. "Forgive the intrusion at this hour, mademoiselle. It is unavoidable, I assure you."

The eyes of the lady on the gallery widened in appalled recognition before she swung back to her sister. "What is the meaning of this, *chère?* Explain at once!"

"Naturally," Juliette answered, her voice mild. "We shall be in the salon when you have had time to dress."

Paulette Armant's face tightened. It appeared for a moment that she might storm down the stairs in defiance of propriety and her sister's reminder. Then she whirled and vanished back along the gallery in the direction of what was apparently her bedchamber. The door slammed behind her.

"My twin," Juliette said, and gave a small sigh.

"So I had supposed." Nicholas could not prevent the smile that tipped one corner of his mouth.

Answering amusement rose into his betrothed's eyes for an instant. "Indeed, it must be obvious, though we are really not so much alike. Paulette is more vivid in her coloring, also her personality."

Not a shred of envy colored Juliette's tone, Nicholas thought; she was merely stating the matter as she saw it. It was possible that she was correct but the look in her eyes troubled him. "There is much to be said for the subdued and serene."

"If they can ever be seen or heard." She went on at once, as if determined to allow no further comment. "Come upstairs to the salon while I see if *Maman* is awake. Perhaps you would care for café au lait while I inform her that we have a guest."

"Wait," he said, as she began to turn away.

She swung back again, her gaze inquiring.

"You expect this to be unpleasant?" He searched her features, noting again the drawn look around her eyes.

"A little uncomfortable, to say the least. They, my mother and my sister, thought never to see me married, you understand. It can only be a shock, presenting them with a fiancé that I did not know myself until a half hour ago."

"And a gentleman they may not find at all acceptable."

Her eyes as she met his were dark and earnest with concern. "I hope you will not take offense if they say so."

"I will endeavor to keep my temper in check," he said gently.

"If you please. My mother is excitable enough without…"

"It was a jest, *chère*." He reached to lay a finger on her lips, aware as he did of their softness, their heat and dewy moisture that made his own feel suddenly parched.

"Oh. Of course."

She hesitated a moment, as if she would say more. Then turning from him in an abrupt sweep of skirts, she moved up the stairs. Nicholas trailed after her, his gaze on the straight, dignified line of her back and gentle sway of her hips while his groin burned and his brain grappled with impulses too dissolute to be borne.

He refused the offer of a breakfast roll but was on his third cup of coffee when the ladies finally joined him. He set his cup aside and rose to his feet, feeling somewhat awkward in that small salon whose original *Directoire* stateliness had been spoiled by the current style of covering every surface with figured India muslin set with bric-a-brac. As Juliette introduced her parent and her sister, he made a formal obeisance then waited until the ladies were seated and his hostess had indicated that he might take a chair before sitting in their presence.

The room was silent except for the rustle of clothing as the three women settled their skirts. Since it was not his place to initiate conversation, Nicholas used the time to take stock of his opponents. It was a habit from the fencing strips, that careful weighing of strengths and weaknesses, one that had often stood him in good stead.

Madame Armant was a matronly lady who seemed content with the role. Her hair was dressed in a neat fashion but had been allowed to gray naturally under her lace cap; no application of strong coffee or brown-tinted pomade for her. The morning gown she wore was à la mode without being ultra-stylish. The rounded shape of her face, arms and bosom suggested dedication to the pleasures of the table; certainly she had no obvious regard for the vogue of existing on coffee and toast to maintain an air of thin frailty. Her features, however, were lined with worry and her eyes red-rimmed from sleeplessness. She was also a prey to nerves if the fidgeting way she played with her handkerchief was any indication.

Her daughter, Juliette's sister Paulette, showed no such agitation. Her demeanor was glacially superior as she sat upright in her chair. She had taken her time with her toilette, having her hair put up in ribbon-threaded ringlets caught on either side of her face and donning a walking costume of wavering rainbow stripes that, set on the vertical, emphasized her slender waist and perfectly shaped shoulders. Her gaze upon him was tinged with suspicion, he thought, possibly because she knew his identity.

"*Maman*," she said now, her voice shaded with impatience.

"Yes, of course, *chère*." Madame Armant jumped a little as she came to attention. "I was merely ordering my thoughts. The situation is hardly… hardly commonplace, you must admit." Turning in Nicholas's direction, she went on. "I am sure that you are quite welcome in this house, Monsieur Pasquale, but I am at something of a loss to understand how you came to arrive in Juliette's company—or indeed, how or where she could have met you. If you have an explanation for these events, I should like to hear it."

Nicholas sent an inquiring glance in Juliette's direction. She shook her head, from which he took it that she had told her mother nothing beyond his name. Her steady regard was also a reminder that it was he who had requested this interview. Now she waited with the others to hear his announcement.

The situation was so unusual that few rules existed for it. All he could do was to speak his intent as simply as possible. "Madame Armant, I am here to seek your blessing upon a marriage between your daughter, Juliette, and myself. This may be unexpected—"

"No!" That cry came from Paulette, who sat forward with her hands fisted in her lap. "It can't be."

"I do assure you—"

"It's a hoax, some cruel joke."

"Not at all," Juliette began with an almost imperceptible glance of support in his direction.

"How can it not be?" Paulette gave a sharp laugh. "It's utterly ridiculous!"

"I will grant that it is unusual, but—"

"*Chère*, the man is a mere fencing master."

"A fencing master?" Madame Armant put her handkerchief to her mouth as she gazed in horror from her daughter to Nicholas and back again.

"Just so, *Maman!* A teacher of fencing from the Passage de la Bourse with no proper family and no prospects, one who slaughters men to prove his skill and gain custom. He has killed half a dozen men, perhaps more if we only knew! Why, he is worse than a common laborer."

Nicholas clenched his teeth as he endured that description in silence. He knew well enough his relative lack of position in a society where, as with most with any pretense to aristocracy, to be a gentleman of leisure was everything. For a man to earn his living with his hands was considered a disgrace; to go regularly to the dueling ground as most masters were forced to do to maintain their reputations verged on the criminal.

Madame Armant moaned, falling against the sofa back, where she lay with one hand clutching her bodice over her heart. Juliette moved swiftly from her chair to kneel at her mother's feet. Detaching a small, chased silver bottle from the chatelaine at her waist, she screwed off the cap and held the vinaigrette to Madame Armant's nose.

Behind them, the door from the gallery flew open just then and a bulky, gray-haired servant woman with nutmeg-gold skin pushed inside. "What passes? Someone is sick? Shall I send for Dr. Labode?"

"No, no," Juliette said over her shoulder. "It's nothing."

"Nothing?" Paulette demanded, rising to her feet so that Nicholas was forced to stand as well. "Nothing, that you bring a killer into the house? Nothing, that you sit there and allow him to upset our mother by suggesting that the two of you will be wed?"

"It was you who upset her," Juliette said distractedly.

"I did not bring such a one into this house! How are we to believe you intend a real marriage with this man? It's nothing more than a trick to get your hands on the marriage chest." She flung out a hand in the direction of a small, highly ornamented chest the size of a camel-back trunk, which sat on a table between the front windows.

Juliette did not even glance at her irate sister. "I assure you any marriage between us will be quite as binding as yours to Monsieur Daspit."

Paulette moved to stand over her kneeling twin. "You dare to compare Jean Daspit to this...this sword master? He is worlds above him!"

"I said nothing against your betrothed, but since you have brought him into this, I will point out that he is a gambler without prospects."

"At least he is a gentleman of known family!"

"That doesn't prevent him from being a fortune hunter as well."

Paulette raised her hand as if she meant to strike Juliette. Nicholas took a swift, lithe step to move between them even as his heart beat heavily from the unexpected boon of hearing himself defended by his future wife. The elderly servant woman, in a blue dress topped by a voluminous white apron and with a crisp white tignon over her hair, advanced into the room as well. For an instant, they stood in strained tableau.

Madame Armant struggled upright again, stretching out a hand to each of her daughters. "Please, please, do not quarrel, my dear ones. Oh, this is my fault, all my fault entirely." She wiped her watering eyes and blew her nose. "*Mon Dieu*, what a coil it is."

"There, *Maman*, don't upset yourself further," Juliette murmured.

"No, but truly, my Juliette," she said, searching for an unused portion of her handkerchief with which to wipe her nose, "it is truly beyond belief, or so I find it. That you who was for so long promised as a bride of Christ might now wed seems a sacrilege. And so it may be, for how is one to tell?"

"I took no vows, *Maman*."

"No, and yet—ah, if only you had sought to ally yourself to a gentleman from a family known to us, an unexceptional man who might become one of us, all might be well. But this...this is more than I can bear!" She fell back again with her wet wisp of handkerchief to her eyes.

"See what you have done!" Paulette cried. "*Maman*, you must forbid this wedding at once."

Madame Armant made a helpless gesture with one hand without looking at them. "How can I, *chère*? What if your sister is truly the elder, as Valara says? Death and destruction are promised if the chest falls into the wrong hands. And I did say that whoever married first should have it, you know I did."

"Yes, but I never dreamed it would come to anything. Juliette had no prospects, while Monsieur Daspit and I—oh, but it isn't fair!"

"'Tis fair, yes," Valara said, pushing out her lips. "Juliette should have the chest. It is her right."

"*I* am the firstborn," Paulette said through her teeth. "I have been the firstborn all my life. If the man I was affianced to at seventeen had not died, I would have been a wife these three years and the chest would long ago have been mine."

"You are not the firstborn," the servant woman said.

"Be quiet," Paulette snapped at her.

"Valara, please," Juliette said at the same time. Her twin turned on her. "Oh, yes, you want to smooth things over now, when it's too late. Valara has already fixed it so you can leave the convent and come here to ruin everything. You love it, don't you? What an escape!"

The servant woman, the *Valara*, who had precipitated the present crisis as far as Nicholas could tell, heaved a great sigh. "Nothing have I done, me, but set things right with my conscience. Always, always, I have known you were the younger, Mam'zelle Paulette. Only Mam'zelle Juliette was the quieter *bébé* and all became confused, as I've told many and many a time. It seemed she might be best for the veil. But then things began to go wrong. When your papa and your fiancé died one after the other, I knew it would be the flames for me did I not speak. *Mais,* you and your *maman* would not listen until it was time for Mam'zelle Juliette's vows, so almost too late."

"If our own mother could not tell us apart, old woman, I don't know why we should take your word!"

"I held and fed both of you and changed your small nappies night and day, *chère*, this you know. Your *maman* was sick near to death with the milk fever for weeks after you were born. She could not feed you, could barely raise her head from her pillow, so you and Juliette were left to me. I know you and I know her, believe me, and I tell you for the last time, she is the one for the chest."

Paulette's face turned a mottled and unattractive red as she stared at the woman Valara. "You always liked her better. She always did everything right and never gave you any trouble—I've heard it over and over until I am sick to death of her goodness. But she will not have the marriage chest. It's mine and I will have it or no one will!"

Whirling, she ran from the salon. In the silence she left behind, they could hear her heeled slippers clattering on the gallery, then the opening and closing of a door followed by distant sobbing.

Juliette pushed erect and turned to sit beside her mother. She took her hand, holding it tightly. Her eyes were troubled and her features flushed with embarrassment, Nicholas thought, as she looked up at him.

"You will have to forgive my sister, Monsieur Pasquale," she said. "This is all so new for her. She cannot grow used to my being at home again or the change in our circumstances. I'm sure she will be sorry, later, for her rudeness."

Nicholas thought privately that it was unlikely. Paulette seemed to him to be a lady used to having matters her way and unwilling to settle for less. He could hardly say so to her sister, however, so only inclined his head. "This was not such a good idea after all," he said quietly. "Perhaps I should go away and come back later for a more formal visit."

"As you prefer."

He waited for her to add something more, since it seemed to hover on her tongue. When she did not, he said, "I could see myself out, but would be pleased if you could walk with me."

She glanced at her mother, who waved a hand in dismissal. With a murmur of reassurance for her parent, his future bride took the hand he offered to help her rise, then waited while the woman called Valara handed him his hat and gloves. The two of them left the salon and went down the outside stairs. In the courtyard with the tall street door in sight at the end of the tunnel-like entranceway, she paused.

Nicholas turned to face her with his hat held against the stripe that decorated the leg of his pantaloons. "Your mother and sister can't approve of me, and I can hardly blame them," he said, his voice abrupt. "It appears unlikely that a marriage between us will have their blessing, now or later, and I know it will be difficult for you to proceed without it. If you should decide that you don't wish to continue, you have only to tell me."

"That is very kind of you, monsieur."

"No, merely sensible. It's a major step we are contemplating, and a permanent one."

"You have much right there, yes. And I suppose I should extend to you the same favor."

"Unnecessary. I gave you my pledge."

"So you did." She gave a small shake of her head. "Still, I would not blame you for drawing back after meeting my family."

"My skin is thicker than that, I promise you," he said with a sardonic smile.

"I am glad to hear it."

She might be glad, but she had not said that she would continue to stand beside him against her relatives, or even that she considered herself bound by their agreement. What he had expected, Nicholas wasn't sure. It wasn't as if he required her reassurance to ease his mind.

"Until tomorrow then," he said, and settled his hat on his head. Bowing most formally, he left her there.

Minutes later, as he strode toward his atelier on the Passage de la Bourse, he stopped abruptly in is tracks. A sailor ambling along behind him almost ran him down, but veered away at the last second. Nicholas muttered an apology with hardly a glance in the tar's direction.

He was to be married. He would wed a novice from the convent, if not a nun. He would take as his wife a woman who did not want him for himself but for a morass of reasons that made little sense and seemed a direct offense to his pride. He was marrying neither for love nor carnal pleasure, but to obtain a mother for Gabriel and others like him. He was pledged to a female he had met a mere two hours ago now but had promised to keep forever.

And the worst of it was that he was actually content with the bargain. He could not wait to assume the responsibilities of a husband. The mere thought of his future duties made his heart beat high and strong in his chest and his body ache with desire.

More than that, every urge toward protective vigilance he had ever felt was far surpassed by the exalted purpose that surged through him. He was needed. It was enough.

He was, against all odds, a contented bridegroom.

3

"Why, *mam'zelle?*" Valara asked, standing with her fists on her ample hips as she met Juliette at the top of the stairs. "Explain to me. I know you are worried for your *maman*, but there are other ways to find a man. No need to drag one in off the streets."

"I didn't, I promise you I didn't," she answered with a wry grimace. "The match seemed right at the time."

"*Zut alors!*" The old nursemaid threw up her hands before turning to lead the way toward a secluded area at the far end of the gallery. "Come, I must hear all that passed between you."

Juliette had expected no less; Valara had always shared her secrets and given good counsel in exchange for them. When she had finished the story of her prayer and its answer, the nursemaid stood leaning with her broad hips against the gallery railing and her arms over her chest. Finally, she gave a slow nod. "You think it a miracle that this Pasquale appeared in front of the church and immediately proposed marriage to you?"

"How could I not? And yet…"

"Now you wonder."

Juliette gave a low sigh. "I don't know. I knew *Maman* and Paulette would not be happy with Monsieur Pasquale, but hardly expected such a commotion."

Valara snorted. "Paulette would make the big scene if you brought home St. Anthony himself. Her nose has been out of joint from only thinking you might make the marriage and take the chest. That you seem ready to do it makes her so mad she is like to bust."

"I honestly can't think why it should. She has had everything her way since we were born."

"It's because of that very thing, *chère*. She thought to have it her way for always, to be first in all matters. Now things have changed."

"You changed them, dearest Valara."

"I could not see you take the veil from a mistake, no. It wasn't right."

Juliette met her nurse's deep-set dark eyes that were clouded with concern. "You are quite, *quite* sure that I wasn't born second?"

"As sure as sure can be. No, our Paulette came screaming into the world, and she is screaming still. But why do you ask? Is it that you want the convent?"

Juliette put three fingers to her forehead, massaging her brow where a headache had formed, pounding behind her eyes. What did she want? She was hardly sure herself. "I think it might be simpler if I return to the nuns."

"You know what would happen then."

Juliette suspected it, which amounted to the same thing. Paulette would marry Daspit. The two of them would open the chest as soon as their vows were spoken. Paulette would do it from rampant curiosity, and Daspit from avarice and lack of respect for family tradition. If her mother learned of it, which she was certain to do eventually, she would be prostrate. Already, she was making herself ill with worry. If the worse came, and some tragedy befell them as tradition said it must overtake those who desecrated the treasure chest, then she might have a seizure of the heart, one from which she would not recover.

"The voodoo curse will get them," Valara said with a wise nod of her head. "That's a thing of power, it is. I've seen things, seen them brought on by spells with my own eyes, things you would never believe."

"They work on the minds of believers, or so the priests say."

"Makes no difference how it works, only that it does. My old granny made the spell, so it's said, long years ago. The master freed her for what reason we will never know. She put the papers saying this in the box when her young mistress married and told her to keep them safe. Then she put the curse on whoever might take them out. My *maman* was always free because of it, for sure, and I'm free today. There's a blessing in that curse for those that do right, but powerful anger among the spirits for the wrongdoers."

"You don't think that Paulette would destroy those papers, do you?" Juliette asked, frowning.

"Might if she was mad enough. Who can say? But I don't put nothing past that Monsieur Daspit, not me. He's a wild one, never steady. He might sell me for a slave because I make trouble for him in his marrying Mam'zelle Paulette."

"Never. *Maman* would not allow it, nor would I." Juliette thought a moment. "But has he actually asked for Paulette? I thought it had merely been mentioned between the two of them."

"I think, me, he hopes Mam'zelle Paulette will make it easy for him by going first to your *maman*." She shrugged. "His affairs can't stand much looking at, be it love or money, or so the talk goes over the fences."

"I feared so." Juliette looked down into the courtyard where a red-legged pigeon with a gaudy, iridescent head strutted in front of his ladylove with fluffed breast feathers and soft cooing that had only one object. The bird put her in mind of Daspit in some fashion.

Farther along the gallery, a door clicked open. Paulette stepped out, paused as she saw them, and then walked in their direction with angry strides that swung her petticoats stiffened by horsehair *crin* against the balusters of the railing with a harsh whisper. "So your would-be fiancé has gone," she said. "At least he has the intelligence to see when he is not welcome."

"You made it abundantly clear. He would have been a fool not to notice."

"And he is not that, is he? He saw very quickly where his advantage lay."

"What do you mean?"

"You are so innocent, one might almost say backward, where men are concerned. You saw a manly form and handsome face, and all thought flew right out of your head. I can account for this ridiculous betrothal in no other way."

"I have seen men before," Juliette said dryly. "But did you think Monsieur Pasquale handsome?"

"Oh, come, how could I not? He is quite striking in his way. Those shoulders, the chest, the legs— even I will admit that regular practice on the fencing strips adds attraction to a man."

For an instant, Juliette wondered if her twin might not be a bit envious of Nicholas Pasquale as her prospective husband. There was no question that he outshone Daspit. The gambler was quite the dandy with his tall form, elegant clothing and perfumed side whiskers, but his shoulders lacked breadth, his chest was deep rather than broad, and he walked with a swagger that was as pronounced as it was ill-advised.

"That's very generous of you," she said warily.

"Oh, yes, all my friends sigh over these sword masters—Messieurs O'Neill, Blackford, Llulla, Rosière and even Croquère. It's quite the thing, you know. But one would never dream of marrying them."

"Monsieur Rosière is married already, I believe, as is Monsieur O'Neill, and to a lady of irreproachable character and family connections."

Paulette's eyes flashed with annoyance at the reminder. "Madame Moisant was a widow, a different thing altogether."

"I fail to see it."

"Because you are determined to be difficult. You know very well the match is unacceptable. You are clutching at straws so as to steal what is rightfully mine."

Juliette started to shake her head, then stopped as it began to pound with pain. "I am only trying to do what is best."

"You think it best to make a laughingstock of our family by bringing a *maître d'armes* into it? You think it best to allow him the position of head of this household, which he will inevitably take as your husband? You think it best to place in his keeping our most treasured family heirloom and repository of our health and well-being? If so, my dear sister, I spit on your best!"

Anger, as strange to her as it was real, stirred inside Juliette. "I want nothing of yours, Paulette, but neither do I see why I should give up what is rightfully mine. You have had the position as first twin all these years. You've had the parties and balls and fine gowns and flirtations—"

"And you have been jealous of them!"

"No, truly," Juliette said in quick denial. "I'm only saying that you've had so much until now. Why begrudge me this?"

"The chest, that's why! I've wondered all my life what was in it, thought all this time I would one day know. If you wed first, I'll never have the answer. It's intolerable."

"How can you say that when you looked—"

"You lie! I didn't, I wouldn't, never, never."

Paulette's face was pale as she spoke and there was a species of terror in the back of her eyes. Others might not be able to see it, but Juliette knew her well, so well. "You did, you know you did. I was there."

"You closed your eyes so you wouldn't see. I was only pretending, barely lifted the lid. It was not enough to see anything at all, not enough to matter."

"But Papa died, and so did Charles Yves, whom he had arranged for you to marry."

"A coincidence."

"Still, if *Maman* knew…"

"You would never tell her such a thing!"

"No, I wouldn't for she would be far too upset, but are you sure you want to risk something of the same happening again?"

"I never looked, I tell you. Besides, Jean…Monsieur Daspit…says that it's all superstition, nothing will happen anyway."

"This Daspit," Valara said. "I never liked that man, me. He is the complete rogue."

"This Pasquale of Juliette's is the rogue!" Paulette cried. "Women fall all over themselves for him, and what does he do? Why, he picks them up, of course. He will never be faithful to you, my dear sister, never in this world. Such a man requires fire and passion in a woman, and you have neither. He will make you unhappy, as unhappy as you deserve to be for trying to take what is mine."

"It wasn't my choice," Juliette protested.

"But you aren't fighting it, are you?"

Juliette was silenced. What her sister said was true in its way. She had left the convent with no more than a token discussion with the Mother Superior, one in which she pleaded her mother's health and the duty to her family. She had been told to pray over her decision, and she had done that, but without excessive fervor. "The church was never a vocation of my choosing," she said after a moment, her voice not quite even. "This is, in its way, a test of my resolve. If you should marry first…"

"Yes? If I marry first, you will return to the convent?"

"I didn't say that." Something inside Juliette resisted that capitulation, though it was impossible to tell whether it came from anger and fear or pride and hope.

"It would be an excellent thing," Paulette said, her eyes bright. "In fact, I believe it may be the only solution. You would not like living here with Daspit as head of the household when we are married, nor can I think he would enjoy having you as a pensioner. I shall have to speak to *Maman*."

"Mam'zelle Paulette," Valara said in tones of protest.

"Come, what is wrong with such an agreement? It was she who decided that the first of us to wed should claim the chest. The one heaven smiles upon in this matter must be the eldest, yes? She believes it, therefore it must be so. And if heaven chooses me, then surely that is a sign that my sister was meant to be a bride of Christ? *Maman* will see it that way when I am done, I know it. She is nearly as afraid of reneging on her vow to give a daughter to the convent as she is of waking the spell on the chest."

It was a clever twisting of the situation to achieve Paulette's ends. Juliette resented it for that reason, but also because it said plainly that her sister cared nothing for what became of her so long as she got what she wanted. Left to herself, Juliette might well have decided to forego the quarreling and ill feelings, might have chosen the convent, after all. Now she was loathe to accept that defeat and fade quietly back into the dubious comfort of stone walls and wimples, prayers and good works.

"First," she said distinctly, "you must marry ahead of me."

"I shall," Paulette said flatly.

"And if you do not, what then?"

"What do you mean?"

"If *Maman* is so determined to give a daughter to the church and you are proven by heaven to be the second born, then perhaps you should take my place."

"Never!" Paulette cried, her face flushing scarlet. "I've never pretended to a vocation."

"And never had one planned for you from birth, either," Juliette said with a tight smile. "Difficult, isn't it?"

"We shall see what *Maman* says about it."

Paulette grabbed the front of her skirts and sailed around, heading toward their mother's bedchamber. Juliette watched her go with a clenching sensation in her stomach.

"That one will talk and cry, and cry and talk till your *maman* agrees with her," Valara said.

"I fear you are right."

"Of course, I am right, me. Am I not always?" The old nurse's smile was grim. "So what will you do?"

"I think," Juliette said slowly, "that I must do my best to make certain Monsieur Pasquale keeps to our bargain."

"You will marry him?"

"I believe I must," she said.

"Must?"

"Will," Juliette corrected. "I think I will take Monsieur Pasquale, the so terrible La Roche, as my husband. But first, I have to make certain that he doesn't decide he will not have me as his wife."

"This will be a great task, you think?"

"I don't know." She looked away from the shrewed eyes of her old nurse. "His proposal was a challenge made in jest, Valara. He didn't mean it. I think…I think he was too much the gentleman to take it back once I had accepted."

The old servant hummed low in her throat as she tipped her head with its snowy tignon. "This has promise."

"You think so?"

"I do, yes."

Juliette caught her bottom lip between her teeth for an instant. "He is a man of much attraction to women, just as Paulette said. I may not have the… the passion he requires."

"You know not what you have inside, my Juliette. You have always done what was expected of you, always bowed to the will of others. I think you can do and be anything you want if the desire is great enough here in your heart." She put her massive fist about the center of her apron-covered bodice. "But first you must learn to fight."

"Fight? Oh, surely not, Valara."

"Not like a man, mam'zelle, with steel and hard blows. Still, you must arm yourself." She paused for a frowning instant, bending a speculative look upon Juliette. "I think the place to start may be at the modiste."

Juliette glanced down at her gray gown. "You mean with a new ensemble?"

"Many of them, *chère*. The *saison des visites* is at its peak. You must shine in it, you must glow. This you cannot do while wearing the demimourning left from your papa's death. New bonnets you must have, too, not that thing from three seasons ago. And then there is your hair."

"My hair?" Juliette lifted a hand to smooth the strands pulled back from her center part.

"You should not hide it, mam'zelle. Men are drawn to hair as surely as horses to oats, and yours is lighter and finer than Paulette's."

Was it? Juliette had no idea. Vanity of any kind was frowned upon at the convent, discouraged with such vigor that in time it vanished altogether.

And yet, she had been steeling herself for some months for the prospect of having her hair cut short when she took her vows. She liked the weight and silken length of the thick tresses, the way it lay over her shoulder when she brushed it, shimmering with her every breath. She was glad that she need not sacrifice it just yet, and possibly not at all. She was so glad, in fact, that she felt positively guilty.

Perhaps she had some small bit of vanity left in spite of everything.

The visit to the modiste was undertaken that very afternoon. Juliette would have put if off for a day or two, but Valara insisted. She was so adamant that it seemed she might decide Juliette did not properly value her advice if they did not set off in good time. Juliette would not have her think that for the world, so disregarded the dull ache in her head and allowed herself to be persuaded.

They didn't go straight to the atelier of Madame Ferret, who had served her mother for years, but stopped instead at the draper, Bourry d'Ivernois, where they inspected a new shipment of fancy goods that included French merinos and muslins and several very nice lengths of printed challis. After much discussion and comparison, they dispatched a bundle to the Armant town house, one containing a shawl of needlepoint and cream *point de gaze* lace, a parasol in black Chantilly, and three pairs of kidskin gloves in pale yellow, pink and blue. Then they waited while several ells of merino and the challis were cut from the bolts, wrapped in paper and tied with string for Valara to carry to Madame

Ferret's shop. Doubtless, there was something health-giving about such labor, for Juliette's headache had miraculously vanished by the time they stepped back out into the street again.

She and Valara were less than three doors away from the shop kept by the modiste when ahead of them, making his way toward them, Juliette saw the long-legged, thin figure of Monsieur Jean Daspit. She glanced around for some way to avoid him, but there was nothing which might serve short of out-right rudeness. He had already seen them and was lifting his hat.

His smile was so warm in his yellow-tinted face that it crossed Juliette's mind to wonder if he had mistaken her for her sister. The possibility was quickly eliminated as he greeted her.

"Mademoiselle, I trust I see you well, and your mother and the charming Mademoiselle Paulette as well."

"Indeed, monsieur." Juliette would have moved on at once, except the gentleman shifted slightly to block her way.

"You are to be congratulated, I understand, though everyone is quite amazed at the swift course of this alliance."

"These things sometimes arrange themselves." She did not for a moment believe that anyone other than the gentleman himself knew of the betrothal. Paulette must have sent a note around to the rooms he kept in a boardinghouse. She wished her sister had not been so prompt.

Daspit moved closer and deliberately bent over her as if to make her aware of his superior height and strength. Her attention was taken instead by the citrus scent of the pomade he used to comb back the straight brown hair that sprang from his forehead, and also the odor of tobacco on his breath as he continued. "Haste should be avoided, regardless."

"No doubt." She stepped back, bumping into Valara, who was just behind her.

"How very disagreeable for you if you should discover the man you have married is not as expected. That is the great value of having a male head of the family, you know. We so often have greater knowledge of our own kind that any female may acquire. I should feel remiss in my duty if I did not warn you that the man who seeks your hand is unworthy of you."

"You are acquainted with Monsieur Pasquale?" She was curious or she would not have asked. It was a failing.

"Not closely, but one hears things. He is a nobody, you comprehend, an Italian who came to the city only two years ago. It's said that he cannot with certainty name his father." Daspit lifted his shoulders in mock sympathy. "What would you? He is quite unsuitable, I fear."

"Thank you, monsieur, for your opinion," she said

in chill accents. Once more, she tried to step around her sister's intended. Once more, he prevented it.

"I have expressed myself concerning this sword master, but there is more to be said, Mademoiselle Juliette. You will forgive my frankness, but just as some men are unsuited to marriage, so too are some females. They are made of finer clay, therefore more fragile and easily damaged. They should avoid the crude emotions and unpleasant duties of the marriage bed, for they are unlikely to survive their rigors, much less take joy in them."

"Monsieur!"

"You are distressed. I am sorry for it, yet I warn you for your own good. You are such a one, mademoiselle. Ignore it at your own risk."

Juliette carried the usual green parasol against the slanting rays of the sun that were so poisonous to the complexion. Now she snapped it shut and lowered it like a sword, pressing the ferrule to the breastbone of her sister's future fiancé. He reached to close his gloved fist upon the parasol's ribs, and she thought for an instant that he would try to wrest it from her.

It was then that a deep voice came from behind her. "Mademoiselle Armant, I had not thought to see you again so soon. Might I be of assistance?"

The velvety timbre of the voice, the trace of amusement like a decorated sheath over tempered steel, the liquid syllables and courteous phrasing could belong to only one person. "Monsieur

Pasquale," she exclaimed, turning with what she feared was too obvious relief, "well met."

"For me as well. You are on an outing of moment?"

"As it happens. I was about to visit Madame Ferret just there."

"And you require my considered judgment in helping choose a new gown or two. Naturally, I am at your service."

He bowed, managing somehow to elbow Daspit aside so the way before them was clear again. Then he took her parasol and handed it to Valara, nodded to Daspit with all the affability in the world, and strolled away with Juliette on his arm.

Juliette could feel Daspit's frown on her back as they walked. Her voice a little strained, she said, "I thank you most sincerely for the rescue, but fear you have made an enemy."

"Daspit? I won't lose sleep over it."

"No, though he might have challenged you just then, you know. He is quite capable of it."

"I should think so, considering his opinion of me. In fact, I might have more respect for him if he had."

"Meaning?"

"I should not be speaking to you, much less offering you escort." He released her, indicating with a bow that he expected her to pass before him into the modiste shop.

She stopped. "You feel he should have resented that?"

"As your future brother-in-law, most certainly. I should have in his place."

"What an odd thing to say."

"Isn't it." His smile was bleak. "He is right, you know. I am not suitable."

"You must let me be the judge of that."

For an instant, something hot, unguarded and not without pain shone in his eyes. It gave Juliette an odd sensation, like a sudden blow to the solar plexus. Then it was gone.

"As you please, mademoiselle. Now I must leave you."

"But you were going to give me your opinion of what I should wear."

"White, mademoiselle," he said immediately. "White silk cut with simple lines, no lace, shirring or other furbelows. And a cloak of white satin lined in cloth of silver and edged with swan's down if it can be found. Something lovely, pure and ethereal, hovering on the brink of flight."

Startled, she lifted her eyes to his. "Flight?"

"A man can be a scoundrel, and still be right about many things," he said roughly. "Perhaps you should heed Daspit's warning."

He turned then and left her, walking away down the street with long, firm strides. He did not look back.

"*Mon Dieu*," Valara said in tones of wonder.

"Exactly," Juliette murmured. "*Exactement.*"

4

Nicholas strode along the shaded banquette with temper riding his shoulders and a scowl on his brow. He stood aside for the wide skirts of the ladies with minimum politesse, stepped around vendors of coffee and rice cakes squatting on street corners, nodded to shopkeepers, removed his hat for a priest, exchanged bows with acquaintances in form, but could not have said with certainty any single person he saw in the four blocks that he covered.

His thoughts were on the woman he had just left and the man who had accosted her. The urge to knock Daspit's teeth down his throat was so strong he clenched his fists with it. The man had no right to so much as speak to Juliette Armant, much less crowd her on the banquette. He was unworthy of breathing the same air, treading the same ground, being warmed by the same sun. If the blackguard came so close again, he would face a challenge couched in the most stringent terms. It would be a distinct pleasure to teach the man manners with a judicious slice or two. Someone should have done it long ago.

The need to stay behind with the lady who would, perhaps, be his wife was so strong that Nicholas shuddered with it. It was impossible. What if she should decide she couldn't bear to associate with him so intimately, after all? He dared not compromise her by being seen dancing attendance upon her in public.

Regardless, he would have given much for the right to stroll at her side along the rue Royale, to pick up a trifle here, a trifle there that might give her pleasure, to be allowed to venture into the modiste shop and help her choose those fabrics and styles which would best enhance her simple elegance of form and face.

Mon Dieu, what a fool he had been to suggest white for her. Angelic she undoubtedly was, but there was far more to her. She was nurturing, compassionate, as serenely maternal as any painted Madonna shown with a babe at the breast. Light seemed to shine around her. He would love to see her in the colors of an Old Master, perhaps lustrous green velvet edged with gold lace. Foolishness, of course, especially since that cloth was reserved for married women. Why was that, he wondered, unless it was too sensuous for the unwed, inviting touch in a way that could well lead to explorations beneath the heavy fabric?

It was not wise or good to think of Juliette Armant in velvet. The image did things to his rampant male impulses that should be prohibited by law. The French were a realistic race. Recognizing the inherent weakness of human nature, they sought always to circumvent it. It was, perhaps, a good thing.

The day was fine, as sometimes happened in January, one of sunshine and cerulean skies with high white clouds, neither too warm nor too cool. Regardless, Nicholas felt so overheated that his thoughts turned to *glaces*, those sweet concoctions made of milk and flavorings beaten in buckets set in ice cut in the far north and shipped on their long journey downriver in blankets of sawdust. An Italian ice-cream maker had his shop on St. Pierre, between Royale and Bourbon. He knew it well, since Tony, the proprietor, catered to his sweet tooth. Tony made more money on ices during the winter season than any other time, perhaps because people expected ice to arrive by steamboat from the north at that season. He swore that his family had been making *gelato* since the Roman emperors had first commanded that ice be brought down from the Alps to Rome. Nicholas believed him; the concoctions were that good. Resolutely, he turned his steps in that direction.

He was just dipping into a bowl of ice cream flavored with grated vanilla bean, sitting at a sidewalk table of wrought iron, when he looked up to see Caid O'Neill coming toward him. Hailing his Irish friend, who had once kept a fencing salon on the Passage near his own, he indicated the ice cream with a gesture. Caid declined with a shake of his head, instead putting his head inside the shop and shouting for Tony to bring him an espresso. That done, he pulled out the chair opposite Nicholas.

"Good news," the Irishman said, as he stretched his long legs out before him. "Rio and Celina will be back in town soon. I had a letter aboard the *Dundee*, and they should be no more than a day or two behind it."

"Excellent. It's been too long." Nicholas had missed Rio. He had gained many friends since coming to the city but few he trusted as he did the man who had been Rio de Silva before he regained the use of his real name, Damian Francisco Adriano de Vega y Riordan, and become the conde de Lérida. The Passage de la Bourse had not been the same without him. Not that Rio would be reopening his fencing salon, of course, now that he was a family man.

"They would have come in November, except that Celina was about to give birth. Again," Caid said with a low chuckle.

"The oldest must be nearly walking by now, yes?"

"And trying to talk, or so I imagine."

"They are done with Spain?" Nicholas scooped up

the last of his *gelato* and pushed the bowl away, then nodded his approval to Tony, who brought an espresso for him, unasked, along with one for Caid.

"For a few years, at least. There is much unrest in Barcelona with this disturbance over who will be the regent until young Isabella can take the throne. Rio hired a Scotsman to look after the estate. Now he will be a Louisiana sugar planter, looking after his crops in the summer and fall and making merry in town during the *saison de visites*."

"When not making more little de Vegas."

"A fine occupation," Caid said with a grin.

"Without doubt, since you and Rio seem to spend considerable time at it. And how is the lovely Lisette today? And little Sean François?"

Caid's smile was warm and a little wicked. "Sleepy. They were still tucked up in bed when I left just now."

For a brief instant, Nicholas felt a pang of envy for that image of marital bliss; a wife in rumpled nightwear with a sleeping baby tucked in her arms after, perhaps, an early morning of sweet and easy love. "You may congratulate me, if you please," he said abruptly. "I am to be married."

Caid just sipping his coffee, choked and coughed, almost strangling. "What? Say again?"

"Married, yes. At least, I believe I may be. The lady may decide against it." Nicholas leaned back in his chair, his gaze on the rich, black brew in the tiny cup he held in his callused fingers.

"You've kept this mighty quiet. I think I'm insulted."

Nicholas gave his friend a brief smile. "No need, I promise you. I only met the lady this morning."

"And you have already—" Caid sat blinking at him for a long moment. "I know an Italian accent gives you an unfair advantage when it comes to the fair sex, but this is… Explain. At once."

Nicholas did so, leaving out nothing, though the more he talked, the more fantastical the whole thing sounded to his own ears.

"Don't do it," Caid said.

"I gave my word." Nicholas lifted one shoulder. "Besides, there is Gabriel."

"You can tame that young scamp without marrying some strange female to mother him."

"I'm not so sure. He needs more than I can give him, more softness perhaps. The lady has need of me as well."

"She may have difficulties with the sister, I'll grant you that much, but there are other ways to solve them."

"You mean a visit from the Brotherhood of the Sword? Brandishing a blade does little to discourage females who cannot, or will not, see reason."

"It might get Daspit's attention."

"Removing him as a fiancé would be a temporary solution. Only a husband for Mademoiselle Juliette will settle the matter once and for all."

Caid stared at him for a long moment, his green gaze considering behind his lashes. "What does she look like, this Mademoiselle Juliette?"

"A nun," Nicholas said, and gave a short laugh.

"No, I mean really."

"She isn't stunningly beautiful, if that's what you are suggesting. No, she's…" He paused, unable to find the words he wanted. "She is…"

"Indescribable, I see."

"She makes me wish I had more to offer her— wealth, position, a name worth having."

"Good God," Caid said, staring at him.

What he had said was the exact truth, though Nicholas knew he had done less than justice to Juliette. She was attractive enough, just not in the accepted manner of flashing eyes, dimpled smiles and masses of black curls. She made him long for the home that was a distant memory, when it was only him and his mother in a cottage on his grandfather's country estate, in exile because he had been born of an impetuous affair between his mother and a sailing man.

When he was five, a marriage had been arranged between his mother and a distempered lout with a noble name and penchant for the whip. They had moved to Rome, a younger brother had been born, and the lout had determined that Nicholas should be consigned to the stables where he could embarrass no one. Nicholas had run away, making his home on the streets, visiting his mother and brother only by night when he knew his stepfather was away. Sometimes on chill and wet winter evenings, he would stand in the alley behind the mansion with a great emptiness inside him that had little to do with the hunger that gnawed at his belly. He stood and stared at the windows where lights shone, music played and those of his blood, if not of his name, laughed and sang and ate bounteous meals they could not share. But he did not cry. He never cried.

"*Mon Dieu*, yes, just so," he said in wry acknowledgement of his folly.

"I thought you had no use for marriage."

"I can't imagine what gave you that idea."

"Nor can I," Caid said frankly, "but it seemed you scorned it as a trap."

"For a woman, yes. For a man, it is otherwise. Most come and go at will, as far as I can see, and take their pleasures where they may."

"You disapprove."

"It's a bachelor's life when one is no longer a bachelor."

"A cheat, in other words."

"When a man takes all the comforts a woman adds to a home and gives nothing in return except a string of painful births and the occasional escort to the opera? Yes, a cheat."

"You, on the other hand, will be an exemplary husband, sitting at the fireside with your lady at your side and children on your knee while you discuss teething and dressmakers and the best way to make candied violets."

"You doubt it?" His voice was cool.

"I'm only trying to picture you with teething marks on the velvet collar of your jacket, drool dripping from your watch chain and a wet spot on your pantaloons." Caid's eyes narrowed as he surveyed him. "Your collar is torn, by the way. Did you know?"

Nicholas blinked, pulling at the offending piece of velvet, trying to see the damage. Then a chuckle rumbled in his chest. "She tore it. I had forgotten."

"She?"

"My bride-to-be."

"Whose charms you have been contemplating so closely that you forgot your sartorial splendor? I have to meet this woman."

"So you shall. At least I hope you may, eventually."

"And you were doing what at the time of this disaster? Or should I ask?"

"Attempting to get under her skirts of course."

Caid sat back in his chair with a thump. "A nun?"

"It seemed necessary at the time. She attacked me in retaliation."

"Your famous address with the ladies having deserted you, I suppose."

"As it happens. Or no, now that I think of it. This

little contretemps took place before that, when she thought I meant bodily harm to Gabriel."

"She waylaid you over that imp of Satan?"

"Some women have a stronger maternal streak than others."

Caid stared at him for a long moment then gave a short nod. "So that's it. You're marrying her to give your brood a mother."

Was he? Nicholas wasn't sure. It had seemed a good idea once, but now he wondered. He had no chance to answer, however, for a shadow slid across their table. He glanced up to see the elegant form of another friend in silhouette against the morning sun.

"Blackford, *mon ami*," he said, squinting up at him. "Either join us or stand so you make a useful sun blind."

"Reduced to the status of an awning, and it's not yet noon," Gavin Blackford lamented. He glanced at the milky residue in the bottom of the bowl in front of Nicholas with a pained expression, shuddered at their espressos, then sat down without refreshment. "This is a chance meeting, I presume? Or might it be the start of some noted quest of valor or vengeance?"

"Quest?"

"The business of the Brotherhood, what else?"

Blackford meant the unofficial quartet made up of Caid, Nicholas, the absent Rio and himself,

Nicholas knew. Only a few doors down from here, on an evening two years ago, they had sworn to extend their secret protection to the weakest members of society in the Vieux Carré and surrounding area, the women and children who were preyed upon by men without principle during this time when the city was divided into three competing municipalities with disorganized police protection. With crossed swords, they had each chosen their watchword, vigilance for Rio, valor for Caid, verity for Blackford and, for himself, vengeance. In the months that had passed since that day, some seventeen men had answered at sword point for their misdeeds. Most had been injured with varying degrees of severity during duels held without fanfare. Many had left town afterward, some had been injured a second time when they failed to mend their ways, one had died in an excess of choleric rage over the interference in their affairs and the summary judgment upon him.

"Nothing is on the table at the moment," Caid answered, his face a little grim.

"Too bad. Croquère spoke to me again last night while we strolled at the Marine Ballroom. The Brotherhood is whispered of everywhere—did you know? And he remembers quite plainly the day he walked in on us as we brandished our swords in salute to good intentions. He would join us, if he may."

Blackford looked from one to the other of them,

his gaze questioning. He knew, as did they all, that Croquère was not only touted as the most handsome man in New Orleans but was arguably one of the best swordsmen along the Passage de la Bourse, the street of fencing masters, close in line behind Rio, Caid, Nicholas and Pépé Llulla. Blackford should be included in that list in all probability, though there was no way to be certain of it. He avoided the tournaments that might prove such a thing, and refused to meet any of his companions in even a friendly bout on the fencing strip. The most important point, however, was that Croquère was a mulatto. His blood degree had no bearing on his qualification for joining them, but could affect how useful he might be. In Paris, where he had been educated, he had fought a number of duels, but it was different in New Orleans. Men who would gladly face off against him in his fencing salon or accept his criticism of their fighting form with gratitude would decline with regret any challenge he tendered. The Code Duello specified that a gentleman need not meet one he did not consider his peer. They all were well aware of the standard. More than that, Croquère was aware of it.

"He has a special case in mind, perhaps?" Nicholas inquired.

"I think it likely. He mentioned a gambler who blamed his mistress for a run of bad luck and sought to change it by sending her back to her mother with no settlement, no arrangement for her future, nothing except hard words."

"A quadroon then."

"Croquère thinks it was an excuse to be rid of her without embarrassment to the gentleman's pocket-book. The man's name, if I recall, was Daspit."

"Daspit," Nicholas repeated, his interest suddenly as sharp as a stiletto.

"A man seen often in the gambling hells. I met him there last month." Blackford tilted his head. "Sharp eyes, long nose, extra length of leg—I was put in mind of a large heron."

"He is unlikely to give Croquère satisfaction."

"Perhaps he will, perhaps he won't, but there are others who have the same scant care for these ladies of the half light. Croquère would be an able champion."

Nicholas glanced at Caid, who returned his look for long seconds. The Irishman saw, as he did, that the quadroons, free women of color with only a quarter or less of African ancestry who lived by becoming the mistresses of white men, were hardly in a position to demand fair treatment. Only tradition and the opinion of a man's peers forced him to provide for them, and the children he had by them, when they were set aside. These forces were strong, but could be flouted if the gentleman cared little what was said of him. The quadroons could use a champion.

"Yes," Caid said in agreement before turning to Blackford. "Tell him to choose his watchword."

The Englishman smiled. "He has it already, in anticipation. Supposing that he doesn't change his mind, it is to be vindication."

Vindication, an interesting choice, Nicholas thought. No doubt it held some special meaning for the mulatto swordsman. He only hoped it did not bring him more trouble than he could handle. Not that he would be left to face it alone. Once a part of the Brotherhood, he would have all the support he required.

They set a time and place to induct Croquère into their cadre, and Blackford agreed to make the appointment known to their newest member. Afterward, they spoke of a number of things, including President's Tyler's troubles with his cabinet members, the events in Florida following the recent end of the Seminole Indian war, and the massacre of a British garrison in Afghanistan. Their main preoccupation, however, was the situation in Texas just across the Louisiana border where the clouds of war were gathering with a vengeance.

Santa Ana, the infamous general who had directed the massacre at the Alamo during the War of Texas Independence a few years back, had been in political disgrace for some years but managed to return as president of Mexico following the ouster of Bustamente the previous fall. His counterpart across the Rio Grande in the Republic of Texas was the hero of San Jacinto, Sam Houston, who had himself just been reelected president following an interim out of office and in a campaign fought amid a manure storm of charges ranging from cowardice and public drunkenness to outright theft. Houston had been backed by the Peace Party, ruled by the rich cotton planters of the southeastern section, but his immediate predecessor in the president's chair, Mirabeau Buonaparte Lamar, a poet, excellent fencer and visionary who was hailed for a time as the Napoleon of Texas, had succeeded in stirring up Mexico prior to leaving office. Santa Ana was making noises designed to maintain his country's claim of sovereignty over Texas and to prevent further incursions into Mexican territory similar to last year's ill-fated march against Santa Fe. It was rumored he would send an expedition across the Rio Grande with the spring, making it appear Houston would soon have a war on his hands.

"Any news from Galveston?" Caid asked as he signaled for a refill of his espresso cup.

Nicholas shook his head. "The *Neptune* out of that port arrived at the mouth of the river yesterday but ran aground on a sandbar. The passengers were to come on aboard the *Octarara* this morning, I believe. I feel most sincerely for old Monsieur Gardette—his son is among those captured at Santa Fe and imprisoned in Mexico, you'll recall. He comes for his lesson every

time I open the doors, determined to perfect his swordplay in anticipation of joining some attempt to rescue
the boy."

Caid grimaced, but made no reply. What was there
to say since they both knew Texas lacked the power
to retrieve the prisoners and the government in Wash-
ington would mount no such military effort. The abo-
litionists in Congress had managed to avoid the
annexation of the Texas Republic as a slave state these
six years and more; they would have nothing to do
with any conflict with Mexico that might force the
issue.

The Santa Fe expedition had occasioned much
excitement in the city and any number of recruit-
ment rallies at Hewlett's Exchange, the unofficial
gathering place for political meetings. Texas President Lamar, then still in office, had thought to
persuade the New Mexico territory to align itself
with Texas, thus increasing trade with the U.S.
along the Santa Fe trail and, eventually, forcing
Mexico to recognize the Rio Grande as a southern
boundary. His scheme, it seemed, included a
Republic of Texas that stretched to the Pacific
Ocean. To set it in motion, he gathered a force of
some 360 soldiers and traders with their goods and
dispatched them to Santa Fe. Several of those
making up that unofficial invasion force had been
from New Orleans, young hotheads who could not
wait for a formal declaration of war before heading

off to join Lamar's ranging militia, or Ranger companies. They had expected an easy victory over a sleepy Mexican garrison with the aid of a citizenry inclined to throw in their lot with the Texans. The march across the plains had covered thirteen hundred miles of burning hot and inhospitable territory, however, with Indian attacks, hunger, thirst, illness and near mutiny dogging every step. Weakened and demoralized by the trip, they were persuaded to give themselves up to the Mexican commander at Santa Fe. In retaliation for the attempted coup, the ranks of the survivors were formally decimated, with every tenth prisoner dragged in front of a firing squad. Afterward, the rest were marched overland in chains and under grueling conditions to the Mexican state of Vera Cruz, where they were shut up in the fortress of Perote. There they still languished while the relatives of the Louisiana recruits searched the newssheets every day, hoping for news by way of the steam packet from Galveston. The incident had left a bad taste in the mouths of Vieux Carré citizens and spurred enlistment in the various militia companies.

Frowning silence held them for long moments. It was Caid who broke it finally as he turned to Blackford. "You must congratulate our friend here, if you please. It seems he is to acquire a wife."

The Englishman turned a skeptical gaze in his direction. "Unlikely."

"Not you, too," Nicholas complained, though glad of the change of subject. "There's no reason whatever that I shouldn't be wed."

"Does the crowing cock take a single hen to himself? Does the bumblebee choose a single flower, forsaking all others?"

"No, but swans mate for life and a hummingbird will guard a single flower until it fades away," Nicholas answered with asperity. "Though what the devil fowls and bugs have to do with me is more than I can see. I have not, I think, failed either of you, nor have I ever broken a pledge made in faith and solemnity."

Blackford looked at Caid. "Testy, isn't he, and sincere with it. Who can this bride be?"

"A nun."

"Faith and solemnity, yes. I do see where it might be required."

"She isn't a nun," Nicholas said through his teeth.

"Almost a nun," Caid amended, "and maternal in the extreme."

"Nicholas is the last man to need a motherly sort for a wife."

Caid agreed. "Which leads me to think there is something more to the affair than he has said so far. I feel a great need to meet this lady who has no beauty worth mentioning but can captivate in a single morning."

"It wasn't like that," Nicholas protested.

Blackford paid no attention. "We could call but are unlikely to be admitted. A lady such as Madame O'Neill, however…"

"A splendid idea." Caid slapped the table with his open hand. "Particularly as my Lisette will be even more curious than I am. Tomorrow should be a fair day for it, or the next day at the latest."

Nicholas rose to his feet with a scowl. "Excuse me. I have better things to do than provide amusement for the two of you."

"A man about to be married has many cares," Caid told Blackford in grave instruction. "The weight of the world is about to descend on his shoulders and he must make ready."

"Yes," Nicholas said. "Perhaps I should ask Lisette how you are managing so far."

"Don't go," Blackford said. "I was thinking of making an offer on those magical matched rapiers you won some while back. From Coulaux et Cie in Paris, were they not? You won't need such superior blades if you are to take a wife."

"How so?"

"She will object to a husband who appears on the dueling ground too often. And you will be closing your fencing salon anyway, or so I thought, since you came into money."

It was true, though Nicholas preferred to disregard it for now. "It hasn't happened yet."

"Well, then, seeing that you're still free, we could

travel out to the lake this afternoon. There is to be a fight between two champions of fisticuff, you know."

"Another time. I must see to young Gabriel just now, since he's still running wild."

"Squirrel and the others will take care of him."

Nicholas gave a rueful shake of his head. "If anything happened to him, they would be heartbroken, besides blaming themselves for something not their fault."

"I don't know how the welfare of a bunch of street boys became your responsibility."

"Because I made it so," he answered shortly.

"A wife to hand it over to may be an excellent solution, after all."

Nicholas gave Blackford a jaundiced look, not at all certain that there wasn't a point behind the too casual comment. Playing devil's advocate was not unknown for the Englishman. He had become increasingly contrary in the past months, since acting as a principal in an unfortunate duel in the country, in fact. Morose and recklessly high-spirited by turns, his temper was so uncertain that it was difficult to know how to take him.

Nicholas made no answer now, but picked up his hat from the extra chair seat, settled it on his head and strode away. Of what use was it to tell either of his friends that he wasn't sure he wanted to relinquish his duties with the boys?

That motley gang waited for him when he reached his atelier, squatting on the stones under the arcade that made a tunnel of coolness along the front of the long row of fencing salons of the Passage and cast a deep shade over his outside door. With them, he was relieved to see, was young Gabriel. As he approached, Squirrel rose to his feet, a frown between his eyebrows and his hands on his hips.

Nicholas eyed the boy, wondering what had he had on his mind. At the same time, it occurred to him that he was growing up. Squirrel must be nearly fifteen now, but looked older, having shot up over the past year, with a height and rangy build probably inherited from some Kaintuck, as the river boatman were called. Soon, he would have to leave off running with the street boys and take up a trade. He was already of a size to make shopkeepers and night watchmen nervous. There had been a couple of incidents where Nicholas had been forced to intervene—nothing of real consequence, a few cakes missing at a patisserie, a pair of boots from a dry goods store, but troubling nonetheless. If Squirrel should fall into real trouble, the law would treat him as an adult. He could be thrown in to prison or hanged, and few would notice or care.

He would care, Nicholas thought grimly. For better or worse, Squirrel reminded him of himself at that age. Something had to be done about him.

Caid and Lisette, to give them their due, would be

concerned as well. Squirrel and the others had entrance at their town house, which they took advantage of on days when it was raining and Nicholas was giving instruction with much coming and going at his atelier. They were also apt to show up on the mornings when the O'Neill cook baked for the week. Still, Lisette and the Irishman had their own family now, and though they had never discouraged the street boys from coming around in any way that Nicholas was aware of, the gang turned up more and more often as his place. A part of it was probably the lessons in swordplay that he gave when he had the time. Squirrel, in particular, was an apt pupil, and it seemed possible that he might one day make his living at the trade. It seemed fitting, since Nicholas's own introduction to it had come from hanging around the salon of another master in Rome years ago.

If he closed the salon and gave over the lease of the atelier to another master, where would it leave Squirrel and the others? The only answer he saw was to adopt them all. A wife to help see after them and lend the motherly touch seemed a practical addition. Yet his problem to this point had been finding a woman he thought would be willing to accept such a family of misfits. Juliette Armant might need him as much as he needed her, but he was half-afraid any suggestion of what he had in mind would make her call off their agreement on the spot.

"*Bien*, M'sieur Nick, so you return."

"As you see. Have you been waiting long?" Nicholas flicked a glance over Squirrel's face, noting the belligerent thrust to his lower lip.

"Long enough." He looked away, looked back again. "Gaby said you chased him this morning."

Nicholas grimaced. "He was eating slops out of the gutter, and smelled like it. A bath seemed in order."

"He thought you might thrash him."

"Did he indeed?" Nicholas glanced at the small boy who was trying to hide behind the rest of the crew. "If he gets sick, it will be far worse than anything I might do."

"He is my lookout since I found him," Squirrel said, squaring his shoulders. "No one touches our Gaby."

It was certainly true that the gang had found the child. He had been curled up asleep in a wooden crate, apparently abandoned behind one of the cribs on Gallatin Street, in the area known as the Swamp. It was a section of the city so dangerous that even the gendarmes avoided it. No one seemed to know where he had come from or who he belonged to, though the best guess was that he had been the child of a prostitute who had died or been killed.

Though frightened and crying when Squirrel and the others had brought him to the atelier, he did not seem to have been mistreated. His sobs had died away at the first sight of food, and he seemed to grow more robust and full of mischief every day. Just over four weeks had passed since he was found, and no one had inquired about him, no one arrived to claim him.

Nicholas unlocked the door and stood aside for the boys to pass into the rooms of the lower floor, where he stored barrels of wine and spirits, also the casks of the olives, sausages and brandied fruits that he sometimes served to clients. There was a kitchen, never used, which opened onto the grassy area behind the atelier, and where the boys slept at night on nests of old coverlets. He let them in every evening and out again in the early morning after sharing his usual sketchy meal of bread and coffee with them. It was the best Nicholas could do for now, and better than letting them fend for themselves on the streets.

"Are you hungry?"

It was a stupid question, Nicholas knew, even as it left his mouth. They were always hungry. He asked it to let them know he had something to give them, though it was only bread with cheese and sardines and a piece of nougat candy each. Still, their grins and small grunts of anticipation gave him a warm feeling near his heart that lasted well past the time it took to parcel out the food in exact portions on the scarred kitchen table.

"Gaby said there was a lady."

This came from Squirrel again, though his eyes remained on his food. The question was meant to be offhand, but the teenager's face was red. It was also telling that he had called Juliette a lady, Nicholas thought, instead of only a woman, or worse.

"There was indeed. She also thought I meant to harm Gabriel."

"He said she was *très belle*, like his mother."

"A boy of taste, our Gabriel." Nicholas glanced at the youngest among them but he was eating his nougat, paying no attention. His sweet tooth had proved every bit as strong as Nicholas's own.

"You think so?" Squirrel asked

"That's she's beautiful? She is certainly attractive in her way."

"You gonna marry her?"

Nicholas blinked in surprise. "What makes you ask that?"

Squirrel shrugged and swallowed, though it appeared the effort might choke him.

"Who told you?"

"Heard it. People always know. People talk."

"Yeah," one or two of the other boys said, backing up their leader, eyeing him and the man who stood over them from under his lashes. "People talk."

By people, Nicholas knew, they meant slaves attached to nearly every house in the Vieux Carré.

One might hear a snatch of conversation, another catch a piece of an argument, a third receive the confidence or complaint of a mistress or master. The different things were put together and, more often than not, the truth came out. Annoying, it might be, but it was also inescapable.

"What if I did marry her?" he asked, crossing his arms across his chest.

"Would she live here with you?"

Nicholas shook his head. "We would need another house."

"Something bigger," Squirrel said with a nod of understanding. "More rooms."

"Just so."

"You could go to the Armant house to live."

So he knew the name, Nicholas thought. He might have guessed that he would. "I don't think so."

"They have no man. And there's the treasure to guard."

A frown snapped Nicholas's eyebrows together over his nose. "What do you know of a treasure?"

"What people say."

Of course, what else? "I have no plans in that direction."

"But a wedding will be held."

"I don't know," Nicholas said in exasperation. "It isn't decided. Perhaps when it is, you will tell me."

"You marry Mam'zelle Armant and go to live in her house, then you won't have no place for us."

What the boy meant was that he didn't expect Nicholas to be concerned with them afterward. That the rest of them felt the same, had doubtless discussed it among themselves, was plain from the sudden quiet that fell among them. "That isn't so," he said, moving to the table and placing his hands flat on the surface. He hovered there until they looked up one by one to meet his eyes. "You will have a place with me always, all of you."

"What of mam'zelle?"

"If she cannot agree to it then there will be no marriage."

"You swear?"

Nicholas looked around the table, studying the doubtful faces turned in his direction. The boys, like the swordsmen of The Brotherhood, were of a number of different bloodlines. Faro had a Spanish look about him, while Weed was almost certainly from Irish parents, given the carrot-colored mop of curls that topped his head. Cotton had the pale hair and blue eyes of some Nordic ancestry, probably mixed with English. Buck's black skin had a blue tint, though his features suggested the Arabic north of Africa, and Wharf Rat was small and quick, with cinnamon-colored skin that had a gray tinge from embedded dirt—born of free parents, both boys stayed that way due to Nicholas's protection. Molasses appeared to have the liquid brown eyes and curling dark hair from the Italian or Greek peninsula. Then there was Gabriel, the child of an aristocratic French mother if his refined features were any indication. Yet they clung to each other, this gang of boys. They might squabble among themselves, but, again like the sword masters, they turned as one to ward off an enemy. Ranging over the city, they lived mainly in the middle of the French Section, but were yet not of it. And if they were not actively scorned by its elite, they were certainly not welcome in their homes or their hearts.

They were right to doubt the charity of Mademoiselle Juliette Armant. Nicholas was not certain of it himself. If he had been, he would have mentioned all of the boys who had become dependent on him instead of only young Gabriel. Yet he had given his pledge to marry the lady.

How could he swear now that he would not if she failed to accede to his wishes in regard to these boys?

Nicholas looked away from all the young faces, where hope burned in their eyes so valiantly, in spite of everything. "I will work out something," he said. "That is, if there is a marriage at all."

Silence followed his words. The boys ducked their heads, looked at each other, stared at the table. They did not look at him. Finally, Squirrel tossed the last crust of his bread on the table and got up from the bench on which he sat. "You don't need a wife. We were fine without one. We'll be fine again if you don't get one now."

"Without doubt," Nicholas answered, since it seemed that some reassurance was necessary.

Squirrel gave a hard nod then looked beyond Nicholas's shoulder while his lips twisted to one side as if he were biting the inside of them. Finally he spoke again. "Faro heard something, come from the Swamp."

"Yes?" The Swamp was that area where Gabriel had been found.

"Man on Gallatin Street, name of Old Cables, owns some cribs. He's a lily-livered snake of a coward, and mean with it."

"More than usual, you mean?" Nicholas asked in dry tones. The locale was not known for its kindness.

"They say he's quick with a whip. Likes it. Likes it a lot with a woman."

The other boys were looking at the table, the smoked ceiling, their grubby hands, anywhere except at him, Nicholas saw. "A woman?" he asked softly.

"Gaby's mother, maybe. He hits 'em, like. He makes them do things. He…"

"I understand," Nicholas said, his voice grim with his dislike for the knowledge in Squirrel's eyes of things no boy, even one his age, should know, much less accept.

"Something oughta be done," Squirrel went on, his voice breaking in the middle of its gruffness. "Mothers ought not die."

They shouldn't, no, and yet the boys who sat at his table almost certainly had not a living mother among them. The grief of it was in all their faces, regardless of how hard they tried to hide it. The sight did something to Nicholas, so his heart felt as if it had been sliced out of his breast with a rusty knife.

"I will see to it," he said. "This, I promise."

"Yeah."

Squirrel collected the other boys with a glance and jerk of his head. "We gotta go."

The street gang didn't argue but snatched up their food and filed from the kitchen. Once out the door, they could be heard muttering among themselves. Gabriel was the last, but he crammed half his bread and sardines in his mouth and grabbed his cheese in one dirty hand before scampering after the rest of them.

"Wait," Nicholas said, starting after the child.

The boy didn't stop, didn't look back until he reached Squirrel and dropped into step behind him, trying to match his short stride to that of the youth who had become his hero. Nicholas guessed that Gabriel would scratch, bite and scream like a wild thing if he tried to lay hands on him, and the others would likely come to his aid. He had little doubt of his ability to overcome their objections, however violent, but what then? He could only hold the youngest of their number safe by locking him away from the others, and this he was reluctant to do. Gabriel had been mistreated enough in his young life.

"Squirrel," Nicholas called. "Look after the boy."

The tallest of the street boys stopped, turned his head. "I'll do that," he said, his voice cracking a little on the words. "I swore to take care of him."

Nicholas cursed softly as he watched them go, but it did nothing to make him feel better. Nothing at all.

5

Juliette had neither seen nor heard anything of Nicholas Pasquale for the best part of three days. She had not expected him to sit on her doorstep, still it was disquieting. It was possible that he had reconsidered, taking fright as some men did at the thought of being tied to one woman for the rest of his life. If so, he should at least have had the decency to let her know.

The bare possibility existed that he was awaiting a summons from her; he had left the matter in her hands, after all. And yet it was the gentleman who was supposed to call on the lady. To send a note saying she required his presence could make her seem desperate. Which might be the exact truth, but she was loath to appear in that light.

It was also lamentably true that she wished for an excuse to wear one of the gowns delivered from Madame Ferret. The first of them had been delivered that morning, and she and Valara had lost no time in releasing them from their boxes and tissue paper wrapping and spreading them over the bed in her bedchamber.

The only time Juliette had been so enchanted by anything to wear had been as a child, when trying on her mother's shawls and capes, bonnets and headpieces. She and Paulette, one rainy afternoon, had discovered the lovely things in a dressing room trunk. They had draped themselves in them, traipsing up and down, preening and pretending to be on their way to the opera. There had been a coronet of roses made of silk, Juliette remembered, pink blooms and buds set on combs to be tucked among highpiled curls.

How their mother had scolded when she discovered them. She plucked the combs from Juliette's hair, pulling out a shining strand of five or six hairs in the process. As Juliette's eyes stung with tears, she had been told that such things were not for her. Paulette would be presented at the opera when she was of marriageable age, but Juliette would continue at the convent following her schooling there, beginning her training as a nun. She might be allowed a crown of roses at her communion, but they would be white—white for the purity of heart and soul— and that would be the end of it.

White.

Juliette had dreamed of pink roses for years afterward, though she had never dared say so.

One of the gowns sent by Madame Ferret was the

white silk suggested by Nicholas Pasquale. She had ordered it just as he had said, though without much enthusiasm. To please Monsieur Pasquale must be an object with her, however, and so here it was, complete with its cape lined in cloth of silver and with a hood framed in swans down.

The silk was like touching a cloud. The bodice, with its mitered pleats that narrowed at the pointed waist, fit perfectly. She was ready to admit the elegance of the ensemble, and even its effect as a frame for her coloring. She would wear it as a matter of course. Regardless, it didn't please her.

The other ensembles were much better. A particular favorite was a simple morning gown made of the rose-patterned gold challis bought at the draper's, a color which brought out the gold in her hair. But the most pleasing one of all was an afternoon gown of heavy grass-green silk taffeta with an *ombre*, shadow, weave that changed from green to golden brown in the folds as the light shifted across it. Its small, upstanding collar was edged with gold embroidery, and the skirt had a front opening edged with the same embroidery, which parted to reveal a gold silk underskirt.

Juliette almost rewrapped the green gown to be returned, for it was certainly nothing she had ordered. Madame Ferret had either made a mistake or thought to foist upon her an extra purchase while Juliette was in a generous mood. The odd color of the silk was most intriguing, however. Before she knew it, Valara was settling the gown over her head.

The fit was perfection, the color amazing. Her hair seemed to shimmer, with strands of gold among its many shades of brown, and her eyes took on mysterious depths. The gold lace reflected against the skin of her neck and shoulders with a gentle glow, while the taffeta outlined her shape with such fidelity that every rise and fall of her breathing altered the color from gold to green and back again.

"*Très belle,*" Valara said, standing back with her hands clasped in front of her. "I like this, me."

"So do I," Juliette murmured.

Madame Ferret really had chosen well, she thought as she turned this way and that in front of the long looking glass that reflected her bedchamber with its motley collection of cast-off furnishing, a crude, handmade cypress armoire, plain wood bedstead covered by a mosquito *baire* that draped from a ceiling hook and a large Turkish ottoman of tufted burgundy brocade that had once graced her father's study. How different she looked in the taffeta, as if she no longer belonged in the simple room always reserved for her visits home. It was vanity, foolish and unremitting, but her appearance made her heart swell with pleasure. What a change it was from the dull black and white and gray that had been all she was allowed for so long. She almost wished that

Nicholas Pasquale could see her now, at this moment.

She would keep the gown. She really must remember to compliment the modiste on her next visit, and also to settle with her on its cost.

Behind them, the door of the bedchamber swung open. Paulette came into the room with an impetuous step and a folded note in her hand. "The most terrible thing, *chère*—oh! What on earth are you doing?"

"Checking the fit of the things sent by the modiste," Juliette answered, her face flushing with an odd embarrassment and also a shade of anger that she should feel such a thing. "What do you think of this one?"

"A most peculiar color." Paulette pursed her lips.

"Isn't it."

"Not at all fashionable, I fear."

Valara, with a muttered comment under her breath that it seemed best to ignore, turned away and began to put the challis ensemble into the armoire that sat against the wall. Juliette, her enthusiasm a little dampened, gave her sister a wry look in the mirror. "Nor am I, I fear. Fashionable, I mean to say."

"It seems strange to see you in anything so…so…"

"So vivid?" Juliette supplied.

"It makes you look quite ordinary instead of as one destined for the church."

"That is to the good, don't you think, since it is no longer my fate."

Paulette gave her a brief smile as she moved to stand behind her, twitching at the green gown's skirts with one hand, as if they were not quite right. "A temporary reprieve, *chère*. I'm sorry if the prospect distresses you, but that is the way it must be. You were meant for good works. Remember how you used to be like a little mother to me when I was ill? It's in your nature to devote yourself to the care and comfort of others."

Juliette remembered the vast amount of noise and trouble Paulette had always made at the least hint of illness and how no one else could quiet her. That had been particularly true the summer they had all been taken ill with a virulent stomach complaint. Their mother was not at her best in the sick room. Any hint of gastric upset made her queasy in sympathy so she tottered away and hung her head over the chamber pot, sending at once for the doctor. Valara had been apt to dose those who fell ill under her care with simple, pleasant-tasting remedies, unlike the tonics and purgatives prescribed by the doctor, whose bitterness was in exact proportion to their supposed efficacy. Juliette had taken them obediently while spurning the more bitter draughts, which was perhaps why she had been less sick than the others. When she was able, she had persuaded her twin to do the same, begging her to take small sips of Valara's tisane. That was after her younger brother and sister, dosed by the doctor, had died and Valara had thrown his nostrums out the window in her rage. Juliette had saved her twin, or so Valara said, but she mourned that she could not save the others as well.

"Devotion," she said now with care, "is as required of a mother as it is of a nun."

Paulette tilted her head to one side. "I never knew you had any thought of being a mother."

"You never asked." Juliette avoided her sister's eyes. There was so much that no one had ever asked.

"I'm not sure I want babies."

"No?" Juliette glanced at her sister then, but Paulette was frowning at swans down on the white gown that lay across the bed.

"Women die in childbirth. Remember Louise Marat who married old Monsieur Begnaud? She succumbed just last week."

Juliette made a small sound of compassion, but Paulette seemed hardly to notice.

"They say there was blood everywhere. Her mother is distraught, for what use that may be. Therese didn't want the marriage, you know, and begged not to be forced to it. They insisted, and this is the result. Poor Louise had no will to live after being affianced to one she could never hold in affection or even respect. She died for love, they say, or want of it."

"People always say that. It makes it more romantic in a ghoulish fashion."

Paulette's eyes, a truer green than Juliette's, were as clouded as emeralds. "Yes, but what if it's true? I could never wed where I did not love, never!"

"And you love Jean Daspit."

"Madly, Juliette. I cannot tell you how much."

"You're quite sure it isn't mere infatuation? I mean—what if he isn't right for you? What if his interest is in your dowry and the chest? You must be sure."

"I must be sure? I? Dear heaven, Juliette, but you are maddening! You always think you know what is right. You are sure you know the best thing to be done for everyone. What a little prig you were when we were growing up, the chosen one, the perfect little nun. And you haven't changed one bit!"

Was it true? Juliette thought with chagrin that it might be so. She had been outside the family and social circle for so long that she had come to look at things with a certain detachment, to see the mistakes and failings of others as something that could be remedied if they would put emotion aside. Living as she had, in constant anticipation of life as a *religieuse*, she had, perhaps, considered herself an authority on what was right and wrong.

"I'm sorry if I seemed—" she began.

"Oh, please! Don't be humble for that I dislike in you above all things. Be human, my dear sister, if you can!"

Valara, behind them, made a grunting sound,

then went ponderously from the room as if unable to endure more in that vein. Juliette glanced at her sister, at the hectic color in her face and the way she was creasing the folded paper she held in her hand. In an effort to smooth over the awkward silence that had fallen, she said, "You had a note for me? Or something you meant to tell me?"

"A note? No, no, this came for me." Her sister thrust the paper square toward her. "But I thought you should know at once what it says."

Something in Paulette's manner gave her a wary sensation in her chest. "Yes?"

"My Jean has been injured in a duel of the most dastardly kind. They say he was taken by surprise in the dark by a swordsman of skill most *extraordinaire*, in fact by your Monsieur Pasquale."

"Impossible!" Juliette swung to brave the accusation in her sister's eyes. At the same time, she could not think the matter desperate or else Paulette would have been prostrate. "He was badly wounded?"

"A slash in his sword arm near the shoulder. Only think if it had reached his heart!"

"You can't really believe Monsieur Pasquale was at fault."

"Who else can it be? Who else had reason or would choose such a method? It's a miracle he was not killed. My Jean was struck down to prevent our marriage, and the man behind the sword was your precious husband-to-be they call La Roche!"

"He would not do such a thing."

"How do you know what he would or would not do? He is a stranger to you, a man who came from nowhere."

That certainly could not be denied. "He was all consideration when we met, his conduct everything that was honorable."

"Then how is it that Monsieur Daspit accuses him? For he swears it was this Pasquale who struck him down without warning."

"Without warning? But you called it a duel."

"He challenged him, yes, invited him to step outside at some affair where they came across each other. What could Monsieur Daspit do but accept— even if the man was masked. A gentleman of courage can hardly refuse even such an irregular match. But there were no seconds, no doctor, no witnesses at all, and the first attack ended it."

"I should think refusing would have been easy if one's adversary wore a mask."

"They were both masked," Paulette said with a pettish shrug.

"A subscription ball then. But I had not heard one was to take place." It could not have been a private masquerade, Juliette was sure, since a mere sword master would never have been extended an invitation.

"How should I know? There are places gentlemen go which a lady does not question. The point is that

Monsieur Pasquale accosted my Jean, intending to kill him so the treasure chest might come to him through you."

"I would remind you that Monsieur Pasquale has little use for Marie Therese's treasure given his lottery winnings. There must have been another reason. In any case, it seems plain Monsieur Daspit suspected who the challenger might be but thought he could take him."

"What man is so rich he would not have more, especially when it comes so easily?" Paulette demanded. "Oh, what does it matter exactly how it happened? The thing is that Pasquale came at him by stealth, a man of diabolical skill. He cried out something, some word of black magic. And when he left my Daspit for dead, he carved in the dirt beside him the letter *V.*"

"In the dirt? And this was outside the ball room? Then it could not have been located on one of the principal streets." It sounded, in fact, as if the affair might have been a quadroon ball, one of those entertainments offered for the delectation of young men about town where the only females present were those of mixed blood. There was, it was said, much decorum to the proceedings, with the young women closely chaperoned by their mothers or other relatives. Still, a man who saw a woman he liked could arrange, forthwith, for her to become his mistress. Such liaisons were common, just as it was common for ladies such as Paulette to pretend to ignorance of them.

To think that Monsieur Pasquale might have been present at such a ball, and for what reason, gave Juliette no pleasure. She wished that she could have remained ignorant of it as well.

"Is this a tale that monsieur tells for your ears only, or has he spread it abroad?"

Paulette gave another shrug. "What difference can it make?"

"If Monsieur Pasquale comes to hear of it, Monsieur Daspit may be forced to meet him in truth."

"Impossible, since my Jean is laid up in his bed. Besides, La Roche would not like to have their quarrel brought out in public."

"Nor would Monsieur Daspit, I believe. He might have challenged him days ago if he had wished."

"Impossible. For what cause?"

"Your fiancé was behaving discourteously toward me. I didn't want to tell you, but…"

"It's a lie!"

"I swear on the cross that it isn't. Oh, *chère*, are you certain you wish to marry that man? He dared speak to me of the rigors of the marriage bed, as he styled it, on a public street. It was meant to frighten me."

Paulette searched her face, her own expression doubtful. She hesitated an instant, then said, "Were you frightened?"

"By thought of what occurs between a man and a woman? Other women endure it and smile about it later."

"Yes, but…"

"My feelings aren't the point, *chère*. Monsieur Daspit may have annoyed me, but was soon put to rout by Monsieur Pasquale. What disturbs me is that you intend to marry a man who speaks of the wedding night as a rigor to be survived. I pray you will think carefully."

"Unnecessary, I promise you! Monsieur Daspit is a gentleman in all he undertakes, including his kisses."

"Paulette! You haven't allowed him to kiss you?"

"Don't look so shocked, *chère*. We are almost betrothed, after all."

Her sister was correct, Juliette realized. A chaste kiss or two might reasonably be permitted, though the hectic color in Paulette's face suggested that these kisses of which she spoke had been a bit more daring. But if she was allowed to be alone with her fiancé for this intimacy, then that meant she and Monsieur Pasquale would have a similar privilege.

The sword master, when next he presented himself, might kiss her. He had every right to expect it.

Juliette's breath caught in her chest, lodging behind the stiff bodice of her new gown. Heat bloomed in her abdomen and spread outward in a fiery wave, tingling below her waist. She was abruptly aware of being a female as never before in her life. It was an odd sensation, uncomfortable and yet exhilarating.

Turning from her sister in a swirl of skirts, she said over her shoulder, "You accuse Monsieur Pasquale of wanting the treasure chest. Are you sure that isn't Monsieur Daspit's object?"

"Of course it is," Paulette said with a brittle laugh. "A gentleman without fortune must be practical in these matters. But that doesn't mean it's the only thing he values in this house."

She meant herself, of course. "You have told him about the chest then? Told him what's in it?"

"Oh, Juliette, not that again. I told you I didn't look, not really."

"I only wondered how much your fiancé knows of the contents."

"Well, wonder no more," Paulette said in brittle tones. "He has no idea exactly what is in the chest, and no more do I. You shut your eyes and covered them with your hands that day or you would know I barely peeped inside. You may stop blaming me for Papa's death and that of Charles Ives. The small glimpse I had of a few old papers could not have caused them to…to die."

Juliette, hearing the shudder of dread in Paulette's voice, moved forward to take her in her arms. "Oh, *chère*."

"You think it my fault, I know it. Everyone would

if they knew. But you won't tell, will you? You will never tell?"

"Never," she murmured, smoothing her sister's back.

"I think…I think sometimes that I am being punished. All this unhappiness is a judgment on me—Papa and Charles, naturally, but also Valara saying that I'm the younger, *Maman* being so upset, you bringing home a sword master. I didn't mean it to be this way, Juliette. You know I didn't mean it."

"I know, I know." And she really did, Juliette thought. Paulette was willful and impulsive, acting without reflection. She had not meant to test the old superstitions surrounding the chest. Once she had, however, she was no more immune to the fear of what had been unleashed than was Juliette. They had both been brought up by their mother, after all.

"Do you really understand?" Paulette asked, raising an anguished face. "If so, why can't everything be as before? Why can't you simply tell *Maman* you don't feel you are the eldest and really long to go back the convent? She will accept that as a sign, I know she will."

"How can I do that when Valara has sworn otherwise?"

"You don't want to do it, do you? You want what is mine. You've always been jealous of me, always. Now you have these new gowns and the interest of a man who thrills you, and you think to take my place as the elder."

"It isn't like that," Juliette began, even as unwanted guilt assailed her. She was thrilled, at least a little.

"I think it is," her sister said, breaking free and backing away, wiping the tears from her eyes with the edges of her hands. "I think you would like to poison my mind against Monsieur Daspit so I will give him up and you may win. Well, I won't do it. I will go to the altar first, see if I don't. We have made plans, Jean and I. As soon as he is well again, we will meet with the priest to discuss marriage and begin the announcements in the church. And what have you done toward being wed? Nothing!" She turned away, skimming to the door, where she paused for the final word. "For all I can tell, you really have no bridegroom. And what is more, I don't believe you want one!"

The things Paulette had said, the way she had looked at her, remained with Juliette long after her sister had gone. She tried to decide if she really were envious of her sister and the beautiful things she had been given as a matter of course, had perhaps always resented the gaiety of Paulette's life compared to the austerity to which she had been consigned. If she were honest, she might have felt a few pangs. Oh, but why should she not? She had been like any other young girl. It was natural to yearn after what was bright and lovely, to hope and to dream. Such things were difficult to suppress.

Yet she had tried. She had wanted to be as pure of heart as everyone imagined her. She had prayed that she might not disappoint her mother or the nuns who tried so hard to make her suited to their order. The remorse she felt when she failed, as she sometimes did, had been painful.

There had been a particular gown made for Paulette, she remembered. The bodice had been dark blue and fastened down the front with bows of white lace. The same lace had edged the sleeves in the Parisian fashion, and lace petticoats had foamed at the hem of the overskirt that was light sky blue. How she had yearned to at least try on that lovely concoction. It would have fit, she knew, since she and Paulette were so near in size. She had seen herself twirling in it in imagination, felt it moving around her, whispering in its silken splendor.

She had not even asked. Her mother would have frowned, Paulette might have refused, and the weakness of her avocation would have been revealed. It was better, she had learned, to suppress such longings, for they only made the temptation harder to resist.

Oh, but how little her sister or her mother knew of her to think she had never yearned. How little they cared for what she felt or thought that they could not understand how drawn she was to all the things they took for granted.

Juliette touched the green gown, cupping her

hands at her breasts then sliding them downward to the narrow turn of her waist. The silken glide, the sheen and smoothness of the sumptuous fabric was like an ache deep inside her. The sensuous whisper of it made her shiver and break out in tiny goose bumps. The green-and-gold ensemble dazzled her eyes and delighted her soul, filling it with glorious color. The way she appeared in the looking glass, the smallness of her waist and pale roundness of her bosom, discomfited her a little, but also stirred some instinct inside that felt deliciously wanton and even a little wild.

Her sister, Daspit and even her mother were so sure that she was not meant for the marriage bed. They thought to frighten her away from it. How could they know what realms of curiosity they roused in her instead?

She had been released from her duty to the convent, a duty that should never have been hers. To take its place, she had a duty to marry, and she did not shrink from it. To accomplish it, she needed a groom. Paulette was mistaken if she thought she feared accepting one.

The one who had been offered to her was Nicholas Pasquale. She would have him if at all possible. Yes, she would indeed.

Leaving her bedchamber, Juliette made her way to the salon. A *secretaire* sat against one wall, a tall piece with a leather-covered writing surface, small shelves holding writing paper, pens and ink and a glass-enclosed cabinet above where books were kept free of dust. Seating herself in front of it, she took down the cut-glass ink bottle, removed its cork stopper, then chose a pen and inspected the nib. She sat for a moment, touching the end of the pen to her chin. Then she dipped it and began to write.

It was late afternoon when the entrance bell clanged, jumping on its metal spring that hung near the foot of the stairs. Juliette felt her heart throb against her ribs at the sound. As Valara went to answer it, she put away her utility sewing in the basket beside her chair, then jumped up and ran to the pier mirror between the two front windows. Her hair, put up in a mass of curls on top of her head, rather than the dangling spaniel's ears ringlets that were the current mode, seemed neat enough, her cheeks flushed with color. She pressed her lips together to make them pinker, then hurried back to the sofa to arrange her skirts as she heard footsteps on the stairs.

The tread was most definitely that of a man. It was Nicholas Pasquale come in answer to her missive. It had to be him.

Then the door swung inward and he appeared. His shoulders filled the opening, his smile made the room seem warmer. For an instant, Juliette felt a little lightheaded from sheer relief that he had actually arrived. It was that or the unaccustomed tightness of her corset, for it could not be the mere sight of the powerful and elegant sword master.

"Monsieur," she said, holding out her hand as he moved forward. "It was kind of you to come so quickly." At the same time, she was aware of Valara stepping from the room with the gentleman's hat and cane, no doubt going to inform her mother of the new arrival so she might join them for propriety. With any luck, she had a few moments in which to be private.

"Not at all. You must know that I have been waiting these endless days for your summons." He bowed over her hand, his clasp warm even through his gloves.

"I didn't…that is, I wasn't sure how this affair between us should be managed."

"Other than with dispatch?" His expression was gravely amused.

A small laugh bubbled up from inside her and she relaxed a degree. "Without doubt."

"Then you have decided the marriage will suit, after all?"

"I have. That is, if you have not…I mean, if you are sure of it as well."

"I am. Wait here one small moment, please." He turned and went from the room, returning a moment later with a basket.

It was a *corbeille de noce*, the nuptial basket always

presented to the bride as a betrothal gift from her prospective groom. Juliette had never expected to receive one in her life. Certainly, she had not thought Nicholas Pasquale would go to the trouble of filling one under the circumstances.

She was incredibly glad that she had taken the time to don one of her new gowns. It seemed his gesture required that extra measure of recognition.

"I would have brought this inside at once," he said with humor in the dark coffee-brown of his eyes as he set it at her feet then lowered himself to the sofa at her side, "except that I could not be sure there was need for it."

"I hardly know what to say," she whispered, her gaze on the extravaganza of woven Italian straw lined with a paper whose intricately cut gold edging reminded her, for an instant, of the gold lace on her new green gown. The basket appeared heaped with treasures.

"Nothing is required. It is your due, after all."

"Oh, no, it can't be, not when we are being so very practical."

"Are we?" he asked, his voice grave. "I thought just the opposite."

She met his eyes, aware of a strong current of understanding between them, and something more that caused her pulse to leap and her blood to course through her veins like warm wine. Then the sound of approaching footsteps sounded in the connecting room. Before she could answer, Nicholas rose and turned away, standing tall and rigidly correct at Juliette's side as her mother glided through the doorway.

"What a surprise, Monsieur Pasquale. We had begun to think you had deserted us."

"I apologize if I seemed derelict in my attentions," he said gravely. "There were arrangements to be made."

"I see." Her mother's her gaze rested a moment on the basket at Juliette's feet. She turned to Valara, who hovered behind her. "Ask Mademoiselle Paulette to join us. She will wish to be present for this."

Juliette bit back a protest. She would have preferred to lift out the gifts chosen for her one by one, taking them from their wrapped paper with only Nicholas as witness. They were for her alone, and she could hardly remember a time when that had been true, when she did not have to divide with Paulette. It was selfish of her to feel disinclined to share the enjoyment now, and she was sorry for it. However, she was also reluctant to have her pleasure tarnished by the disparaging glances or comments she feared might be directed her way.

The time passed slowly. Juliette rather expected Nicholas to be ill at ease, but he kept up a flow of small talk, entertaining her mother with just the kind of rumor and tittle-tattle about city officials and happenings at plantation house parties that she liked to hear. The only indication that it was not his usual conversational theme was the sardonic gleam in his eyes when he glanced in Juliette's direction. Madame Armant sat forward in her chair, the better to hear, and once forgot herself to the extent of giving a small titter of laughter. So engrossed was she, that she actually frowned as Paulette sailed into the room.

"What is this?" Paulette asked, her voice a little high as her gaze fell on the telltale basket. "How very beforehand of you, Monsieur Pasquale."

"Your sister should have every observance," he answered, his voice even.

"You are a romantic. How droll."

"Paulette, *chère*," their mother said in feeble reprimand.

In that same moment, Valara entered, bearing a small tray on which was balanced a glass of claret of the kind offered to gentlemen callers and three glasses of *eau sucré*. Juliette's sister said no more, but moved to a chair and dropped down onto it, folding her hands as if seeking patience.

There seemed nothing to be done except explore the contents of the basket. Leaning forward, Juliette took out the first small bundle that came to hand.

It was a pair of tortoiseshell side combs with gold filigree trim. After admiring their workmanship and saying everything appropriate, she passed them to her mother for inspection. Following these came a box of almond-and-rose soap, and a pair of kid gloves embroidered with violets and roses. These were followed by a silk handkerchief embroidered white on white, and a set of needles with gold eyes enclosed in a painted and gilded case.

"*Alors*, monsieur!" Juliette's mother exclaimed. "You would pierce this marriage like the stab of your sword?"

"Madame?" The man beside Juliette lifted an eyebrow in puzzled inquiry.

"One never makes a gift of a knife to a friend or loved one, for it will cut the relationship, nor of needles, for they will surely put holes in it. Everyone knows this."

Nicholas reached at once to take the needle case from Juliette's hand, tucking it into his coat pocket. "My apologies, madame. I did not realize. There now, they are gone." He reached for the glass of claret that had been set on the side table near his elbow, and took a small sip.

Madame Armant gave a cry so sharp that he flinched, almost spilling the wine. The glance he sent Juliette was a clear request to know what he had done now.

"*Maman?*" she said with as much patience as she could manage.

"He uses the left hand, *chère*. Tell me he does not do the devil's work."

Juliette gave him an uneasy look. "Monsieur?"

"My regrets, but I am indeed left-handed, mademoiselle. For that, there is nothing I can do."

"Oh, my poor daughter," Juliette's mother moaned, drawing out her handkerchief and holding it to lips. "My poor daughter."

"*Maman*, please," Juliette said. "Many people favor the left hand as you well know. And it is only a day's work for the devil that's required because of it."

"But which day, I ask you? It isn't natural, and with all the rest…"

It was often best to disregard her mother's starts of this kind, Juliette had discovered. Suppressing a sigh, she turned back to the basket before her. From it, she drew a fan with sandalwood sticks and a hand-painted scene of leaves blowing in the wind. Next came a cashmere shawl woven in a paisley pattern and so fine it could be pulled through a ring, as the saying went, followed by a brooch of coral carved like a miniature rose bouquet. Finally only one item was left. As the paper was lifted away, a jewel box appeared, which opened to display a pair of bracelets.

Paulette gasped, a sound echoed by Juliette's own swiftly caught breath of amazement. It was the only sound she had made to that point, but it said plainly how startled she was, and how beguiled.

The bracelets were impressive indeed, wide bands

of gold set with pearls and coral in an intricate rose pattern highlighted by tiny emerald leaves. Such jewelry pieces were the current rage to cover the small stretches of bare wrist between the sleeves of a day gown and a lady's short gloves. They were also a fashionable version of the traditional gift given by the prospective groom to his future bride.

Rose blossoms and buds carved in rose-pink coral. She had her pink roses, and they would be hers forever.

"Allow me," Nicholas said, setting his claret glass aside and taking the velvet-lined box with the bracelets from her. Snapping them open, he fitted them, one after the other, onto Juliette's wrists and fastened the catches.

The touch of his hands, the intimacy, and the finality of the act made Juliette's heart beat faster. She feared he could feel that hot throb in the pulse points on the undersides of her wrists, knew he could when he looked up and met her eyes while the centers of his own turned dark, and darker still.

Madame Armant waved her handkerchief in a gesture of determined bravery. "You have been more than generous, Monsieur Pasquale. I am sure Juliette is grateful, as I am for her sake."

"Yes," Juliette said quietly. Never in her life had she received such beautiful things. She had no words to express how precious every item in the basket was to her, particularly the bracelets, or how grateful she was that he had troubled to buy them for her.

"*Bien*. We will leave you, Paulette and I. That is to say, it is usual for a betrothed couple to be given a few minutes for private communication on these occasions and I do not begrudge them now." Her mother rose to her feet, wavering a little before regaining her balance. "I fear—I mean, I feel sure you will wish to set a date for the nuptials."

"A date," Paulette echoed. "But *Maman!*"

"It is necessary, *chère,*" their mother said with an air of great bravery in the face of tragedy.

"It isn't fair. Monsieur Daspit is laid up in his bed so unable to select items for my *corbeille de noce* or proceed to dates, and all because of Monsieur Pasquale."

Nicholas frowned. "Pardon me?"

"It was you, you know it was," Paulette said, her face pale as she made the accusation. "Who else would try to kill him while hiding behind a mask?"

A strange expression crossed Nicholas's face, one that came and went so quickly that Juliette could not name it. Still, it left her uneasy.

"I would not take that advantage, mademoiselle."

"You would say that, of course."

"Nor am I accustomed to having my word questioned."

Madame Armant walked to the door. "Paulette. Come."

"I will never forgive you for this attack, Monsieur Pasquale. Never!"

Paulette ran from the room behind their mother.

The connecting door was left open, however, and it was plain from the sound of their voices that they had gone no farther than the next room. Juliette was acutely conscious of that fact as she turned to the man she was to marry.

"I hardly know what to say," she began. "Paulette—"

"Then say nothing," he interrupted. "How your sister sees me is of no importance compared to other matters that should be settled. Would you like the usual alliance rings between us, or would you prefer something different?"

It was considerate of him to take so little notice of her family's blatant disapproval, though he must be accustomed to it by now. It was Juliette who minded it, for his sake. With an effort, she turned her attention to his query. He referred to the customary interlocking double rings for bride and groom. These were usually engraved inside with their initials and the date of their marriage. One ring of the pair would be worn until the wedding, then it would be locked together with its mate following the ceremony and worn forever after.

"I...the alliance rings would be lovely, if you care for them."

He inclined his head. "I will call for you in the morning to escort you to the jeweler then, so you may choose exactly the style you like. That is, if you have no objection to being seen with me."

He meant in public, because of the speculation it would cause, and the gossip. "It will be as well if people become used to the sight, will it not?"

"There is that," he answered with amusement threading the surprise in his voice. "Perhaps you will have a date for the engraving in mind by that time."

"Have you no preference?"

"I am at your disposal."

"We must consult with the priest to receive his counsel and his blessing." She was trying to be prosaic about these arrangements, though it was difficult with him so close beside her.

"I will be there. Arrange it as needed."

"Yes." She paused. "Monsieur…"

"I wish you would call me Nicholas."

"It isn't the usual thing, even after the wedding."

"Still, I prefer it."

"Nicholas, then." She hesitated again. "About… about the injury to Monsieur Daspit…"

"I had no hand in it. Must I swear it to you?"

She searched his face, noting the clearness of his dark eyes with their thick fringe of lashes, the arch of his eyebrows—particularly on the left side where it just missed being permanently sardonic—and the firm set of his lips. He was sincere, she was sure of it. And yet something remained.

"You know something about it, perhaps?"

His face changed, and he gave a slow shake of

his head. "That isn't the same as being responsible. I do promise that the matter has no bearing on our marriage."

His manner was still relaxed, but the lines of his face were set, giving nothing away. It would have to do, she thought. "Very well."

His smile was like the summer sun easing from behind a cloud, a gathering blaze of heat and beneficence. "You are a rare woman, Juliette Armant."

"I somehow doubt it."

"Believe me, it's true." He got to his feet with a lithe movement, and turned toward the door. "I will call for you in the morning."

"Wait, I haven't thanked you for all the lovely things you gave me, or for thinking of the basket." Rising, she moved after him.

He stopped, turned back. "There is no need. It was your right, and my honor."

It was gallantry at its most facile, she knew, but no less affecting for it. Greatly daring, she put out her hand to touch his arm, the lightest brush of her fingers. "Regardless, I am grateful."

They stood there for endless seconds, her fingers barely tethering him to her, her betrothal bracelets gleaming gold at her wrists, her skirts brushing his half boots. Their eyes met in silent query and answer. Then he glanced at her mouth, drew a breath and held it for endless seconds. A soft oath left him. He bent his head and touched his lips to hers.

His mouth was smooth and warm, and tasted of claret and some rich, sweet essence that seemed his alone. It held hers, molding it to his touch, his desire. The gentle pressure and delicate savor of it made her feel as if there were nothing in the world except the two of them and the clinging surfaces of their lips, as if some deep, soul-stirring communication of blood and sinew took place between them in that brief meeting of breaths and mouths and beings.

Seconds later, it was over. Valara was there, almost palpably discreet as she handed over the visitor's hat and cane. Nicholas took them and went lightly down the stairs while Juliette watched him go. She moved out onto the gallery, standing at the railing to see him disappear into the shadowy opening of the entranceway. Slowly, she lifted her hand to touch her lips and the pulse that throbbed there. And she knew beyond the possibility of doubt that everything had changed.

She could never, ever accept with complacency the fate decreed for her at birth. Only the most dire circumstances could force her to go back to being a nun.

6

How he could have ever thought the lady he was to marry plain was beyond his comprehension, Nicholas thought on the following morning as he and Juliette strolled along the rue St. Louis with Valara following three steps behind them. She didn't stun the senses on sight, as some beauties were wont to do, but she had a presence that crept in upon the consciousness like the glow of a rising moon. Her attraction was without artifice. She was serene and unaffected in her manners. Her smile was genuine. Everyone who passed her on the street smiled in return without realizing it.

Few of them looked on her escort with pleasure. That dimmed Nicholas's enjoyment of the outing but could not destroy his pride and pleasure in having Juliette on his arm.

She was most soignée this morning in a walking costume of blue silk faced with pink and with pink silk shirring, and pink flowers under the brim of her bonnet. Her hair was covered, except for a chignon in the shape of a figure eight that nestled at the nape of her neck...still he had seen it uncovered just yesterday. Far from being ordinary brown, it was highlighted with gold, streaked with auburn like rich molasses, and touched here and there with shimmering hints of blue. The need to see it down, swirling around her shoulders and across her breasts made his fingers itch to search out and remove the pins that held it in place. That prospect was one of the things that made him inclined to have the wedding take place as soon as might be possible.

Another reason concerned the gang of boys who followed them at a safe distance on the opposite side of the street. The bonnet Juliette wore prevented her from catching sight of them, Nicholas was almost sure, but they were inspecting her from the crown of that smart straw confection to the tips of her blue leather slippers. No doubt they were intent on seeing what sort of mother the lady might make, and if they could abide her, after all. Gabriel, Nicholas noticed, seemed to have no such doubts. He would have run after her if Squirrel had not held him back.

The boy had good instincts. Nicholas had spent some time the evening before in contemplation of the part Juliette would play in making a home for them all. His thoughts had drifted to a son of his own blood, perhaps with her unusual green-and-gold eyes. That had led, not unnaturally, to the lovemaking necessary to bring about such an end, to the thought of her hair caressing him like silk, her breasts smooth and round against his chest, her legs twined around his, and her hands, ah, her hands…

It had been a long and uncomfortable night. Knowing that he was hardly fit to touch the hem of her day gown, much less her undoubtedly chaste night wear, made no difference whatever.

Thinking of it now added nothing to his ease, either. Cashmere pantaloons of the kind he had donned that morning with a gray frock coat were not designed to conceal the effects of virulent male imagination. It was time he turned his attention to other things.

He opened his lips to ask if Juliette had any interest in the new comedy to be given for the first time at the St. Charles, something called *A Lesson for the Ladies*, but she spoke at the same time.

"Would you mind very much if we stopped off a moment at Madame Ferret's? There is a small matter that I must take up with her."

"As you wish," he answered, even as he sought some way to avoid the detour. If her purpose was as he suspected, he would rather be elsewhere when she questioned the modiste. "However, I must admit my time is limited as this is my day at the salon."

"Your day?"

"We sword masters alternate days when we are available, you understand. It allows for time to recover between bouts of exertion and permits clients to patronize more than one salon."

She stopped on the banquette. "You have men waiting on you at your atelier? Oh, but you must join them at once."

"A good friend is occupying them at the moment, so all is well." The friend was Croquère. Nicholas hoped sincerely that no friends of Jean Daspit came looking for him while the mulatto was in charge. He didn't want his fencing salon torn up, even if he did intend to give it up at the end of the season.

"Then I shall just stop in at Madame Ferret's after all. It will only take a moment."

Nicholas bowed to the inevitable. With luck, Madame Ferret would be occupied with a customer so only a sales clerk was available for inquiries. He might yet brush through this unscathed.

His luck was out. The modiste came bustling from the back with her smile showing a large quantity of pink gums and yellowed teeth and the pince nez on her nose fairly quivering with her eagerness.

"Mademoiselle, monsieur, I trust I see you well. How may I be of service this fine morning? Please say all was in order with the gowns delivered for mademoiselle."

"Indeed," Juliette said with a smile, "but I must bring to your attention one that I did not commission. I should have returned it at once, but it is, unaccountably, made to my measurements. You will remember it, I'm sure, if I tell you the fabric was of an unusual green."

"But yes, *ma chère*, how could I forget?" The modiste exchanged a sparkling glance with Nicholas, who immediately shook his head, trying to signal discretion.

"You mean there was no error?"

"None at all. How very fortunate you are, *ma petite*, to have the advice of a gentleman of such taste and refinement. So many who interfere in these matters have neither, you understand."

"A gentleman."

"But of course." She glanced again at Nicholas, her smile secretive yet knowing.

Juliette turned to him. "You ordered the green-and-gold gown, monsieur?"

Nicholas said a small prayer and pinned his best smile on his face. "An uncontrollable impulse, I fear. If you don't care for it…"

"I do, very much, but that is not the point. Who paid for this order?"

Now how was he to answer that? If he said it had been charged to her mother's account, then he would not only be guilty of extreme presumption but might easily be found to have told an untruth. If he said it was to his own, he assumed a right that would not be his until after they were married. If they ever were married after such a gaffe.

At least she approved his selection. He had that satisfaction.

He had hesitated too long. So much for his vaunted charm. Where it went when he faced Juliette Armant, he could not begin to guess.

"To whom have you charged the cost of this gown?" Juliette demanded, turning again to Madame Ferret.

"Why, as to that, mademoiselle…" the modiste began, her complexion visibly paler as she stared from one to the other of them, clearly realizing she had made an error.

Nicholas could not allow the modiste to suffer for his impulse. "To me," he said in firm tones. "I commissioned it and I paid for it. I will apologize in any way you like for daring to think you would accept it, mademoiselle, but the silk reminded me of you when I saw it in the window and I could not resist."

"You have no right."

"Agreed."

"You must know I cannot accept such a gift. Or did you think I had ordered so many gowns I would not notice another?"

"I thought you would be beautiful in it. That was all."

"Was it indeed? And did you think, perhaps, that I might be as compliant as the other women for whom you have apparently selected such things in the past?"

That she had so little understanding of the respect in which he held her stunned him. That she could feel any slightest hint of jealousy, as suggested by her question, almost robbed him of speech. He glanced at the old nurse, Valara, who had followed them silently into the shop in her capacity as chaperone, but her impassive face gave him no hint of how to escape from the situation he had created.

"The ladies in question have been the wives of my good friends," he said, choosing his words with extreme care, "and my part in selecting their gowns was merely as an advisor. The reckoning went to their husbands. I will admit to anticipating the role of a husband in this case, but would remind you that we are soon to be married. Under the circumstances, I could not feel that a little more irregularity would be of moment."

She lifted her chin, her gaze meeting his squarely. He held that regard though it was one of the most difficult things he had ever done.

"Mam'zelle," Valara said, clearing her throat with a rasp. "Remember, if you will, the Plauchet *soirée*."

Juliette glanced at the nursemaid and a frown pleated her brow. Abruptly, she turned to the modiste. "You will strike out the amount put to the account of this gentleman, if you please, and add it to my mother's."

Madame Ferret glanced at Nicholas, who gave a resigned nod. "But yes, *certainement*, Mademoiselle Armant," she answered, "at once."

"Considering the nature of this misunderstanding, I'm sure I need not ask that no word of it should pass beyond the door of this establishment."

"*Mais non*, mademoiselle."

Juliette's features relaxed a fraction. "I shall have need of a gown suitable for a wedding shortly. I may count on you to provide it, yes?"

Madame Ferret's assurances were fervent and voluble, and followed them from the shop and into the street.

Nicholas hardly knew whether to risk further recriminations by continuing with his apologies or stop while he was to the good. Valara, thankfully, relieved him of the problem.

"It's as well you did not return the green gown, *chère*," she said in a low rumble from where she walked behind them. "You would have nothing to wear to the Plauchet's, for the white and silver is too elegant, too much for the opera."

"Yes, I'm aware," Juliette answered over her shoulder.

"So that's why you accepted my gown," Nicholas put in with the glimmer of a smile. "You had need of it."

She gave him a clear look. "I accepted it because I like it. Also because you are quite right in saying that nothing about our betrothal is as usual."

"Do you mind that?" His amusement faded as he waited for her answer.

"What good would it do? Some things can't be changed."

"So must be endured? I'm not sure I like that approach. We could, if you like, try for more normality."

"Flirtation and formal visits, you mean?" she asked with a quick glance. "Sitting in the salon with my mother while I speak in platitudes and you concoct elaborate compliments that mean nothing at all? I prefer it as we are, I think."

"Where we hardly see each other and you ignore my compliments when we are together?"

"Did you pay me one?" she asked, her eyes widening a fraction.

"You thought it an excuse?"

"Frankly, yes."

"I can see that flirtation is definitely required. May I accompany you to this soirée?"

She looked a little self-conscious and a hint of color touched her cheekbones. "It is a private affair, mostly family. You would not care for it, I'm sure."

What she meant, but was too kind to say, was that he lacked the credentials to be invited, being without family background or a name that could be traced to the *ancien regime*, and a *maître d'armes* to boot. He did not press it, but was aware of a sudden burning need to be present.

Ordinarily, Nicholas would have been indifferent, but this was a challenge. One way or another, he was going to see what his bride-to-be looked like in the gown he had chosen for her. It was a matter of curiosity, he told himself, and possibly of pride, but nothing more. No, nothing more.

The call at the jeweler on the rue Chartres took no time at all. Nicholas was hardly surprised by now, yet it disturbed him in some fashion that he could not pinpoint. Most women would have at least glanced at the display of fine ladies time pieces in gold and silver fastened by lapel pins or with chains to hang from the neck then pin at the waist. They would have hung over the glass-enclosed mahogany cases where lay the complete jeweled parures, from rings and bracelets and necklaces to earrings, each piece set with topazes or rubies, emeralds, sapphires or diamonds, or else the individual brooches or chatelaines to keep handy the needle cases, scissors and thimbles, perfume bottles and tiny notebooks and so on displayed beside them. Juliette passed them by with hardly a glance, walking straight to the ring case. There, she chose an alliance set of simple elegance in the traditional gold set with rubies, neither the most expensive shown to her nor the least. She tried it briefly for fit, then asked Nicholas's opinion, pointing out with inescapable logic, when he deferred to her taste, that he must wear the masculine mate of it. He signified his satisfaction and the jeweler, Monsieur Muh, complimented their selection, as did Valara. There were no rapturous sighs, no sidelong glances and certainly no tender kisses to seal the choice.

Afterward, they returned to the Armant town house, stopping neither for a pastry or an ice since Juliette refused to be the cause of further neglect for his salon. And that was that.

The whole business left Nicholas on edge. Why that might be, he was not certain. The arrangement between Juliette and himself suited him. He was of an age when marriage was logical and he had need of a wife. He appreciated decisiveness and dispatch in a lady, and he did not regret the outlay for rings and other furbelows. He was no callow youth, mooning over a pretty form and face and writing bad poetry to commemorate his lady's shell-like ears.

What in hell was the matter with him?

The remainder of the day at his salon did not go well. He was so distracted that he allowed a mere stripling to come within an inch of touching him in a practice bout, then returned an attack from another with such ferocity that the poor man stumbled backward over his own feet and fell on his backside. He offered the cigar box to a man known to turn green at the first whiff of tobacco, and poured wine over the fingers of one so fastidious that he changed his linen six times every day. A few more like incidents and he could close his salon long before the wedding because he would have no patrons left.

Being blue-deviled and at loose ends as evening drew in, he walked over to the rue Royale and dropped in at the O'Neill town house. It was the Moisant town house, of course, strictly speaking, since it belonged to Caid's wife who had been the widow Moisant. Regardless, no one had called it by that name since their marriage.

Caid was not at home, but Nicholas was shown into the salon where Lisette and her longtime companion, Agatha Stilton, were entertaining a visitor, a lady dressed in the dark and elegant style of the Spanish aristocracy. The caller, disregarding her stiff finery, jumped up and ran toward him the instant he stepped into the room.

"Nicholas!" she cried, casting herself into his arms. "I've been so longing to see you!"

"And I you, *condesa*," he said on a husky laugh as he finally stepped back, gazing down with real affection at Celina de Vega, *née* Vallier, who was just the same as when she had left New Orleans, with her sherry-colored eyes and fine, golden brown curls. "When did you get in? Where is Rio?"

"This noon, finally, and I thought we should never arrive. I always forget how endless the river is, once its mouth is entered from the gulf, and nothing to see except swamp and cane fields. As for Rio, the wretch has deserted me, gone off with Caid to visit old haunts. You would think he had been a New Orleanian from birth to see how much he misses the city.

He meant to surprise you at your salon, I think. It's amazing that you didn't run into him on your way."

"I'm glad I did not," Nicholas returned, smiling down at her, "for I would surely have missed such a warm greeting."

"*Parbleu!* As if he would care that I embrace the man who once saved my life."

"That was his doing, and you know it."

"But your sword which finished the thing, deny it how you will. Come, sit down. I have been hearing the most astonishing tale about you from Lisette, and won't rest until I have the straight of it from your very own lips."

He greeted Lisette, Caid's sensible and much adored wife of the lustrous auburn hair and smoke gray eyes, with the traditional salute on either cheek, bowed over the hand of her angular, New England-born companion and scratched behind the ears of the Lisette's little dog, Figaro, curled up in a corner of the settee. Then he knelt an instant to greet young Sean François O'Neill, who stared back solemnly from where he sat in the arms of his nurse-maid, apparently being displayed to Celina.

Rather than answer Celina's quizzical comment, Nicholas asked after the children born to her while in Spain, a son who put in an appearance a few months after they arrived there and a daughter born a short time before they left again for Louisiana. While he listened, he declined the offer of claret in favor of the cool drink made with lemon syrup that the ladies were enjoying. After the descriptions of the de Vega progeny, whom he was entreated to visit at his earliest convenience, he was regaled with tales of the sojourn in Spain, the glories of Catalonia, the vapid yet strained nature of the Spanish court under the recently reinstated Queen-Regent Christina and the alternating terror and tedium of steamboat travel across the Atlantic in winter.

"But enough," Celina said finally. "You were going to tell me about this marriage of yours."

"Tell us both," Lisette said, "for I've only heard it from Caid. Though a prince among men, he is most unsatisfactory when it comes to the details of a story."

"I will give you all the details your hearts desire, but would beg a favor in return."

"You know you have only to ask, *mon cher,*" Lisette said at once.

He had been almost sure of it, which was why he dared broach the subject. His smile carried warmth and gratitude in equal measure as he said, "Then you may proceed with the interrogation."

The pair of them took him at his word, bombarding him with questions until he was sure he had no secrets at all remaining in his life. At last they fell silent, watching him with something unnervingly like compassion in their lovely, knowing faces.

"Oh, Nicholas," Celina said after a moment, "are you sure this is what you want?"

"It is."

"And you care nothing for this lady," Lisette asked, tipping her head to one side. "You are certain of it?"

He thought of his reaction to Juliette's nearness this afternoon and felt perspiration break out at his temples. "As to that…"

A smile lit her eyes. "You do care, admit it. You took one look at her and were struck by a *coup de foudre*, the thunderbolt to the heart, which destroys reason and makes fools of us all. This is why you are so eager for the match. It has nothing to do with little Gabriel or the street boys."

"I almost wish you were right," he said with a wry smile and a shake of his head. "I would like to think the happiness of my friends could be mine. But, alas."

The two women looked at each other, and Nicholas felt his stomach muscles clench at the prospect of further questions. If he had not given them carte blanche to ask them, he would be ready to leap up and make his escape. Something of his feelings must have communicated itself to them, or else they decided to take pity on him. When Lisette spoke again, it was to revert to their promise.

"You spoke of a favor in return for your story. What could we possibly do for such a self-sufficient gentleman?"

"I had thought to throw myself on your mercy in

the matter of an invitation, *chère*, but am reminded
that Madame Celina is related to the Plauchets." He
turned to Celina. "I have that right, yes?"

"Indeed, if you mean Etienne and Sonia Plauchet.
Sonia is my cousin."

"So you might prevail upon Madame Plauchet to
add another name to the invitation list for her
soirée?"

"Yours, for instance?"

He inclined his head. "Mademoiselle Armant will
be there, you see, and I have a notion to see how she
fares after being away from the social scene for so long."

"I'm sure Sonia would not mind at all, but her
husband is rather a stick who frowns on anything in
the least unconventional."

"You could persuade him, I know."

A considering look appeared in her mist-colored
eyes. "Perhaps, if they thought they could have Rio
as well. It would be a feather in their caps to be the
first to entertain the Count de Lérida on his return
to the city."

Nicholas heard the anticipation in her voice
without surprise. Rio had been a sword master before
gaining his Spanish title and so denied such entertainments among the elite in the past just as
Nicholas was now. To be elevated to the position of
social lion could not but be gratifying, even if he had
been lounging around the Spanish court. "You think
this privilege might allow the entrée for a friend?"

"I don't see why not. Rio would be pleased to twist Robert's tail a little. He was rather odious to him when my brother was injured in the fire at the Hotel St. Louis, you know."

"I remember something of that," Nicholas said. He had been busy fighting the fire that had ravaged the hotel but well recalled Rio's angry despair over the situation. The hotel had just opened again after its rebuilding and he wondered briefly what Rio would think of the new version. He said nothing of what passed through his mind, however, but expressed his gratitude in suitable terms for the prospect of an invitation.

Lisette, eyeing him as he fell silent again, said, "Stand up, Nicholas. Let us look at you."

He lifted an eyebrow, but it went against his principles to refuse the request of a lady. Setting aside his glass, he came to his feet with a pretense of ease.

"Turn, please."

He held out his hands and revolved, though he could feel heat gathering under his collar and cravat.

"A visit to the tonsure parlor, yes?" Lisette said with a glance at Celina. "The hair is a bit long, which is fine in a poet but a little threatening in a sword master."

"Threatening?" Nicholas's voice held pained inquiry as he faced them again.

"Too romantic to be respectable," Celina said. "You already have the appeal of a man dangerous to know. You need not add macabre fascination."

"It wasn't my intention to add anything."

"You do it whether you intend it or not," Lisette said with offhand frankness. "It's this fascination with death so popular of late. Everything is ruins and catacombs and weeping willows and black crows." She shuddered, looking at the same time at Celina for support. "A gray coat, I think, very simply made without braiding or other decoration, and worn with a white waistcoat, or perhaps a striped one."

"And pantaloons that are not quite so stylish," Celina said.

"I believe you are right. It won't do at all for him to outshine the other gentlemen."

"At least not by too great a margin," Celina said judiciously.

"Ladies," he said in warning tones.

"We must consider his betrothed," Lisette said. "She will not wish him to be too attractive to other women."

"Decidedly not. Some way must be found to minimize all that Italian charm."

"Maybe I should just keep my mouth shut and let you two do all the talking for me," he said, crossing his arms over his chest. "Otherwise, I may seduce some poor mademoiselle by accident and cause a terrible scandal."

"He might, you know," Celina said, looking wide-eyed at Lisette. "His smile can be as lethal as his riposte."

"Humorous," he said with no smile at all. "Though what need I might have with some coy maiden when I will have such brazen ladies at my side is more than I can see. Between you two and my betrothed, I shall be spread extremely thin."

The door opened behind him at that moment and two gentlemen lounged into the room. "Bring out the rapiers, *mon ami*," one drawled in a deep voice tinged with a Spanish accent. "This dastardly Italian is seducing our wives and must be taught a lesson yet again."

"You're certain it's necessary? It appears to me the ladies have him at a disadvantage."

"In which case, we should certainly run him through as a menace to society and be done with it."

"What you can do is save me from these two harpies," Nicholas said to Rio and Caid with real relief. "They are tearing my character and my wardrobe to shreds, so I am left with nothing except to seduce them in self-defense."

"Oh, well, in that case," Rio said magnanimously.

"Hah!" his wife exclaimed. "Wait until tonight when I have you alone!"

"I am all anticipation."

Rio's eyes were filled with heated promise overlaid by affection so deep that it transformed his face, Nicholas saw. The sight gave him an empty feeling inside that he could not explain and didn't care to examine.

* * *

The Plauchet soirée turned out to be a musical affair, with a string quartet culled from the orchestra of the St. Charles Theater and an exhibition by three members of the corps de ballet currently appearing at that venue. Afterward, there was to be dancing, of course, since the city was mad for the latest Viennese waltzes of Herr Strauss.

Etienne Plauchet was a sugar planter who had a sizeable plantation on Bayou St. Jean. The town house he maintained was in keeping with that white gold wealth. Its second-floor ballroom was rather ostentatious in a city where private entertainments were usually small enough to fit into a salon or else the larger room created by opening the sliding doors between double salons. Pale colors of the kind popular during the reign of Louis XV had been used in the décor. The delicate palette made an excellent foil for the refined colors chosen by the ladies for their gowns. The ballroom was warm with the coal fires that burned at either end, and scented by the combined effects of smoke, perfume, Macassar oil favored by the gentlemen and the China roses that hung their heads in tall vases set between the windows.

Nicholas had plenty of time to study his surroundings; he was present with the party of the conde and condesa de Lérida for a good quarter hour before the Armant ladies put in an appearance. With them, he noted with grim displeasure was Jean Daspit, looking like a great crane with his bony arm in a sling of white silk. His attention could not be held by that gentleman for long, however. As Daspit stepped aside, he revealed a vision in green and gold.

To Nicholas's immense satisfaction, the gown he had chosen for Juliette was as perfect as he knew it would be. The color brought out the rich lustre of her hair and pearl-like sheen of her skin while the gold lace made her eyes seem as bright as stars. She appeared strikingly elegant, and every inch the lady of fine family which she was without doubt.

Celina, coming to stand at his side, leaned close to speak in low tones. "That is your lady?"

"It is."

"She doesn't have the look of a nun."

"She did," he said. "Until now."

She looked, in fact, much more like her twin sister than she ever had before. Nicholas was not so sure that was a beneficial transformation. Yet to look at Paulette left him unmoved, while watching Juliette stopped the breath in his chest and made his brain feel hot in the cauldron of his skull. It ignited a fierce, burning ache of possessiveness unlike any he had ever known.

"You had best get her to the altar quickly, or you may find yourself cut out."

It was an intolerable thought. "You may well be right," he said, moving in Juliette's direction as if drawn by invisible cords before the words were half out of his mouth. "Excuse me, if you please."

He thought the condesa de Lérida gave a soft chuckle as she watched him go, but did not look back to be sure.

Madame Armant and Paulette, with Daspit at her side, were greeting the Plauchets as they stood near the door to receive their guests. Juliette stood to one side, which suited Nicholas just fine. He inclined his head to those he passed, trying to look as if attending such affairs was a boring and unexceptional necessity. His attention was for his betrothed, however, who watched his approach, appearing immensely entertained but not particularly surprised to see him.

"Nicholas," she said, extending her hand, "how very glad I am that you are here."

"I return the sentiment a thousand times, though I must tell you that it is unwise to allow a gentleman to know so easily how you feel." His manner was grave, and he did not release her hand, could not bring himself to forego the pleasure of feeling its warm clasp through the double layer of his own gloves and hers.

"Now why is that?"

"It could cause him to think that he need not exert himself further to fix your interest."

Her smile was bright, lighting her eyes with an impish quality he had not seen before and which gave him an odd feeling behind his breastbone. "Since we are to be wed, I cannot imagine more exertion would be useful to you."

"That only shows how you underestimate me, *ma chère*," he answered at his most suave. "Flirtation between a gentleman and a lady is an agreeable art that can lead to many interesting discoveries."

"Such as?"

She watched him with great care, he saw, and could not suppress a smile. "Now that is well done as an introduction to the game. I congratulate you. But such as…? Why, likes and dislikes, thoughts, dreams, what makes the other laugh, or not."

"So we would talk."

The enjoyment in her face was enchanting. He wished that he could keep it there longer, but her sister was glancing their way with the glitter of anger in her eyes, and Daspit had turned in his direction with a thunderous expression on his beaklike face. "Among other things, Mademoiselle Juliette, among other things," he answered. "Dare I hope for the first dance?"

"It is yours by right," she said, "and as many more as you wish."

"I would take them all if I dared."

"And why would you not dare?"

"Fear of becoming more unpopular than I am already, perhaps. To give cause for being removed as a nuisance is not my object."

"Unlikely, I should think," she replied with a wry smile. "Who would risk a meeting over a few dances?"

"Any gentleman here with eyes in his head," he answered, bowing over her hand before releasing it at last.

She gave a light laugh, though a pink tinge kissed her cheekbones. "I think I could come to like this flirtation."

So could he, if only for the satisfaction of watching her bloom under it, Nicholas thought. "Until the music starts, then," he said, and turned reluctantly to give his attention to the gentleman who had moved to stand at his elbow.

"If I might have a word," Paulette's fiancé said in tones that were barely polite.

"As you please." Nicholas indicated a nearby alcove with a brief gesture. Instinct warned him that the interview might turn ugly, and he'd as soon not distress Juliette by making a public display of it.

Daspit moved ahead of him, turning just inside the draped enclosure. "What I have to say will be brief. You tried to kill me in order to clear your way to Paulette's treasure chest. It didn't work. Next time I'll be ready, and it's you who will be removed from the competition."

"I had no part in your injury," Nicholas said with precision.

"You think I don't recognize a professional

swordsman when I square off against one? If it wasn't you behind the mask, then you sent him."

"I assure you—"

"Don't," Daspit recommended. "You aren't wanted in the Armant family. It's best you remove yourself before you do irreparable harm. Paulette's sister was meant for the church and will return there, that is if you don't despoil her before—"

"Stop there." Nicholas spoke with a sword slash of finality in his voice. Only the sling on Daspit's arm prevented him from demanding satisfaction for the insult.

"A *maître d'armes* with principles, now there's a farce for you." Daspit gave a crack of laughter before thrusting his sharp face toward Nicholas. "I will say it again, Pasquale. Remove yourself from this ridiculous race for the treasure chest or accept the consequences. You sought to be rid of me with a sword. I am not a man to attack with impunity. Being a gentleman, unlike some I could name, I deliver to you this warning. It is the only one you will have."

Daspit spun on his heel and strode from the embrasure. Nicholas took a step after him, then stopped, clutching a handful of the velvet drape and holding it aside while he watched the man stalk back to join the Armant party.

A brooding thoughtfulness rode his brow and his lips were set in a straight line. He did not rejoin the soirée until Celina came to find him to sit with her and Rio for the ballet performance.

7

Juliette sat watching the pas de deux with its pantomime of lovers as they met, advanced, retreated and surrendered, but the ballet dancers had scant hold on her attention. She longed to know what had passed between Daspit and Nicholas. That it was not pleasant seemed plain from the expression on the face of Paulette's fiancé. She only hoped that it had not led to a challenge.

Her sister's involvement with the man mystified her. He was possessed of the necessary social graces and exerted a certain saturnine charm in his pursuit of her sister, but displayed little warmth in his affection for her. He was passable in looks, but not nearly so handsome as Nicholas Pasquale.

Of course, few men were.

She stole a glance to where Nicholas sat with the conde and condesa de Lérida and a small tremor ran along her nerves. His shoulders were so wide compared to most, his long legs more muscled; his profile that was turned to her could have graced some ancient statue. His perfectly tailored gray evening coat, black waistcoat striped in silver-and-black pantaloons gave him an air of European sophistication that far surpassed the attempts at stylishness of the other men present. Just looking at him gave her a melting sensation in the pit of her stomach. That she had dared accept the offhand proposal of such a man disturbed her in ways she could not comprehend.

She was also annoyed that he had not chosen to sit with her. Paulette and their mother had not made him welcome, of course, and he could hardly claim the place by right since their betrothal had not yet been made public. There had also been that small contretemps with Daspit, seated beside Paulette, who with their mother hemmed Juliette in on either side. Between the strained relations and physical barriers, it would have been difficult for Nicholas to make a place for himself with her.

She liked to think that he did not want to draw undue attention to her just yet by the attempt. It was always possible, however, that he had no wish to enjoy the ballet performance at her side.

The prima ballerina was a sylph of a thing, with enormous eyes and hair as sleek as winter sable. She appeared to know Nicholas, for she smiled often in his direction and batted her darkened lashes at him. The sword master inclined his head slightly in acknowledgment at least once, for Juliette saw him.

To be disturbed by that byplay was ridiculous, in spite of the alliance ring now being engraved at the jeweler's shop. Juliette had heard the whispers of his reputation as a Casanova. High moral standards were not usually associated with those who made their living in the theater and opera. An amour in that direction should be no surprise, she told herself with a determined attempt at sophistication.

Proof of it was unwelcome all the same, she had to admit to herself. It made her think of young Gabriel and the woman who bore him. What had become of her that Nicholas was concerned enough with his love child to marry for his sake? Had she died? Did she desert him? Had he loved her and did he love her still? Or was it guilt that made him see to her son, guilt that he had not cared enough to marry the woman?

Perhaps he had married her. What if Gabriel was not a love child at all, but his true son? She had no way of knowing, Juliette realized. How little she knew about this man she was to marry, after all.

She had almost forgotten how practiced were his wiles, and his charm. How foolish of her to be so affected by his flirtation earlier. It must be second nature to him to make a conquest of every woman he met. She must not become one of them, for she feared that way lay heartbreak.

Quite a number of guests arrived after the ballet, some of them coming from other entertainments, others interested only in the dancing. Among these late arrivals was a gentleman of such gold-and-blue splendor that he stood out easily among the crowd. His coat of dark blue merino was superbly cut and molded to his sveltely muscled frame, his buff pantaloons fit without a wrinkle, his evening shoes gleamed with polish, and his hair, cut short so it waved close to his head, had the metallic gleam of pure gold.

Juliette noted his entrance from where she stood near her mother, who was commiserating with a friend of hers draped in black silk who spoke with many tearful asides about the loss of her husband two years before. With little else to hold her attention, Juliette allowed herself a moment's speculation about the newcomer. She was not alone, for a pair of young matrons who had been gossiping at a great rate just behind her noticed him as well.

"La, is that not the Englishman from the Passage de la Bourse?"

"Indeed. One must wonder what the world is coming to with two such masters here tonight."

"One concerns the other, you may depend on it," the first lady said in patronizing accents. "At least this one is the cadet of a noble family instead of a nobody like the Italian."

A cadet referred to a younger son, Juliette realized. The two women were comparing Nicholas unfavorably with the newcomer. Her fingers tightened on the gold silk fan she carried.

"Why, not only is this Pasquale person of questionable family, but I am sure I heard he was born on the wrong side of the blanket."

"Revolting," the second lady snapped. "Someone should take this one aside and explain that he isn't welcome here."

"I should not like my Pierre to feel he should correct his manners. To lose a husband in such a way would be a great tragedy. Still, what a pity that we are forced into the association. We are being overrun by these sword masters who dare to marry into the best families, *n'est-ce pas?* First the Valliers give them countenance, then Lisette Moisant."

The first woman gave a sharp laugh. "It was just as well that she accepted him as a husband since she had already taken him into her bed."

"La, how wicked you are. Not that it isn't true, or so one hears. Now poor Sonia must have her evening ruined by this *parvenu* who is hanging out after the Armant girl, if rumor is to be trusted. What a detestable coil. Next, we shall be expected to acknowledge introductions. I believe I shall be struck down by headache and leave early."

"Let us hope that these *maîtres d'armes* have better sense than to approach a young lady of marriageable age, else some gentleman may risk his life to explain the error after all."

"Oh, *chère*, these sword masters support each other amazingly. If one is challenged, the others feel called upon to stand with him. I shudder to think of what may happen before this is over."

So did Juliette. Even so, she was incensed for Nicholas's sake. Such snobbish nonsense, to assume he was not fit company for those assembled under the Plauchet roof. He was a gentlemen to his finger-tips, much more so, in fact, than many of the country farmers from upriver plantations who exercised their company manners only during the *saison de visites*. She was strongly tempted to go to his side and parade the room with him, presenting him to all they came near. The only thing which prevented her was the fear that she might cause the very con-tretemps the ladies behind her feared. That would do Nicholas no good at all.

While the Plauchets greeted the late-arriving guests and the ballet troupe gathered their props and prepared to leave, several manservants set to work clearing the chairs used by the audience during the performance. The more elderly among those attending followed these seats to that end of the salon reserved for chaperones, and the infirm and those who would not be dancing. Other guests stood here and there in groups, or else began to promenade the room, seeing and being seen.

Paulette and Daspit were among those who made the circuit, while Madame Armant retired to the chaperone's corner with her widowed friend. Juliette could have followed either of them, but did not move from the spot where she had retreated out of the way of those who cleared the floor. She glanced around covertly for a glimpse of Nicholas, but instead saw the English sword master coming toward her in the company of the celebrated count de Lérida.

"Mademoiselle Armant," that titled gentleman said as he bowed before her, "permit me to present Monsieur Gavin Blackford, a good friend of mine and of your future husband. I trust you will ignore the irregularity since he particularly wished to make your acquaintance."

"Certainly, *Monsieur le comte*," she said with a bit more cordiality than she might have moments earlier. Giving her hand to the Englishman, she said, "*Enchanté*, monsieur."

"You are too kind, mademoiselle." The Englishman bent his head over hers while the gaslight from overhead slid among the close waves of his hair in golden gleams. "But then, I should have expected nothing less from the lady my friend calls an angel."

Juliette could feel the heat gathering in her face, burning across her cheekbones. That Nicholas had spoken of her to his friends was surprising enough, but that he had used such a term left her at a loss. "He exaggerates," she said, lowering her gaze to the gentleman's precisely tied cravat that was held in place by a fine sapphire pin.

"Undoubtedly, from time to time," Blackford said with a smile, "but I try to make allowances."

"I didn't mean that he isn't truthful…"

"Then you are indeed angelic?"

She gave him a quelling stare as she removed her hand from his grasp. "I only mean to say that he has an exalted idea of my character."

"But you were about to become a bride of Christ."

"Which, being human, doesn't make me without sin except immediately after confession. Monsieur…"

"Delivered of the required prayers and suitably shriven, you are then holy enough to take on the care of young Gabriel? I had not realized motherhood required such preparation."

"I believe it requires more than that," she said tartly, "though perhaps a bit less when the child is your own."

"You object to the parentage of Nicholas's young orphan. Then you can't be the angel he thinks."

"Orphan? A strange way to refer to a child who may have lost his mother but still has a father."

"I should doubt the poor mite ever had a father that could be named, least of all by the woman who left him behind."

A frown gathered between her eyebrows. "What do you mean, she left him?"

"By death, most likely, or merely from despair.

It makes no difference to Nicholas so why should it to you?"

She put a hand to her throat, in part to hide the pulse that throbbed there. "Can you be saying that Gabriel is not his son?"

"Never in this life or the next," the Englishman answered with wry humor rising in the blue of his eyes like a stream of bubbles in the sea. "Nicholas has more sense and less conceit than to allow that to happen. He took the boy in because—well, because he needed rescuing, like all the rest. Still, if you thought the boy was his and agreed to mother him regardless, then you are, just possibly, as saintly as described."

Juliette snapped open the fan that hung from her wrist and used it to cool her face. "I assumed his relationship with Gabriel was much closer. That only makes me foolish."

"I see it quite otherwise, as would Nicholas if he knew. You might tell him, since he is here to protect you from my wicked tongue and, no doubt, claim his dance."

Blackford bowed once more, tipped an ironic eyebrow at Nicholas as he approached, then moved away with unhurried grace.

"Something has upset you, I think," Nicholas said, his gaze on her face. "What was Blackford saying?"

"Nothing of importance." It was difficult enough

to adjust her thinking concerning him without having to explain it at the same time.

"You are certain?"

"Of course." The music of the first waltz began at that moment, and she reached out to place her hand on his arm.

He seemed to accept her reassurance, or so she thought. In any case, he turned with her toward the cleared area in the center of the room. She moved beside him with her head high, aware of the many gazes that followed them. Then she faced him while he placed his free hand at her waist and swept her into the waltz.

It was nothing like waltzing with Paulette or even Monsieur Devoti, the popular dancing master who had come to the town house for private lessons just this morning to repair this neglected area of her education. Nicholas was much stronger and infinitely more assured. She could feel the warmth of his hand where it rested at her waist, sense by the vibrant tingling the spots where every fingertip touched her. Though he held her at the prescribed distance, her skirts brushed his thighs and knees with disturbing intimacy. The circle of his arms was like an embrace; she felt surrounded by the heat of him and the scent of freshly pressed linen combined with an elusive spice scent that she thought might come from his shaving soap. His guidance in the movements of the dance was unerring so they kept well away from the other dancers. His rhythm was measured perfection yet effortless, as if as natural to him as breathing. She wondered in distracted confusion if this was the secret of his success with women, that he brought the same strong and effortless capability to all the undertook, including the act of love.

She also realized in some dismay that she was proving herself to be an extremely sensual person. She would not be so affected by his nearness or his touch otherwise.

"You are very quiet," he said, a quizzical look in his eyes as he gazed down at her. "I think my good friend Blackford must have been maligning me if whatever you were discussing has reduced you to silence."

"Oh, no," she said in the coolest tones that she could manage, "the opposite in fact."

"Singing my praises instead? That doesn't sound like him."

"He was telling me that I have been much mistaken in my notions about Gabriel, that he is not your son at all."

He drew back a little. "You thought he might be?"

"You suggested that I apply myself as his mother, if you'll remember, becoming your wife to take on the job. That suggests that he makes his home with you, and how should that be unless he is your child?"

"You thought I had a father's duty toward him. I see. Are you disappointed?" He watched her, his eyes as black as jet behind the thick screen of his lashes.

"It is no concern of mine," she answered, then ruined the declaration by going on at once, "though I confess I see no reason why you would require a wife if he isn't your son."

"I thought to adopt him, something that should be more acceptable if I have a household that includes a female for the maternal touch."

"No doubt. But he truly has no blood connection to you? He isn't the result of some conquest?"

"You think I might have been littering the town with my by-blows?"

A hard note underscored in his voice, one she had never heard before. It made her a little nervous, but she would not be deterred. "You cannot say that you have had no liaisons."

"I won't insult your intelligence by such a claim. But I have made certain, insofar as it's in my power, that no child pays the price for them."

"Very considerate, I'm sure. And intelligent of you not to deny it, since I saw the way the prima ballerina looked at you."

He gazed down at her a long moment from under the slanting darkness of his eyebrows, then his expression smoothed and warmth rose in his eyes. "*Ma chère ange,*" he said, "can it be that you are feeling just a little possessive?"

Was she? She could not think so, since she had shared everything with her twin all her life. She had wondered, very briefly, if there might be anything about her that might attract him in a way similar to his other women, but that was different.

"My concern is for our agreement," she said in precise tones. "I am not an unreasonable person, I hope, but I will not share my husband with other women, nor will I become a drudge who stays at home caring for the children while he amuses himself with his friends."

"Fascinating," he murmured, "particularly the reference to children in the plural."

Heat flooded her face. "Well, I assumed…that is to say, I thought ours would be a normal marriage, which would surely include—"

"So do I expect it," he interrupted. "I should like to have a child by you."

Hard on the words, he spun her into a breathless series of loops and turns, which was just as well since she had no words to answer him. She followed his lead with instinctive grace, however, responding to his every movement, every touch, every glance as if they were of one mind and body. It was gratifying that she could match his pace. It was exhilarating, a sudden effervescence in the blood. Her feet flew, she swayed and bent to his masterful guidance while purest pleasure rose inside her and she clutched the ridge of muscle under his sleeve for support and balance, and for the deep, internal gratification of it.

Too soon the music ended. Nicholas bowed, she curtsied, and he walked with her back toward where her mother sat with her friends.

Juliette inhaled as deeply as possible against the press of her whalebone corset while she sought to recover her breath and the serenity she had struggled so hard to perfect. Before she had regained either, Nicholas spoke abruptly.

"If you were to receive an invitation to the literary salon of Madame O'Neill this week, would you come?"

"I should be very pleased," Juliette answered. She had heard these literary evenings mentioned. They sounded intriguing.

"Excellent. I shall see that she invites you. I think…that is, it seems the more often we are able to meet before our marriage, the better."

He did not quite meet her eyes as he spoke, something she noted with surprise. Could it be that he was not quite so positive of the direction of their odd betrothal as he seemed. "That must certainly be true."

A smile tugged at one corner of his mouth, perhaps for the judicious tone of her voice. "It will be as well as if we reveal all our faults and foibles, sins and secrets in advance."

There was no time for more, since they had

arrived at the chaperone's row. It was only as they reached that point, where the only conversation between them must be polite and innocuous, that she realized he might have some hidden reason for his invitation, some secret or sin that she had yet to discover. She also recognized that he had never answered her challenge, had never promised to foreswear any part of the life he now led as a carefree and dangerous master at arms.

Nicholas left the Plauchet house after his second dance with Juliette. He feared making her more conspicuous than he had already, for one thing, but the gathering was not the most enjoyable he had ever attended, either. He was used to being stared at and discussed behind his back; that kind of interest went with occupation of *maître d'armes*. There were always those who made men like him out to be vicious and depraved because it gave them the vicarious pleasure of being seen in such dangerous company. He was not used to being looked on as a pariah, however. Juliette's twin, in particular, had stared at him in contempt, as if he were the lowest of the low. It had not been easy to bear, considering the way she hung on the sleeve of Daspit, who was known to be considerably less fastidious in his conduct.

Nicholas would have liked to escort Juliette home, but his presence had not been requested and she could not be separated from her family. Instead, he must allow Daspit that honor in place of the male head of the household that the Armant ladies lacked. It went against the grain, but matters would not always be thus. When he and Juliette were married, he would have a great many more rights.

Best not to think too deeply on that subject. The hot heaviness it brought to his groin was a handicap he did not need on this outing.

The streets were dark and still. French Creoles were a quiet lot, in the main, those who were not abroad on their various entertainments. Not for them the raucous shouts and fistfights of the Irish section, the hurdy-gurdy tunes that blared forth from the barrel houses and dives of Gallatin Street or even the shouts and hurtling carriages of the American section uptown. A violin played in some quiet absinthe house, a gentleman strolled homeward whistling the march from *Norma* that had been presented at the St. Charles Theater a few days past, a small dog yapped nearby, as if resenting some by passer, animal or human, and that was all.

The night was cool, with a chill wind off the river. Nicholas turned up the collar of his cape and tugged his gloves higher over his wrists. Then he walked briskly toward his salon on the Passage de la Bourse.

At his atelier, he stripped off his evening wear, changing quickly into gray knit pantaloons tucked into soft black leather boots and a black shirt, leaving off his cravat. Strapping a plain leather scabbard at his waist, he drew out the sword it supported halfway then shot it back with a snap to be sure it was well settled. Swinging a short gray cloak around his shoulders, he took a half mask from its inside pocket and slipped it over his eyes and went quickly back down to the dark street once more.

A short while later, he was striding through the dark back alleys of Gallatin where few men dared tread alone. He avoided the gutters with care, since what passed for drains here were never cleared of their accumulation of slops except by scavenging pigs or the annual spring floods. Every sense was alert for furtive movement or untoward sound. He passed gin mills where the rotgut served bore no resemblance whatever to real gin, dance halls where the male customers were too drunk to do more than shuffle around the floor and pleasure palaces where anything could be had for a price except true pleasure. Reaching a ramshackle building that had once operated as a boardinghouse, he slipped in at the back entrance.

Just inside, he paused, assailed by the odors of cheap perfume, unwashed bodies and unemptied chamber pots. The room where he stood, most likely a parlor at one time, had been fitted with a narrow hall of sorts from which opened six cubicles on either side that were scarcely larger than the single mattresses which lay on the floor inside them.

Lengths of dirty sacking hung over the openings, sagging on lines of limp rope so they concealed nothing of the evil-smelling and lumpy pads, the mismatched bowls and pitchers that sat on the floor, the smoking lamps on rickety tables in the corners or the women who plied their trade in such vile surroundings.

"Come in, dearie," one slattern called, brushing back her mass of greasy hair from her face. "I'll treat you fine, I will."

"Thank you, no. I am in search of a man called Old Cables."

"Bent on mischief, are you?" She gestured briefly toward the mask over his face.

"Nothing that need worry you."

"Oh, I'd not worry if you carved out his liver and used it for a pillow."

"You've no love for the man."

"Who does? Or could? Except himself of course, who sees a whoreson in the mirror and calls him a wise man."

"Then you've no reason to warn him of a visitor."

She gave him a weary yet conniving smile. "Visitor? I've seen none, not in weeks. Though he's not here, love."

"But he'll be back."

"As sure as the wagon comes for bodies of a night, my handsome friend. He always comes back for the money."

"In the evening?"

"Oh, aye. And the morning."

"Soon?" He took out a coin and flipped it toward the woman who sat on her mattress with her head resting against the wall.

She looked at the Mexican silver dollar she caught and her eyes widened. Then she bit down on it, displaying gray teeth. Satisfied of its authenticity, she gave a quick nod. "An hour. Could be less. And could be I might help you pass the time, if you were minded."

Nicholas made no answer, but moved to the stairs that rose against one wall inside what had once been the front door. Mounting them with his back to a crazed plaster wall, he divided his attention between the upstairs landing and anyone who might be inclined to follow him. On the second floor, he discovered another set of cribs on one side of the upper hall and a single room on the other. Unsheathing his sword, he approached the door of the room and eased the flimsy panel open with the tip.

Nothing moved; the place was empty. He stepped inside and closed the door until only a thin shaft of light was visible from below. Skirting the bed, avoiding a slipper chair that was surely a faded relic from some ladies boudoir, he made his way to the window. There, he shoved up the sash and leaned out, holding it with one hand while he took great gulps of marginally cleaner air. After a moment, he set in place the stick that lay ready to hold the sash open, and seated himself on the sill to wait.

He had picked away the street mud from around the soles of his boots with the point of his sword, stabbed a large cockroach that sought to investigate his presence, and slapped at several hundred mosquitoes by the time he heard footsteps on the stairs. His mood, never cordial, had gone from sour to disgusted, and from there to an abiding contempt that left him as surly as a swamp moccasin.

He didn't move as he heard Cables downstairs, berating the women who worked in his cribs, slapping those who answered back and threatening to turn them all into the streets. The goading, superior tone of his voice grated on Nicholas's nerves, rousing as it did an echo of his stepfather denouncing his mother for her sin of lying with a man before she was wed. By the time Cables appeared in the bedchamber door with a lamp in his hand, Nicholas's anger was like acid, corrosive and painfully destructive. Still, he remained where he was as the man walked to the table that sat against one wall and placed the lamp on it.

"You think a great deal of yourself for one who makes his living from the toil of women," he said then, the words even.

"What the hell?" Cables dropped the money he clutched in his right fist and reached inside his coat.

Nicholas came off the windowsill like a rope uncoiling. His sword whispered of death as he whipped it from its sheath. Long before the man he had come to see could bring out the small pistol that nestled in his waistcoat pocket, he had the silvery point of the blade at his throat.

With his sword held steady in his left hand, Nicholas reached with his right to grasp Cables's pocket pistol by its grip and lift it into view. He tossed it toward the open window without even a glance in that direction, and was satisfied when it hit the ground below with a small thud.

Cables's face was purplish red and a sheen of sweat appeared in its creases, dripping down his jowls that rolled above his tight collar. "You can have the money—"

"Thank you, but no."

"What do you want then? Who are you?"

"Who I am matters not at all. What I want is your life."

"Don't kill me! Please, I'll do anything."

"Very wise, *mon ami*. Unlike the poor female wretches who slave on their backs for you, I am unimpressed by threats."

"I don't know what you mean."

"You are a whoremaster. I am in search of one of your women, though not for the usual reason. I believe her name might have been Marie."

"Marie? I've known a dozen Maries."

Nicholas pricked him with the sword so a bright

drop of blood shone in the lamplight. "Think. Think very hard about a woman who was here until a month or so ago. She had a child, a misbegotten mite called Gabriel whose father neither knew nor cared that he was conceived. Unless, of course, that man was you."

"That Marie. She's gone, long gone."

"Gone?"

"Dead. She died by her own hand, cheating me of a week's food for her and her brat."

"Dead, rather, of your abuse, spite and greed, I would say. And when she had found the only peace allowed those who fall to these depths, you put her child out to die as well."

"What else was I to do? I'm not running an orphanage."

"It's abundantly clear that such charity is as foreign to you as honor. I would hand you a sword and allow you to defend yourself if you had any notion of upright conduct. As it is, I would as soon challenge a dog."

Cables licked his full lips. His voice was hoarse when he spoke. "I know nothing of swordplay."

"What do you know of justice?"

"I've committed no crime."

"Except that of preying on those weaker than you and less able to protect themselves. Yes, and then scorning them for the place the world has assigned them."

"They are whores! Who cares what becomes of them?"

"I care, and you will care as well if you value your miserable hide. You will treat the women here as tenderly as you might your own flesh and blood from this moment. You will do it or pay the price, this I promise you. If they feel pain then so shall you, if they bleed you will do the same." Nicholas's voice dropped to a soft growl. "And if they die, I can promise you will not see another morning. I will spit you ready for the devil to roast in the fires of hell which you so richly deserve."

"You can't do this! I have friends, men who will protect me and what I own."

"Go to them," Nicholas said. "Complain, if you will. They mean nothing to me. I will find you wherever you hide, follow wherever you run. You will not escape my vengeance for I have sworn it as my watchword and will hold to it as long as I have breath. You will die. This I swear. Heed me well. You will die."

He stepped back with an abrupt movement and made a swift slash, first one side, then the other, in the soft wood of the rickety table to form the letter V in imitation of the mark said to have been left by Croquère. Then he turned with a whirl of his cloak, stepped out the window where he had been sitting and twisted as he fell to catch the sill, hanging from his fingertips for a second before dropping to the ground. Seconds later, long before Cables's shout for help echoed up and down Gallantin Street, he vanished into the night.

8

The invitation Nicholas had promised arrived at the Armant town house the following afternoon. It was brought by a manservant who insisted on delivering it personally into Juliette's hands. On heavy velum and inscribed in a looping and elegant feminine hand, it said simply that Madame Caid O'Neill requested her presence at a literary evening to be held on Thursday between the hours of eight and twelve midnight. She would be extremely pleased if Juliette would arrive an hour in advance of the given time for a private chat and light refreshment.

The tone of the note was casual and friendly, recalling the lovely and rather elegant lady she had met the previous evening, and Julianne smiled in anticipation of the treat. A part of her pleasure was the prospect of seeing Nicholas again—she was honest enough to admit that, at least to herself. It was weak of her to succumb to it, perhaps, but she couldn't seem to resist it.

She wondered if she dared ask Lisette O'Neill about the other women in his life. As the wife of his best friend, she must surely have some idea of who they had been, what they had looked like and how the affairs had ended. Juliette knew she should not care since they were in his past; a wife was supposed to turn a blind eye to such things even when they occurred after the wedding. Still, she wasn't sure she could be satisfied until she had definite answers.

She was also curious to know what these ladies had meant to Nicholas, if he had been affected at all by the end of whatever had been between them. She could not imagine being intimate with someone, as a man and a woman must in such a case, yet feel nothing when it was over. Men, so it was said, attached little meaning beyond the physical to the joining of naked bodies in passion, and yet how was that possible?

She still wondered what had attracted him to those women as well, and if there were anything about her that might conceivably stoke his desire. He was unfailingly kind and astute enough in the ways of women to indulge in a little flirtation, but his attitude held such respect that she could not flatter herself she appeared to him in the light of a lover.

It wasn't that she wished him to be mad with passion, of course; she knew better than to expect such a display. Still, it was bad enough to marry for practical purposes without having to feel that her husband might see bedding her as a chore.

"What have you there to cause such a frown?"

Juliette looked up, startled by Paulette's voice from just above her bent head when she had no notion that her twin was anywhere near the salon. She'd thought her still abed, and it was clear that she had only just climbed from it. Her hair hung down her back in a bedraggled braid, her feet were bare and she wore only a nightgown of white batiste under her open Gabrielle wrapper.

"Nothing," she said, folding the note and slipping it into the pocket that hung from her waist. "Just an invitation."

Paulette made a moue of distaste. "From your fencing master, I suppose."

"Actually, no. From Madame O'Neill."

"The same thing, no doubt. So now you will be joining the circle of ladies who have married fencing masters. How charming."

"Circle?"

"So some style it. The thing is Madame O'Neill's doing, I believe. She is known to be outré in her quiet way, holding her literary salon each week to which flock all those who pretend to enjoy exercising their minds. She has no people of her own, poor thing, so gathers around her all the resident intellectuals and dissidents, including her husband's friends who make their living by the sword, turning them into her family. Her salon is quite something in its way. Not that it matters, since the beau monde cannot be bothered to attend."

"She sounds an interesting person." Privately, Juliette thought the majority of the beau monde too frivolous in its pursuits to enjoy the kind of circle Paulette described.

"You would think so, of course." Paulette smothered a yawn as she moved to a fauteuil and subsided gracefully onto its seat. "I would not become too involved with the crowd, were I you," she went on. "Such friendships as you may form there are unlikely to persist when you return to the convent."

"I am gratified by your concern," Juliette said in dry tones.

"Oh, *chère*," her twin said with a shake of her head. "I didn't mean to annoy you, truly, I didn't. I don't at all begrudge you this last fling, as it were, at romance. In fact, I quite see the appeal of your sword master. He is formidable in his strength and such a handsome gallant, more than enough to turn a woman's head. But I know you, my dear sister, and you can never be happy at my expense for it simply isn't in you."

She had a point, one that had caused Juliette to toss and turn in the night and rise early. "I dislike very much that it has to be that way."

"It doesn't, you know. All you have to do is renounce this unfortunate marriage. You will be far better off, I am sure of it."

Her sister sat forward in her chair, her face earnest, intent. It was possible she believed what she was saying, Juliette thought, or had convinced herself that it was true. But was it?

"I'm sorry," she said with a small shake of her head. "I would not cause you pain for the world, but if your future happiness depends on inheriting Marie Therese's marriage chest, then I can only think there must be something very mercenary in your attachment to Monsieur Daspit."

"You would say so, if only to get your own back at me. But you cannot help knowing wealth is an important consideration. If a gentleman has none, then he must marry to mend the situation. This is only common sense, however hard it may be on those concerned. Now Jean says his mother is displeased. She feels my dowry was misrepresented if the chest must be subtracted from it. I had not meant to tell you for I know you will think it reflects badly on the man I am to marry, but Jean told me afterward that he must reconsider the alliance between us if there is to be no inheritance from the chest."

"Oh, Paulette," Juliette said softly. She was not really surprised, but felt for her sister all the same, particularly as she saw the distress she was trying to hide.

"I understand the position he is in, really I do, but only consider the shame, Juliette. To be deserted so close to the altar, cheated of a wedding for a second time? I should be mortified beyond words. People will begin to say that I am jinxed, a bad luck bride. I could never hold up my head again."

"Surely Monsieur Daspit would not do this to you. You will hardly be a pauper without the chest. There is the settlement left by Papa, and you know *Maman* would be more than pleased to have you live with her."

Paulette pushed her fingertips back through her hair at the temples, frowning as she dislodged more strands from her braid. "I don't know, *chère*. Jean isn't himself since this business of the strange duel. He is distressed over his mother's disapproval and consumed with the need to be avenged against Monsieur Pasquale for his injury and the ridicule he has suffered."

"Ridicule?"

"The circumstances are just peculiar enough for people to snicker and say unkind things behind his back."

"It wasn't Nicholas. He has sworn to me that it was not."

"And you believe him as a matter of course."

"Why should I not? No one has said he is not a man of honor."

"What does that make my Jean, then?"

"Mistaken," Juliette said firmly before a thoughtful frown crossed her face. "Has he never said what this odd meeting was about? I mean, the reason it took place?"

"A gentleman does not discuss such things with a lady." Paulette's tone was austere.

"No, only his intention for revenge after what appears to have been a fair meeting, in spite of its irregularity."

Paulette gave her a dark look. "As if a meeting can ever be fair between someone of such expertise and a gentleman who is merely proficient."

"Are you suggesting there was more to it? That it might have been in the nature of a punishment?"

"I said nothing of the kind," Paulette declared, sitting stiffly erect. "That would be to admit fault in Jean's conduct."

"If you have no idea of the cause of the meeting, then you can't know there was none."

"I know, because I know the man I love!" Paulette leaped to her feet, her hands clenched at her sides.

"Yes, but what if he is seeking revenge against the wrong man?" Juliette asked, clinging to reason. "What if he injures someone who had done nothing to him?"

"It's unlikely that he can harm your Monsieur Pasquale. The man is a master, after all."

"Possibly, if you mean in a fair contest, but you have just said Monsieur Daspit could never defeat him that way."

"You are suggesting that Jean would attempt something less than fair?"

She had, rather, spoken her fear aloud, Juliette thought. Nicholas Pasquale might be difficult to defeat, but he was not invulnerable. She thought there might be a number of ways he could be hurt, from the manner of his birth to his feelings for the child, Gabriel. And she could not think that she was the only person to note these things. "I spoke in haste. Forget it, if you please," she said with a vague gesture, then went on as another thought occurred to her. "But Paulette, if you are overset by the possible shame of a broken betrothal, perhaps you aren't really in love with Monsieur Daspit."

"I never said that was all. I love him madly, passionately, and with every fiber of my being. I will be desolated beyond imagining if there is no marriage."

"Surely, if he feels the same—"

"He does, of course he does. He has said so a thousand times."

Juliette pressed her lips together a second, trying to think how to ask what she felt could be vitally important. "And does he show you without words? What I mean to say is, does he..."

"Does he make love to me? Is that what you want to know?" Paulette demanded.

"Something of that sort. You said before that he kissed you. But does he speak of love as he holds you?"

"You can be sure of it. Yes, and as he does much more, I do assure you."

"More?" Juliette, taken aback, could not prevent her disapproval from shading her voice.

"My dear innocent sister, you can have no idea of how the touch of a man of experience can make you feel, or how abandoned a lady can become when she is alone with such a man."

Juliette could feel her face burning. "But *Maman* has always acted the strict chaperone, I know. How can this be?"

"There are ways to evade such supervision."

"And this is usual? I mean, others you know, your friends, do the same?"

Paulette gave a low laugh, though rich color rode high on her cheekbones. "Those who dare. Such stolen moments are thrilling beyond anything. I should not tell you of things that must be forbidden to you, but you did ask."

So she had, and the knowledge she had gained disturbed her, though not in the way that Paulette envisioned. It confirmed her feeling that there was something lacking between her and Nicholas Pasquale. They were not in love, it was true, but it seemed improbable they ever would be without something more in the way of physical contact between them.

She was also concerned for Paulette. It appeared that she might be putting her good name at risk and that Jean Daspit was abetting her, if not actively persuading her to it.

Did everyone play at decorum in public but do what they pleased in secret? Was she so naive, had she been so protected because of her vocation, that she had never seen it?

No, that could not be. French Creole ladies of their station were known for their fidelity and circumspection—even the Americans, who found much they considered sinful about the Vieux Carré and its inhabitants, allowed them that. The place of females in the society in which they lived was too restricted, the expectations for them too high and social consequences of straying too dire for the kind of looseness Paulette described. Some few of the more daring might venture such things, but that was surely all.

"Be very careful, *chère*," she said slowly. "A gentleman often loses respect for a lady who cannot, or will not, keep to the rules that protect her."

"What do you know of it?" Paulette cried as tears sprang to her eyes. "Nothing and less than nothing. And you never will. You never will!" Clutching her wrapper around her, Juliette's twin fled the room. Her bare feet thudded along the gallery, then faded away as her bedchamber door slammed behind her.

Juliette sat still, her brow furrowed in thought. It seemed her sister, for all her protests, might well fear that Monsieur Daspit had grown cool toward her for the exact reason just stated. How tragic if it should prove true.

Juliette also feared that her twin might know more of this dueling affair than she was willing to admit. What she knew troubled her in some fundamental way as well, or so it seemed. That didn't mean that Paulette was right and Nicholas was somehow involved.

It didn't mean she was wrong, either.

The evening visit to the O'Neill town house began according to convention. Juliette walked the short distance with Valara as her companion as the lamplighter began to climb to the streetlamps on the corners of these main thoroughfares, setting their gas jets aflame so long shadows were thrown across the streets. Nicholas had offered his escort but she had thought it best to avoid unnecessary meetings with her mother and sister until after the wedding. The O'Neill butler let them in, leading the way along the dim *porte cochère* to where it opened into a large courtyard. Juliette left her old nursemaid to gossip in the kitchen while partaking of coffee and shortbread. Alone, she mounted the stairs that led upward to the gallery. Her hostess met her at the top with the traditional kiss on either cheek, then conducted her along the railed enclosure to where several wicker chairs were spaced in a comfortable grouping on this mild evening. There, she was greeted by Madame O'Neill's companion, Agatha Stilton and also by Nicholas, who rose to take her hand.

He was breathtaking in a frock coat of tobacco-brown broadcloth worn with fawn pantaloons and a waistcoat of cream, striped in brown. His eyes were compelling yet warm with approval, and carried such conspiratorial amusement in their ebony depths that she felt her heart shiver inside her chest.

It might have been her discussion with Paulette, but the meeting without her mother's knowledge, or even Valara's near presence, suddenly had the feel of a clandestine rendezvous. She was irresistibly reminded of the things her sister said sometimes happened during such assignations. Not that she expected to be left alone with Nicholas here in the midst of the O'Neill household, yet who knew what he might have in mind?

His manner was exactly what she might have wished for from a lover. He held her hand for that bare second longer than was necessary, sending a tingling sensation from her wrist to her elbow. Then he ejected Lisette's small dog, who answered to the name of Figaro, from the extra chair, brushed the seat with his handkerchief and seated her as if she were made of the most delicate of porcelain. Juliette saw Madame O'Neill glance at her companion and smile with the lift of one eyebrow. It was meant as a comment of some kind, she was sure, but of what variety she could not tell.

"How lovely it is to have a private moment," Madame O'Neill began, her calm gray eyes bright

with amusement. "I have been wanting to congratulate you on bringing Monsieur Pasquale to such a delicious standstill on the morning you met. To hide
his little protégé from him under your skirts while
he stood fuming! How I should love to have seen it.
No other female has managed to flummox him, I
promise you."

"A thousand thanks, madame," he said in wry
protest. "I'm sure my betrothed needed to have that
information at her fingertips."

"You feel she will use it against you?" Lisette
O'Neill inquired.

"I would not, of course," Juliette said quickly, "especially as it did not happen in just the way you
describe."

"Monsieur," Lisette said, turning on him. "Can it
be you lied to us?"

"Not in the least."

The lady swung back to Juliette. "He was not
forced to listen to a lecture from you on his methods
of child rearing? He did not suggest that he would like
to exchange places with Gabriel under your petticoats?"

Juliette glanced at Nicholas and then away again.
"Well, as to that…"

"He did, I am certain of it. And if he did not
hint at other liberties he might take, I know these
sword masters not at all—or only your goodness
prevented him."

Juliette's face burned as she remembered Gabriel's skimming touch along her limbs below the knee and Nicholas's suggestion that his would be different. She sent him a flickering glance from under her lashes, but he was favoring Lisette O'Neill with a stare that seemed to promise retribution. If it disturbed their hostess, however, she gave no sign, but only grinned at him with every appearance of enjoying his discomfiture.

"I'm not sure who was most affected by that small contretemps, Monsieur Pasquale, Gabriel or myself," Juliette said with precision. "At least it ended well."

"Indeed it did, since it propelled the great, the invincible La Roche toward matrimony."

"Please," Nicholas said with a pained expression. "I've asked you not to call me by that name."

"But it so suits you," his hostess protested.

"Now there I can't agree with you," Agatha Stilton said, joining the fray. "A man more animated would be hard to discover."

"But that is what makes it so perfect, don't you see, like some great monster of a man who might be called T'Jean."

The companion sighed, though her eyes twinkled as she looked at Juliette. "I confess that I have never understood this French Creole habit of giving everyone a *petit nom* while ignoring the perfectly good names assigned at baptism."

"It's a failing, I know," she answered, "but what

would you? A bit of informality is surely permissible in such a formal world."

Lisette leaned forward in her seat a trifle. "As to that, I hope you don't mind the lack of ceremony for this small meeting before the evening begins? There are those whom Monsieur Pasquale desired you to meet in a place less open to view than the public streets. This seemed the best location for many reasons, among them friendship and shared interest in the welfare of those who may become your concern."

"I'm not offended, no, but confess I haven't the least idea what you mean." Juliette looked from Madame O'Neill to Nicholas, her gaze wary.

"I'm sure you don't," the sword master said, "for which I must apologize. I had intended to postpone this business, but am persuaded since coming to know you better that it will serve best to be quite honest."

A species of alarm seeped through Juliette as she noted the serious cast of his features. "Honest?"

It was then that the bell of the iron pedestrian gate in the porte cochère clanged out a summons. Nicholas made no reply to her query, but sat quite impassive as the butler emerged from the courtyard kitchen below and moved with unhurried treads to answer it.

Nicholas wished he had been allowed more time to prepare Juliette for what was about to take place.

It was his own fault for delaying, and he knew it well. He had procrastinated, afraid of what she might say or do. Perhaps it would have been better to present her with a fait accompli, after all, saving this meeting until it was impossible for her to back out.

Too late.

Lisette was on her feet, walking toward the head of the stairs with Figaro frolicking around her skirts. Halfway there, she realized no one was following her and turned back. "Come then, Nicholas, and bring Juliette. There is no point in putting off the moment any longer, you know."

He did know, but that didn't make it any easier. Offering his arm to Juliette in grim foreboding and punctilious form, he led her toward what he feared might be a fatal test.

The boys filed into the courtyard, laughing and talking among themselves, shoving each other in good-natured horseplay. No doubt they had been promised a treat. Nicholas thought briefly of offering to reimburse Lisette for it, but knew she would probably take his head off at the mere suggestion. She was fond of his street rats, and they of her, though they would never give her the instinctive trust that they gave him unasked. The problem was that she was too far above them, at least in their eyes. Toward him they had no such reverence, and needed none.

Lisette reached them first, touching a shoulder

here, ruffling a thatch of hair there as she greeted them and asked after one or two small hurts among them. Her little dog followed, making them welcome in his own way. Nicholas glanced at Juliette as she moved down the stairs at his side. Her face held curiosity, he thought, and the shadow of a smile for the obvious affection between Lisette and the visitors, but nothing more. If she suspected that this gathering had been arranged for her benefit, or had any special significance, there was no sign of it.

They reached the bottom of the stairs. Lisette turned to indicate the leader of the boys. "Juliette, may I present someone you should know? This is Squirrel, and with him are the other members of his street cadre, Faro, Cotton, Buck, Molasses, Wharf Rat and, of course, Gabriel, whom you know. Boys, the lady on Monsieur Pasquale's arm is Mademoiselle Juliette Armant, who may well become essential to your welfare."

Squirrel crossed his arms over his chest, scowling, while the others whispered among themselves behind him. Long, silent seconds slipped past while they glanced at Juliette from the corners of their eyes, looked away without quite meeting her gaze, then quickly sneaked another peek.

Nicholas caught the questioning look on Juliette's face as she turned her head in his direction. He said nothing, did nothing, but only waited to see how she would manage. His breath seemed trapped in his chest and the tension in his muscles could not have been more concentrated if his life had been hanging in the balance.

She swung back to the others after a moment, stepping forward with her natural, innate grace. Warm interest gleamed like gold in her hazel eyes as she held out her hand to Squirrel.

For a long moment, Nicholas thought the boy would fail him and his teachings. Then Squirrel took her fingers and bent his upper body over them in a bow that was a credit to his instructor.

"Mademoiselle," he said, his low voice cracking just a bit on the last syllable.

That brief greeting set off a flurry of imitation from the other boys. Juliette went down the line, accepting their awkward salutations as if they were offered by the most polished of gentlemen. That was, until the very last, when young Gabriel stepped from behind Wharf Rat and held his arm at his small waist, bowing until he doubled over so far that he lost his balance.

Juliette caught him up before he could tumble to the paving stones, setting him upright again with such a natural and quick caress on his small, dark head that anyone not watching closely might have missed it.

Nicholas was watching, however, and the hard lump that rose in his throat was something he had not felt in years. His pride in his chosen bride was so powerful that it amazed him. She was perfect, his Juliette, so perfect for his purpose that he thought she might well be right, that the Holy Mother must have sent him to her.

Her perfection went beyond her maternal instinct, however, as much as he valued it. Her sweet allure enthralled him, set him to longing for things he had given up as impossible long ago. The sheen of her hair, held this evening by the combs he had given her, the lush curves of her mouth, the gentle swells of her breasts and turn of her slender waist were enticements that kept him in such a state of tumescent agony that it was proof positive that he did not deserve such divine grace.

Abruptly, Squirrel stepped in front of her, putting a hand on Gabriel's shoulder and pulling the child behind him. *"Mais non,"* he said, his young voice as hard and challenging as any sword master's defending his honor, "you will not have Gabriel, no. He belongs with us."

Nicholas stepped forward, as did Lisette, but Juliette held up a hand to ward them off. "Is it you who sometimes takes care of him, Monsieur Squirrel? You have done this while he was on the streets, yes?"

"Aye."

"You have kept him safe, a fine thing."

"I have, and so it will be always."

"I mean him no harm."

Squirrel's face remained impassive. "You may not mean it, but it will happen."

"How can you say so when you don't know me?"

"It's the way of it. You will make him care then you will go away. He has cried enough."

Juliette's eyes grew soft and liquid before she spoke. "I wouldn't do that."

"You might not think to do it, but things change. People change. People die."

The words were stark, with much hard, painfully gained wisdom in them for one so young. Hearing them, Nicholas was reminded of what Squirrel had said before, that mothers die. The boy's fear, he thought, was that something might happen to Juliette if she should take on the care of Gabriel. Nicholas understood it very well, for he felt echoes of it somewhere deep inside him.

But what of Juliette, who had known little of sorrow and nothing of hunger or the vast terror of belonging to no one and having not even a roof over her head? Could she understand what lay beneath the boy's words or, understanding, accept it?

It was too difficult a test. He should intervene, Nicholas knew. Yet he could not bring himself to move, needed to know how she would answer, not only for the boys who stood before her but for himself.

"I know," Juliette said. "People turn from you who should care only that you are happy. It's the way of the world. But I will not be one of them. I will not hurt Gabriel nor will anyone else, not if it's within my power to prevent it. If you doubt me, then you are welcome to come and see him whenever you wish."

"When you and Monsieur Nick marry."

She seemed a little taken aback that he knew, but covered it instantly. "Yes, just so."

"La Roche needs no wife. We are fine as we are."

"Squirrel," Nicholas said in warning tones as he stepped closer to Juliette.

"Well, we are." The boy looked around at the others, who dutifully supported him with mutters of agreement.

"But we will be better," Nicholas answered. "You shall all be welcome under our roof, and in any way you like, as long as you like, either as our guests or as sons of our house."

"Sons?" Squirrel said, his voice cracking again.

Juliette's lips formed the word also, though no sound came from them before she swung to face Nicholas, her eyes a swirling mix of jade and emerald, peridot and topaz, like jeweled mosaics in the sun as she searched his face.

Lisette, who had been watching the byplay, looked from one to the other of them, then quickly turned to the boys. "Come, now, all you young rogues. I believe Monsieur Pasquale and his future bride have much to discuss if things are to turn out as they should. Cook has made a fresh batch of molasses cakes that require tasting. I think he used too much butter but you must give me your opinions."

They went with her, though eyeing him and Juliette askance and whispering among themselves. Figaro cavorted at their heels, ecstatic that they would be staying, or perhaps only that their path took them in the direction of the kitchen.

Nicholas took Juliette's arm and walked with her back to the stairs, where he mounted them at her side. As he moved, he tried to think how to say what he must, but anything he could contrive seemed lacking. Starting with an apology was indicated, but from there nothing appeared likely to suffice except plain words.

"I'm sorry," he said, his voice even. "I should have told you about the older boys before, and would have, except—"

"Except you feared that I might run screaming back to the convent."

"I suppose," he agreed with a grimace as he heard the cool note in her voice.

"But you decided to be—what was the word? Honest, I think."

"The risk had to be taken. I could have waited until after the ceremony, but that was hardly fair, and I preferred not to prejudice you against the boys because of something I had done."

"As if I could not decide who to blame." Her voice was uncompromising.

"Oh, I am of course. But now I must ask whether

you will stay or go since you have an understanding of what I plan." He waited, holding himself with as much detachment as he was able, though his neck ached and his shoulders were so stiff that he thought they might creak with the effort.

"You expect me to mother four or five boys from the streets as well as little Gabriel."

"Six, actually, seven in all."

"This is really why you decided to go through with that jest of a proposal in front of the cathedral, because of pity for them?"

"Pity, no. I admire their courage, their resourcefulness and ability to look out for themselves and each other. But the streets are a dangerous place to be, particularly for a young man half-grown with others who depend on him."

"You fear for them."

He had thought to save his other reasons for later, when she was less distrait. Now it seemed best to put them all on the table. "I grew up on the streets myself, much as they are doing now. I know too well the temptations, and the consequences."

She studied his features, her own serious. At least there was no disgust there that he could see, no immediate rejection.

"What do you intend to do? I mean to say, where would they all stay?"

"You heard my promise to them. I thought to buy a house if you will choose one."

"I?" She stared at him, the pupils of her eyes widening, crowding out the green until they were almost black.

"It will be your home, the place where you will spend your time. It might as well be to your order."

"But what of your preferences?"

He could tell her of those, particularly a large bedchamber with a soft bed located far from where the boys would sleep, but it seemed best not to press his luck. He had given her enough cause for dismay. "I have none, except that there is room for all and you are content."

"You have none because you don't expect to be there any more than necessary." She lifted her chin in apparent challenge.

He smiled and reached to graze her cheek with the knuckle of his forefinger, being careful not to scrape her soft skin with the ridge of calluses that came from constant sword practice. "I thought we settled that before. I will be there. I may be there more than you will like, certainly more than you may prefer."

"What if I prefer you to be constantly at hand?"

He watched the flush that colored her face with shades of pink and rose, wondering exactly what was in her mind but not quite daring to hope it was the same erotic image that flared to life in his own.

"Then it shall be as you choose," he said quietly. "In all things, it will be as you desire it."

9

He had no right, Juliette told herself in despair. To touch her with such gentleness, making her heart ache inside her chest, was grossly unfair while he was also telling her that he had no need of her except as someone to establish a home for his charity children.

Oh, she honored him for his determination to take the boys in off the streets. It was the measure of any man, much less a swordsman, that he should have a care for those weaker and in need, that children and animals could be comfortable in his company. She was even flattered in a way that Nicholas felt her suitable to aid him in this undertaking. Yet she had almost come to believe in his smiles and his promises of something more meaningful between them.

Not that she had reason to complain. She could hardly claim to be desperately in love. She was using him as a means of gaining Marie Therese's chest just as surely as he was using her. That he was not repugnant to her must be plain to both of them. She had his respect, she knew, perhaps more than she deserved. If he desired her a little, then that was all to the good, wasn't it? She must be satisfied with these small signs of favor.

Oh, but she longed for so much more. She wished that she did not, that she could be the kind of woman who looked at such matters with a truly realistic eye, the kind who might accept whatever her husband offered, endure his embraces, bear his children, manage his household and allow him to come and go as he pleased while she found her satisfaction in the family life she created.

Once, she might have been that way. She might have accepted it as her lot in life along with so many others, just as she had accepted the church, because it was expected of her. Circumstances had changed, she had changed. Having been freed of the yoke of expectation, she discovered that she no longer felt obligated to please those around her. She yearned, just this once, to please herself.

Selfish, it was so very selfish of her, just as Paulette said. And what did it mean, anyway? She did not object to Nicholas Pasquale as a husband. In fact, the prospect made her shiver somewhere deep inside whenever it crossed her mind. Her heart went out to the boys he wished her to mother; they were so brave and gallant with their bows in exact imitation of the man who was so obviously their heroic pattern card.

In truth, they reminded her very much of her brother René, who had died when barely their age. He had been ten and just as rough-and-tumble as those street boys, just as engaging when he grinned, just as enticed by sweets. He had always come to her with his cuts and scrapes because, though she was only slightly older, she was less likely to go into hysterics at the sight of blood than their mother and more apt to be sympathetic than Paulette. She had often helped him get ready for mass or to go out visiting, washing his face and ears for him and standing on the low Turkish ottoman in her father's study to comb his hair. When he had died, she had been so distraught, so ill, that they had called in the priest, thinking she would join him in his grave. She still missed him.

In an odd way, tending these boys as their mother, if they would have her, might be like having René back again. They certainly required someone to care for them. Though they had washed their faces, the streaks left by those halfhearted ablutions remained, and they all needed their hair trimmed and brushed.

"Very well," she said abruptly, "Did you wish to buy a house or lease one?"

"Buy it." His answer was just as swift and the dawning of anticipation lighted the dark depths of his eyes. "I have always wanted to be a property owner."

"In the city, I suppose. Does the address matter to you?"

"It would be pleasant if it were not too far away from my friends, friends who will also be yours." He gestured briefly at the house and courtyard around them.

"Excellent," she said, thinking that it would be convenient to her mother as well, so she could visit her often after Paulette married. "You are aware of my need for haste. We are to meet with the priest for his counsel tomorrow, and must ask that the betrothal be announced at the cathedral on Sunday."

He inclined his head in agreement.

"The announcement will be read three times then we may be wed. There is barely time before Mardi Gras, as we said before, so the ceremony must be immediately after the last announcement."

"Must it?" he asked, tipping is head to one side while a teasing light gleamed in his eyes. "We could always make a Gretna escape."

He meant they could cross the river to the little town of Gretna that was named for the amenable judge born in Scotland who performed ceremonies with no questions asked. She hesitated, since it was so simple and obvious a solution. Such a marriage was hardly respectable however, being a civil ceremony only. It smacked of embarrassing haste to the Creole mind, giving rise to all manner of questions and counting on fingers if children appeared too soon afterward. Most of all, it lacked the solemnity of a union blessed by the church.

"I would much prefer the cathedral," she said. "There will be enough talk of the marriage between us without giving cause for more doubt."

"Arrange matters as it pleases you, then," he said quietly, his expression somber once more. "I will make myself available."

She studied his features for long seconds. It seemed that some reply was expected, though his gaze drifted to her mouth, resting there so intently that the surfaces of her lips tingled as if in anticipation of a touch, a taste. "That is…very generous of you. Thank you."

He glanced away over the gallery railing where they stood, but Lisette and the boys were inside the kitchen that occupied the ground floor of the *garçonnière*. Mademoiselle Stilton, Lisette's companion, was nowhere in sight, and must have retreated into the salon. Returning his gaze to hers, he said, "Not so generous, after all. I require, I think, some token of our agreement."

"Token," she repeated, certain she knew what he meant but afraid she might be wrong.

"This," he said, and cupped her face in his left hand, angling her lips to meet his.

It was a tender possession, a gentle ravishment, a bittersweet acknowledgment of what was to come between them. His mouth was warm, so warm and smooth, and masterful in the way he wooed her lips to part for him. She drew breath, sharp and deep, as she felt the incursion of his tongue, yet its smooth glide, its heated probe, was beguiling. She swayed, and he drew her against him. She felt the strength of his arm at her waist, the spread of his hard swordsman's fingers in rays of heat across her back. She pressed her palms to his chest, sliding them upward over the hard musculature beneath his coat, measuring the width of his shoulders, touching in tentative exploration the taut column of his neck and the thick curls that grew low on his nape.

Her breasts touched his chest, flattened against him as he caught her closer still. She was boneless, trapped in the rapture of his incredible hardness where she was soft, his sureness where she was hesitant. His scent of spice, pressed linen and his own unique male essence made her giddy. She could not think, could only lean against him in urgent, aching need, never thinking to protest, her breath caught deep inside as she waited for a more intimate touch, a more definite possession.

It came, his warm fingers at the curve of her breast. And it was so truly what she required, so certainly the move for which she longed, that she shuddered with a low moan deep in her throat.

He paused, drawing back by slow degrees. She let him go because she would not make a display of her need, and because she must never cling.

"Three weeks," he said with a husky note in his voice. "It will be a long wait."

"Yes."

The word was whispered, and heartfelt. Even as she spoke, it was impossible to say if she were answering a true expression of yearning impatience from him or only an artful pretense made from simple courtesy. Casanova, to whom Nicholas had been compared, would never have been so maladroit as to allow a lady to feel undesired. At least her feelings seemed to matter enough to make an effort worthwhile.

The sad thing was that it made little difference either way. She was going to marry him no matter what he thought or did not think, regardless of what he did or did not do. She would be his wife, in spite of everything.

Lisette's literary salon was crowded as usual, Nicholas noted, and also as usual, the vast majority of those attending were men. The ranks had been swollen over the past couple of years by sword masters who had managed to get themselves invited, but also by members of the militia company with whom Nicholas and Caid trained every week at the Place d'Armes. The militia itself had increased in size, with several new units added and constant notices in the newssheets for drills. The original numbers were not all there, however, as quite a few had left for Texas to join the army Sam Houston had begun gathering against the threat from Santa Ana.

Lisette had grown into an accomplished hostess. Conversation never lagged, though it centered more and more on political conditions, particularly the Texas situation, the slavery policies of President Tyler, who had taken office after the newly elected Harrison had died last year from pneumonia contracted during his inaugural speech in cold rain, and the rising crime rate in the city that was still divided into three sections, with little cooperation between the different police departments. Of course, it didn't hurt that she and Caid served excellent Bordeaux and punch cups to the gentlemen and orange- and lemon-flavored drinks for the ladies. On this evening, she also had great wheels of cheese garnished with vine leaves on silver trays and crystal bowls heaped with hothouse grapes, chunks of coconut, nut meats and fingerling bananas just off the boat from Havana.

Nicholas watched his friend Caid circulate through the room, exchanging a quip here, giving a measured opinion there, pleasantly at ease with everyone. He envied him his home and its gracious atmosphere, and the affection that made the Irishman glance around now and then to find Lisette, allowing his gaze to rest on her until she looked his way and smiled into his eyes.

Nicholas was by no means sure that two years of witnessing such scenes had not contributed to his decision to take a wife when the opportunity offered. Allowing himself a sardonic smile for that bit of self-knowledge, he turned his head to scan the room, searching for Juliette. She was deep in animated discussion with Celina, Rio's wife. Nicholas watched her for long moments, willing her to look his way even as he admired the simple gown she wore of pale gold challis woven with a pattern of cream and green and set off with cream lace collar and cuffs. What it would prove if she did, he didn't know, but still he could feel the quickening of anticipation inside him as he waited.

"Careful, my friend," Blackford said as he strolled up to stand at his shoulder. "The *on-dit* will be that you are in the lady's pocket."

Nicholas gave the Englishman a droll glance. "I can think of worse places to be."

"As it happens, so can I."

"But you will not attempt the climb." The warning was quiet, but no less exact for it.

"Rabid jealousy, I might have known. One of the advantages of a Latin heritage, no doubt, a complete lack of self-consciousness in affairs of the heart."

"I wouldn't say that."

"After making your claim clear with a verbal stake through my chest? What then?"

"I wasn't aware that I was so obvious."

"Stand a moment in my shoes."

"I doubt they would fit," Nicholas said, allowing incipient annoyance to shade his voice.

"You'd be surprised." Blackford went on with

scarcely a pause. "One hears that a certain man of business in a less savory section of town was visited by a gentleman wearing a mask. I am aware that Croquère found it necessary to don a disguise, but thought the Brotherhood had agreed the practice was too melodramatic to become a habit."

"You and Caid agreed, as did Rio, but I don't remember adding my pledge. Besides, it seemed a good idea to muddy the waters a bit where Croquère's activities are concerned. He has need of a mask for obvious reasons, but allowing him to be singled out by it is not good strategy."

Blackford inclined his head, his face pensive. "I take your point, and may try the effect myself next time. Am I to assume that the marks left in the floor beside your victim were for the same reason?"

"A warning couched as a calling card of sorts, again to replicate Croquère's touch. But what do you mean by my victim? I left Cables alive."

"Then some other crime caught up with him. He was most thoroughly dead, stabbed through the heart, when found."

Nicholas met the Englishman's turquoise gaze, his own steel hard. "I've no objection to accepting blame for deaths I achieve, but am damned reluctant to take credit where none is due."

"An unforeseen consequence of our pact, I believe," Blackford said. "We make such convenient scapegoats."

"Yet the greater the number on our score sheet, the more likely we will attract notice from the gendarmerie. We've only escaped so far because of the divided nature of the city with its different police forces."

"That, and a high degree of caution," Blackford agreed. "I somehow feared the last might have gone to the wayside with you."

"Be assured that I have more reason than ever to practice care."

"As a man about to take on a ready-made family, yes, I see," the Englishman said with a considering glance toward where Juliette sat. "Speaking of which, Jean Daspit seems determined to make both the care and the wedding difficult. He can't be satisfied that you weren't at fault in his injury. Shall I pass the word that you were elsewhere at the time?"

"I doubt he will believe it without the name of the man who bested him. And the kind of revenge he might contemplate if he were to discover that it was Croquère is best left to the imagination."

"So you will chance whatever he may do to you?"

Nicholas shrugged. "I am in his black books anyway."

"Then watch your back, *mon ami*."

"Always," Nicholas said with a tight nod. "Always."

It began to rain after the first hour, a steady downpour that drummed on the roof and sheeted down from it onto the balcony facing the street.

Such a common occurrence did little to dampen the spirits of the gathering. They simply raised their voices above the noise as they listened to a report that Monsieur B. F. French planned to open his private library of 7500 volumes to anyone desiring to make use of it. This soon degenerated into more complaint against the three-part municipal system, which worked to prevent a municipal library, and Nicholas wandered away from the male-dominated argument to where the ladies of his acquaintance, Juliette, Celina and Lisette, had withdrawn to themselves. They were talking of a new shipment of books, including a French translation of Dickens's *The Old Curiosity Shop*, at Monsieur V. Hebert's bookshop, and also Hebert's landscape wallpapers and English floor coverings that were all the rage.

His opinion on the latter was solicited purely as courtesy, he was sure. He liked the wallpapers, disliked the rather florid floor coverings, and said so in a way he hoped would offend no one's sensibilities. Afterward, he added a comment or two to the talk about the lithographs of the painting by Inman of Fanny Essler as Florette in *La Tarantula* currently displayed for sale, and the recent recital which had featured Schumann's Symphony No. 1 in B-flat Major.

"Oh, I must tell all of you that I am giving a ball in a few days time," Lisette said as a small silence fell. "Or rather, I've persuaded Caid to host it."

"My poor friend," Nicholas mourned.

"Not at all," she corrected him with a tilt of her head. "He enjoyed the process immensely, I do assure you."

"That is, of course, quite different."

Lisette's smile was reminiscent. "Yes. It's to be a subscription ball in celebration of the residency of our very own Spanish count and his lady, and the place the new Louisiana Ballroom at the St. Louis Hotel. What think you, *mon ami?* Will you stand as a sponsor?"

"A *maître d'armes* as a sponsor for a subscription ball? You can't be serious."

"Oh, please, times are changing."

"But not that much. Put my name on the subscriber list and your ball will be doomed before it begins. No one will darken the doors. Or at least no one who is anyone."

"But you will agree regardless? It's to be a grand *bal masque* in the Venetian style, the most glorious of the season, I promise. I must have sponsors to help with the guest list and to keep order."

"Not to mention to help pay for everything?" he asked with a wry smile.

"Oh, I don't count that," Lisette answered with a light laugh and more disregard for money than Nicholas had yet managed to acquire, in spite of the amount of his lottery windfall.

"You and Caid should not have to manage alone,

chère," he answered. "It would give me pleasure to help welcome home our friends and keep peace at this masked affair. Only leave my name off the subscription list, and I'll undertake to keep my face covered throughout the night."

"Done," Caid's canny wife said at once, then turned to the other two women. "There. Didn't I tell you he could be cajoled into it?"

Nicholas closed his eyes with a melodramatic shake of his head, though it was mere form. He cared not at all that he had succumbed to feminine blandishments; it was his pleasure to be of assistance to one who had done so much to make him feel at home in New Orleans and accepted into the circle of her friends and relatives. Still, it seemed he should have some small return for his compliance.

When the opportunity presented itself, therefore, he lifted an eyebrow in Lisette's direction with a small but meaningful tilt of his head toward Juliette. The lips of Caid's wife twitched and she exchanged a sparkling glance with Celina. Almost immediately, she excused herself to see to some supper detail in the kitchen while Celina discovered a sudden need to check on her offspring who were asleep in a *garçonnière* bedchamber.

"Alas," he said to Juliette with a mock sigh, "it seems we have been left to entertain ourselves. Shall we stroll to a window and watch it rain?"

She glanced at the hand he was holding out to

help her rise from the settee. "What a conniver you are, monsieur. Was it really necessary to send my companions away in order to speak to me?"

"Apparently not, but how was I to know that I had only to ask?" He watched her closely, aware of an intense, febrile pleasure in being private with her that threatened to escape him in a wolfish smile.

"You couldn't…can't… That is to say, though I may not be willing to accede to your every request, I am perfectly able to accept a casual invitation."

"And what if there is nothing casual about it?"

Color rose into her face. "If you are thinking of another of your tokens…"

"I wasn't but they appear to be on your mind. You will discover, my Juliette, that I am always happy to oblige in such matters."

"I have no doubt!" she said, her gaze accusing.

"Excellent." He reached to take her hand, drawing her up to stand beside him before strolling with her toward the nearest window embrasure. "Such understanding makes a fine start to our getting to know each other."

Her movements were rigid for the first few steps, then she slanted him a quick glance and fell into a more relaxed pace at his side. "Something similar was in your mind when you asked that I come tonight, I believe—that is, over and above the introduction to your young protégés. You wanted me to pass some little time with your friends."

"And they with you. Do you mind?" He turned with her inside the embrasure where a current of cool air, moist with rain and scented with the smell of the river, swirled around the edges of a lazily billowing curtain of printed muslin. Even as he faced her, however, he was aware that the motives she imputed to him were not nearly so clear or disinterested. He had thought to introduce her into the circle of his friends, yes, but more than that, he simply wanted her near him.

"Of course not. I like them very much though they seem rather intellectual."

"Not at all, or at least very few pretend to it. They are just a group of like-minded people with more on their minds than gossip and gambling, fashions and the latest waltz music."

"They, or at least your particular friends, the conde and condessa and Monsieur and Madame O'Neill, seem very genuine and happy in each other's company, if I may say so."

"You may say anything you like," he answered, "though I'm glad you approve as this may soon become your social circle, likely the only one available to you."

A small frown pleated her brow. "Because of your occupation, you mean. I have not been used to a large acquaintance, you know, so will not mind in the least. Sometimes of late it feels as if I no longer belong in my own family so I am grateful for the offer of another. More, I believe that to be denied the pleasure of an evening such as the one we are enjoying is the loss of those who may hold themselves above it."

The easing of the tightness in his chest came from relief, Nicholas realized. Until that moment, he had not understood how much it mattered that she be comfortable among his friends. That she could see their finer qualities, appreciating them even as he did, seemed more than he deserved. "I've often thought the same," he agreed as lightly as he was able before going on. "I am glad of this opportunity to enlarge on our acquaintance as well. I feel certain you have questions since the French Creole preoccupation with family history and lineage is well known. Pray ask whatever you like and I will try to give you answers."

She met his gaze, her own dark there in the embrasure while the sound of the rain falling close behind them was an endless obbligato. She moistened her lips with the tip of her tongue, a movement that drew his attention to their luscious curves, their enticing softness. The drawing sensation in his lower body that resulted was so intense that it was a second before he could attend to the words she spoke in softly musical tones.

"I have been curious about one or two things concerning you, since you bring it up. For instance, is it true that your father was an Englishman?"

"Quite true." He should have known better than to offer her carte blanche. Self-effacing she might be, but that did not mean she was without daring. Her demure pose could well be a mask, or so he thought with sudden insight, one she donned to conceal the person she was inside, the person she might have been but for the peculiar circumstance of being born to a pious and superstitious mother.

"But you never knew him."

"Is that another way of asking if I bear his name? The answer is no, of course. His union with my mother was not legal in nature, therefore I am the bastard in truth that I am sometimes called behind my back. Being born at Easter, I settled on Pasquale as fitting when it came time to choose a suitable *nom de guerre* of the kind usually taken by fencing masters." Since he had decided on honesty in this arrangement, he might as well make it complete.

"It's said you had a brother, that he is the reason you came to New Orleans."

He turned to put his back to the frame of the embrasure and the outer drapery of winter velvet that had been swung open on its short metal rod. "A half brother, to be exact. And yes, I came because of the man who caused him to commit suicide. Or one of the men."

"One of them?"

"Rio's uncle, who styled himself the conde de Lérida, was a swindler who involved my brother in his schemes then left him to take the blame. I arrived in New Orleans on the trail of this count, to be revenged."

"And you were."

"Yes," he said simply.

"The other man who...who caused his death, what of him?" Her gaze was on the rain that caught the candlelight in small gleams as it ran from the eaves, splattering onto the canvas-covered floor of the balcony outside.

"He was my stepfather, my brother's true father, and a beast in the form of a man. He enjoyed tormenting those weaker than himself, those in his power. I ran away from him as soon as I was able, since anything was better, even the streets. Stephen, my young brother, never made his escape."

"And your mother?"

"Nor did she, except by death."

She was silent, her gaze pensive. After a moment, she said softly, "So you have no one. No one, that is, except your street boys."

"There you have it."

"I see why you feel for them, I think."

"I doubt it," he answered, his voice suddenly tight. "There is no maudlin pity in it or mere desire to see them clothed and fed. The streets are a place of death where you either learn to die or learn to kill. No child deserves that lesson."

She reached across the space of the embrasure to

lay her hand on his arm. In that silent gesture was comfort without pity, compassion without disdain. The touch of her gloved hand, the warmth of it through his coat and shirt sleeve, seemed to reach into the darkness at the center of his being, easing some long held pain there.

And he worshiped her in that moment with sudden passion and unbounded gratitude, as a wounded cur might venerate the mistress who took in him from the cold, who fed his need, tended his injuries and gave him at least the outward sign of tender acceptance. That adoration knew no bounds, admitted no hindrance, no despair.

He would have her, he vowed in quiet determination, would keep her, hold her forever, whether she willed it or not and regardless of those who might attempt to take her from him. She would be his, yet she must never learn what he felt for her in the days and weeks which lay ahead of them. It was too powerful and sharp a weapon, one which could cut too deep. To hand it over without a hedge of defenses was clearly unthinkable.

That was a lesson he had learned long ago. To remain alive and well, it was necessary, always, to protect the heart.

10

Juliette detached herself from the Armant party and entered the ballroom while her mother and Paulette were still removing their cloaks, collecting their dance programs and shaking out their costumes at the cloakroom at the head of the entrance staircase. The maneuver was deliberate. She wished to be truly anonymous this evening, and the best way to do that, or so it seemed, was to distance herself from Paulette. They were too much alike even in differing disguises; the two of them together would be instantly recognizable.

Where this impulse came from Juliette could not say with certainty. She only knew that she chafed under the restrictions that bound her. The life she had lived, her expectations and responsibilities, had changed so dramatically that she was still trying to catch her breath. Everyone thought they knew her, what she was like, what she needed and what she should do. Their expectations stifled her, made her feel pulled in too many directions. To be on her own for a short time this evening seemed like an intoxicating glimpse of a freedom she had never known, might never have again.

That she dared embark on it was due solely to the demi-mask of flocked green velvet that covered the upper portion of her face. There was something about a masquerade, she thought. Hiding behind a disguise allowed the more daring inclinations of one's nature to come to the fore. It permitted the wearer to become someone else, the person they had always dreamed of being, at least for an evening. She needed that somehow.

If her costume was anything to go by, her most secret fantasy must be to play the daring lady of the *ancien regime* at the court of the fabled Sun King, Louis XIV. Vague family rumors claimed that had been the position of her ancestress, Marie Therese of the bridal chest, and so it seemed a natural choice. The deciding factor, however, had been that Madame Ferret had a fashion doll dressed in that manner and from which she could draw inspiration on short notice.

Her bodice *à la Polonaise* was of palest green silk embroidered in pink and rose with poufs at the hips resting on a framework of panniers. Beneath it was a sensuously soft skirt of a darker blue-green, which swayed with her every movement, and was short enough to show her clocked white silk stockings and heeled slippers that were set with ruched rosettes. The corset she wore was longer at the bust and waist than the current fashion, with the effect of making her waist appear wasplike while pressing her breasts up over the edge of her bodice in a manner that might have been indecent except for the pink ruched insets on either side of the pearl buttons that fastened the front. These twin insets were the exact shade that her nipples would be if they chanced to pop into view. Other than this small outré touch, the costume was demure enough.

She could not wait to see Nicholas's reaction. That was, of course, if he recognized her. He might not, and she was by no means sure that she would make herself known to him.

Paulette's costume for the evening bore no resemblance to her own, for which Juliette was grateful. Her sister had abandoned petticoats and stays for the freedom of Roman drapery edged with a band of purple-and-gold braid and with a gold fillet holding her hair in a simple arrangement and a purple demimask over her eyes. So long as some little distance was kept between the two of them, Juliette thought there should be nothing to give away any connection with her twin.

The ballroom was resplendent for this affair, a symphony in cream and white and pale rose. Located in the St. Louis Hotel that had replaced the old hotel of that name that burned two years ago, it still smelled of fresh paint and newly sawn wood. An

enormous crystal and bronze d'or chandelier filled
the oval dome that made a cave of the ceiling, its
fluttering gaslight throwing a myriad of wavering
shadows over the walls and polished wood floor. On
a dais at one end of the room, a pianoforte aug-
mented by string quartet and French horn was being
readied for playing, their assorted sounds creating a
jangling discord. As the night was unseasonably
warm, the French doors that lined the walls stood
open to the evening air with their rose brocade draperies looped back and only their swaying gauze under
curtains to discourage the insect life.

Many guests had already arrived, peopling the
room with kings and courtiers, bishops and nuns,
queens and devils, harlequins and Columbines, and
dozens of other fanciful personalities. In less than a
moment, she spotted Nicholas, or a man she was
almost certain was he.

The cavalier on whom her eye had fallen was of
commanding height and athletic form and wearing
a loose shirt with full sleeves and lace-edged cuffs
tucked into doeskin breeches and complemented
by high-topped boots with turned back cuffs. A
tunic of French blue sewn with the arms of a *mousquetaire* of Louis XIV topped this ensemble, while a
short cape hanging from one shoulder and a wide hat
with the brim pinned up on one side and worn over
a wig of black curls finished it off. The crowning
touch was the rapier that hung at his side, something

that would ordinarily have been surrendered at the door along with the sword canes and pocket pistols men often carried. Since it was a part of the costume, and ornately ceremonial, he had apparently been allowed to keep it. So splendid was he, so very dashing, that shivery heat rose in her midsection at the mere sight of him. It seemed, for an instant, a terrible shame that the style of dress he had chosen was no longer in vogue.

Beside the bewigged gentleman was another dressed as a horseman of Andalusia who could be the conde de Lérida. Even as she watched, a St. Patrick with snake's head staff in hand and the look of Monsieur O'Neill moved to join them. Yes, the *mousquetaire* was definitely Nicholas.

High-pitched laughter trilled from behind her just then. Juliette glanced over her shoulder to see her mother, gowned as the Empress Josephine, being escorted through the wide doorway by Monsieur Daspit in a domino and Venetian vulture's mask while Paulette clung to his other arm. Juliette lingered no longer, but strolled away, moving around the edge of the floor with an attempt at languid, Eighteenth-century grace in spite of her haste.

The air was thick with the scents of perfume and hair pomade, warm bodies and the cedar chips and camphor used to prevent the depredation of moths upon silk and wool. Dancing had not yet begun, and Juliette moved in an informal promenade of those wishing to see and be seen. Conversation mounted up into the dome to echo overhead like the drone of a bee swarm, and the deeper she went into the ballroom, the warmer and closer it felt.

No one seemed to be paying her the least attention, for which she was grateful. She curtsied to a short and rotund Napoleon, who was almost certainly Governor Roman, bowed to a Goddess Minera whom she suspected might be Madame Sonia Plauchet, and exchanged brief remarks on the décor with a lady in the powdered wig and excessive paste jewelry of a Duchesse du Barry, but that was all. Or so she thought, until she noticed that she had picked up a train of sorts.

It was not one man who trailed along behind her but two—a pair of young gentlemen costumed in the dark blue coats and pantaloons and black leather helmets of the gendarmes, and with the cudgels of their trade swinging at their sides. Swaggering even as they attempted to look official, one was compact of body and swarthy of complexion and the other pale, sandy-haired and lamentably pockmarked below his mask. Neither was long past their majorities, as proved by the juvenile manner in which they winked and nudged each other with their elbows.

Juliette walked a little faster. Perhaps her sortie alone was ill-considered, after all. Her experience was only with private balls among family and close friends, where everyone was known and the chance of a distressing encounter absolutely nil. A subscription ball such as this one was different, she knew, since tickets were sold rather indiscriminately to the gentlemen acquaintances of the sponsors. Ladies were not required to have tickets, and it was assumed any attending would be the wives, mothers, sisters or other near relatives of the subscribers, with no unaccompanied ladies admitted. Certain it was that such ladies sometimes infiltrated the ballrooms, however, since the newssheets were sometimes obliged to print notices to the effect that they would be denied entry. That anyone might assume she lacked a protector in the ballroom had not occurred to Juliette, just as she had neglected to consider that she might be accosted. She had not been in the habit of thinking of herself as the sort of female who might attract unwanted attention.

Ahead of her was a family group with three young ladies, apparently sisters, dressed as shepherdesses. Juliette skirted them, and then wove her way in and out among another group who had selected ancient China as their inspiration. The ploy seemed to delay the two in her train, since they were apparently known to the shepherdesses. She breathed a sigh of relief.

Her progress had brought her to within a short distance of Nicholas and his friends, though an Egyptian pharaoh and his embonpoint Cleopatra served to shield her from them for the moment. Their voices reached her, however, in snatches of bass rumblings. Then her attention was caught by a few disconnected words in the accents of the conde de Lérida.

"…this business of conducting your affairs from behind a mask disturbs me, *mon ami*. Necessary, it may have been, but I trust you are done with it?"

"For the moment," Nicholas drawled. "Blackford told you?"

"He was concerned for you, as any good friend would be. As for the man you are thought to have injured, he is no idle bon vivant, apt to respond at once to an ungentle reminder of his manners. He'll want your scalp if he can get it."

"First he has to find me."

"You think another mask enough to confuse him? Don't be daft. Your accent combined with that magical sword of yours would tip off a blind man."

Masked. The word rang in Juliette's mind while a sinking sensation invaded her chest. Nicholas had accosted someone with sword in hand while his face was covered. Who else could it be except Daspit? And yet Nicholas had sworn that he was not the masked swordsmen who had attacked Paulette's future husband. What did it mean?

In her distraction, she failed to notice that her pursuers were back on her trail. The first she knew of it was when the darker of the two spoke at her elbow.

"Mademoiselle, a moment of your time, if you please."

She turned away at once. "You must excuse me."

The other gendarme lifted his cudgel and used it to touch her arm, bringing her to a halt. "We must insist, really we must."

They were inebriated, she realized as the liquor on their breath reached her, though perhaps not so much that they crossed the line of what was allowed in female company. Still, they blocked her way, grinning with vast bonhomie and no small interest in her décolletage. She slanted a quick look at Nicholas and saw that he had noticed the confrontation. His face was turned in her direction though the strip of black velvet with eye holes that he wore made it impossible to tell if he recognized her.

"Fair incognito," the pockmarked gendarme said on a hiccough. "Most earnestly, we beg leave to sign our names to your program for a waltz. That is, if you have any left?"

"As to that…"

"You cannot refuse the law, you know. Attempt it, and we may take you away to the calaboose."

Juliette, annoyed by their familiarity, drew herself up. "Your pardon, messieurs, but the choice of dances belongs to my fiancé, and he is waiting for me. Let me pass."

The darker gendarme stepped closer. "Mademoiselle, attend to us. We are the law, and you must show respect. Only one small dance each, we beg. Is that too much to ask?"

"Far too much."

It was Nicholas who answered, shouldering his way in front of the pair then stepping closer to Juliette with one hand on the hilt of the jeweled rapier at his side. "Mademoiselle Incognito has given her answer. Do you question it?"

"*Mais, non*, monsieur." The pockmarked one stepped back in haste, lowering his cudgel, trying to hide it behind him while his nervous glance fastened upon Nicholas's hard stare. He jerked his upper body in a bow. "We apologize profusely, mademoiselle, don't we, Gaston, and pray that you will forgive and excuse us."

His friend, stammering, added his apologies and obsequies, then tugged his companion away before Juliette could do more than murmur her acceptance. The two of them backed a few steps, then turned and hurried off.

Juliette watched them go, aware at the same time of Nicholas staring after the pair with a brooding set of his mouth. Then he turned to face her. She sustained his searching black gaze with some effort, at the same time both impressed and disturbed by the ease with which he had dispatched the two young men. It was his manner, she thought, dangerous, protective, yet as natural as breathing. Her would-be assailants might not have recognized him as the *maître d'armes*, La Roche, but they had known to retreat before the unconscious threat he represented.

She knew who he was, this perfect musketeer in his severe costume with its ancient military insignia. She knew, and was amazed that he wanted her as his wife and mother of his children, had pledged to marry her regardless of who opposed them. Regardless, she was not entirely satisfied. Something inside her wanted more from him than mere ballroom gallantry, duty or the exaggerated respect that she sometimes caught on his face.

"You are all right, fair Incognito?"

Had there just a shade of emphasis on the name she had been given? She could not be sure, but hearing it spoken solidified an impulse inside her. She had greatly enjoyed their brief flirtation of the other night, and would have more of it. In addition, she was not quite ready to relinquish her small share of freedom. Since she was unknown behind her mask, she would remain so for a while longer.

"But yes, perfectly, monsieur," she answered, lowering her voice to a sultry purr by way of disguise. "Your intervention was most timely."

"It was my very great pleasure, though I trust I have not overstepped my bounds."

"There should be no bounds for one who effects a rescue."

"None?" he asked, his voice pitched low and deep as he tilted his head in inquiry.

She gave a light, breathless laugh, and snapped open the fan that hung at her wrist, waving it to cool her warm cheeks. "Well, hardly any."

"I would look into that statement more closely, mademoiselle, did I not fear to trespass as surely as the pair I just sent on their way."

"Very wise of you. But then I'm sure you have more address than to fall into such a trap."

"What do you know of my address, fair one?"

It was time to retreat a bit, perhaps. "Nothing at all, monsieur. I judge merely from appearances."

"If that is to be our measure, then permit me to say that you appear far too lovely for superficial acquaintance."

"Indeed? Meaning you have no desire to dance with me?" Her smile, she feared, had turned a little arch.

"Oh, indeed I desire to dance with you, mademoiselle. But also more, much more."

His meaning was plain, and if it had not been, the look in his dark eyes behind his mask would have made it clear. She felt an answering rise of heat inside, a purely feminine reaction to the suggestion that hovered unspoken between them. A *frisson,* an intense thrill of delight for his response to her delicate enticement, shivered over her.

Even as she reveled in the exchange between

them, however, she was disturbed by it. He was betrothed to her yet was casting out lures to what appeared to be another woman. She had not expected eternal fidelity, but a modicum of circumspection until after the wedding was surely due his future wife. Why had she not considered this possibility before she began her attempt at coquetry? The truth was she had not anticipated so instant and decisive a response. She had, in her deepest being, expected fidelity from him simply as a matter of honor. To discover that he would not reserve that for her was a disappointment.

He was offering his arm as the first strains of a Chopin waltz began. She took it, moving with him onto the floor, allowing herself to be swept away to the music even as an odd pain spread inside her.

"We are well matched as to time period, you and I, mademoiselle," he said with a glance over her costume before his warm gaze returned to her face. "Yet I fear your grandeur surpasses the pretensions of a simple musketeer."

The caress in his voice rippled over her skin again, and she felt her nipples tighten, unbelievably, under her bodice from the deep, rough sound. With wry sadness in her heart, she resolved to play out the subterfuge she had begun, especially since she had no wish to hear excuses, just now, for his conduct. With luck, she would be able to make her departure from the ballroom without revealing that she had been his flirt of the evening. "There are times," she said softly, "when riches and position no longer matter."

"All well lost for love?" he inquired. "A noble concept, but one that seldom survives everyday life."

"I meant, rather, that all differences are extinguished in the dark."

She felt his shoulder stiffen under her hand and was not surprised. She had amazed herself with the comment. Then he drew her closer as they swayed together, closer than was at all proper.

"A temporary obliteration, I fear, but one of stupendous appeal."

"Besides," she went on as if he had not spoken, "there are also times when a lady of fine lineage has need of a man with certain dangerous skills."

"For which the honored musketeer might be given a reward?"

"A boon, perhaps—or is that the same thing?"

"Both, or either, are acceptable, and their promise more than enough to stop my poor soldier's heart."

She gave him a look from under her lashes even as her heartbeat threatened to suffocate her. "Now why do I doubt that?"

"I can't imagine. I am the simplest of men beneath my surplice, and regardless of my much vaunted skill with a blade. I can love, or die for the lack of it. Or die in a moment because of it."

Something in his voice gave her a panicky feeling

in her chest. She drew back a little to stare at him, frustrated by the mask that prevented her from guessing at his meaning or the sincerity of it. His eyes were almost black, their rich tobacco color eclipsed by the wideness of his pupils. She drew a quick breath that lifted her breasts and made her ribs ache with the pressure against her corset. Before she could speak, his grasp tightened at her waist and upon her hand.

"Come away with me," he said in quiet entreaty. "Come now, while no one is watching and we are protected, at least in part, by our masks."

To ask such a thing of her was to presume she was a light skirt who might succumb to his blandishments in a place less public and minus supervision. She should refuse at once, should do it with cold disdain that he would dare insult her so.

The words would not come. It wasn't just that she wanted to know how far he would go in betraying his betrothal, nor was it merely the sensual temptation, though that was strong and heated inside her. No, she was entranced by his desire for her, for the woman she was pretending to be behind her impersonation of a lady from another place, another time. She longed for a taste of the subtle mastery that women whispered about when they spoke his name. She wanted to know his touch without the reverential gentleness that he used with her because she had once been promised to the church.

"Where shall we go," she asked, the words a mere whisper in her throat.

Tivoli Gardens was their destination, several acres of pleasure grounds on the edge of town, beyond the Faubourg Ste. Marie, that had been laid out in imitation of those of Paris and Copenhagen, which were, in their turn, copied from the Villa d'Este in Italy. They traveled by carriage, an elegant landau with driver that had been borrowed, Juliette suspected, from one of his friends, probably the conde de Lérida. They clip-clopped along the city streets, passing from one dim, golden circle of lamplight to another. The night air was rich with the scent of the sweet olive trees that had been planted to cover less pleasant aromas. Beneath it, however, could still be discerned the odors of street offal and the occasional chicken or rabbit run kept by some frugal householder. Dampness was in its breath, too, as if from distant rain.

They said little. Juliette could think of nothing that would not give away her identity or else be so banal that silence must be preferable. Nicholas appeared preoccupied, his manner somber though exquisitely correct as he rode beside her.

As they passed beyond the streets of the Vieux Carré, however, he took her hand in careful fingers and turned her wrist to the light of a street lamp's passing glow. With disturbing competence, he released the buttons of her glove, exposing a diamond-shaped patch of skin. Bending his head, he pressed his lips to that bare area where her pulse throbbed with a staccato beat. His mouth was heated and she felt the faint and intriguing prickle of beard at its ridged edge. For the briefest of instants, his tongue touched that fluttering evidence of her rapid heartbeat with hot, wet erotic testing.

She jerked a little with a small sound of surprise catching in her throat. He chuckled, she thought, though it was such a low rumble that she could not be sure. Then he did up her glove again and sat with her hand captured in his on the seat between them until they reached the gardens.

Music greeted them as they came through the entrance gate. Its rhythm was less exalted than the operatic arias and waltzes they had left behind them in the French section, featuring instead polkas, mazurkas and Acadian country dances played on concertinas, fiddles and rattling percussion instruments. It was toe-tapping music, however, and it added a jaunty swing in their steps.

They followed the sound to the open air dance pavilion that centered the gardens, a large building with only stretches of railing between its massive wooden columns, which supported a cypress shake roof. The shuffling of feet on the cypress boards of its raised floor created fine sawdust that hung in the air, permeating it with the unique, woodsy fragrance.

Paths led off from the pavilion like radiating

spokes. Some routed strollers to a series of booths where food and drink were served, others to a maze, a small zoo for children, a carousel and lake for sailing toy boats or row boats. Between these wider lanes were quieter walkways laid with crushed oysters shells and overshadowed by large live oaks. Niches holding classical statuary were set into them here and there, and vine-covered arbors offered daytime shade for cast iron benches.

Nicholas suggested refreshment, but Juliette declined. Eating or drinking would be difficult to manage without removing their masks, something she could not contemplate just now. In any case, her throat was much too tight. They wandered away from the aromas of fresh bread, coffee, baked meats and sugary sweets, from the noise and music, taking at random one of the more deserted paths.

Their footsteps crunched on the oyster shells. The chalky whiteness underfoot allowed them to follow the twists and turns of the shrubbery-lined walk. Flaming torches set at sparse intervals also provided guidance, though not enough to detract from the sense of seclusion. The sounds of revelry grew fainter behind them, the shrubbery crowding the walkway darker.

A vague trepidation touched Juliette. She had heard rumors of attacks and other disturbing events taking place in the back reaches of these gardens at night. Mothers and chaperones did not ordinarily allow their charges to ramble away into its dark environs. Still, Nicholas was so close beside her that she could feel the brush of his tunic as he moved, the warmth of his body wafting around her. He was such a solid presence that she felt safe there with him, even as the distance from other people increased.

"You are warm enough?" Nicholas asked after a long moment.

"Perfectly." She had stopped long enough before leaving the ballroom to retrieve her hooded merino cloak, which swirled and dipped now at her heels. Its folds were more than adequate to ward off the night coolness.

"I would not want you to take a chill."

She gave him a quick look as she heard the grave note of his voice. "It doesn't seem likely."

"Too bad, since it also removes any excuse to gallantly offer my cape—or to warm you."

He was teasing, a novel thing where she was concerned. The problem was that she didn't quite know how to answer. A blue-white flicker in the distance presented itself then as a distraction, and she seized on it with gratitude.

"Look there, above the treetops."

"Where? What?"

"Lightning, I think."

Nicholas stopped, turning toward her. She slanted him a quick glance as she lifted a hand from under her cloak to point out a black mass of clouds to the northwest.

"Yes," he said, his voice rich with satisfaction as the flash came again. "I can see it in your eyes."

His voice, the cadences of it, seemed to brush against the nerve endings under her skin, causing them to spring to life with exquisite sensitivity. She felt the oddest sense of dislocation, as if she were outside her body, watching her movements from a great distance. She was not herself and she knew it. This heedless abandonment of reason and scruples belonged to someone else. And yet the shivery anticipation at what might happen in this secluded area of the gardens was hers alone.

Still, she wished somehow that she had not embarked on this deception, had not hidden her identity from him. How lovely it would be to simply stroll along these paths in the dark while knowing that whatever advances he might make would be from desire for her and not for some faceless female who had the audacity to be private with him.

As she stood there, annoyance with him seeped into her mind. How could he do this, disregarding the pledge he had made her? Of course he had not said he would have no other women, only that he would not draw back from their agreement. It was not the same thing. She had no real right to complain, but the urge was fierce inside her.

"Mademoiselle? Is something wrong?"

"I was only thinking that you seem exceedingly familiar with these surroundings."

"I have a fondness for outdoor entertainments," he said with amusement threading his voice, "perhaps because I spend so much time indoors."

"At your atelier, I suppose."

"So you do recognize me. That is an unfair advantage, you know."

Answering that charge was not in her plans at the moment. "You would be difficult to mistake, monsieur, especially after you begin to speak."

"You are saying I have an accent?"

"A slight one only, but quite disarming."

"Is it indeed?" he asked, an intrigued sound in his voice.

"I find it so."

"Then I can only be glad, for disarming you is certainly my object."

"So I supposed."

"Do you mind?"

A shudder caught her, one that traveled down her backbone, shaking her to the core of her body. Never in her life had she been so aware of a man or her femininity. It felt as if she hovered at the edge of a precipice where one false step could spell disaster, while some angry, exultant, passionate, half-mad need urged her to jump.

"Not at all, Monsieur Pasquale," she said, her voice not quite even. "I had hoped you would."

His reply was long in coming, then was a deep and vibrant whisper. "Ah, well. Never let it be said that I disappointed a lady."

He reached to take her hands, lifting them to the smooth, warm surfaces of his lips. The heat of his mouth through her gloves was so affecting that she curled her fingers around his in a convulsive clasp.

"You are chilled, after all. Perhaps we should go back."

"No," she whispered. "I'm not cold, only…"

"Frightened, perhaps?"

She gave a quick shake of her head, then faltered. "Perhaps a little."

"It may be I have the remedy," he answered, the words like a caress.

Gently, he straightened her cramped fingers then flattened her hands against his chest, brushing aside the lapels of his cloak so only the thickness of his tunic and shirt lay under her palms. She could feel the rock-solid bands of muscles beneath the cloth layers, feel also the steady throb of his heart. She pressed harder, absorbing his heat, his strength, enthralled by the firm musculature of his body that was so different from her own.

It was stunning, the naturalness of her impulse. She had thought always to be denied the experience of touching a man in an embrace. Now she was captivated by her own boldness and also by the swift, hard breath that he drew in response. His warmth and hardness invaded her senses, tingling along her arms to flow through her with an effect like strong wine taken in haste. She swayed a little, even as she lifted her gaze to his.

His eyes were black gleams through the slits of his mask. They rested on her lips, she thought. Releasing one hand, he laid it against her face, caressing her cheek with hard fingertips. Then he dipped his head toward her, hesitated, leaned nearer. His mouth touched hers and she lowered her lashes, closing out everything except the incredible sensation of his lips upon hers.

It was a gentle salute, a careful fitting and molding of sensitive surfaces. There was no harshness in it, no sudden movements, no demand or domination. He savored her and the moment, or so it seemed, taking pleasure in them without need for more. Beneath such tender contact, she felt something unfurl deep inside her, opening in warm, willing response. And in that moment, she knew she could trust him not to rush her into more than she intended. If there was to be a seduction, it would be infinitely skilled, delicately prolonged and dependent entirely on what she required. He might ask but would not demand, nor would he take without permission.

That knowledge was heady beyond anything she had ever known, so liberating that it seemed to loosen her hold on her own desires. With a low murmur, she turned her hands and grasped the edges of his tunic to draw him closer against her. She felt the shift of his thighs against the flat front of her skirts, knew the moment when he lowered his arms to her waist, enclosing her in their iron circle. She reveled in their strength and leashed power, in the solidity of his body. His aura of dangerous masculinity was like a magnet, and she acknowledged a reckless urge to give in to its drawing force, to allow him to do what he willed.

The touch of his tongue at the line where her lips came together was tentative, as if he were wary of shocking her. Yet how should that be when he doubtless thought her a masked coquette bold enough to drive here with him? She had been so sure his tenderness toward his future bride was due to misplaced reverence. That he might have the same care for the sensibilities of a strange female disturbed her. It was irrational, perhaps, since she was deliberately concealing her identity, but the thought rose like a dark shadow in her mind.

Even so, the sensations he roused were so entrancing that she parted her lips for a sighing breath. He took advantage of that access, teasing the delicate surfaces at the entrance of her mouth into tingling sensitivity while also allowing her to know the flavor of him.

It was as hot and intriguing as some exotic spice. She wanted, needed, more of it. With an instinct she hardly knew she possessed, she slanted her head on her neck to avoid the rasping together of their masks while allowing deeper penetration, fuller exploration. At the same time, she pressed closer against his enticing firmness.

His heart thudded under her wrists with a more powerful rhythm. The muscles of his arms became as taut as steel hawsers. His tongue glided over hers in slick yet grainy abrasion.

She should be appalled, even aghast at such intimate invasion. Rather, she was beguiled. A part of her mind knew and accepted this deep kiss as an imitation of greater consummation even as every ounce of natural feeling in her body hovered, waiting to see what would come next.

He released her mouth, his chest rising in a deep, almost winded breath as he rested his chin against her temple. "*Cherie,*" he began in tones that had the tenor of apology.

"Don't," she whispered in her sultry, camouflaging register.

Seconds stretched into a minute while he stood unmoving except for a slow rocking, as if he felt the need to console her. Then he gave a single nod. "You are quite right. No words are required for what is between us."

Turning his head, he pressed his lips to her hair, then leaned to blow softly in her ear before tasting the lobe with warm lips and tongue. He eased away a little as he continued in a searing path of small kisses that trailed along the edge of her mask then down her cheek and jawline to the tender turn of her neck. She felt his fingers cup her shoulder, kneading it an instant, before dropping lower to where her breasts pressed against her neckline.

"Your costume is lovely, *ma chère,*" he said with laughter like a ragged edging to voice, "but these bits of pink just here are pure enticement. How are they called?"

"Cockades, ribbon cockades," she murmured, glancing down as he flicked the offending decorations with his thumb.

"Whatever they may be, they are driving me mad. Forgive me, but I must..."

Bending his head, he pressed his lips to the creamy swell of her breast at the edge of her décolletage, then caught the edge of one cockade with his fingertips and pulled it outward and down, lowering her neckline to expose the tight rosebud of her nipple. An instant later, he bent his head and she felt, incredibly, the wet heat of his tongue in a licking caress.

"Sweet, so sweet," he whispered, "like delicious little candies."

She was so shaken by that unexpected foray, so inflamed by the touch on the tip of her naked breast that her knees threatened to give way. She gasped, swaying so that only his arms held her upright. With an exclamation under his breath, Nicholas swept her into a nearby bower. There, he dropped onto the bench within the dim enclosure and pulled her down onto his lap.

Swift protest rose to Juliette's lips, but died away unspoken as he caught it in his mouth and drew her close again, rocking her against him. He kissed her chin, the hollow of her throat, and leaned lower to seek out the damp and strutted nipple he had released, applying warm suction.

She melted, leaning into him with all the pliable softness of warm candle wax. She threaded her fingertips through his hair while simmering, liquid quiescence gathered in her lower body, flowing, expanding with his every movement. Fire surged along her veins so she ceased to feel the night coolness, knew nothing except the tenuous, waiting stillness inside her, the half-wild anticipation of some further incursion, some greater advance in his possession.

It came moments later, the brush of his hand as pushed her cloak aside then slid the cap sleeve of her gown down her arm, freeing the full globe of her breast for his attention. He cupped it in his warm grasp, molding it to a perfect fit, then he circled the small hillock with kisses before fastening his mouth upon the peak again. Mere seconds later, he released his clasp and lowered his hand to her knee. She felt him gathering her skirts with unhurried movements, drawing their fullness higher. Then the warmth of his hand came down upon her pantaloon-covered thigh as he slid it beneath the layers of silk and lace-edged cambric.

Her breathing grew quicker, taking on a frantic edge. He soothed her, trailing up and down from her thigh to her knee in hypnotic rhythm, letting her feel and accept the sure weight of his hand before sliding it higher. He reached her upper thigh, kneading with slow assurance, ran his fingertips around to the sensitive inner surface where the two halves of her pantaloon legs were split for customary convenience. Delicately questing, he delved inside, laid his palm over bare skin, and soft curls.

She stiffened with a sound of protest catching in her throat. It was not fear of the intimacy he had undertaken that distressed her, however, but rather the ease with which he made that move. His very assurance that had seemed so calming moments before was a sudden affront. He was entirely too familiar with female apparel, too experienced with dalliance in the dark, too much the legendary lover.

More than that, he was using his wiles on a woman other than his betrothed, a nameless, virtually faceless female. It was not her he desired, but any woman with a willing body and no inconvenient scruples. She disliked that intensely in him at that moment, distrusted it to the point that it quite extinguished her desire.

Juliette put a hand to his chest, pushing against his hold. She thought for an instant that he might not let her go, but he opened his arms in abrupt compliance and even steadied her as she teetered off balance before surging to her feet. Stepping away several paces with her back to him, she straightened her bodice, readjusted her half mask and shook her skirts into place.

"If I offended you, fair Incognito," he began.

"No. No, I simply came to my senses." If she could have fled on foot, she would have done so rather than turn to face him again, even in the near darkness. That would gain her nothing, however, as she had no way back to the masquerade other than in the carriage that had brought them. "I would like to return to the ballroom now."

Silence. Then his deep voice spoke the words she feared and longed to hear.

"As you wish."

She heard the rustle of his clothing as he rose and moved to her side. He flung back his cape to offer his arm, and she accepted that support without looking at him. A slight trembling ran through her fingers and he reached to cover them, holding them on his shirt sleeve. They moved away from the bower, in the direction of the faint lights and music, with no sound between them other than the grinding of their footsteps on the crushed shells of the path.

Strain held them. Juliette thought Nicholas hovered at the edge of some comment or question though he did not speak. For herself, she had nothing to say, wanted nothing more than to leave the gardens as soon as possible, returning to the masquerade where she might convince her mother to go home as soon as possible. Her greatest fear just now was that some chance word or gesture might reveal who she was to Nicholas so she would be obliged to face him without the protection of her mask. That would be unendurable.

She walked as quickly as she could without being obvious about it, her eyes focused on the lamplight that glowed above the shrubbery of the winding walkway. She did not so much as glance at the man beside her, concentrating instead on holding to her composure until she was well away from him in the privacy of her bedchamber.

The two men rose up like phantoms, hulking figures in rough garb appearing from the ambush of the thick greenery on either side. One grabbed Juliette's arm with a hard hand, throwing her to the ground. She cried out, feeling the sharp bite of broken shells on her hand and elbow as she caught herself. Above her head, Nicholas grappled with the other attacker, his cloak swaying and dipping around him. Abruptly, he shoved free, reached for the sword at his side. It came free of its jeweled scabbard with a slithering scrape, leaping to his hand. Silver fire ran starlike from hilt to tip as it caught the distant light. With a discordant clang, the blade struck metal and scraped free again.

The assailants were armed with swords as well, she realized in stunned horror. What could it mean? A sword was a gentleman's weapon, requiring money for the purchase and training to make it useful. It was not the weapon of footpads and robbers who roamed the night to prey on the unwary.

The attack was planned and directed at Nicholas. Had he been struck in that first savage assault? She strained her eyes in the dark but could not tell.

"Run," he called out to her as he faced the two men from his swordsman's crouch. "Go now."

To obey that low command might be the intelligent course, but she could not bear the thought. Instead, she pushed to her knees on the shell path, her gaze burning as she looked from one man to the other.

The two assailants were not so eager to close with a known *maître d'armes*, one some called the greatest in New Orleans, now that he had sword in hand. They circled him, crouching, weaving on their feet as they sought some advantage.

Nicholas appeared disinclined to allow them one. He caught the excess fullness of his cape, swirling it around his right arm as a makeshift shield as he followed their movements with narrowed eyes.

The initiative of the ambush had changed, or so it appeared to Juliette. The position of the brutes who had essayed it was weaker, not only because they had lost the element of surprise but because it was more difficult to take on a man in the position sinister, left-handed, than one who wielded his blade in the right hand. Yet they were still two against one.

The heaviest of the pair growled an oath and rushed Nicholas. Steel rasped against steel in a shower of sparks. Nicholas swirled free, lunged to the attack. There came the flash of blades in parry and riposte too quick to follow in the dimness though she stared with aching eyes. Then the slighter of the two men, seeing his chance, darted forward to join the fray. Nicholas danced backward to gain room, at the same time leading the fight away from where Juliette knelt. Set once more, he took on the blades of both men in an attack of powerful, blinding speed. Illusive, cunning, he seemed invincible. Yet Juliette's heart was in her throat and an ache of empathetic vulnerability invaded her midsection.

She longed to do something, to aid Nicholas in some way, but how? She could not intervene without becoming a handicap as he was forced to consider her position there in uncertain light. The best thing she could do, or so it seemed, was stay well out of the way. In truth, the attackers looked almost clumsy compared to the power and grace of the man they faced. They hacked and slashed with little finesse, almost as if aiming for Nicholas's sword arm instead of his heart.

Suddenly, Nicholas swept into an attack of slashing ferocity. It drove the two men back, stumbling, desperately parrying the lightning-fast, bell-like blows of his steel. Juliette saw her chance. She snatched up her skirts and thrust out her foot.

The nearest attacker tripped and fell backward, arms windmilling. His sword slashed the face of the second man, who howled as he reeled away before plunging to one knee.

Immediately, Nicholas was there, knocking away the protective hand of the first man with the flat of his sword before leaning to press the point to his throat. Behind him, the other attacker stared an instant, then scrambled to all fours before plunging away, staggering off into the night.

Nicholas, his sword arm unmoving, spared a glance in Juliette's direction. "You are unhurt?"

"Yes, quite," she answered in clipped tones. "And you?"

He made no direct reply, asking instead, "What shall we do with this *canaille?*"

"The gendarmes, perhaps?" She tried to see his face, alerted by some shade of meaning in his question other than the obvious, but his mask prevented it.

"A course that could occasion more discussion than either of us cares to undertake at the moment."

"Oh. Yes." It was unlikely she would be required to speak to anyone in an official capacity since ladies were spared such ordeals, but it would undoubtedly come out that Nicholas had not been alone. Keeping her identity secret might prove difficult. "It…it was you they meant to injure, therefore the decision is yours."

"I'm not so sure."

"What do you mean?"

"Never mind." He lifted his sword with an abrupt gesture and stepped back. "Up, scum," he said to the man on the ground. "Run, tell your master that his plan did not succeed and he will have to try again. Tell him to plan well, for next time I will not be so lenient."

A slicing hint of death was in the quiet voice of Nicholas Pasquale. That the defeated attacker heard as well was plain from the whiteness of his face before he crawled to his feet and lumbered off down the path.

When his footsteps had faded away, Nicholas sheathed his sword with a metallic hiss and clang then moved to extend his right hand, pulling Juliette upright so quickly that she caught his arm for balance. Her fingers tangled in the cape that still wrapped it, pushing through a narrow rent in the blue cloth.

A quick exclamation sprang to her lips. "You were slashed! Where? Is it deep?"

"A nick only. Think nothing of it."

"You are certain?"

"I swear it."

He swung his cape back into place and stepped away from her lifted hand as if unwilling to have her touch him. That was the height of irony, since, quite suddenly, she wanted that almost more than she could bear. That he had come so close to death, had been forced to defend his life, affected her with a deep, near primitive need to be close to him, to take him into her body as if he might be safe there. It was, no doubt, the result of lingering passion from moments before, but it was strange beyond anything she had ever known. A tremor ran over her as she fought the sensation, but still it seemed to lodge in the lower part of her body with a throbbing anguish of need.

Something of her distress must have been communicated to Nicholas, for he stared down at her a grim instant. When he spoke, his voice was without inflection. "This was a mistake on all fronts, coming here with you. Believe me, please, when I say that I regret it beyond imaging. Amends will have to wait, however. The best thing to be done now is to return you to the ballroom as planned."

"Yes," she whispered.

He took her arm again and steered her toward the area where they had left the carriage. She went with him without protest, almost without noticing her concentration on the feelings that shifted through her.

How had she come so close to passionate acceptance of this man who cared for her not at all beyond her usefulness as a mother figure? How could she want him so desperately when he stood closer to death than to life? How could she long to turn back the clock and live again those few minutes of ecstasy, changing their outcome, when she knew the terror of attack must follow?

These questions remained with her as he escorted her back to the St. Louis Hotel ballroom. They were with her still as she rejoined her mother and sister and made her way homeward. They haunted her as she lay staring into the gathered canopy of mosquito netting above her bed hours later, listening to the storm that finally broke above the city and the rain that pounded on the roof before splashing into the narrow courtyard.

She thought of her fiancé's voice and his face, remembered the touch of his hands. The kiss they shared repeated in her mind a thousand times. She considered what she might have done differently, wondered what would have happened if she had stayed in his arms. She congratulated herself on her escape one moment, and wished that she had not effected it the next.

It was long hours before she slept.

11

The four sword masters stood looking at the bed as if they had never come across such a thing before. In truth, they had not seen one on such a massive scale. Done in rosewood of a fine satin sheen, it had opulent curves and fine carving on the headboard. The four soaring, treelike posts supported a tester that scraped the ceiling, with shirred silk stretched inside its massive frame. Obviously designed for cotton and sugar planters with deep pocketbooks to match their exalted ideas and neoclassical mansions with extremely high ceilings, it was a bed to give any red-blooded gentleman ideas.

"Do you think Celina will like it?" Rio asked in a dubious tone without taking his gaze from the Mallard showpiece.

"When she stops giggling over your obvious intentions," Blackford answered.

"Thank you." Rio gave him a scathing look. "Caid?"

"Are you sure it wasn't her idea in the first place?

I mean, did you happen upon this thing yourself or have you received gentle hints over the past few days?"

The conde gave him a wry smile, but didn't bother to answer the allegation. "Nicholas, *mon ami?*"

"She will adore it. And I'm wondering what Juliette would say if I should order one like it."

"Your little nun will undoubtedly agree with whatever you choose," Blackford said, turning away to inspect the armoire that was a matching piece to the bed.

Nicholas laughed with a short sound. "I wouldn't count on it."

"Meaning?" The Englishman sent him an intrigued look.

"Nothing," Nicholas said shortly. He was disinclined to discuss his betrothed in masculine company, but he was also aware that he had no idea what Juliette's reaction might be to his purchase of such a hulking monster of a bed. His own response to the thought of her in it was certainly not a subject for public conversation.

They stood in the *Magasin de Meubles* of Prudent Mallard on the rue Royale where the smell of sawn wood, coming from his workshop just around the corner, permeated the air like incense. Mallard, a distinguished gentleman in his early thirties whose French still held the accents of Paris where he had learned his trade, was occupied with a country gentleman and his lady, leaving them to decide on the purchase.

It was Rio who had steered them to the furniture maker. He was presently refurbishing the bedchamber allotted to him and Celina at the Vallier plantation as a birthday gift for his bride. They had already visited the display rooms of Francois Seignouret, where they had looked at a suite in finest mahogany that included a bed, armoire and pair of fireside chairs. However, Rio had decided to compare the prices of Seignouret's nearest rival in skill and fashion.

Rio, his gaze on the design that was Mallard's signature, said, "Yes, but which do you prefer, Mallard's eggs or Seignouret's S curves?"

"For myself, Seignouret's work," Nicholas said with a gesture of the sword cane that he had been leaning on. "I will be furnishing a house on a smaller scale after all and Juliette may prefer the refinement. For your country place, Mallard's designs may be better."

Caid, standing nearby, reached to clamp a hearty hand on his shoulder. "So you're really going through with this marriage."

Nicholas stiffened, drawing a hissing breath through his teeth as he dropped his sword cane from numb fingers. He could not speak for the pain spearing into him, but lifted his right hand in a quick, warding-off gesture.

Caid exclaimed and released his hold as if he had grasped a nettle. "You're injured?"

"Nothing of any moment, just a slice through the flesh under the arm, but it's a trifle sore."

"So I would imagine." The words were dry. "You were all right earlier last evening, so it must have happened while you were absent from the masquerade."

Nicholas dipped his head in a nod. "We— I went to Tivoli Gardens, not the wisest of choices, as it turned out."

"We?"

He should have known Caid would catch that small slip, Nicholas thought. Now he would be satisfied with nothing less that the whole tale. "I took a lady for a drive. We sauntered a few minutes in the gardens but were set upon by a pair of thugs."

"Armed with swords?"

"As it happens."

Gavin Blackford picked up the sword cane that had rolled to his feet, hefting it his hand. "You must have been well away from the crowd. What on God's green earth possessed you?"

"Oh, the lure of conquest, what else?" Nicholas drawled.

"I'm sure. And who was this beleaguered lady in danger from churls and seducers on all sides? Or should we guess?"

"She was incognito." It was true enough as far as

it went, Nicholas thought. Still, he had known it was Juliette from the first, could not have failed to recognize the unique coloration of her eyes or the lush curves of her mouth. Fascinated by her refusal to let him know her and the hint of the coquette in her manner, he had played up to what had seemed an innocent charade.

That had been a mistake. How great a one had been brought to his attention during a long and painful night during which the ache under his arm seemed a minor annoyance compared to that in other portions of his anatomy. Worst of all was the turmoil in his mind.

What had she been about, concealing her identity yet smiling with infinite promise in her eyes as she agreed to his suggestion to slip away from the protective presence of her chaperones? Why had she gone with him so willingly along that dimly lighted pathway? Had it been a game to see if he could penetrate her disguise? Was it simple curiosity of a sensual kind that had been denied to her all her life? Or was there something more?

"Incognito?" Blackford asked. "And we are to believe you could not, did not, unravel her mystery?"

"Believe what you will. I can't stop you." Nicholas's voice was curt as he flexed his arm and found the ache had eased a fraction.

"I would rather administer lessons in self-control and the courtesy due the woman you are to marry, except that you seem to have been punished already."

"You have no idea," Nicholas said, his smile wryly self-deprecating.

"These hooligans who set upon you," Caid said with a frown, "you think it mere chance that they caught you where they did."

"By no means. They struck for my sword arm."

"And knew which to choose," Caid said in grim tones. "We can assume they knew you would be there…." He paused as Nicholas shook his head, then added, "Or else followed you from the masquerade."

"Where they may have known you would appear," Blackford put in, following the thing to its logical conclusion. "So who have you offended of late?"

"None who might seek such underhanded revenge."

"Not even Daspit?" Caid asked. "I'm assuming he still blames you for his injury instead of Croquère."

"I prefer to give him the benefit of the doubt."

"Since he may become your brother-in-law, yes," Rio said, then pursed his lips. "The purpose could have been to give you a handicap."

"Making it easier to dispatch me on the field after a timely challenge?" Nicholas shook his head. "I could always reveal the injury and delay any meeting until it had time to heal."

Rio gave him a sardonic glance. "Yes, but would you?"

Nicholas declined to answer, since he could not swear to that much intelligence.

"Just so," Rio said. "I suggest you avoid any situation that seems likely to lead to differences, at least for the next few days."

It seemed good advice. The problem, Nicholas suspected, might be in following it.

Rio opted for Mallard's artistry for his bedchamber furnishing, and stepped aside with the furniture maker for the usual spirited bargaining over price. Caid left them, since he had promised to drive out with Lisette for a round of afternoon visits. Nicholas and Blackford did not linger, either, but waved to Rio and went out into the street.

They turned in the direction of the Passage and their ateliers. Neither had clients scheduled, since their salons were closed for a day. Fencing was a strenuous art, and pushing too hard by opening every day could result in strained muscles and other injuries. Besides, they were both obligated for weekly training with the militia as part of the Louisiana Legion, and it was necessary to keep time clear for that activity.

Blackford strode along with a frown between his gold-dusted eyebrows and a stranglehold on Nicholas's cane that he still carried. The two of them wove their way between sellers of pralines, pecans and greens and past ladies protected from the sun by veils of fine green *barège* with matching green gloves on their hands and sloe-eyed maids trailing behind them, bowed to acquaintances and skirted a dog fight. The Englishman scarcely seemed to notice. It was plain to see he had something on his mind, but Nicholas, suspecting what it might be, was not inclined to give him an opening for expressing it. If he thought to escape through such denial, however, he was to be disappointed.

"To bring the tender joys of the bedchamber to every woman in New Orleans is a worthy ambition, no doubt, but may prove exhausting even for you," Gavin said with acid condemnation. "Far better if you confine your urges in that direction to their proper target."

"Meaning?" Nicholas asked in mild inquiry. As they came to a corner, he crossed over and turned down the side street in the direction of the river.

"Mademoiselle Armant is a lady worthy of any man's consideration, amorous or otherwise."

"You think so."

"Not being an idiot."

"I suppose you would take my place, given the chance?" A raw edge seeped into Nicholas's voice against his will.

"Don't be a nod-cock. Unlike some, I am able to admire a lady without the urge of possession. But what maggot of the brain made you vanish in the glooming with a female of easy virtue when you should have been attending on the woman who will be your wife?"

"How do you know her state of virtue?"

"Like a wart on a toad, some things spring to the eye. You may call her a lady if it pleases you, but the circumstances make it doubtful."

"She may have been too innocent to understand my purpose."

"Which would make you doubly the villain and a fool into the bargain." Blackford paused as they turned again, this time into the Passage. "Was she?"

"Being a gentleman," Nicholas said with soft amusement, "I cannot tell you that." It was more than any code of honor that kept him from exposing Juliette's part, however. He preferred that no one else learn of her lovely daring.

"Of course not, bedding a willing wench having nothing whatever to do with marriage to a nun. You swoop and play and strike, occasionally, for the kill, but hold it all close to your heart. Or I suppose you must, if you have one."

"Oh, I have one."

"Display it then, or you may lose the one female who might save you and your misbegotten brood from whips, gallows, dark specters in the night and other such ills."

Nicholas stared at Blackford, wondering what he had said or done to cause him to think such a thing. "And if she has no use for it?"

"It will be no more than you have earned."

"A fine pronouncement from one who hasn't, so far as I've seen, bothered to form any kind of romantic attachment during your time in the city," Nicholas said as his temper finally began to flare.

"For which restraint, its women should sacrifice a dove on every altar. Not that my affairs, or lack of them, are of moment here."

Nicholas stared at his friend, wondering at the pain that lay like drowned hope under his swift flow of words. To question a man about his past was not a tenant of the swordsmen who resided on the Passage nor of the Brotherhood, however, and so he kept his curiosity to himself. "Will it satisfy you, *mon ami*, if I say that no action of mine will cause grief for Mademoiselle Armant?"

"Meaning you expect a pallid union based on convenience on one side and conformity on the other, so without tiresome sentiment? She deserves better in return for leaving behind her visions of peace and heavenly approval."

"I would not deny it. But the reason for your concern, again, is what?"

"A dislike for careless cruelty."

That was very close to insult, and Nicholas felt his hackles begin to rise. The only curb on his temper was knowledge of his English friend's convoluted way of thinking. It was not beyond reason to think the slur might have been delivered to draw out a declaration of his feelings for Juliette, though why they should matter to Blackford was difficult to fathom.

It would not be forthcoming, in part because he was not at all sure what he felt after the night before.

That Juliette Armant might not be the reserved lady he had thought, that she might have a hidden side to her nature, was a disturbance in his mind. It also excited him beyond imagining. Her eager responses, her lovely acquiescence in his arms, made his heart swell with a painful joy to think about them. And yet he also felt guilty for touching her, ashamed that he had gone so far, come so close to despoiling her.

He had thought to test her intentions and even, perhaps, her resolve. She had not disappointed him since she had called a halt to his advances, almost shoving him away from her. Regardless, there had been something uncontrolled, even a little wild in her participation until that moment.

Any rational man would be overjoyed to discover that his betrothed was capable of such a sensual awakening. And he knew it was no more than that for her kisses, though sweeter than spring nectar, had been untutored. She had touched him as though the body of a man was unknown territory to be investigated with care. Her tentative explorations had excited him even as they affected him with tenderness beyond anything he had ever known.

The problem was within himself, he thought. He had seen her as the mother of his strays, a gentle soul, angelic, pure, uncomplicated and endlessly compassionate. He had thought to defend her with his strength and aid her with the protection of his name. He had desired her, but as a simple hunger that had in it the need for her gentle and unconditional acceptance. That she was not as he had seen her disturbed him in some fundamental way that he could not quite grasp. She had shocked him or something very near it.

He, the legendary lover of women, the epitome of experience in the bedchamber, the man who enjoyed women in all their infinite variety, could not comprehend this woman who had almost become a nun. It seemed that she desired him, was drawn to that part of his nature that was most sensual, and yet how could that be? Most disturbing of all was that his desire for her was not so worshipful as he had thought but as carnal as any he had known. Since the evening before it had become a living thing, eating away inside him.

She had been a novice and he had somehow corrupted her.

He must be depraved.

There was also the fact that she had stayed behind to help during the attack instead of running as he had commanded. It was the last thing he had expected when she should have had nothing except disgust for him.

Yes, but now she thought he had betrayed her with another female since she could not know that he had recognized her from the moment she walked into the ballroom. That being so he was torn asunder by the choices available to him. Was he to reveal his knowledge and allow her to realize how much he wanted her? Or should he keep it from her, maintaining his distant adoration?

Which would she prefer? Or which did he prefer, for that matter?

He had not the vaguest idea.

They were almost at his atelier, drawing within a step or two of the arcade, which shaded the stairway to his upper rooms. A shadow moved in that dusty gloom, gathering, elongating until it took on the shape of a man.

Blackford sprang forward with the power of a great golden cat. Sliding the sword cane from its sheath, he whirled to stand between Nicholas and the source of danger in a single fluid movement. He crouched there, tense of muscle and lethal of purpose.

The man under the arcade stood loose-limbed and at ease, a half smile forming on his face. Even so, he moved not a muscle.

Blackford straightened. Then he stepped to one side as he reseated the sword cane with a snap.

"Well, now. I guess you must be a sword master," the gentleman who had apparently been waiting for them said with an admiring shake of his head. "If I'd been looking for trouble, I expect I'd be whistling through a few extra lung holes about now."

"Or be as silent as a sieve," Blackford answered. "Do you play hide-and-seek or have you business here?"

"Oh, business, of course," the man replied, his good humor unimpaired as he stood with his feet slightly spread, ready for trouble, but with his hat in his hands. "Though it's with the gentleman next to you, I'm thinking. Not that I doubt your ability, but he comes with a higher recommendation."

Kentucky was in the accents of the man before him, Nicholas thought, and in his rangy, long-limbed frame as well. He was all surface affability, with a shock of barely tamed oak-brown hair and a bland look in his eyes the dark gray shade of old slate. Still, something in his manner put Nicholas on alert. The gentleman was not the bumpkin he might wish to appear.

Even as he made that lightning assessment, however, he frowned at Blackford's interference. What had possessed the man to step in front of him? He might have a small injury but was hardly incapacitated. His friend's concern was excessive. He really was taking too much on himself.

Moving forward so that Blackford was forced to step aside, Nicholas asked, "You would see me, monsieur?"

"If you're Pasquale, the one they call La Roche."

"I am."

"Kerr Wallace, at your service, sir." The stranger put out a large, square hand.

Nicholas stared at the hand an instant, then reached to take it in lieu of a bow. He half expected an attempt to crush his fingers as some of the Americans uptown attempted on occasion. The contact, instead, was firm, dry and brief. The eyes above it were level and assessing, not at all those of a stupid man.

"A Scots name, unless I miss my guess," Blackford said.

"My folk came from there long years back," their visitor answered, "though we make our home in the Smoky Mountains now. But you, sir, sound as if your arrival was more recent."

"Just so."

"Nothing to do with Jacobean sympathies as with my grandfather, then, but I'm sure there was a reason all the same."

Blackford glanced at Nicholas with something between annoyance and amusement in his eyes before he answered. "One that makes no difference here."

"Well, now, we could all say that, couldn't we?"

Nicholas liked the simplicity of that answer, which effectively put an end to further questions. His smile for Blackford was a little crooked before he turned back to his prospective client. "Perhaps you would care to step upstairs where we may be more comfortable. I can offer you a glass of Bordeaux if you have the time."

"That's right kind of you, sir."

"Not at all." Nicholas, turning toward the stairs that rose against the back wall, half expected Blackford to make his excuses and continue to his own salon along the way. Instead, he stood aside to allow the Kentuckian to precede him then followed after them.

The unlocking of the salon door released the odors of sweat and metal polish, stale wine and tobacco smoke. They were so familiar to Nicholas that he hardly noticed them in the regular order of things, but did so now as he saw the stranger take them in along with a fast, comprehensive survey of his surroundings. He glanced at the long room that fronted the Passage, with its tall French windows that could be opened for maximum air circulation, brackets on the plastered walls holding epees and foils, and polished floor laid with long canvas fencing strips, and wondered if it were alien to the Kentuckian or might have some familiarity. Nothing in the man's face gave any indication, one way or the other.

Nicholas led the way through the main salon to the sitting room, where he poured wine from the tray on a console table while they took their seats.

Handing around the glasses, he joined them, waiting until they had tasted the libation before he spoke.

"How then may I be of service, monsieur?"

The Kentuckian stared down at the glass he cradled in his fingers for a long moment, then looked up to meet Nicholas's eyes. "You can teach me how to handle a sword."

"Willingly, but may I ask for what purpose?"

"The usual, I expect."

"You have had a meeting forced upon you, perhaps. I pursue this, you understand, not to pry into your affairs but to learn how quickly you need to acquire this skill."

"You're talking a duel? No, what I want is to kill a man."

Nicholas spared a glance at Blackford, who merely lifted an eyebrow. To the Kentuckian, he said, "A worthy object, I feel sure, but there are other, more certain ways to arrange it."

"Not without getting hanged for it. Besides, I don't mind giving him a fair chance at me."

"You apprehend that the purpose of a duel is not death. It's an affair of honor usually satisfied by first blood."

A smile flitted across the Kentuckian's mouth, one that did not reach his gray eyes. "You're telling me nobody ever sets out to put paid to a score?"

Nicholas was forced to concede that point. "This man you would meet is a swordsman?"

"He is."

"Not a professional."

"Like you, you mean? No, but he's been at it a while."

"He has experience and, I would assume, considerable skill, but you would still meet him."

"I figure you can show me what I need to know."

"We are not talking days, but weeks, even months of hard work."

The Kentuckian lifted a wide shoulder. "I've waited some little time so a bit more won't matter. And I've never been afraid of hard work."

The last was undoubtedly true, Nicholas thought. Kerr Wallace had the look of a man who understood the purpose of his muscles. "Forgive me, monsieur, but with all the will in the world to aid your cause, I cannot be a party to murder."

"You won't be. As I said, he'll have a chance at my hide. And so will a bunch of other yahoos unless I miss my guess."

"You contemplate other meetings?"

Kerr Wallace grinned. "Sounds that way, don't it? But no, I'm not that bloodthirsty. Fact is I have a mind to join old Sam Houston against this Generalissimo Santa Ana that's raising a dust on the other side of the Rio Grande right now. Seems he'll likely make a stab at claiming Texas again to the show the powers in Europe he hasn't thrown up his hands."

"It's Santa Ana you are determined to kill."

"Wouldn't mind that, but no." Wallace looked away, then back again. "All right, I suppose you should have the whole sorry story. My oldest brother and a friend hightailed it to the Texas country a while back, all fired up about independence and freedom and all such that appeal to hell-raisers. They joined up with Lamar's Rangers and were sent off on that damned wild-goose chase to Santa Fe."

"Ah," Nicholas said.

"Exactly. Mack's friend was a so-called gentleman from Louisiana. When things got too hot out on the plains, he stole Mack's food and water and snuck off in the night to join the Mexican Army that was trailing them. Mack, being the idealistic fool that he was, refused to take anything offered him to replace his supplies. It was his fault he'd lost his, he said, because he had no more sense than to trust the wrong man."

"He died," Blackford said, his voice soft.

It was, Nicholas thought, a fairly brutal comment, but a kindness all the same since it saved the Kentuckian from having to speak the words. He said nothing, but waited for the answer.

"He...went off his head, I guess, or maybe just decided to sell his life for a good price. Anyway, he led a sortie to replenish their horse string and never came back, or so said the letter that finally reached Kentucky a couple of weeks ago. It was written from a Mexican prison by a man who survived the march and the killing afterward, so took a while to get to my mother. Mack had asked him to write, you understand."

Yes." Nicholas understood all too well, for he had traveled halfway around the world on a similar mission. He clapped his hands together, his gaze steady on the man who had come to him for instruction.

"And this traitor, this Louisianian is the man you would kill."

Kerr Wallace inclined his head.

"*Bien*. We will start these lessons tomorrow."

"Nicholas," Blackford said with a warning in his voice.

"I thought maybe today," Wallace objected.

"My salon is closed," Nicholas answered pleasantly, ignoring the Englishman.

Blackford cleared his throat. "Your problem last evening…"

"I'd just as soon these instructions be private," Wallace said in firm tones.

"That will, naturally, be more expensive."

"Let me assure you, sir, that I can stand the price."

"This trifling wound of yours, remember?" Blackford insisted.

Nicholas gave him a quelling stare as he said to his new client, "In that event, we can start this afternoon."

"Capital," the Kentuckian exclaimed with the

first genuine smile since he had appeared at the salon. "You won't regret it."

Nicholas rather doubted that, but a man had his pride and it was, in any case, too late to worry about it now.

It was just then that they heard the pounding of steps on the outside stairs. There were a number of them though they had little weight and lacked the clatter of booted heels. As they neared, the strain of hard, gasping breaths could be heard, a sound that brought Nicholas to his feet with a frown. Before he could reach the door, it burst open.

His street boys spilled inside like a pack of leaping hounds. White-faced, wide-eyed, they raced toward him on grimy feet, all talking at once. In their midst was Squirrel, half running, carrying a small limp form in his arms.

"M'sieur Nick, M'sieur Nick!"

"It's Gabriel, M'sieur Nick. Do somethin'."

"He's dying, M'sieur Nick."

"You got to do somethin' now!"

12

"Juliette!"

She heard her name called from what sounded like the courtyard and turned quickly from the armoire where she was counting sheets and inspecting them for tears and insect damage that might require mending. It was Nicholas; she would know his voice anywhere. What she did not recognize was its note of concern verging on alarm.

Stripping off the apron she wore, she thrust it and the list she had been making into the hands of Valara, who had been helping her. Her fingers shook a little as she smoothed her hair into the chignon she wore at the nape of her neck. Whether that was due to the unannounced visit or the memory of the night before that skittered through her mind, she could not tell. She only knew she was suddenly fearful in a way she had not felt in a long time.

At the door that opened onto the gallery, she stopped in a flurry of skirts. Paulette was there, standing at the railing. Her chin was lifted, as were her eyebrows, and her arms were folded over her chest. She was staring down into the courtyard in cold disdain. Then as Juliette watched, she turned her back and moved away.

"Juliette!"

It took only an instant to realize what was going forward. Nicholas had seen Paulette, mistaken her twin for her and called out to her. Paulette, instead of correcting the error, meant it to appear that Juliette had snubbed him. It was a petty trick, one that sent a shaft of anger through Juliette. Still, the feeling that gripped her hardest was a pained lowering of spirits. It was clear that her fiancé could no more tell the difference between her and her twin than he had been able to identify her beneath her royal court lady disguise. He saw only the surface with no appreciation for what lay beneath it.

Nicholas, hard on his last call, came forward from where he had stopped in the shadowy archway of the porte cochère. Abruptly, Juliette saw the small body that he cradled in his arms, and also the other boys who crowded behind him.

"Here, Nicholas, I'm here," she cried, stepping swiftly to the gallery railing and leaning over it. "What is it?"

"It's Gabriel. He's ill."

"Bring him up to my bedchamber, bring him at once!"

Along the gallery from where she stood, her twin

exclaimed in annoyance. Juliette gave Paulette a hard stare with all the condemnation in her heart behind it. Then she pushed away from the railing and, calling out to Valara for her help as she ran, hurried to meet Nicholas at the head of the stairs.

Gabriel, the poor little mite, was burning up with fever, his breathing fast and shallow, and his eyes ringed by circles as dark as bruises. That he suffered from a stomach complaint was plain from the odor that rose from him, coming from the filth that stained his dirty shirt and encrusted his skinny little legs. Valara took one look and began to issue instructions in her deep and firm voice. Juliette listened, nodded, then saw to it they were carried out with all possible speed.

A tub of tin lined with zinc was brought and set up in Juliette's bedchamber, then cans of warm water carried up from the kitchen. Together, Juliette and Valara stripped the child and lowered him into the bath, gently washing away his dirt. Then they held him there, in spite of his moans and thrashing, while more cans of water were brought, cold this time, and poured into the tub to make the water cooler and cooler still.

Once, Juliette heard a moan from the doorway and looked up to see her mother standing there. Distress and painful memories pulled her face into deep lines of age, and she waved a handkerchief in a feeble gesture of distress before holding it to her mouth, making gagging sounds behind it.

"It's all right, *Maman*. Don't concern yourself," Juliette said, her voice a little abrupt.

"I'm so sorry, *chère*, but I can't, you know I can't."

"Are the other boys still here?"

Her mother nodded toward the courtyard. "Out there."

"Could you see that they have something to eat and drink?"

"But *chère*…"

"Please, *Maman*."

"Yes, of course, if you insist. Never let it be said that I have not a tender heart."

Juliette gazed after her mother a long moment, then she set her lips and turned back to the child who needed her attention.

Shortly thereafter, when a can much fuller than the others was poured into the tub from over her head, she looked up again. It was Nicholas who had brought it, spelling one of the maidservants. She gave him a brief smile for no other reason than to allay some of the dread she saw in his face. He returned it, though the look in his eyes remained grim. Oddly enough, that instant of silent communication seemed to quell something of her own fear.

When Gabriel's teeth were chattering, his lips blue and his skin cool and pebbled with goose bumps, Valara signaled that he could be lifted from the tub. It was Nicholas who did that, while Juliette wrapped him in a large square of Turkish toweling then gathered him into her arms. Moving to a rocking chair before a small coal fire, she held him in her lap, crooning as she soothed him, uncaring for the dampness that seeped into her gown and petticoats.

Valara watched her a moment, then exchanged a long, unsmiling glance with Nicholas. She went from the room and down the stairs to the kitchen to make one of her tisanes, the concoctions she always stirred together when anyone was ill.

The silence as Juliette was left alone with Nicholas was unnerving. She kept her gaze lowered, rubbing the hair of the child she held to dry it, smoothing the silk of it away from his small face while an odd tenderness grew around her heart. He was so small, so vulnerable to have been living hand to mouth in the streets. It hurt her to think of it.

"Thank you," Nicholas said with his voice a mere rasp in his throat. "You really are an angel."

"No." He meant well, but it was not what she wanted to hear.

"But yes. Anyone who could think otherwise would be a fool."

She pressed her lips together, but then said what had to be said. "He may not live. This is much like the malady that took my sister and brother."

"You think I should go for the doctor?"

"Valara says not. He came with his purgatives and bitter pills when the others were sick. My mother allowed him to physic them, but Valara tossed his remedies out the window when they began to decline, refusing to give them to me and Paulette. We lived. The others did not. I trust her and will give Gabriel her tisane. Then it will be in the hands of God."

"How long…?"

He didn't finish the questions, but there was no need. "We will know by morning, I think."

"Yes." He drew a deep breath, as if his chest was too tight.

"You should go and change, perhaps. I will send for you if…if anything should happen."

He glanced down at the stains on his coat and grimaced, then shook his head. "I'll go, but would like to return."

"Immediately, you mean?"

"If I may."

How could she object? He had every right to be concerned, no matter how difficult it was to have him near. "I doubt that my mother will forbid it, as long as Valara is here."

"Excellent. I won't be above an hour."

She nodded, watching as he backed slowly away from where she sat as if reluctant to go. His dark eyes were on Gabriel, but flickered also to her face before returning to the boy. At the door, he turned finally and strode away down the gallery.

When she was certain he was gone, she drew a

deep, uneven breath and let it out on a sigh. She held Gabriel, cuddling his small, slowly warming body closer against her as if for her own comfort.

She had dreaded seeing Nicholas after the evening at Tivoli Gardens. Somewhere inside her had been an insidious fear that he might have recognized her and would think less of her for her near surrender or have second thoughts about the marriage. Why she should think so, she could not say; he was hardly in a position to cast stones. Wasn't he known as a lover extraordinaire, one for whom midnight trysts were an everyday, or every night, affair? He had been in that garden bower just as she had, had engaged in every kiss, every touch. Why should it be the woman who must feel as if she had behaved like a wanton, or that she was wicked for enjoying those moments in the dark?

She had reveled in them, had felt the most beneficent languor, thrilled to an amazing impulse to throw caution to the winds and be wanton indeed. Only the knowledge that Nicholas thought her some unknown female had prevented her. Well, and also the fear of stepping out of the role she had been cast in so long, that of the good sister, forever pure, untouched and untouchable. It had been how she was, how she thought of herself, for so long that she hardly knew what she might become without it.

Her best hope seemed to return to her pose as the pious future wife and mother. Nicholas needed her,

wanted her in that role, and so did the boys he had
adopted as his own. He would expect her to come
to him as pure and untouched as any Madonna. It
was how he saw her, what he required of her, so that
was how she would be. And afterward would have
to take care of itself.

Valara returned with her elixir, a concoction
made of lemon syrup, salt and a small amount of
grenadine stirred into a quart of boiled water.
Coaxing and pleading, they roused Gabriel enough
to take a little of it from a spoon. He seemed to like
it, since he licked his lips even though his eyes
remained closed.

"'Tis a good sign," Valara said, standing over the
rocking chair, watching the child through narrowed
eyes. "Or it will be if he can keep it down."

Juliette murmured in agreement, and closed her
eyes to say a little prayer even as she rocked gently
back and forth.

Moments later, when it appeared that the elixir
would be retained, they fed him another spoonful,
then another and another until he had taken at
least a half cup of the liquid and would take no
more. Juliette would have shaken him awake yet
again, but Valara put a hand on her shoulder.

"Let him sleep, *chère*. It's the best thing. It will
comfort him, I don't doubt, that he is being held
against your heart."

"I hope that it may," Juliette answered quietly.

The old nursemaid smiled. "The little ones, they squeeze our souls, yes? And he has much need of you."

"Perhaps I have need of him."

"And what of the man who claims him?"

"I don't know what you mean."

"I'm an old fool, but not blind. You are made for love, my sweet Juliette. It's there in your smile, in your walk. You have too much life, too much joy inside to be shut away from it. You could tend the children of others and pray for them, yes, but were made to have children of your own, and to love their papa as a woman loves a man."

"And should he not love me?"

"He will, if it is God's plan, and if you wish it."

"Why would I not?"

"Ah, *chère*, sometimes it feels safer to go without love than to ask for it. Only the brave learn what is in the heart of one who comes to them in a marriage such as you will make."

Juliette rested her cheek on the top of Gabriel's head. "I should not like to know that I am only tolerated for the sake of the boys."

"Then you must take the chance."

"How?"

"You will know when the time comes."

It was not a satisfactory answer, but all she was going to get, Juliette thought. She said no more, but sat rocking, rocking, as the morning crept slowly away.

* * *

Nicholas had not returned by the midday meal that her mother served at the usual hour of three o'clock. Juliette wondered briefly what had kept him, but had little time to worry about it. Gabriel became fretful and almost delirious, crying and calling for his mother. Juliette could not leave him for an instant, could not put him down without him crying after her. He would only swallow Valara's elixir if she held the spoon, and if any attempt was made to force him to take more than a sip at the time, he became violently ill.

It was Paulette who made that last unfortunate discovery during the short interval she sat with him while Juliette ate her dinner. Paulette had been sure Gabriel would not notice the substitution of one twin for the other and that he was being coddled for no reason, errors which made it necessary for her change her clothing from the skin out. Since it also kept her and her snappish comments about charity children and their diseases well away from the sick room thereafter, Juliette could not help thinking the incident had some benefit. The hour reserved for afternoon calls brought Monsieur Daspit to be the recipient of Paulette's indignant complaints and peace reigned once more.

Juliette had finally persuaded Gabriel to take another half cup of the elixir, rocked him to sleep, then put him down on her bed, when she heard measured footfalls coming along the gallery. She turned expectantly from covering the child, ready to impart news of his slight improvement to Nicholas. Instead, she saw the shadow of a man narrow of shoulder and with the bat-wing shape of a sling on his arm pass the window. Her lips tightened as Paulette's intended stepped into the bedchamber.

"How very touching." Daspit's gaze swept the boy on the bed, paused for a frowning instant before he looked toward Juliette. "I suppose it hasn't occurred to you what an imposition it is to foist this little guttersnipe onto your *maman* and your sister?"

"He is sick and has nowhere else to go. What should I do, turn him back out into the street?" She stepped away from bed toward Daspit as she spoke, afraid their voices might wake her patient.

"Send him back to the one who brought him here. Send him to an orphanage where he belongs. Send him to the devil, for all I care. But you should not be spreading his contagion to those who should be dearer to you."

"Why, monsieur, one would think you fear this childish complaint," she said, driven to anger by his presumption. "Though what affair it is of yours is beyond my comprehension. You are not yet head of this family, not even, insofar as I am aware, officially betrothed to my sister."

"Long friendship and honest intention give me the right to speak. Your sister is grieved by your stubborn attempt to usurp her place, and now by this lack of consideration for her welfare or that of your mother. This is but one example of the disruption you have caused in their lives, and I fear it will grow worse before it gets better."

"Don't speak to me of consideration, monsieur. It is you who told my sister that you may draw back from a marriage between you if she cannot bring the marriage chest to it. If she is upset, you must look there for the cause."

"She told you this, did she? It only proves she understands the practicalities of the matter and joins with me in the search for a remedy."

Juliette gave him a hard stare. "Well, you may search all you like but will find it difficult to get around the fact that I am the elder by several minutes. And should you choose to desert Paulette because of that circumstance, it's my belief that she will be better off for it."

He gave a short laugh. "You would think so, given your lack of experience."

"I fail to see what that has to do with it."

"Your sister undoubtedly uses a different measure. Between a man and woman are matters of the flesh which—"

"Which should not be discussed with my sister, much less with me. I cannot imagine where you found the nerve or the opportunity to bring such things to her notice."

"Nerve is a commodity I have in abundance, Mademoiselle Juliette, and opportunity can be created from nothing if one has the will. But then, I would expect you to know nothing of such things. How typical of you to prefer they aren't mentioned." He smiled with a knowing look, which set her teeth on edge. "I warned you once that you were unfit for these pleasures. You should have heeded me instead of encouraging this bastard sword master. You force me to demonstrate my meaning, and have only yourself to blame if it is too shattering."

He took a step toward her but Juliette held up a hand to ward him off. "My fiancé is expected at any moment, monsieur, and will certainly object in lethal fashion to finding you alone with me. In any case, you are quite mistaken in considering me ignorant of what passes between a man and a woman. I see no purpose in further demonstration, at least not from you."

"Now this is interesting," Daspit said, tilting his head as he clasped his wrist at the edge of the black silk sling supporting his injured arm. "Am I to understand recent experience in that direction has found favor with you? It may be I've been courting the wrong sister."

"I hardly think so." He could not be suggesting that he might transfer his affections. Could he?

"I have always thought you the more attractive, particularly in temperament."

He was only trying a different means of alarming her, she thought. If so, he was succeeding. That he might withdraw from his agreement with Paulette in order to pursue her sent dismay skittering along her nerves. "Must I remind you again that I am betrothed?"

He shook his head, watching her through narrowed eyes. "I am the better *parti*, you know. My mother's people were of the nobility who escaped to New Orleans from the Terror, as she will tell you if you ask. Pasquale is a mongrel in comparison to my birth and breeding."

She thought he flicked another glance at Gabriel with the last, an imputation which brought sharp anger to her voice. "One with much experience on the dueling field."

"That need not trouble you. A lady may say what she will with impunity, may disavow an engagement without fear of reprisal."

She stared at him a long moment before she spoke again. "It's the chest, isn't it? You believe it to be right-fully mine, after all, and think to change brides in order to claim it. You must look elsewhere for a fortune, monsieur, for I have no interest in your birth and breeding and would never serve my sister so under-handed a trick as to accept you as a suitor in her place. That is, of course, if I didn't have a fiancé already."

"You know very well this marriage to Pasquale is a mere convenience, a means to grasp the prize before it gets away from you."

"You can know nothing of my wedding arrangements, but I assure you they are as valid as any you may make."

"A nice piece of sophistry, under the circumstances," he said on a laugh.

"No such thing. I will wed Nicholas Pasquale and that will be the end of it."

Jean Daspit opened his mouth to reply, then scowled and closed it again as he glanced toward the door. Juliette followed his gaze, half expecting to see Nicholas. Instead, it was Squirrel who stood there, with a shoulder propped on the door frame and his arms crossed over his chest. On the young man's face was a look of such knowing contempt that Juliette blinked to see it.

"M'sieur Nick won't like you talkin' like that to his lady," the boy said, never taking his eyes from Daspit, "won't like you talkin' to her at all. You best take care."

"If you think I fear your M'sieur Nick, you are much mistaken."

Squirrel twitched a bony shoulder. "Your funeral."

It looked for an instant as though Paulette's fiancé might resent the boy's interference in some violent manner, but a glance at the warning in Juliette's set face seemed to dissuade him. "I will not stay here and bandy words with a mongrel pup. Mademoiselle Juliette, we will speak on this matter at a better time." He sketched a barely civil bow. "Until then."

Squirrel stood aside to let Daspit pass. Juliette thought he almost spit on the floor where Paulette's betrothed had walked, but apparently thought better of it. When he turned back, he searched her face, as if expecting a reprimand.

"Come inside," she said with a quick gesture of welcome. "It's Gabriel you wanted to see, I expect."

He looked awkward in a way he had not before, as if he didn't know what to do with his hands and was reluctant to tread on the Aubusson carpet with his dirty and broken boots. He stared, unblinking, at the small, still form on the bed. "Yeah. It's just that…I mean, it's been some little while since he cried or made any noise."

"He's asleep, only asleep," Juliette said quickly.

"You sure?"

The dread that lurked in his face made her chest ache. She touched his arm. "Come closer and see for yourself."

Squirrel approached the bed and stood looking down. After a moment, he rubbed his eyes, as if pretending they itched. "He's goin' to be all right, you think?"

"It's too soon to say for sure, but I think he may."

"That's…that's good." He put out a hand, as if he would touch Gabriel's head, then glanced at it and drew back, rubbing his palm up and down the leg of his ragged pants.

"I doubt you will wake him."

Squirrel shook his head. "He's so…I mean, he looks nice, real nice."

What he meant was that the child was no longer dirty. Juliette swallowed against the thickness in her throat, wishing suddenly that all Nicholas's street boys could be as clean and comfortable. And why should they not? She could see to it. That much, at least, was within her power.

"Tell me, Squirrel," she said quietly, "do you have another name, one given when you were born?"

He opened his mouth, closed it, then tried again. "My mother…she called me Nat. It stands for Nathaniel."

"That's a good name. Perhaps you will allow me to use it one day."

He gave the idea some thought, then bobbed his head. "Maybe."

"Do the other boys have such names?"

"Some do, some don't."

She nodded her understanding while making a promise to herself to see that situation changed as well. "You can sit here with Gabriel for a time, if you like."

Squirrel looked at the rocking chair she indicated, then at his clothes. "I'd better get back to the others, tell 'em what's what. But Mam'zelle…"

"Yes?"

"That Daspit, you won't let him get too close, will you?" He looked at her then away again as if to hide the raw knowledge in his eyes. "He's not a nice man, not always. You don't want nothin' to do with 'im."

"I suspect you're right. And I will be very careful."

"That's good then. Somebody's likely to kill 'im one day, but until they do…"

"I understand." He seemed to be something more than familiar with Paulette's suitor and his reputation. It occurred to Juliette that he might have other knowledge. "You saw Monsieur Daspit's injury. Do you know, by chance, how he came by it?"

"Oh, sure, Mam'zelle. Croquère, he pricked him right good."

"The sword master, Croquère? You're sure of it?"

Squirrel gave a firm nod. "'Twas about the way he sent away his woman, his *placée*."

She had not known that Daspit had a *placée*, as the quadroon mistresses kept by young gentlemen were called. She wondered if Paulette was aware of it. Not that it was at all unusual. It might have been more surprising if he had not kept one.

Did Nicholas have such a woman in a house somewhere? Odd, that the idea had never occurred to her.

"Why then does he blame Monsieur Pasquale?"

"Croquère wore a mask. 'Sides, he'd never admit being bested by such a one."

It was very true. Pride would not allow Daspit to admit to defeat by the mulatto. "You think he won't find out who really was his opponent?"

The contempt she had seen before flashed over Squirrel's face again. "He's not over-full in the brain box. And M'sieur Nick, he wore a mask, too, when he—"

"When he what?" she asked as the boy came to an abrupt halt.

"Nothing."

"You saw him at the masquerade, perhaps."

Squirrel would not be drawn. He only set his lips in a tight line as he shook his head then turned and trotted back down to where the others waited. It was frustrating in the extreme.

Something was afoot among the *maître d'armes*; she was almost sure of it after what she had overheard in the ballroom. What it might be, she could not guess other than that it involved Nicholas and it was dangerous. This business with Daspit and Croquère, and also the attack upon Nicholas and herself at Tivoli Gardens, were almost certainly part and parcel of it.

As the affianced bride of a sword master, she should know the dangers her husband faced, all of them. There had to be a way to find out. She would have to think about it.

She would have to think long and hard.

13

It was late afternoon before Nicholas was able to return to the Armant town house. Not only was it necessary to bathe and change his clothing from the skin out, but he discovered that the strain of carrying Gabriel had opened his wound so he had to send for a sawbones to put in a few stitches and bind it up again. He should have had it sewn up in the first place, he knew, but had hoped to get away without the trouble. It would not do to bleed all over his linen, however; he had a limited number of shirts for changes, after all. And the last thing he wanted was to give Juliette reason to question the state of his health. She was disturbed enough about the attack the evening before without learning that it had been a serious attempt to disable him.

He had hardly made himself presentable again when Kerr Wallace appeared on his doorstep. The Kentuckian would have released him from his promise of a lesson, but Nicholas had given his word. Actively facing the tall backwoodsman on the fencing strip was not possible, but there was much to be taught concerning the lore of fencing as a sport, respect and caring for the various types of weapons, exercises to strengthen the body, and reasoning behind the traditional swordsman's positions. They made a decent beginning, even if the lesson was cut shorter than normal.

Nicholas arrived in Juliette's bedchamber in time to make himself useful in the effort to get more of the old nurse's concoction down Gabriel's small throat. It was a success, though he thought several times that he might have to change his coat yet again. The boy was fretful, tossing and turning with the rise of his fever as the day waned, and Nicholas finally gathered him up off the bed and carried him to the rocker as Juliette had done before. Gabriel quieted at once, much to his surprise and pleasure. Holding him close, Nicholas rather grandly commanded Juliette and Valara to go away and rest while he saw to him. That they obeyed was almost as astonishing as the fact that he could settle Gabriel.

Juliette paused at the doorway to look back at him. Her smile was rueful, Nicholas thought, but it was also approving. He felt as if he had been awarded a medal.

Time crept away, marked by the rattle of an occasional dray or carriage on the paving outside, the cries of flower and coffee vendors, and the murmur of female voices that drifted along the gallery beyond the door. He thought he might have dozed a little, the effects, perhaps, of his late nights recently and the stiff shot of brandy the doctor had pressed upon him before plying a needle to draw the edges of the sword slash together. He came to with a start to discover evening had descended, taking the light.

Someone was just entering the bedchamber. A slim figure dressed in gray, she carried a tray from which came a most tempting collection of aromas. She placed it on the table at the far side of the bed, then turned and came around it toward him.

"Juliette…"

She didn't speak, but gave him a small smile as she reached to gather Gabriel into her arms, smoothing her hands intimately down Nicholas's chest as she picked up the boy and transferred him to the high mattress of the bed. Swinging back, she returned to lean over him with a soft gleam in her eyes. She put her hands on his shoulders then bent her head to press her lips to his.

Surprise and disappointment held him immobile for long seconds. Then he put his hands to the slender indentation of her waist and set her back a step before rising to his feet. The move effectively broke the kiss. Before he could speak, however, she grasped his lapels to pull his head down. He resisted while catching her arms, moving his fingers to her wrists. She made a small sound of annoyance and dropped back down to the flat heels of her slippers, her head tipped back on the stem of her neck as she stared up at him.

The glow of a candle that had been steadily growing brighter slid into the room just then. A cool voice spoke from the doorway. "Excuse me. I thought a small meal, and a light, might be required."

The woman who stood beside Nicholas swung toward the doorway. "Oh, Juliette, I brought food for Nicholas as well. And then…we are so sorry. I don't know what came over us."

Nicholas was caught between anger and chagrin, courtesy and self-defense. There had been no *we* to the business; Paulette had deliberately approached him as if she were Juliette. He could not exonerate himself without implicating her, however, and to accuse a lady of improper conduct was not the act of a gentleman.

"It was a mistake, I'm sure," Juliette said shortly. "I have noticed before that Nicholas has difficulty telling us apart."

"Not on close contact," he replied with the precision. "I was about to point out that your sister had apparently mistaken me for her fiancé."

"Were you indeed?"

"I promise you." He held Juliette's eyes there in the candle glow, his own gaze steady.

Paulette set to her hands on her hips. "There has been a rash of mistakes today, or so it seems to me. Jean had quite a long conversation with you this morning, my dear sister, almost longer than he had with me."

Nicholas glanced from one sister to the other. "I trust this discussion was not of the same nature."

"He was concerned that I was imposing upon my mother's good nature by turning her house into a hospital." Juliette glanced down at the tray in her hands, which held the glowing double candlestick as well as an assortment of dishes. "At least you need not go hungry now. Sit down, please, and eat. I would have sent a tray earlier except that it seemed a shame to wake you."

"And to disturb Gabriel, I expect."

"Just so. I added a little chicken broth for him along with your food, and it would be good if he could take it now. I hope to persuade him while you have your meal." She turned away, moving to transfer the double candlestick to the bed table, then put the tray down beside it and take a small bowl and a glass from it.

She was evading the issue; Nicholas was almost sure of it. He could think of several reasons for it, from the need to keep peace with her sister to reluctance to be the cause of a duel. It seemed best not to call her on it under the circumstances, but he did not intend to forget it.

That was not all, however. Behind her quiet composure, his bride-to-be was incensed with him. The cause was not hard to guess. She thought he had betrayed her with a masked siren, yet could not accuse him of it without questions about how she knew of it. Being the person she was, she had forgotten his supposed treachery earlier in her concern for Gabriel, but remembered it now that the boy was getting better.

Dissatisfaction sat on Paulette's features as she looked from him to her sister. No doubt she had expected to cause more dissension between them than she had managed. As he lifted an eyebrow in her direction, she exclaimed under her breath then flounced from the room.

"I believe she is disappointed," he said in contemplative tones. "Do you think she expected you to call off our engagement?"

"Who can say."

He moved around the bed to stand at her shoulder, leaning a little to see her face. "You do believe that I had no designs upon her just now?"

"Yes, certainly. As I said, it's easy to confuse us."

Her voice was brusque. Listening closely, however, he thought he heard a note of dejection in it. "I was not confused. Do you really think I can't tell you from Paulette?"

"From a distance, yes."

"She was as near as you are now." He shifted slightly to brush his lips over the nape of her neck.

"Don't!" She shivered a little, hunching her shoulders as she played with a small silver spoon that she no doubt meant to use to feed Gabriel. "I'd rather not talk about it."

"We must, I think."

"Your food is getting cold."

"Let it. Some things are more important."

She turned to face him, the fullness of her skirts piling against his boots with the swiftness of her movement. "If you knew who she was then why did you kiss her?"

"I didn't," he said, his gaze steady of her face. "As much as I regret having to say so, it was quite the other way around."

"Oh. But then…"

She believed him, or seemed to at any rate. The gratitude he felt for that simple boon was far in excess of its reason. It was also an indication of how uncertain he was of where he stood with her.

He waited a moment for her to go on. When she did not, he said, "Paulette is your sister, your twin whom you know better than anyone. Was what she did just now from mere pique, because Daspit sought you out this morning? Was it in hope of causing a rift between us that would allow her and her fiancé to win the prize? Was it at Daspit's behest? Or could it have been—"

"Curiosity about the Casanova of New Orleans?" she supplied as he stopped in his turn, uncertain how to word what he meant or the wisdom of voicing the possibility.

"Don't," he said quietly.

"Why not? You earned the title, I believe. Or so I'm told. To sample such famous expertise must be the secret dream of half the women in the city, especially those committed to men less expert in the art. Paulette may believe I have unfair access. Or she may feel it's her right. After all, I have always shared everything with her."

"And you would rather think that than suppose she would deliberately hurt you."

Her gaze remained on the level of the plain silver stick pin in his cravat. "I suppose I must."

He searched her face, but could gain no inkling of what she really felt. Rather than press it, he said softly, "I have no wish to be disobliging, *chère*, but I must tell you that I object to being shared."

She lifted her eyes, clouded by doubt, to his face. "You do?"

"Definitely. Nor am I inclined to share my future wife."

A wild rose flush bloomed on her cheekbones. "If you are speaking of Daspit's advances, then you may be sure that will not happen."

"So he did make one of some description. I thought as much."

"Only to discover his chances of exchanging one bride for another should my claim to the marriage chest prove more valid."

He allowed his gaze to roam over the oval of her

face, the curves of her enticing mouth, her hair where curling wisps had escaped the severity of her chignon to give her a disheveled look that hinted of bedchamber intimacy, the lovely line of her breasts where they curved to the narrow turn of her waist. The heat that rose inside him added fervor to his voice as he spoke.

"I doubt that was all."

"If you mean…but he has Paulette."

"And she is attractive in her fashion but is not your equal in sweetness and inner fire. Daspit is obviously an idiot where the hearts and minds of women are concerned, still he has eyes in his head."

"Thank you very much," she said with asperity, "but I don't believe—"

"I mean it, you know."

Her eyes flashed green-gold fire at him. "Of course you do, every time you say it to a woman. Nevertheless, Monsieur Daspit's interest is purely in the treasure chest. This, I do assure you."

"And yours?" he asked, driven by what demon inside he did not know, but one that might have been roused by her conclusion that he lacked discretion in his dealings with women. "Was there no curiosity about his advances?"

The look she gave him held utter disdain. "None."

He was forced to believe she meant what she said. That seemed to indicate her response to him the night before had been unique, for him alone. The fierce gladness that shook him was a revelation, yet with it came a matching resentment.

"You will find that I am a possessive man," he said with quiet precision. "For Daspit to attempt laying hands on the chest in this particular manner could be a most dangerous aim."

"So Squirrel told him."

"Squirrel? He was there?"

She related the tale, including the derogatory name applied to Paulette's suitor, and his concern mounted with every word that fell from her lovely lips. Daspit would not take kindly to being reprimanded by the young scamp, and Squirrel, for all this defiant courage, had few defenses against a gentleman of the ton who might decide to punish him for his temerity.

"Where is he now?" Nicholas asked.

"Monsieur Daspit has left the house. Or if it's Squirrel you mean, he is in the laundry below with the others. I offered beds, but they seem to prefer pallets on the floor."

"They have eaten?" He should have seen to that matter earlier but had not realized the boys were still on the premises, had expected to find them at his atelier when he returned there.

The look she gave him had ice around the edges. "Of course."

"My apologies, but there is no 'of course' about it, not with most people."

She gave him a small nod, then turned away to pick up the bowl of broth. With it and the spoon in her hands, she sidestepped him as if she thought the discussion between them was over. He reached to put a hand on her arm, and she paused, looking up at him in inquiry.

"And what of you," he asked, his voice a low murmur in his throat. "Have you no curiosity concerning the peculiar talents of the Casanova of New Orleans?"

She met his gaze for a burning instant before looking away again. "I should not have called you that. I'm sorry."

"Don't be. It's been said before. But that is not an answer to my question."

When she looked at him again, the pupils of her eyes were wide, like dark mirrors reflecting the candlelight. She did not speak for long moments in which he became aware of distant voices, the rattle of an evening breeze in the banana tree growing in the courtyard and the sleepy cooing of a dove. After an eon, her lips parted for her to speak. "And if I do?"

"It would be my duty, and my very great pleasure, to satisfy it."

Color flooded her features, though it was impossible to say whether it was from resentment or embarrassment. "When we are married," she said evenly, "it will be my obligation to allow it."

Her tone carried a warning not to trespass, or so

he thought. She was still angry then. He might have guessed. But was that all? It was entirely possible that whatever curiosity she possessed had been appeased at Tivoli Gardens. It could also be that she had felt nothing else, that his ardor had frightened her so she had drawn away from him at the end. Neither was a pleasant thought, or a comfortable one.

"Just so." He released her as he inclined his head, and was glad enough to let her go. And yet, he could not resist a riposte, did not try as it came to him in razor-sharp instinct, more lethal than anything learned on a fencing strip.

"I did miss you at the masquerade last evening. What kept you from it?"

Dull red color flooded her face, though she met his eyes without flinching. "I was there, but remained only a short while."

"Oh? And why was that?"

"The falseness was much too painful."

He made no answer. What was there to say? But he acknowledged in grim rectitude that it was possible for a so-called master of the sword to be cut more deeply by his own weapon than any other.

Gabriel roused enough to swallow a little of the broth that Juliette urged upon him. His color was better, his fever less virulent, and he had lost the boneless, rag-doll feel that had been so terrifying earlier. It made Nicholas's chest ache to see the

valiant way the boy tried to smile as he lifted him
onto his lap to help Juliette feed him. That, as much
as her assurances, made him feel the worst might be
over. Even so, he coaxed and bullied him into taking
more of Valara's lemon water concoction after he'd
had as much of the broth as he and Juliette could get
down him. He hated doing it while poor Gabriel
whimpered and tried to go back to sleep, but it was
better than losing him.

When they had ceased to plague the child, he
dropped into a deep slumber again. It worried
Nicholas but Valara, when she came to look in on
them, waved away his concern. To sleep was best for
him, she said; the *pauvre petit* was as tired as he was
ill. He felt safe for the moment and so could rest easy.

The pronouncement made sense and Nicholas was
grateful for it. He was left with a lingering sense of
guilt, however, as if he should have done more to
provide that sense of security. On reflection, he was
not sure it was possible in his bachelor lodging. It
required something more than mere cleanliness, a
bed and decent food. The main ingredient was the
calm and gentle care Juliette had provided, and her
loving presence. He had done the right thing,
bringing the boy here. It would be even better when
he and Juliette were married.

Valara went away after a time and did not return.
Perhaps she went to her evening meal, perhaps she
felt Gabriel's presence served in place of a chaperone

or that the betrothal removed the need. In any case, Nicholas and Juliette were left alone.

He was more aware than he wanted to be of their seclusion in her bedchamber. The bed where Gabriel lay was where she slept in her virginal nightgown, doubtless embroidered in white-on-white by the nuns. He could picture her there, warm and soft and unprotected, could picture the things he might do if he joined her on that high mattress. She would be so sweetly tender and compliant....

Compliant.

Why was it that promise left such a taste of ashes in his mouth when he knew well that it was all he could expect and more than he deserved? And why could he not control his more rampant urges and lascivious visions concerning this lady who was so far above such carnal images?

Clearing his throat where he sat behind the tray she had arranged for him, he asked, "Have you eaten?"

"I don't remember," she said, her gaze unfocused, as if her thoughts had been elsewhere.

"There is more than enough here for two." He took a roll and some of the baked ham and sliced cheese from the bounty before him and nudged it in her direction.

"I'm really not hungry."

"Eat. Or shall I take you on my lap and feed you like Gabriel?"

She gave him a long look then reached for the food.

Nicholas was gratified, even if it did indicate that she preferred not to risk his touch. After a moment, he spoke again. "If Gabriel is better by tomorrow evening, perhaps we should keep our next appointment with the priest."

"Yes, I suppose."

She grimaced as she spoke, but he was almost sure it was for the prospect of further lecturing by the elderly cleric. Their first visit had set arrangements for the wedding in motion, but the priest seemed less than satisfied with their commitment, recommending prayer and extensive counseling. "You haven't changed your mind?"

She gave him a steady look. "No."

He could have wished for more animation. At least he could be satisfied he had not made the prospect of being his wife too repugnant to her. "Then there is the matter of a house."

"I've made a few inquiries, but wondered—what would you think of living here?"

"In your mother's home?"

"There is ample room, and she won't care to live alone once Paulette and I are both married."

"Ample for everyone?"

She took his meaning at once. "Including all the boys, yes."

"And what will she think of sharing living quarters with a former *maître d'armes* and a bunch of hooligans?"

"She will grow accustomed once away from the influence of my—that is, once matters are settled. She is quite taken with Gabriel."

Nicholas put his plate aside, his appetite suddenly sated. "He is small and imminently loveable in much the same way everyone enjoys a new puppy. But they grow up to become the mongrels Despit named them, in the main, like their benefactor."

"You are no mongrel," she said sharply.

"Nor am I purebred by any standard. You need not come to my defense," he went on as she frowned and opened her mouth to speak. "I know what I am and make no excuses for it. But I will not have Squirrel and the others made to feel they are here on sufferance."

"I was only thinking they could begin staying at once instead of waiting until after the marriage to come to us."

"I honor you for that thought," he answered quietly, "perhaps more than you may realize. Still, I prefer to have them near me until that time, particularly Squirrel."

A small smile tugged at one corner of her mouth. "Nathaniel."

"He told you? That's a mark of great favor."

"So I perceive. But you are concerned for his safety?"

"You could put it that way."

She looked at her hands and reached for a napkin

from the tray to wipe them. It was, he thought, a ruse to gain time for considering that point, or else to avoid looking at him. Finally she said, "You may have reason, I am forced to admit. Still, to have the boys here would relieve my mind."

"You fear a repeat of Daspit's importunities?" he asked, frowning in his turn. "Or is it your concern for the safety of this famous chest that's at the heart of the matter."

"You need not speak so slightingly."

"That was not my intention. I suppose that having only heard of its wonders, it's difficult to attach the same importance."

Abruptly, she rose to her feet. "Wait here."

He would have protested, done more to make her see that his interest in her inheritance was slight, but she was already whisking from the room. She returned moments later bearing the wooden chest taken from its pride of place in the salon. The size of a small camel-backed trunk, it seemed to have some weight, considering the strain on her arms. Nicholas rose to his feet at once to take it from her and lower it to the floor.

"We can't open it, of course, since that it the crux of what *Maman* calls the family curse, that bad luck will descend on those who dare. But you can see that it's quite old and has value of itself."

It was true enough, from the little Nicholas knew of such things. The carving that covered the surface was beautifully executed, the wood carefully matched and polished where the pieces were joined. The surface design was of stylized leaves and vines set with flowers that had petals of inlaid ivory, and it's clasps and hasp looked like chased silver. It had an exotic, almost erotic look in its Arabesque curves and curls, and the wood appeared to be the Far Eastern species known as *palissandre*, or violet ebony. It was not the sort of thing that might have been owned by a peasant girl, he thought, or even some Parisian merchant's orphaned daughter. This was a treasure from the *ancien regime*, a piece of the life of some lady who had come down in the world in her journey to New Orleans, perhaps torn through disaster or death from some noble family and sent across the sea to what had been New France.

Or she might merely have had some connection to such a family from which she had, just possibly, stolen this particular wedding chest.

"Your ancestress to whom this belonged…" he began.

"Marie Therese."

"Marie Therese, yes. What happened to her?"

"Before she came here, I don't know. After the journey, she and the other brides stayed with the Ursuline nuns. The men of the colony who desired wives came to court them under the watchful eyes of the holy sisters. Most of the women were impatient to become mistresses of their own homes and settle in their new lives. They had nothing and no one who cared about them so were not hard to please, nor were they encouraged to be particular by those who had sent them. The most attractive among them naturally had the greatest choice of suitors and went to the altar first. Marie Therese was sought after by a captain of the guard, a government official and a planter. She chose the last."

"They resided in the city?"

"Actually, no. He took her to his indigo plantation on the river. She preferred that, had no desire to mix with what passed for society. It was her daughter who came to town later, and her granddaughter who built this town house."

"They seem to have prospered, so must have looked after the chest well."

"One of them allowed her husband to rifle through it, or at least did not prevent him. She and her six children fell ill with cholera. Only one, the eldest daughter, recovered. Another took something from it as a token to be worn by her daughter on her wedding day. The girl's groom was killed in a steamboat accident while journeying upriver to visit relatives, so it was the daughter from a second marriage who inherited."

"A deadly curse, then."

"Sometimes, not always. My mother's younger brother became obsessed with looking into the box since he had been told only his sister would have that privilege. He was eight years old at the time. The day after he sneaked into my grandmother's room to look, he fell and broke his arm while trying to walk the gallery railing."

Nicholas shook his head, unable to suppress a smile. "He sounds a regular hellion who would likely have had accidents anyway."

"He was, from what I remember of him. He drowned years later while trying to cross the river during a flood. I was small at the time, but remember well how distraught my mother was over it. She blamed the curse for that as well, of course."

"My grandparents were not without their superstitions, or my mother if it comes to that. They believed in the evil eye and the power of a mother's spittle to protect her children and much more. Still, I should tell you that I have little patience with such things. Bad things happen. No mythical curse is required to cause them."

She watched him, her gaze serious. "But you would not go against the superstition just to prove it?"

"I would not go against it at all, if that is your wish. My only interest is to see why Daspit is so determined to have the box in his possession, whether it's something about it or a need we cannot see."

"And what do you think?"

The chest had been fairly heavy, Nicholas thought, but not so much so that it was likely to contain gold or silver. Jewels were the most portable form of wealth but he would have expected anything of the sort to have been removed long ago. No, he suspected from his knowledge of females that the chest was filled with the kind of useless memorabilia that usually filled the jewel and bonnet boxes of older women, tattered handkerchiefs and ribbons received from long dead admirers, broken fans and shoe buckles, yellowed letters tied with ribbon, bits of lace and carefully saved buttons of wood, bone or mother of pearl; darning eggs, tangled embroidery silks and rusted needles. Some of it might be interesting because of its great age but would hardly constitute a treasure unless one was a direct family connection.

"I think I must look closer into the affairs of your sister's fiancé," he said finally

"You will be careful, will you not? He…I believe him capable of extreme measures in order to protect his interests."

Nicholas flexed his sore arm a little, thinking of just how true that could be. "I will take every care. But the hour grows late. I should leave you now. Before I go, would you consent to allowing all the boys to look in on Gabriel?"

She glanced at the child where he lay sprawled in sleep, exactly as she had left him. "I see no reason why they should not."

"I will bring them. Oh, and for the visit to the priest, I shall call for you, with your permission."

"I should be glad," she said, the words sedate in spite of the flush that made its way slowly to her hairline.

He would have liked to stay and explore the origin of her increased color, see if it had any relation, possibly, to the progress toward their marriage. However, that seemed a temptation best resisted under the circumstances.

The boys weren't asleep, which didn't surprise Nicholas. They made their own hours, often remaining on the streets as long as there was anyone coming and going, any chance of a coin from those leaving the theater or opera house or a stale crust that might be handed out the back doors of restaurants. Rising from their pallets with alacrity, they followed him upstairs where they stood in a solemn row, staring down at Gabriel where he lay sprawled on the soft mattress. Squirrel must have related to them the progress in the sickroom, for the others seemed content enough merely to look at him without questions or comment.

As quiet as they had tried to be, however, there was some inevitable noise to their entrance, the creak of a floorboard, shuffle of their bare feet before they reached the carpet, a cleared throat or snuffle. Gabriel stirred in his slumber, turning his head on the pillow. A moment later, he opened his eyes. Like a nail to a magnet, he turned his head to find Juliette. As he found her, a smile of radiant joy spread over his small features.

"*Maman,*" he whispered.

The soft intake of Juliette's breath was perfectly audible in the quiet. She stood as still as tomb angel for long seconds, then she moved closer and took Gabriel's small hand in gentle fingers. "Here, *mon petit.*"

The sighs of the boys who watched seemed to flutter the candles on their wicks. Their faces, in the dim glow, reflected a thousand dreams and hopes and forlorn wishes aligned to an infinity of disappointments. Nicholas, watching, felt his vision blur for a single instant.

A sharp exclamation cut into the soft silence. "Juliette, *mon Dieu!* What goes here? I saw the chest taken from its place, but never dreamed... Have you gone raving mad that you would expose it to these creatures? They might...they might do anything!"

It was Juliette's mother who stood in the doorway. Her sweeping glance of condemnation did not exclude him, Nicholas saw. Juliette had, apparently, been optimistic about her acceptance of the boys. He opened his mouth to reassure them, but it was too late. They scattered like chickens before a runaway carriage, pushing and shoving past their hostess on their way out the door. Their footfalls could be heard thudding down the stairs to the courtyard.

"*Maman!* Look what you have done," Juliette cried.

"What I have done? Look at you, *ma fille*, risking everything for the company of these little ruffians. Monsieur Daspit is right in saying you are too unworldly, too easily taken in by any scoundrel."

Juliette drew herself up. "I am not the one who is being taken in, I promise you."

"How can you say so when it is clear that you have been making this man you intend to marry free of the contents of the chest? I was never so shocked in my life!"

"I was not! He would never ask it, unlike some I might name."

"I have the evidence of my eyes."

"You see nothing, nothing." Juliette clenched her fists, taking a step toward her parent.

"I see that I should never have taken you from the good sisters. With them is where you belong, just as Paulette says, and there you must return when your sister is wed."

"You promised the chest to the first to reach the altar, and here stands my groom," Juliette declared with a gesture in his direction.

"Your sister is the eldest."

"Not according to Valara."

Madame Armant put a hand to her ample bosom. "You would take her word before that of your mother?"

"When I know that it is Paulette who has convinced you Valara is wrong and the chest belongs to her? Yes, I would. Paulette will say anything to make certain of being wed to Monsieur Daspit. He is threatening her, *Maman*, saying that he will not have her at all if the chest does not come with her. She is desperate to have it."

"She says the same of you and this—this sword master."

Nicholas could not let that pass. "In that regard, *madame*, she is certainly wrong. I have little use for the chest. And I would have your daughter if she came without a picayune to her name or a stitch on her back."

Madame Armant fell back with a gasp, putting a hand to her throat. Juliette flung a glance of reproof at him before she started toward her mother. At that moment, Gabriel began to cry, upset at being abandoned by his friends and the loud voice over his head. Juliette paused, half-turning, obviously torn between the two of them.

His presence was only making matter worse, Nicholas saw. "Forgive me," he said, his gaze on her distraught face, "but it seems best I take my leave. My presence isn't useful here, in fact quite otherwise. You need not see me out, nor should you be concerned about the boys. I will see to them as usual. And I will come for you tomorrow as arranged."

"Yes, thank you," she said, relief plain in her face. "We will talk more then."

Nicholas turned on his boot heel and went from the bedchamber. A black frown sat on his forehead as he left the house and turned in the direction of the Passage. This retreat was not as he had planned. In imagination, he had pictured a slow walk with Juliette along the *porte cochère* to the entrance gate, with perhaps a kiss of surpassing sweetness to speed him on his way. He was also loathe to leave her in the midst of another scene with her mother. The insistence on her return to the convent made the blood boil in his veins. It was such a heartless threat when she was just beginning to wake from years of sleepwalking through a life she had not planned or desired, just gaining a taste of worldly pleasures.

A few steps down the banquette, he caught a glimpse of a shadow emerging from a doorway. His head came up, senses alert, but it was only habit, for he knew almost at once who waited to join him.

"It's all right, back there?" Squirrel asked, shoving his hands into the pockets of his ragged coat as he fell into step beside him.

"In a manner of speaking." The words were dry.

"I heard the old witch say Mam'zelle would go back to the convent."

Squirrel had listened at the door, or possibly from the courtyard. Nicholas wasn't surprised. The outcome of that particular quarrel had become important to the boys. "It seems a possibility."

"Can't you stop them from makin' her do that?"

"I can try, but it must be the lady's decision in the end."

Squirrel was quiet for several steps before he said, "You have to marry her quicker than the other, yeah? So why not take her across the river."

"I suggested Gretna, but the plan did not find favor."

"What's to keep t'other lady and that bastard Daspit from stealing a march on you?"

It was a question that had troubled Nicholas for some time as well. "Nothing except a similar reluctance on the part of Mademoiselle Paulette to be married in such a shabby fashion."

"I guess women set a lot of store by weddings," Squirrel said with a shake of his head.

"They do."

"Be a shame if you don't get hitched first. I mean, sounds to me they don't want Mam'zelle Juliette marrying at all, and that would be hard on Gaby. He needs her."

Nicholas gave the young man a quick look, but his pale, begrimed face gave nothing away of what he might be feeling. "Everybody does, I think."

"Even you." Squirrel turned his head at that moment, meeting his eyes in the light from the street lamp on its corner bracket.

"That hardly comes into it," Nicholas answered after the barest hesitation.

"But you want her for a wife?"

Nicholas gave him a crooked smile. "You feel I'm sacrificing myself for you and the others? Banish the thought, my young friend. I want the lady. The thing is that I may not be worthy of having her."

"Horseshit."

The comment lacked refinement, but was satisfying all the same. It might have been more comfort if Nicholas could have believed it.

14

Juliette could not decide whether the elderly priest who presided at the cathedral was ambivalent about the marriage between her and Nicholas because of her last-minute failure to take the veil, the disapproval of her mother, who was an active supporter of the church, or the occupation and reputation of the groom. All these things were touched on during the second uncomfortable interview she and Nicholas endured, so it may have been the combination. In any case, the warnings given them to consider carefully the step they were taking seemed even more stern than before.

It made little difference. She and Nicholas were both of age and neither had any impediment to being wed. A date was set for the Monday before Mardi Gras.

It was a great relief to have the matter settled, at least to Juliette. What Nicholas thought of it was impossible to tell. His manner was suitably grave while speaking with the priest, his answers to the questions put to him ready enough, if not particularly fulsome. As they left the priest's study, he offered his arm but it seemed an ordinary courtesy rather than the close gesture of a fiancé who relished the touch of his future bride. She hardly expected anything else, but was still troubled by the feeling that the occasion should have been more momentous.

Before them lay the trampled, open space of the Place d'Armes with its low spiked iron fence and spreading sycamore trees that were already swelling with new buds at the tips of their branches. Nicholas and the others drilled and paraded there with the Louisiana Legion, she knew, though the square was empty this evening except for a few strollers, an elderly gentleman or two taking their evening constitutionals and courting couples with chaperones in tow, much as Valara followed them. It was a reminder, if she needed one, of the life led by the man at her side, one of which she knew precious little. There had been others. On their way here from her mother's house, Nicholas had bowed to half a dozen men who had stepped aside for him on the banquette. One of these had been a young gentleman wearing the precise same waistcoat that Nicholas had on and with his cravat tied about his throat in the same manner. Another was a rotund merchant who actually turned the gray color of overworked pastry as he recognized him.

He was capable of causing such terror and dismay

if he so chose, of using his deadly prowess to intimidate other men and thereby gain whatever he desired. It took a man of strong character to refrain, yet there was nothing of that in his manner. He did not swagger his way down the street, forcing others to give way, did not go first through doorways or expect to be given precedence for the time and attentions of others. For all the notice he gave of his status he might have been a mere clerk or cotton factor instead of one of the deadliest sword masters in the Vieux Carré. He even shortened his stride so that Valara, following behind them, could keep their pace without loss of breath.

"I owe you an apology," she said as the direct results of these ruminations.

His glance was wry. "I can't imagine why."

"Monsieur Croquère, or so I'm told, is the *maître d'armes* who administered the salutary lesson in the conduct of a gentleman to Monsieur Daspit. I should not have doubted you when you denied responsibility in that affair, and I'm sorry for it."

"You accepted my word in the end. It was enough."

His generosity in the matter made her feel worse instead of better. "I did so with reluctance, I fear."

"But since you knew me only by reputation then, even that was a victory."

"Something more in the way of trust is necessary between husband and wife. I hope to do better next time there is a question."

An odd expression moved over his features, though it was gone so quickly that she could not begin to guess its cause. "You believe in perfect honesty in marriage."

"It seems the only foundation for happiness."

"Even if the lack of candor is for the protection of others?"

Was the question hypothetical or could he be keeping something from her? "Others being?"

"Others. Friends, comrades in arms—the wife herself."

She met his eyes, so darkly compelling that she felt as if she were being drawn into their infinite depths. They invited her acceptance, tested her trust, promised realms of possibilities that she was not sure she dared explore. Falling back on the prosaic, she said, "Meaning that you do have something to hide?"

"Meaning that nothing is ever quite as simple as it may seem. But no matter. What shall we do now? I can take you home at once if you prefer, but thought we might extend our excursion for a half hour. Shall we stroll along the levee? Walk to Vincent's for a pastry? Or we have an invitation to drop in on Rio and Celina, if that should find favor."

"I don't know," she said with a small frown. "I would be easier in my mind if Gabriel had been left in Valara's care, only *Maman* wouldn't have it."

"He seemed much better this afternoon, and was half-asleep when we left."

"And she did promise to look in on him from time to time—her way of making amends, I think. She regretted her outburst yesterday, after it was too late."

"So she thought to make it easier for you to talk to the priest about our marriage?"

Juliette could hardly fault him for the doubt she heard in his voice. She had been surprised herself, to say the least. And yet her mother was easily swayed by tender sentiment when not prey to superstition or trying to appease Paulette, and she had seemed so sure she could cope. "Perhaps she saw we were determined to go ahead so has come to terms with it in her mind."

"In which case, I suppose we must allow her help," he returned. "To look in on Rio and Celina should not take long, if you care for it."

"They know of our errand?"

"Yes, though it has no bearing. Celina has only selected this evening for the two of them to be at home to guests. She doesn't aspire to the heights of Lisette's literary salon, but enjoys people and would like to establish that she is not so high in the instep since becoming a Spanish countess that she can't receive friends and acquaintances. It isn't a formal affair, but she promises certain delicacies in the way of edibles that were either brought from Catalonia or the recipes discovered there."

It sounded delightful. Her mother would undoubtedly disapprove, but Juliette would not allow that to weigh with her. "A message could be sent to explain our delay?"

"Of a certainty," he agreed with his flashing smile, and they turned in the direction of the town house of his friends.

The gathering was sparse, but that was explained by the comparatively early hour. Denys Vallier, Celina's brother, was there, along with a few of his friends, particularly the irrepressible Hippolyte Ducolet and more dolorous Albert Lollain. Monsieur Caid O'Neill and his Lisette were ensconced as well with their small son, who was soon sent off in the company of his nurse to join the De Vega offspring in their nursery. In the O'Neill party was the proper Bostonian lady and companion of Madame O'Neill, Mademoiselle Agatha Stilton. Juliette recognized Madame Maurelle Herriot, as well, and Monsieur and Madame Plauchet, whose soirée she had so recently attended. The Englishman, Monsieur Blackford, lurked in one corner, where he appeared to be watching the company with bemused and distant interest. With him was a tall, raw-boned giant of a man whose dress marked him as being from some upriver town or settlement, one of those rowdy Americans whose raucous habits, fondness for fisticuffs and lack of social graces made them the boogeymen used to frighten Creole children into obedience.

The salon where everyone collected had a distinctly European air to Juliette's eyes. Larger by half than the one at home, it featured painted panels on the doors and delicate molding on the plastered walls that created spaces which were painted in muted pastel tones. A great many pillows in exotic, beaded silks were strewn over the settees, and heavy crown moldings drew the eyes toward the ceiling where gods and goddesses reveled in a sylvan picnic. The transformation was new, she thought, for the smell of fresh paint lingered in the room.

The company was found enjoying one of the promised delicacies, blood oranges from Seville. A dozen or so of these golden globes had been sliced into wedges to reveal their dark red flesh, while more made a pyramid in a chased silver bowl. Along with them were black olives, dried currants, shelled almonds, paper-thin slices of smoked ham cut from haunches that still had the hide and hair attached, and trays of small Iberian sausages, all served with rounds of warm bread spread with butter and glasses of Spanish sherry. Not unnaturally, the gathering centered on the table laden with this bounty, where the guests were sampling and talking in Creole fashion, both with equal fervor and at the same time.

Nicholas's arrival was hailed with smiles and cries of welcome, and Juliette received no less as his fiancée. Everyone seemed to know where they had been and why, and teasing comments were many. It was Blackford, advancing from his corner, who put an end to the general raillery. Pausing at the table, he picked up three of the oranges in his long fingers, weighed them a second, then fired them, one after the other, at Nicholas like so many sweet-smelling balls.

Nicholas's reaction was instantaneous, his reflexes unerring, as he lifted his left arm to snatch the missiles from the air, dropping each orange into his right hand as he caught them. The feat was not without cost, however, for he drew in a sharp breath as he raised his arm, and gave a short grunt of pain with each impact in his palm.

Conversation stilled. Movement ceased. No one breathed, or so it seemed, as they waited to see the outcome of such an unprovoked attack. It might be anything, from artillery with oranges to swords at dawn. And no one could guess which until they saw what Nicholas would do, heard what he would say.

The two men faced each other, tall, broad-shouldered, a match in strength and will and arrogance of feature. A match in all things, except that Nicholas possessed some injury that had left him pale and with a white line around his mouth, an injury about which he had told Juliette next to nothing. She could guess, nonetheless, since she had been there when he had sustained it.

Juliette felt cold inside, swamped by terror and

anger, perplexity and chill disdain. And she hated that she was so far on the outer edge of Nicholas's life as a sword master that she had no idea what had caused this confrontation or what to do to keep it from turning deadly.

"Hearty, but not so hale," Blackford said, his voice clear and slicing in the quiet. "I did wonder how went your day of lessons with our barbarian friend, and if you had saved enough strength to lift a glass, much less the skirt of—"

He stopped abruptly, or more correctly, was stopped by the impact of an orange striking him in the mouth.

"Forgive me," Nicholas said in tones as chill as steamboat ice. "I thought you meant to make a game of it. Or was it simply of me?"

Englishman touched a hand to the small split place on his lip then looked down at the blood staining his fingers, "It's no game, not when your pretenses and passions can end in death."

"I am thrilled to the marrow by your concern but fail to see the cause of it."

Blackford gave him a look from under his eyebrows. "I wonder."

"But you need not fear," Nicholas answered. "I have no taste for feats of arms, games or oranges, but only require your amends to the lady for the embarrassment she has been forced to endure from your pique and bad manners."

A short laugh shook Blackford, and he turned his gaze, bright with hilarity, toward Juliette. "Oh, willingly, and with an abundance of groveling. She was only a target in the most distant sense and without the least intent of damage."

"I believe," she said in quiet anger, "that you are quite castaway."

"A good enough explanation," the Englishman said, his humor unimpaired. "And it should be a verifiable truth before the evening is over."

"Why?"

He did not make the mistake of asking what she meant, but only shook his golden head. "I despair of finding reasons that might suit but not shock you. Ask your intended groom."

She lifted her chin, certain that she was being made game of now even if not previously. "I shall."

"Excellent. You might even get an answer if you are properly stern and righteous and refuse to be deflected by gallantry or pretty speeches."

Juliette sent a quick look toward Nicholas, doubtful of his reception of this if he so disliked the other. He was frowning at Blackford, his eyes dark with thought. The Englishman followed her gaze and his own face turned grim. And in that moment, Juliette became aware of a sense of familiarity, as if she had experienced this moment before, or dreamed it. It was false, she knew, yet the room, the two men, the strained tempers amid the smells of oranges and sausages and bread, of wax candles and coal smoke from the fire on the hearth, all seemed part of a time or place she should know well.

The impression lasted only an instant then was gone. In its wake, she felt disoriented, but there remained with her a distinct impression that Nicholas and Gavin Blackford were very much alike under their different attitudes, different personalities. No doubt it was merely the effect of similar height, athletic form and commanding presence, but they almost seemed to favor one another.

Their hostess came forward then in a brisk rustle of skirts. "Enough, if you please, gentlemen," she said with a winsome smile. "I refuse to have it said my entertainments descend into brawls, and absolutely forbid any rips and cuts to my new furnishings. Come and break bread together, *mon chers*, or poor Rio may be forced to eat oranges and sausages with every meal until Mardi Gras."

The moment was pushed aside by the determined tact and conversation of at least half the company. The other half appeared a little disappointed that they were not to see an impromptu passage at arms, the story of which would ensure their welcome at dinner tables for a month.

Juliette was in a quandary. The need to know the extent of Nicholas's injury burned inside her, yet he obviously preferred not to discuss it. That might be normal male reticence in part, but could also be because any weakness in a sword master of his renown could invite a challenge from one who sought to improve his own reputation with minimal risk. He would also be reluctant to reveal where and how he received this wound in front of his betrothed; a mishap during an assignation with a masked coquette would hardly improve his position as a future husband. No doubt that was why he had not spoken of it during the time they had spent together yesterday and this afternoon as well. He would not like to rouse her curiosity. Yes, and she was hampered by the same considerations since she could only inquire into the matter with care for fear of revealing her prior knowledge of it.

How she wished she had never embarked on that foolish deception. It had complicated a situation that was far too strained already, making her watch what she said and did in a way entirely foreign to her nature. If matters continued as they were she would be forced to confess the ruse and get it off her conscience. Yet she could not bear to think of Nicholas learning how far she had strayed from the pure and noble image he held of her.

It seemed necessary to sample the food Celina had laid out for her guests. Nicholas carried the plates for the two of them while Juliette filled them, and then found seats for them on a settee against the wall before heading back into the fray for glasses of wine. She sat holding their food while staring after him, wondering how she was to discover what she needed to know without giving away her own secret.

"Mademoiselle Armant?"

She turned at the sound of her name to see the American with the look of the mountains and backwoods about him bowing at her side. "Monsieur?"

"I had thought Monsieur Pasquale might present me, but since he is otherwise occupied and this is an informal gathering, perhaps you will permit me to introduce myself. Kerr Wallace, mademoiselle, at your service."

"You are an associate of my fiancé?"

"If you mean a *maître d'armes*, no, alas. La Roche is teaching me the art of the blade, or trying. I hope to become proficient before he closes down his atelier."

"*Enchanté*, Monsieur Wallace." His accent was atrocious but his French nimble enough. Perhaps he was not such a barbarian as she had thought. She extended her hand, and he bowed over it with unexpected poise, retaining it in his grasp long enough to be a compliment but not so long as to be an affront. Relaxing a little under the influence of that show of manners, she continued, "I'm sure you will soon gain skill."

The American grimaced as he turned to stand at her side with his hands clasped loosely behind his back. "No doubt, if I can keep up with Pasquale. He's a hard taskmaster."

"Is he?" she murmured, intrigued by that small glimpse into such a masculine world.

"I should say. I begin to dread seeing what he's like when not hampered, as he was today, by a sore side."

"A…minor hurt, no doubt." She was annoyed to think this near stranger knew more of it than she did, but waited with tightness like a ring of steel around her chest for the answer to her comment.

"Apparently. I was glad to see the dispute come to a peaceable end just now, not the least reason being his lack of fitness for any meeting. But it's a sign of internal fortitude, in my view, to refrain from a fight unless there is no other choice."

"You do have a point." Her answer was at random in her relief at his easy confirmation.

"I was also pleased to see that a man need not prick his friends as a result of minor confrontations. If honor should demand a meeting for every dispute, then a man could be down to mere acquaintances before he knows it."

"Very true," she said, surprised into a smile.

He gazed down at her with an engaging grin that showed his teeth bright white against the sun-bronzed skin of his face. "Not that I'm always raring for a fight, you understand. It just seems that your average New Orleans rooster is a mite touchy."

She liked the frank look in his eyes, which were as cool and gray as a winter sky. His tranquil manner was also appealing, though she thought it covered an alert watchfulness that missed nothing of what was happening at various points in the room. "You speak as if you are new to the city, monsieur."

"I've been around a month or so, but stayed on the American side of Canal Street until a few days ago."

"I understand. And now?"

"Now I've left the Verandah Hotel and taken a *pension*—I think that's the word? More of a boarding house than a hotel, at any rate. I liked the company uptown just fine, but it wasn't what I needed."

Nicholas had been waylaid on his return with the wineglasses by a gentleman with enormous side-whiskers and a paunch that stretched the double length of his watch chain from waistcoat pocket to waistcoat pocket like the traces of a dray. Rather than begin eating without him, Juliette spoke again to the man at her side. "Then you have not been going to Nicholas for instruction for any length of time."

"As you say. I could have begun sooner, wish I had in all truth, but I wanted to be certain I had the right man."

"You were looking for him in particular?"

Kerr Wallace's smile flickered again. "I was looking for the best, and found him."

"I believe he scored highly in the last tournament of the fencing masters."

"My informants say he would have won except

that he valued the safety of a young friend of his more. But technical skill wasn't the only measure. I also wanted the most honorable master."

"Now why, I wonder."

"Call it a whim," he said with a shrug. "The finer points of swordsmanship are important, but what's worth more to me is the etiquette. I want to know, when I use what I've learned, that all is done fair and square."

There was something in his mind as he spoke, she was sure, but it seemed presumptuous to question it. "I've no doubt Monsieur Pasquale will be able to guide you in that regard."

"Agreed. I mean, only look at this business of the Brotherhood. Some would take advantage of that idea to settle old scores or maybe put the fear of God into his enemies. Nothing I've heard—which isn't much, you understand, but enough to go by for my purposes—suggests anything at all low about the business. It's done just as if it was broad daylight and before a hundred witnesses."

Juliette could feel her heart plunge into a harder beat in her chest. Here was someone who knew something of what the sword masters were about and was not averse to speaking of it, or else didn't yet understand the inappropriateness of it as a subject for a lady's ears. "I...I've never quite understood how this is different from a duel, particularly if the usual form is followed."

"As I understand it, a duel comes about as the result of a slight or insult to a man, something that reflects on his honor. This Brotherhood, on the other hand, is out to right the wrongs of those who don't usually prattle about such, much less defend it. In the general order of things, you understand, a woman's father, brother or cousins make certain she is protected from harm. But when a female or young one has none to look out for them, that's when these swordsmen turn up to even the score."

"Yes, I do see," she said slowly.

"That's been true from the start, from what I can make out, despite what's said about this business last week."

"And that would be?"

A conscious look crossed his strong features, followed by a frown. It was a moment before he answered and then it was in a different tone altogether. "It occurs to me that as someone near to Pasquale, you should know the answer, and would if he'd thought it fitting that you should hear the tale."

"You need not be concerned with what my betrothed considers fitting, Monsieur Wallace."

His smile was wry. "But I think I must or suffer the consequences. And those, you know, could be drastic."

"You could fail to receive your lessons, I suppose," she said in dry tones.

"Or receive one I hadn't bargained on getting."

His gaze moved past her, to where Nicholas approached. "In any case, I'm saved now from both possibilities. I should take myself off so you can eat— and before I get in more trouble than I can yet handle." Sketching a quick bow, he nodded at Nicholas then moved off with an unhurried stride.

"What was the American saying to you?" Nicholas asked as he placed her wineglass on the table at her elbow and dropped onto the chair beside her.

"Not a great deal," she answered, "merely passing the time."

"Then why were you scowling at him? Not that I mind," he added with a lift of an eyebrow, "since it's preferable to sharing your smiles."

Juliette, seeing an opening for what she wanted to know, took instant advantage of it. "Was I scowling? Then perhaps it was because he seems to know all about your recent sword cut when you have not seen fit to inform me."

The humor faded from his face. "It was nothing, I promise you."

"A mere trifle, I'm sure, only enough to prevent you from your usual method of teaching swordplay or to be an endangerment should you receive a challenge."

"Your concern is gratifying, *ma chère*, but misplaced. A few days, and it will be as if it never happened."

She should let it go, she knew, but something inside her would not allow it. "This American did not say how you came by it."

"My own fault entirely," he said, his black eyes intent yet fathomless as he met and held her gaze. "I was where I should not have been, distracted by something quite beyond...but never mind my excuses. Call it an attack by a pair of thugs who caught me unaware."

Something in his voice, some whisper of emotion, carried her instantly back to that night and its sensual magic. For an instant, she was there again, close in his arms, pressed against him. For the briefest moment she wondered—but no, it could not be. Her fears had been answered, and she must be content with that. Anything else was too dangerous.

"At least the—the distraction was not lethal."

"No," he said gravely, "it wasn't quite that."

It was some time later, when the gentlemen had gravitated to the balcony where they could smoke their Havana cigars while they talked politics and the possibility of war, and the ladies had gathered in a closer circle to compare notes on the most recent scandals, that Lisette mentioned Celina's new Mallard bed. An immediate outcry arose to see it. There being little reticence in such matters among the Creoles, they were soon crowding into the bedchamber to admire the new acquisition.

It was a lovely piece of furniture, quite massive yet graceful with it. The construction was clever as well, as Celina demonstrated by removing the decorative cap from an end post to reveal a cavity where valuables might be secreted. The armoire that matched the bed had its place of concealment as well, one located on the side with access by way of a small door concealed in ornate molding. The compliments to their hostess were most sincere, but Celina would have none of them.

"It wasn't my idea, I assure you, but all Rio's. He's rather tall, you know, and complains that most other beds are too short. But he is not the only one to succumb to Mallard's lure. Caid has commissioned a bed just like this one, hasn't he, Lisette?"

"I fear so, though I doubt the length of it had as much to do with his decision as the sturdiness." The Irish sword master's wife laughed with the others before turning to Juliette. "I hear Nicholas considered one also, but wanted your opinion before placing the order."

"I wouldn't know," Juliette was forced to say. "He hasn't mentioned it."

"No doubt he means to wait until you have settled on a house. First things first."

Lisette seemed to know as much or more of Nicholas's intentions than she did, Juliette thought with some chagrin as she murmured a noncommittal answer. It was not to be wondered at since she and the others had known him far longer. Still, it felt like a failing that they had spoken so little of their future together.

She should also like to know more concerning his other activities. As the ladies began to move back toward the salon in chattering groups, she deliberately trailed behind near Lisette. Just outside the bedchamber door, she touched her lightly on the arm. "Might I ask you something, Madame O'Neill?"

"By all means, if you will call me Lisette."

Juliette searched the face of Caid's wife as the lady paused, her expression expectant in the light of the torch burning in the courtyard below the gallery that served as a conduit between the town house rooms. "It's about Nicholas..."

"Is he all right? He seems unaffected by his wound, I confess, but these things can lay low the strongest of men."

Juliette was glad she need not pretend ignorance any longer. "He says it's nothing, though who can tell? He doesn't appear to be much affected. My greatest concern, however, is this so-called Brotherhood and his activities behind a mask."

"He told you of that?" Lisette's gaze was troubled.

"Not exactly. I heard of it in a roundabout way."

"I suppose it's inevitable that people should talk, though this is the first I've heard of anyone connecting a particular sword master to the incidents."

"What is it about? What is he doing?"

Lisette gave a quick shake of her head. "Nothing in the least dishonorable, if that is your worry. The mask—well, that is Nicholas, always a flair for the dramatic but with reason behind it. He thought to deflect attention from another affair conducted behind a disguise, you know."

"By Croquère, I think," Juliette said, thinking of Squirrel's determination that she should realize his idol was innocent in the business with Daspit.

"As you say."

"You mention other sword masters. What of your husband? Is he one of them?"

"Not any longer. It isn't a calling for men with families."

The prickle of goose bumps ran over her skin. "Because of the danger?"

"Also the consequences of being exposed."

"But you swear it isn't disreputable?" It seemed entirely possible that the sooner she and Nicholas were married with their ready-made family around them, the better it would be from a safety standpoint.

"It's a matter of righting wrongs that can be addressed in no other way, you see, of using hard-earned strength and knowledge of swordplay as a force for good. So many look the other way when bad things happen, telling themselves that it's not their affair, that they have no right to interfere. Stepping forward to prevent suffering can be a noble thing. Regardless, it isn't always legal. There could be consequences." Lisette glanced to where the other ladies had disappeared into the salon again and began to walk that way so Juliette was obliged to walk beside her. "Really, you should discuss this with Nicholas. I'm sure he will tell you about it in detail. Husbands and wives should not have secrets from each other, you know."

Juliette felt a flush creep up her neck to her face as she thought of the secret she was keeping from Nicholas. Lisette, naturally, could have no inkling, would hardly believe it possible, she was sure, not of a former novice at the Ursuline convent. She could hardly believe it herself, any more than she could believe that Nicholas, the Casanova of New Orleans, spent his nights as some kind of masked savior instead of swaggering his way through the bedchambers of the city.

But was that all? Had he been attacked in Tivoli Gardens by chance or was there some other purpose behind it? Was he a seducer of women or their rescuer? Could he be both a sensualist extraordinaire and titular father to a clutch of stray boys? The things were not mutually exclusive, but seemed unlikely to reside in the same man.

The person who had won Squirrel's respect, who had held Gabriel during his illness, was the same man who met others at sword point in the night, the same who had been attacked and injured while in her presence. And he had deliberately kept these things from her. Why was that?

Was she so fragile, so unworldly in his eyes, that he thought she could not bear the truth? Did he expect her to swoon away or else fall to her knees in prayer over his sinful ways?

She was made of stronger clay. In addition, she was tired of being treated as if she were different from other women. To be revered and protected was a lovely thing, but no substitute for being accepted as she truly was inside, with all her faults and foibles. This was an essential truth that Nicholas Pasquale would discover before he was very much older.

Whether she allowed him to learn everything there was to know about her was, of course, another matter altogether.

15

No moonlight illuminated the walk back to the Armant town house, nor could any stars be seen beyond the dim glow of the streetlamps that made pools of light at the street corners but left long stretches in between in darkness. A rising wind from off the river swept the city. It's breath was damp and smelled of coming rain mixed with the normal odors of mud and decaying vegetation. Few people were abroad, though a cat yowled a few streets over and a carriage rattled past with its curtains pulled over its windows.

Nicholas glanced down at the woman who strolled at his side as he made the turn onto the rue St. Louis. She had been quiet during this walk homeward, not that she was a chatterbox at the best of times. Her face in the flickering light of the streetlamp was composed, remote, yet her grasp on his arm seemed a little tighter than was usual and her footsteps faster, as if she were in haste to reach her mother's town house. The need to take whatever was troubling her from her shoulders, to make her smile, laugh, relax against him was a nebulous yet deep inclination. The problem was that he wasn't sure how to go about it, or if he might not be the major cause of it.

Running in tandem with his concern was another impulse, one that involved stopping and pulling her into one of the doorways they passed where he might ruffle her too quiet equanimity, not to mention the tightly buttoned perfection of her clothing. These things were like a challenge, one he longed so violently to meet that he could feel the heat of that desire simmering at the edges of his brain. What restrained him was not Valara who followed along with them as usual, the chance of causing gossip if seen or even Juliette's own cool demeanor. No, it was something within himself, a desperate sense that he had not the right combined with a fear of the great hole that would be left in his future if she should decide not to be a part of it after all.

"I had not thought to be quite so long at Rio's and Celina's," he said, strain making his voice a little flat. "I hope the delay won't cause any upset."

"I see no reason for it."

"No," he echoed, though he was not particularly sanguine about Gabriel being in the care of her mother. It wasn't that he expected Madame Armant to do the boy an injury, but he put no faith in her concern for his health. He would have felt better if Squirrel and others were on the premises, but they had refused to set foot in the house, depending on him for reports from Gabriel.

It would not do to express his doubts, since it could only force Juliette to defend her mother. Instead, he said, "You seemed to get on well with Celina and Lisette. Did the gathering tonight meet with your expectations?"

"It was a delight. Both ladies were most kind and made me feel more than welcome among them."

"You will find they only improve with closer acquaintance."

"I feel sure we will all become great confidantes, sharing all our secrets."

The disquiet that touched him was brief since they were nearing the entrance gate for the Armant porte cochère. Valara had the key in her keeping this evening, perhaps because it was too large and heavy for the ornate pocket that Juliette wore at the waist of her teal walking costume. The servant woman moved ahead of them to unlock the gate, then stood aside for them to enter.

"Perhaps you could run upstairs now and see how Gabriel fares," Juliette suggested as she moved past her. "I'm sure Monsieur Pasquale would appreciate having a report before he leaves us."

Valara nodded in agreement and trundled away down the tunnel-like entrance. Nicholas turned and secured the gate behind them, then gave Juliette his arm again.

Their footsteps rang with a hollow sound on the stone paving. A night breeze, funneling down the dark passage, brought with it the scents of winter jasmine and sweet olive from some nearby garden. Valara's rotund figure vanished from sight ahead of them as she emerged into the courtyard, then they heard her heavy treads crossing the courtyard and ascending the stairs.

Juliette halted in the shadows at the edge of the tunnel's mouth and released his arm. "It's good that we have this moment alone before she returns."

"Indeed?" He paused, waiting. When she did not go on at once, he tried again. "There was something you particularly wished to say?"

"I…I cannot but think that you have the wrong impression of me." She released his arm, knitting her fingertips together as she stood stiffly at his side.

"How so?"

"I am not all sweetness and piety, you know."

She was so very earnest in her demeanor that he felt his mood shift from uneasiness to quirky humor. "No?"

"I have a dreadful temper when roused to anger, and can be quite vindictive when pressed to it."

"Indeed."

"I say this to warn you so you will not be disappointed when we are married."

"You could never disappoint me."

"I might, if you expect a biddable wife who will ask nothing of you and accept your word as law. In all truth, my nature is much…warmer than you may have been led to believe."

"Led?"

"By my mother and my sister, and also by my association with the convent."

"Now that is good to hear. A man does not like to think that his wife will be cold toward him."

"I shan't be that."

What was she trying to say? Could it really be what it seemed? She had suggested before that she would merely oblige him in his more carnal urges, yet now appeared to be hinting at more. The mere idea sent a hot surge of desire through him. He tried to fight it with deep breaths through flared nostrils, but the need to touch her, to taste her was a desperate hunger. Even so, a shadow of disturbance flitted across his mind. His voice not quite even, he said, "My expectations are of no great importance in this arrangement of ours. Whatever your nature is or is not, you must be yourself, nothing more and certainly nothing less."

"It's very kind of you to say so. You will come to realize, I believe, that I am simply a woman. My needs, my passions are those of any human being. I would not have you think my life is lived on some more exalted plane untouched by such emotions."

"Not that, perhaps, and yet you were a nun." Of course she had wants and needs, he knew that, knew also how impractical it was of him to assume it might be otherwise. Still, the resistance he felt inside was a measure of his ambivalence. As idealistic as it might be, he knew something inside him preferred his image of her as his angel—gentle, compassionate and eternally pure.

"The nunlike manner I wore when you first saw me was not one of my choosing but something pressed on me as a child, like a mask I was told I must wear. Now I have taken it off."

For an instant, he caught a tantalizing glimpse of the woman he had sensed that night in the pleasure gardens. She intrigued him almost unbearably. He wanted to know her from the finest hair on her head to the pink curve of her smallest toe. That need brought a fierce, gripping ache that had nothing to do with the stiffness of his side. With his hands clenched into hard fists to refrain from reaching out to her, he said, "I will always remember you as I first saw you, coming from the cathedral."

"Because you prefer it. The question is, why?"

Why, indeed? He stared at her there in the dim entranceway, at her set face and troubled eyes. Then a slow inkling began in the back of his mind, growing steadily clearer. He needed her to be above him on some level, he thought, if not socially, then morally. It was a form of self-protection at its deepest heart. If she was plainly beyond his touch in that sense, regardless of his own base urges toward her, then it made no difference that he was unworthy of the honor of being her husband. He could enjoy her while depending on her benign goodness, her compassion and, always, her forgiveness. Even a fatherless street rat could worship at the feet of a Madonna.

It was not a comfortable insight. He had no need of someone else to make him feel inferior. The stinging pain it unleashed changed to resentment between one hard breath and the next.

He reached to take her wrist, dragging her against him and clamping his other arm around her waist. Spinning then, he pressed her back to the brick wall of the porte cochère, stepping close so his leg nudged between her thighs and his chest absorbed the soft fullness of her breasts. She gasped, lips parting, and he took instant advantage, lowering his head to possess her mouth, plundering its lush sweetness as he released the hard grip he held on his control.

She stiffened, pushing against his shoulders with one hand while twisting the other in his grasp where he held it against the wall. He paid no attention. Slanting his head, he probed deeper, engaging her tongue in a furious duel for supremacy. She sought to elude him, trying to turn her head, but he would not allow it. Releasing her wrist, he cupped her face, holding her immobile for his intimate invasion.

She stilled, then made a small, impatient sound in her throat. An instant later, he felt the nip of small, sharp teeth on his tongue.

His jerked his head back, staring down at her while his mind cleared like the lifting of morning fog. Suddenly ashamed, he opened his mouth to speak but was forestalled.

"If this is an example of your much vaunted expertise," she said, her breasts rising and falling in maddening rhythm against him, "then I don't think much of it."

"I don't blame you. Please, I—"

"Don't apologize. There is no need since I know I made you angry. It would be considerably more to the point if you would accept me as I am and behave accordingly."

She was giving him a chance to redeem himself. Or was she? She might expect him to merely signify his understanding with some pretty speech or gesture.

The hot blood thrumming his veins would not allow it, nor would his real need to erase from her mind the moments just past, replacing them with something that was, hopefully, more pleasing.

This time, when he lowered his mouth to hers, the movement was more controlled and with every intention behind it to bring pleasure. Banishing everything except the passing moment, he brushed her lips with his, absorbing the fragile texture of their surface, feeling the intake of her breath as it feathered across his own. He inhaled the warm, feminine scent of her that hinted at soft, powdery notes of lavender and roses, of pressed cotton and linen. And when he tasted her mouth, its flavor went to his head like some exotic cordial that heightened his senses and brought pure, intoxicating joy bubbling up inside him.

She sighed, melting into his arms. Her hands settled on his shoulders, sliding over the broadcloth of his frock coat to clasp behind his head. Her tongue touched his in tentative advance and retreat, the movements growing bolder as he slid his own around and over hers in sinuous incitement.

Dearest God, but he wanted her, wanted to feel her bare skin against him while she writhed in sweet, mindless passion, wanted to hear her whisper his name while she cooled his hot skin with small, delicate kisses, wanted to merge his body with hers until he could feel the beat of her heart in the life's blood flowing through her deepest recess.

His pulse thundered in his ears and every muscle strained rock-hard with his rampaging desire. And he didn't care if she were pure as April rain or mistress of every art of the bedchamber. He longed to hold the passionate masked woman of Tivoli Gardens once again. He needed her, had to have her, could not bear to think of ever losing this gentle yet wanton angel. More, he wanted her to want him, yearned to show her all the many variations of skill that she so disdained, to use them to effect her surrender.

She was right in thinking that he had disapproved of her stirring desire. The causes were there, yet what right had he to fault her? He could not think of her returning to the convent and its restrictions, so why should he wish to impose them on her outside its walls? It was foolish and possibly self-serving. Other men might adore a Madonna but did not long to possess her.

He did, and would. Whatever he had to do to make her his would be done. Whatever he had to be, he would attempt it. He did not deserve her, but she had been handed to him by grace and superstition, and he would hold her for as long as possible. He could not bear for it to be otherwise.

The desire that racked him when he thought of her, looked at her, touched her was something he would deal with later. And God would forgive him if he chose the wrong manner of it.

It was then that he heard, as from far away, the heavy clatter of feet along the upper gallery and sharp calls edged with dismay. He and Juliette broke apart, staring at each other in the dimness. Then they moved as one, turning in haste to step from the porte cochère into the open courtyard.

"Mam'zelle Juliette! Oh, mam'zelle," Valara cried, almost tumbling down the stairs in her haste. Her face was gray beneath its nutmeg brown and her eyes wide as she ran toward them. "He's gone, the *petit garçon*, that sweet little boy. He's not in his bed, mam'zelle. He's gone."

Juliette moved forward to meet the servant woman, catching and holding her hands. "Calm yourself, Valara. He has to be here somewhere."

"No, no. I looked into every bedchamber, Mam'zelle Paulette's, your *maman's*, the spare one. He's gone."

Before Juliette could speak again, Madame Armant appeared, trailing from her bedchamber with her nightcap askew, its lappets uneven where they dangled under the rolls of her chin. "What is this commotion?" she asked in querulous complaint. "I had barely gone off to sleep and now will be wide awake for hours."

"It's Gabriel," Juliette said sharply. "I left him in your care and now he is gone. What has become of him?"

Madame Armant pushed at her cap in a half-hearted manner that did little toward straightening it. "Why, I hardly know, *chère*. The *pauvre petit* was sound asleep in his bed when I looked in on him after Paulette left for the theatre with Monsieur Daspit and Madame Daspit, his mother. Is he not there now?"

"Apparently not." She turned to her old nurse with a frown. "I thought one of the maids was to sit with him. What of her?"

Valara only shook her head.

"As to that," her mother said with another nervous push at her cap, "he ate a good dinner and seemed so well, and the girl was half-asleep in her chair. Paulette said it was unnecessary to make her stay."

The misgivings that gripped Nicholas turned to alarm. He tried to keep the accompanying anger from his voice as he spoke. "If he woke to find himself alone and in the dark, he might have gone into hiding."

Valara's worried frown lightened a little. "'Tis so, I had not thought. We must search everywhere."

They did just that, looking in armoires and cupboards and under beds, searching beneath the skirts of dressing tables and in the depths of the kitchen where the others had slept before. They called and coaxed, but Gabriel did not appear.

It was Juliette who put the thought into words that had been slowly growing in Nicholas's mind. "Suppose…suppose he left the house. Suppose he went to find the others."

The other street boys, she meant. It was a definite possibility, or would have been except for a few problems. "He was still weak. How was he able to slip away without being seen? Yes, and how did he manage to get through the outer gate? He would barely have been able to reach the lock, much less lay hands on a key and open it."

Juliette shook her head, her fear and unhappiness in her eyes.

"How many keys are there and who has access to them?"

"We—we all have one."

"Your mother? Paulette?"

"Are you suggesting they put him out into the street?"

Nicholas gave her a steady look. "That's what I'm trying to find out."

"Perhaps the gate was left open by accident and he slipped out after Paulette left. Or Squirrel might have returned and found some way to remove him."

If the gate had been left open it had been no accident: Nicholas was fairly sure of that much. Whether Gabriel could or would have taken advantage of it was uncertain. On the other hand, the idea that Squirrel might have spirited Gabriel away had more than a little merit. He could well have felt his Gaby was better off elsewhere.

"I'll check with the other boys," Nicholas said with an abrupt nod. "In the meantime—"

"Yes, in the meantime, we will continue to look for him."

At his atelier, he found Squirrel and the rest of the street gang laid out on their pallets in the rear of the raised basement. They came awake instantly with the wariness of their kind. Nicholas watched them rise to their feet with mingled hope and impatience, but when they stood before him in the light of his raised candle, Gabriel was not among them. They had not seen him since they left the Armant town house, they said, watching him with pale faces that seemed to hold the shadow of accusation since it was he, Nicholas, who had taken the boy there.

"You don't know where he is, didn't help him leave?"

Squirrel gave him a dark look. "Wish I had."

"You think he could have gotten away by himself?"

"Guess he might've. Like a monkey, is our Gaby. But where would he go if not here."

It was a point, Nicholas thought. "The O'Neill town house, perhaps. But no one would have been home there since Madame and Monsieur O'Neill were at De Vega's place."

"Might have slipped in where the party was with all the coming and going, saying he knew where they were. Or that you and Mam'zelle Juliette were there."

"I'll take the De Vega town house," Nicholas said, his voice grim as he turned to the cupboard where his sword cane was kept and took it down. "You and the others can check at the O'Neill place."

Rio and Celina were just seeing off the last of their guests, Caid and Lisette and Blackford, who stood on the banquette. They were surprised to see

Nicholas back again, but grasped the situation at once. Immediately, the six of them split up to search the courtyard and *garçonnière*, the kitchen, laundry, stables and various storerooms. Servants were roused to help make a sweep of the house, in case the boy should elude them by slipping from room to room.

It didn't help. Gabriel was not on the premises. He had not been found at the O'Neill town house, either, since Cotton, the street boys' second-in-command behind Squirrel, came with that news, adding that they were still searching.

"Lisette and I will go home at once in case he shows up," Caid said as they congregated in the porte cochère after their last foray into dark corners.

His wife nodded with a troubled frown. "I can hardly believe Madame Armant caused such a disturbance as to scare away the other boys. Could she not see that Squirrel and the others are Gabriel's family?"

"Women of her sort seldom look beyond their own convenience," Caid said in grim tones.

"Juliette seems different from her mother or sister, I must say," Celina put in thoughtfully. "I suppose it's from spending so much time with the nuns."

Nicholas tipped his head in agreement. "That, and being told at a young age that she must follow a different path."

"She has to be beside herself with worry. Her concern over the boy's illness was very nearly that of a mother. We spoke at length this evening about childhood illnesses and their cures. She seemed fretful about having left him, apparently with good reason."

Nicholas, who had not bothered to relinquish his hat on his arrival, took it off, raked gloved fingers through his hair. "Gabriel seems taken with her, too. I can hardly believe he left her bedchamber since she told him she would return, can't think where else he might have gone, except my place or here."

Blackford, his blue gaze narrow with concentration, spoke then. "You don't think someone might have taken him?"

"Who would do that? He's only a street child, worth nothing to anyone except me."

"And is there nothing anyone might be wanting from the likes of you?" Caid asked in the mild Irish brogue he fell into when at his most serious.

"Ransom, you mean?" Nicholas frowned at the lining of his hat.

"You have recently come into a considerable sum, as everyone knows. Or it might be your absence from the dueling field that's required."

"Not many know of my attachment to the boys. And I have no current challenges."

"For a wonder," Caid said, though his frown suggested the comment was mere habit. "What of those who might want to do you an injury?"

"By striking at Gabriel? But who?"

"You would know that better than we would."

His protest had been mere form, Nicholas knew as he clapped his beaver on his head again. He was well aware of who might do such a thing, though he disliked believing that anyone could stoop so low. He also did not want to accept the corollary, which was that taking Gabriel from the Armant household would have required help from Paulette. "But anyone must know I would discover it eventually and they would then have to face me on the dueling field."

"Or me," Caid said judiciously.

"Or me," Blackford added.

"Just so," Lisette said in a firm tone. "It's time now to cast a wider net, I believe. Caid and I will turn homeward, as he has said, watching for him along the way."

Rio nodded. "Blackford and I can each take a street leading to the river."

"The gendarmes, Nicholas, don't you think?" Celina said, touching his arm.

"For what good it may do." The police who walked the streets knew the boys well, he was aware, but it was doubtful they would go out of their way to look for one of them.

"Don't be so cynical, *mon cher*," she said with the glimmer of a smile. "You have just seen that you aren't the only one who cares for these children."

"Yes, I know," he replied. "It's the one thing which gives me hope."

They set out on their objectives except for Celina, who remained behind at the town house with her children and also to intercept Gabriel if he came there after all. Nicholas soon found the watchman who walked the area, locating him by the thud of his cudgel as he pounded the banquette and called out the hour. The man listened to his story then shook his head. He'd seen nothing of young Gabriel, hadn't for a couple of days, and was sorry to hear that he'd been sickly. He'd keep an eye out, but that was all he could promise.

It was moments like these when it felt perfectly useless to be a swordsman to Nicholas. What good was it that he could walk in cool and dispassionate calm to meet any number of men in the fog-shrouded dawn, face naked steel without flinching or take a wound with only a shrug for the pinprick, when he could not prevent bad things happening to those who mattered to him? He was the premier master at arms in New Orleans, but could not order the massive search it might take to find one small boy, had no power to see that he remained unharmed. Free-flowing anger dogged his steps as he strode in the direction of the river to rejoin his searching friends, it stayed in his heart as they roved the streets, looking, looking, seeking among the waving tree shadows around the Place d'Armes and under the arcades of the *Cabildo*, between the wind-rocked bowsprits of ships and among the stacked merchandise of the dock area that fronted the river levee. It was still with him as Caid and Rio finally turned homeward to check there again while he and Blackford went toward his atelier in hope that Squirrel and the others would be waiting for him with news.

He would not go just yet to the more unsavory parts of town beyond the Vieux Carré, refused to consider that it might be necessary.

It was Juliette who came forward from under the arcade that shaded his doorway. Valara was behind her, carrying a lantern that cast fantastic, elongated shadows against the plastered brick walls. They appeared ghostlike in the wavering light, wrapped in dark cloaks that lifted around them with the strengthening storm wind, their firelight-glazed faces solemn and their eyes like dark pools.

"You've found him?" he demanded, striding forward.

"No—but there is a message." Juliette stopped, catching her bottom lip between her teeth.

"Tell me."

She came closer, searching his face. "He is safe, in a manner of speaking."

Dread, magnified by the doubt of his reaction that he saw in her eyes, made him feel sick. "What is it? What has happened?"

"Paulette did not come home tonight."

"And?" He had little time and scant patience for the indiscretions of her twin.

"She was supposed to be at the theater with Monsieur Daspit and his mother, you know. That was over some time ago. *Maman* grew worried and upset, and I went to her bedchamber for her vinaigrette. In the drawer where it is kept was a note from Paulette addressed to *Maman*. She knew she would be disturbed when she was missed so someone was sure to look there."

"You are saying…"

She swallowed. "Paulette and Monsieur Daspit have eloped."

"A note left behind," Blackford murmured, "the inevitable sop to conscience."

"They are bound for Gretna," Nicholas said in grim acceptance. A low grumble of thunder seemed to echo his words.

"We may be able to stop her before she and Daspit find a boat to take them across the river." Blackford looked as if he meant to fling away on the chase at once.

"He will have had one waiting, depend on it."

"We will have to go after her, then."

"No," Juliette said, stepping forward to put her hand on his arm.

Blackford frowned down at her. "She is your sister. You can't let her make such a mistake."

"I think there is more," Nicholas said, his gaze on Juliette's pale face.

"She said that…that Gabriel is safe with them."

Nicholas clenched his fists at his sides. "Daspit has him."

"I don't think we were supposed to know it. I believe we were to be diverted by the search while they made their escape."

"Or else Gabriel is a hostage to prevent anyone chasing after them."

Pain darkened Juliette's eyes to storm green. "They wouldn't hurt him. Paulette said, that is, she promised no harm would come to him."

"I will kill Daspit if it does," Nicholas said under his breath. "If he puts the smallest bruise on Gabriel, I will personally slice him to pieces like a field hand killing a snake."

Blackford lifted an eyebrow. "He knows that, I imagine. Do you think they will make an extended wedding trip of it?"

"Paulette will be impatient to prove her claim to the marriage chest," Juliette answered with a slow shake of her head. "Daspit as well. They will return."

"But not before it's too late for you, Mademoiselle Armant. It seems a shame when they might be stopped."

Juliette turned toward Nicholas. In her eyes was a question, or so he thought. He inclined his head while holding her gaze. "We might stop them, but there are no guarantees. I will admit that it goes against the grain to let them get away with using Gabriel to rob you of your birthright. Or to send you back to the convent, if it comes to that."

It was long moments before she spoke, then the words were not quite even. "These things matter, but most important of all is Gabriel. I can't believe they would hurt him, at least not deliberately. Still, he has been very ill, and now they are taking him across the river at night in what I can only suppose must be an open boat. What if he takes a chill? What if he cries for me? What if he fights them and falls overboard?"

"You would have me bring him back, then."

"Yes," she said simply, "I would. And I will go with you to do it."

"You cannot. It's no trip for a lady, especially not with rain coming on."

"You can't deal with Monsieur Daspit, Paulette and Gabriel all at the same time. I will go, and Valara with me."

"Mam'zelle Juliette!" The old nurse's eyes widened and she fell back a step.

"I will give myself the pleasure as well," Blackford said.

"You?" Nicholas turned his frown on Blackford since it seemed to have no effect on Juliette.

"I know a man who may take us across the river. Besides, you will require someone to watch your back—in the event this becomes a voyage into a snake's den."

Blackford hinted at a possibility that had not occurred to Nicholas in his concern for Gabriel, that the letter left behind by Paulette was meant to be found, the elopement designed to entice him, Gabriel's protector, away from the city where he might be ambushed and dispatched without witnesses. Such convoluted thinking was Blackford's specialty. Or it could simply be that his English friend knew of the sword slash to his side and meant to stand guard on his left flank.

"Another point," the Englishman continued. "If Mademoiselle Juliette is there, and her maid, then the sister may be able to brush through this without a scandal."

"In case they are stopped short of the wedding, yes," Juliette agreed. "Gabriel may be frightened as well, even if the boat trip in this weather doesn't make him sick again."

What they said made sense, Nicholas knew, and he could hardly stop Juliette short of physical force. Still he wanted to make the situation as clear as possible. "It will be rough on the river as well as cold and wet. We won't know what we'll find until we get there."

"I am not made of spun sugar," she said, her eyes steady.

"Brava," Blackford said applauding with a single clap of his hands. "Nor am I. And I can row."

Nicholas did not turn his gaze from Juliette. "Attend to me, please. If we cannot come upon Daspit and your sister in good time, if they discover we are after them and go hiking off into the country with Gabriel, we must follow on their trail. There will be no other choice."

"I would expect nothing else."

"It could be days before we can come up to them, so impossible to return without everyone in the city knowing we have been away together. Valara might afford some small protection in the matter with any other man, but not, I regret to say, with…with the Casanova of New Orleans." He could speak no plainer than that, he thought, at least not without giving offense.

She lifted her chin, giving him stare for stare. "The possibility seems remote, but given that we are to be wed in good time, the chatter of those not involved in this affair means nothing to me."

Like Blackford, he admired her spirit. Even so, he suspected the concern of the moment was overshadowing her natural reluctance to be the subject of gossip. "You are quite certain?"

"Why are we standing here talking," Juliette demanded. "They are getting farther ahead of us every moment."

Daspit might be a blackguard, but his instinct to run away with the woman he wanted suddenly seemed more than sound to Nicholas. He would love to know that Juliette was insisting on going with him for the purpose of standing before the Scots judge who married couples out of hand. To be assured that the union between the two of them was complete at last, that nothing could be allowed to come between them, not sisterly concern, family duty, not even the church itself, seemed a consummation definitely to be wished. Afterward, he would hold her, caress her, and seek once more the woman hidden behind the serene façade that she wore so well.

"Excellent," he said, tightening his grip on the sword cane in his hand. "We go. But you will please remember this warning."

Her green-gold eyes held his there under the arcade, then an odd smile surfaced in their depths, one that made his heart shiver, for an instant, in his chest.

"I will remember," she said softly. "I will certainly remember."

16

The river was high, as it always was this time of year, swollen with winter rains and the intermittent melting of snow in the territories to the north. The sky that arched above was as black as the underside of an iron sugar kettle. Wind from the southwest pushed the water into waves that lapped hungrily against the levee and shone here and there with the dirty blotches of white caps. They set the waiting boat to rocking so it thudded against its levee-side dock in an irregular rhythm, bucking and dipping like a live thing. Valara, clinging to Juliette's arm as they approached, took one look at the dorylike craft of the kind often carried on ships as lifeboats and stopped in her tracks.

"No, mam'zelle. We can't go, not in that."

"It won't be so bad once we're on the river." Juliette hoped that it was so. Certainly, the giant of a black man who sat at the rudder grinned at them without concern. She did not doubt he was competent; still, the boat did look flimsy in the light of the lantern that Nicholas held aloft to light their way.

"Samson is the best on the river," Blackford said, raising his voice above the rush of the wind and waves. "He's made this run, fair weather and foul, a thousand times."

"Two thousand, maybe more," the boatman agreed in a rumble that had the same base note as the thunder overhead along with a Caribbean lilt. "Folks all the time gettin' married on the other side."

Juliette gave the boatman a quick glance as she realized he suspected an elopement. There was no opportunity to make the situation clear, however, as Valara spoke again.

"We can't go," she said again, her gaze on Nicholas, who had stepped into the boat and, keeping low, waited now to hand the two of them aboard.

"We decided this already," Juliette said with a shake of her head. "I won't back out now."

"I did not decide, mam'zelle. You go, but I can't, not me."

Valara was no slave. Juliette could not compel her obedience, even if she would have done anything so heartless when she was obviously terrified. She glanced toward Nicholas, meeting his eyes for a brief instant. They asked nothing, demanded nothing, yet seemed to hold a challenge in their depths. Abruptly, she gathered her skirts in her right hand, then gave him her left as she prepared to step into the boat. To her old nurse, she said, "Stay if you must, but I am going."

Valara wavered, then stepped back. "Your pardon, mam'zelle. I will tell your mother what transpires with you. Go with *le bon Dieu,* you and Monsieur Nicholas. May he guard you."

It was unclear whether Valara invoked the protection of God or of the swordsman, but it made no difference. Nicholas's warm grasp supported Juliette as he steadied her, then guided her to a seat in the prow before taking his place behind her. Blackford bent to release the boat's shore line and give it a shove away from the small wooden dock built against the levee as he leaped aboard with athletic grace. They were off.

Juliette grabbed hold of the gunwales on either side of her as the river jerked the bobbing craft into its current like a piece of flotsam snatched from an eddy. An instant later, they were riding the waves, plunging, racing forward with the force of Samson's hand on the rudder and the sweep of the oars wielded by Nicholas on the forward seat. Blackford, just behind him, seemed to be urging him to give up his place and allow him this first turn at rowing. Juliette knew a moment's doubt as she considered Nicholas's injury and the wisdom of such straining effort. He seemed not to feel it, insofar as she could tell in the fitful light from the lantern that sat now at Blackford's feet. He only shook his head in answer to Blackford's demands and bent his back to the task. She faced forward again.

The wind was in their faces, as if trying to hold them back. A wave dashed high, splashing over the front of the boat. Juliette sucked in a shocked breath as its cold wetness hit her head-on, showering over her where she sat. Then she ducked her head and huddled into her damp cloak, enduring.

They were being carried downstream. It was not unexpected, of course; all ferry traffic from New Orleans to the towns across the river had to allow for the current. Still, it seemed to Juliette that the drift was too fast. How the boatman could judge, she had no idea. She could see no more than a gray hint of the opposite shore for the darkness, windblown spray and wallowing progress of the boat that dived in and out of the wave troughs.

She thought of Paulette and Daspit, along with Gabriel, ahead of them somewhere in this winter storm. Were they still on the river? Paulette would be beside herself with terror, and the boy as well. Was Gabriel dressed warmly enough? Would Paulette hold him secure against the plunging of the waves and protect him from the spray.

It was her fault that Gabriel had been caught up in this affair, or so Juliette felt. She should never have left him this evening. What if he caught an ague or pneumonia from being out in the weather, then was too weak to recover from its rigors? This mad start of Paulette's could be the death of him.

How difficult it was to believe that her sister would actually drag Gabriel out on such a night. Thoughtless and frivolous Paulette might be, and a little too concerned with her own wishes ahead of others, but she was not a monster. She would not endanger a sick child for no reason, surely she would not. Nicholas seemed to think that she might abandon the boy, but Juliette refused to believe it. The only way she would do such a thing was if forced to it by Daspit.

Forced.

Was it possible Monsieur Daspit had compelled Paulette's agreement to a runaway marriage? Her sister had refused to consider such a hole-and-corner affair. Appearances were everything; it was not in Paulette to regard all well lost for love; the sentiment was too foreign, too melodramatic and disreputable. This instinctive feeling was another reason Juliette had insisted on coming with Nicholas.

Their mother would be beside herself when she discovered what Paulette had done. She could easily make herself ill dwelling on it, imagining every possible disaster, every physical danger and social consequence. Valara would see to her as best she could, but Juliette felt she should be with her.

So many had need of her. Juliette felt the painful wrench of the conflicting duties, also the fear that she might somehow fail them all.

The rain began as a warning patter but quickly became a deluge. It poured down, soaking everything that had not already been drenched by the waves. Falling so heavily that it seemed a solid wall of water, it blanked out the distant black line of the opposite shore. Juliette was grateful for the bonnet which helped shield her face, and also for her heavy cloak that protected her from the worst of it. She did not think Nicholas and Gavin Blackford, in their lighter frock coats, were faring so well.

Turning on her seat, she looked back at Nicholas. A solid, broad-shouldered presence, he wielded his oars without stopping, aiding the steady thump and swish of Samson's rudder. She could just make out his features in the lantern light behind him, just catch the gleam of his eyes.

A grin of pure enjoyment slashed his face as he bent to dig his oars into the black waves again and again. No fear or doubt was in it but only virulent and reckless defiance. He was fighting the elements and watery disaster as surely as he had ever fought an opponent on the dueling field. It wasn't that he didn't recognize the danger but rather he saluted it, smiling in its face.

Suddenly, Juliette's spirits surged upward with matching exhilaration, matching courage. It burgeoned inside her, more vivid than anything she had ever known. All trepidation was wiped away. Never had she felt so alive or so invincible.

A slow smile tilted her mouth in response, becoming a bubble of laughter for the unadulterated joy of being where she was, with this man. Regardless of their errand and her doubt of its outcome, at that moment she would not have changed places with any woman in the world.

Abruptly, a wave smacked into the side of her bonnet. Its force sent the boat's prow rearing toward the sky. She lost her grip, tumbling off the seat. Nicholas swore as he dropped the oars and reached for her with strong hands, going to one knee in the bottom of the boat.

She careened into him, her shoulder thudding into the center of his chest. He gave a short grunt but his arms closed strong and hard around her. Dimly, she was aware of Samson yelling, the boat sheering broadside to the wind, Blackford plunging forward to snatch the trailing oars and fit them into the locks at his own seat. He dug in hard and they began to move forward again.

As in a daze, she felt the rise and fall of Nicholas's deep breathing, sensed the thud of his heart in his chest. The heat he gave off was in such sharp contrast to the chill of her body that she gave a convulsive shiver. He pulled her closer, helping her regain her balance before easing back onto his seat, drawing her up with the flexing of hard muscles to sit beside him.

"Your wound," she began in distress as she tried to move away.

"I will survive."

His firm embrace supported her so she was pressed to him on one side from her shoulder to her knee. His scents of warm, wet linen and wool, a hint of unique spice and clean male enveloped her, mounting to her head like fine brandy. She inhaled sharply, waiting in breathless anticipation for what might come next.

He drew air into his lungs with a soft hissing sound, but did not encroach. They sat still for wind-tossed seconds while matching each other breath for ragged breath. And it seemed suddenly so right, his nearness and the infinite sense of protection he gave her. The boat could still capsize, the rain swamp them, the current take them miles downstream to where there was nothing but endless reaches of water surrounding islands of ancient shells and, finally, the gulf itself. It didn't matter. She was safe. She was where she belonged.

How unbelievable was that feeling compared to her life not so long ago when the round of her days had been supposedly set for eternity, constricted by duty, service and prayer within a convent's high walls. That she had been relieved of those things astounded her anew. If it happened that she had to return there, she would be forever grateful for this taste of a wet, windswept night and another kind of life. She was fiercely glad that she had known it, that she had dared reach for it.

These thoughts slipping through her mind lingered as Nicholas held her close in the hard circle of his arm, there beside him on the seat. Then he spoke against the side of her bonnet.

"The river is getting wilder. It may be best if you stay here beside me where it's safer."

"Yes," she murmured, and relaxed against him. She faced forward but scarcely noticed the darkness ahead. Instead, every iota of her attention was on the man who held her, on the sway of his body as he absorbed the boat's movement, the way the rain ran from the brim of his hat and down his back, the golden slant of the lantern light across the handsome planes of his face as he turned his head, helping watch for debris in the water. She watched, and was mesmerized by his male grace and power while passion and an odd grief swelled her chest. And she wondered in despair if he felt toward her even a minute portion of the fascination of mind and body that he roused in her.

He has kissed her earlier as if he meant it. She had returned that embrace with all the pent desire that was in her. It had been a revelation, the sensations that bloomed inside her, bursting upon her with heat and fury like some internal volcanic eruption. How she had longed to surrender to them and to the man who held her while also learning respect for that intense sensual hunger. It was too powerful a reaction for experiment. She would not chance it again until they were husband and wife.

If, or course, they ever achieved such a union.

The wife of Nicholas Pasquale, most notorious swordsman in New Orleans. Would it be limitless bliss to be Madame Pasquale, to have the right to lie in his arms with nothing between them except honesty and need, hope and possibility? Or would there be only disappointment and inevitable sorrow?

None could say. It might be that she would never know.

The west bank finally appeared out of the wind-swept rain, a gray smudge lying between dark water and sky. By degrees, it grew bigger and darker and pricked by scattered lights. When they were within hailing distance, the boatman Samson reached under his seat and brought out a trumpet made from a cow's horn, which he blew to announce their approach. This was, apparently, the signal alerting a nearby stableman to the arrival of paying passengers, for a horse and wagon rattled up to meet them as they docked.

While Nicholas handed Juliette from the boat and into the wagon, Blackford inquired about another couple with a small boy arriving ahead of them. The wagon's driver shook his head. He'd not been called out, but that didn't mean much. The other boat might have landed farther downstream and its passengers been picked up from a different stable. Sure as certain, he knew the direction of the judge's house, had made many a trip there. He would have them at the front gate in two shakes of a lamb's tail.

He was as good as his word. They plowed through the slanting rain, splashing in and out of mud holes, jostling each other on the hard seats located behind the driver. A short time later, they pulled up outside the gate of a picket fence that fronted a neat two-story house with a bungalow roof and wide steps leading up to an expansive veranda. Nicholas climbed down and helped Juliette alight. Blackford stayed behind to pay the wagon driver and ask him to wait while the two of them entered the fenced-in garden and approached the front entrance. Nicholas knocked and they stood waiting while rain sluiced off the roof behind them. Juliette tried to shake out her wet cloak and skirts, but with little result.

The door opened in short order. An elderly houseman surveyed them, his eyes shrewd, before inclining his head and wishing them a good evening.

Nicholas returned the greeting in curt tones. "We must speak with the judge. The matter is urgent."

"Come inside where it's dry, sir, you and your lady. The judge is with another couple just now, but you may—"

Nicholas pushed past the man without ceremony, taking Juliette with him by the simple expedient of a hand at her elbow. She went willingly enough, for she had caught the low murmur of voices from what appeared to be the front parlor that opened off a long entrance hall in the American fashion. The double doors were flung wide. They stepped inside without pausing.

It was a large room, plastered and painted white above its wainscoting and set about with a number of settees, chairs and tables in comfortable arrangements upon a Brussels carpet. In one corner sat a pianoforte with a woman, doubtless the judge's wife, seated on the stool before it with her hands lifted as if about to play. A cheery fire of logs burned in the large fireplace, and it was here that the judge stood with his back to the flames and a couple facing him. The gentleman of the pair was tall and somewhat damp. The lady was soignée and exceedingly à la mode, in pale blue silk trimmed in lace. Next to her, in place of an attendant, stood a boy whose coat and pantaloons, though clean, appeared to have been tailored for a considerably larger child.

At their sudden entry, the judge looked up briefly from the book in his hand, then returned his attention to the page at hand and completed the sentence he had begun. Then he closed the volume with precision.

They were too late. The vows had just been finalized, judging from the triumphant color in Paulette's face and the satisfaction in Daspit's eyes. Juliette gave them only the barest of glances, however.

"*Maman!*"

Gabriel, breaking free of Paulette's grip, ran pell-mell toward Juliette. She went to one knee, her skirts pooling around her as she caught the boy. She hugged his small body close while a hard lump formed in her throat and she felt almost boneless with relief. She had not known until this moment how afraid she had been she would never see him again, or just how much it would have hurt her to lose him.

"Are you all right?" she inquired in an urgent undertone as she brushed over his back and arms, noting that his clothes were surprisingly dry.

"But yes! We ride in boat. Mam'zelle Paulette was sick. She cry and cry, say she not marry, no, not without pretty clothes. We go to big house. I haf' sweet drink and the boy who lives there gave me this to wear." He pulled at his small frock coat made in imitation of a grown gentleman's. "I handsome, yes?"

"Indeed," Juliette said, her voice not quite steady as she ruffled his hair and smiled into his eyes, "very handsome."

Paulette took a step toward Juliette and the boy, speaking with her chin held high. "If you thought to spoil our marriage by coming after us, my dear sister, you are too late."

"So I see." Juliette climbed to her feet with the aid of Nicholas's arm but did not relinquish her hold on Gabriel. "Are you sure this is what you wanted? Only think of *Maman.*"

Paulette moistened her lips, glancing at her new husband. "It had to be this way. You gave us no other choice."

"But of course she wished to be married," Daspit declared, bristling. "Why else would she be in Gretna?"

"Truly, *chère?*" Juliette asked, taking a step closer.

Paulette's face lost some of its color. "Yes, of course. Oh, not like this, but what does it matter? It's all the same in the end."

Nicholas spoke then. "What just took place was merely a civil ceremony. Without consummation or the sanction of the church, an annulment would be an easy matter."

"Don't listen to them," Daspit said. "They are only after the chest."

"I promise that isn't it." Juliette barely glanced at him, but held her sister's green gaze.

"Then you willingly give it up now that we are the first to wed?"

"As to that…"

"You see?" Daspit's laugh held a wealth of scorn.

"I only meant to say it isn't up to me. *Maman* must choose. But if you will come away with us at once, Paulette, then it may be possible no whisper of this escapade will ever be heard. It will be as if the vows never took place."

Paulette looked from Juliette to Nicholas then to her groom. Finally, she turned to the judge. "Monsieur?"

That dignitary cleared his throat with a rasp, glancing at his wife, who rose from the pianoforte and came to stand at his side. "It can be a solution for those few times when either bride or groom turn out to be unwilling. Yes, or when they discover they didn't know their own minds."

Paulette faced forward again. "But I do know my mind. Monsieur Daspit and I are legally wed, and so we will stay!"

"Consider carefully, mademoiselle," Nicholas urged, "before you go so far you can't—"

"Stand back," Daspit said. A small pistol suddenly appeared in his hand, snatched from his waistcoat pocket behind the cover of Paulette's caped form. Its tiny black bore was centered on Nicholas. "You tried once to remove me as a groom, but there will be no chance of it this time. We are leaving, my bride and I. Get in the way and it will be the worse for you."

Daspit's progress put him next to the window that looked out onto the front verandah. Juliette caught a flicker of movement behind the draperies that closed out the winter night. An instant later, they parted and a melodious, mocking voice fell on the air.

"Ah, sweet love, let us celebrate its glories, singing a psalm of soft and gentle wooing—or marriage, whatever your pleasure. But not of murder, I think, unless the groom dotes on the taste of steel."

It was Blackford, batting aside the velvet drapes

so he sat framed in their folds, one leg over the windowsill with his hip resting on the frame, a whimsical smile on his face and the shining blade of his sword cane resting at the base of Daspit's neck. Juliette distinctly heard Paulette's gasp of shock and the small scream of the judge's wife, even as she drew air sharply into her own lungs.

Daspit whispered a curse, his eyes wide. "What is it to you, Englishman?"

"A bagatelle, really—except that it offends me when my friends are held in danger by a fool with the ripe smell of mistakes and Tivoli mischief about him. Drop the pistol."

Blackford's voice carried deadly intention beneath its musical timbre, but Daspit chose to ignore it. "Remove your sword if you care for your friend."

"Pull that trigger," Blackford said gently, "and I will core your miserable neck with this blade like a gardener looking for apple seeds. It will not be bloodless."

That reached Daspit, for a grimace of frustration crossed his face. After an instant, he lowered his arm a fraction, then a little more. Juliette allowed herself to breathe, but Blackford's grasp on his sword with its point resting just above Daspit's cravat remained steady.

"Be calm, my friend," Daspit rasped as he released the pistol's cocked hammer once it was pointed toward the floor. "I seem to have made an error in judgment. My lamentable temper and the heat of the moment, you know. I must beg the forgiveness of everyone present, including my lady-wife."

The words were smooth enough, but Daspit's face was the color of a ripe plum and the look in his eyes murderous. It was an expedient apology, an unvarnished attempt to regain the ground lost by his show of force. Juliette didn't trust it, but before she could open her lips to say so, Paulette spoke in a rush.

"Of course I forgive you, *mon chéri!* You were overwrought, as who would not be. But we have won, we are the first to wed, even if no one else ever knows. We have only to go and tell *Maman*, then we can be married in the cathedral at our leisure."

She was right, as even Juliette had to admit. The deed was done, and there was no point in denying it. "I came after you, in large part, to act as chaperone for your return. It might be best if we all went back together."

"So I would act the chaperone for you as well?"

"I suppose."

"But all of us in one boat would be horribly crowded. No, I am now a married lady so have no need of a duenna. Monsieur Daspit has made arrangements for us, and we may as well use them."

"But, *chère*," Juliette said urgently. "Be sensible, I beg you."

"Sensible like you? I don't believe you can claim

to be a pattern card of behavior any longer. Only look at you, here at night in company with two gentlemen instead of merely one."

If only she had the means to coerce her sister, Juliette thought. But no one had forced Paulette to bow to their will in her life. "You will go straight home in the morning?"

"Assuredly. As fast as we can go."

"Gabriel remains with us."

Paulette glanced at Daspit, who merely shrugged. "You are quite welcome to him," she said as she turned back to Juliette. "We only brought him because it seemed that searching for him would draw attention away from our departure."

Juliette wasn't sure which angered her more, that the child had been dragged out in such inclement weather for so paltry a reason or Paulette's failure to recognize what she had done. The words clipped, she said, "Then you must do as you please, as always."

Paulette lifted her chin while a rose flush sat on her cheekbones. "I intended nothing else."

She moved ahead of Daspit out into the wide hallway and along it to the entrance door. The rest of them moved after the two, reaching the front porch in time to see them dash out into the rain and through the gate to where the horse and wagon was tied up at the hitching post. Daspit handed Paulette up onto the backseat, then shouted an order to the driver.

Nicholas started forward, calling, "Wait. That's our wagon!"

"It was yours while you hired it. Now it is mine." Daspit swung up onto the wagon seat before looking down at him. "There is one other consequence of this evening, Pasquale. My seconds will call on yours tomorrow."

Nicholas, standing with his hands on his hips, gave a brief nod. There was no time for more. The driver snatched his whip from its holder and cracked it above his horse's head. The animal lunged into the traces. Paulette screamed and grabbed for Daspit's arm. The vehicle spun away, throwing up water from the ruts in the drive as it disappeared into the rain-splattered night.

Monsieur Daspit had just challenged Nicholas. Juliette stood there, still clinging to Gabriel's hand, while the knowledge sank into her mind. It had been done with scant manners and little grace, in front of her, Paulette and even the judge's wife. There were those who would scorn him for that, but all she could think of was the fact of it. Daspit had challenged Nicholas, and that meant that he must know he had been injured, must be aware that he had less than his usual skill with a sword.

Daspit intended to take advantage of Nicholas's weakness. He meant to be avenged for the injury he was so sure he had suffered at the sword master's hands.

Juliette had been expecting this for days, from the moment she had met Nicholas Pasquale and taken him to meet her family. It had been inevitable, a product of his profession and the nature of disagreements between gentlemen in the city. It was almost a relief not to have to fear it any longer.

"What a pity," Blackford said, "that I didn't slit his throat while I had the chance."

"An efficient end, but where would be the sport in it?" Nicholas asked, his gaze thoughtful as he stared down the road where the faint rattling of the wagon could be heard in the distance.

"Oh, it's sport you require? If only you had told me, I could have left you to dodge his shot for the fun of it."

Nicholas gave him a straight look. "Worried, *mon ami?*"

"Annoyed. I don't like acting as second in wet boots. Or hadn't you noticed that we're now afoot?"

"I believe the couple walked here," the judge's wife put in then, "possibly from Widow Burlington's rooming house. Some mention was made of them putting up there."

"Yes, for Paulette to change into her bridal finery," Juliette murmured, thinking as she spoke that the pair had undoubtedly intended to return there for their wedding night. The same realization was reflected in Nicholas's eyes, she thought as she glanced in his direction. Or perhaps not, since he

had problems somewhat greater than her sister's seduction to consider.

"Your honor," he said to the judge, "if we might
prevail upon you to take out your carriage, we would
be most grateful."

The Scots gentleman spread his hands. "My
apologies, sir, but I have none. My good wife and I
seldom venture beyond where our two feet or a river-
boat may take us."

"Direct me to the nearest livery stable, and I'll
arrange transportation," Blackford said. "Though
why I must wade through heaven's tears for it is
beyond me. The ideal solution, as I see it, would be
to put up some other rooming house for the night
and cross the river again in the morning."

"Unacceptable," Nicholas said shortly.

"Because you and the lady are not yet one in
heart, mind and body? The remedy is at hand."
Blackford smiled with infinite charm at the judge's
wife. "What say you, my lady? Is another wedding
one too many? Would your honored husband not tie
the knot for these two?"

"I'm sure he would," the lady said, dimpling under
the Englishman's charm while approval chased the
shadow caused by the confrontation from her eyes.

The judge gave a decided nod. "I should be
honored—particularly as I have serious doubts of any
boatman being persuaded to cross the river again
tonight. You will all have to take shelter. Mrs. Clancy

keeps a respectable establishment a few doors down from the widow's where the others are staying."

Satisfaction shone in Blackford's eyes. "You see? Wed now, rise early, and you may still be the first to reach Madame Armant with news of your nuptials."

"That wasn't our purpose," Nicholas said shortly.

"But why waste the opportunity? The gossips will get wind of this, you know—in fact, Daspit may use it to cloud the issue of his own elopement. You could make wise fact of wicked slander."

"Playing cupid, *mon ami?*"

Blackford tipped his head as if amused by the severity in Nicholas's face. "It seems someone must."

"Don't, please. It's been discussed between the lady and myself and dismissed."

"Wait," Juliette said. Her heart was beating against her ribs like a wild thing trying to escape. Opposing impulses clashed in her mind, threatening to tear it apart. How she dared to speak, she wasn't sure, still less did she know how to put what she wanted to say.

"*Chère?*" Nicholas's eyes were curiously blank as he glanced in her direction.

She turned toward him with one hand still holding Gabriel's small one and the other clenched at her side. "Monsieur Blackford is right. Monsieur Daspit has proven that he cannot be trusted to allow this affair of the chest to end as it should. A Gretna wedding was his idea, and it seems just that he should be defeated by it. It may be that *Maman* will allow our birth order to decide ownership of the chest, as it should, if both Paulette and I present ourselves as wed on the same night." She hesitated then went on with difficulty. "That is, of course, if you have not changed your mind."

His smile was brief and his voice quiet as he said, "It will not avert the duel, you know."

He understood her far too well, but what did she expect? "I am aware."

"I could not accept your sacrifice for such a reason."

"It would not be only for that." What she thought but could not say was that marriage between them would make it less likely Jean Daspit would seek to kill rather than merely repair his honor with a show of blood. But that was not all. "I seem to have discovered in myself a great reluctance to return to the convent at my sister's will. And need I remind you that you gave your word?"

"Never, *chérie*."

His voice seemed to resonate inside her, setting off vibrations so deep in her heart she thought they might never end. She nodded, moistened her lips. "Then if you have no objection, and the judge is willing, I should be pleased to marry you now."

Nicholas watched her a long moment, the dark depths of his eyes swirling with hidden thoughts, hidden inclinations. "You are certain?"

"I believe so."

"There will be no regrets?"

She shook her head as she whispered, "None that matter."

A smile softened the stern lines of his mouth, rising slowly to light the rich brown depths of his eyes. In it was the same reckless defiance with which he had faced the danger of the river. "Then I have no objection," he said softly. "None at all."

17

It took scant minutes to speak their wedding vows. When they were done, Juliette could not have told how they had been phrased or what she had said in answer. She recalled Blackford standing up beside Nicholas and with Gabriel next to her, remembered holding tightly to Nicholas's hand and also the warm and steady look in his eyes as he turned to her and pledged his troth, but nothing else. She smiled and sipped the wine offered by the judge and his wife, accepted the congratulations of Blackford and the tight hug given to her by Gabriel. She heard the rain that tapped against the brim of her bonnet as she walked the short distance to the rooming house on Nicholas's arm while Blackford trailed after, shielding Gabriel under his cloak. She climbed the steps that lead to the door, allowed the scrutiny of the rotund Irish lady who met them with a lamp held high to see their faces, and went without protest to the room they were allotted. She heard Blackford say that he and Gabriel, yawning mightily from the effects of excitement and watered wine, would take their rest in a small bedchamber just down the central hall. Then she was inside the room she and Nicholas had been given, standing in its center while he locked the door behind them.

It was a pleasant enough room, clean, neat with plain furniture obviously made—with more practicality than artistry—from the cypress so abundant in the swamps behind the town. A rocking chair sat in a corner beside a simple, four-square armoire and a rag rug lay alongside the bed. The covers were turned back to reveal fresh linen sheets folded down over a quilt in a star pattern while another lay across the foot of the bed. A pitcher and bowl sat on a washstand, which doubtless hid the inevitable slop jar.

There were no flowers, no tray of delicacies to tempt nervous palates and provide distraction from the purpose of the chamber, no tester bed inset with a bridal *ciel de lit* in celestial blue silk to symbolize the heavenly pleasures now allowed them as a wedded couple.

There had been no altar or candles or sonorous prayers for their fruitfulness and a happy life, nothing except a brief ceremony she could barely recall. Yet the deed was done, she was married.

It didn't seem real. There should have been more to it somehow, considering the enormous change in her circumstances.

Juliette shivered then could not seem to stop shaking. It was her damp clothes and the chill night, she thought, added to the events of the evening. It had nothing to do with being alone with her new husband. Nothing at all.

A fire had been laid in the fireplace. Nicholas moved to light it, using a spill that he held in the flame from the lamp until it caught. The kindling flared up quickly with the black smoke and odor of pine pitch. He knelt on the hearth, rearranging the larger sticks of wood above the blaze. She moved to stand at his shoulder, leaning to hold out her hands to the heat.

He glanced at her and a soft exclamation left him. Rising with lithe strength, he took her trembling hands, enclosing them in his, chafing them a little. "You're freezing, *chère*. I should have known. Come, get out of your wet things before you catch your death."

"I have no maid," she said, giving him a small smile without quite meeting his eyes, "and there are dozens of buttons."

"You have me."

The words were matter-of-fact, as if he played maid to ladies every day. Perhaps he did. How was she to know? "Yes, but…"

"You need not fear I'll be overcome with passion the instant I see an inch of bare skin," he said, his smile droll. "A wife who shivers at my touch holds no great attraction, I assure you."

"No, and it isn't you, really it isn't. I mean to say—"

"I know what you mean. Quickly now, make a start while I go and see if our hostess has anything stronger than a dish of tea in the house. I could use a brandy myself."

Juliette had no idea whether his errand was real or an excuse to give her a moment to collect herself. Whatever the purpose, she was glad of it. When the door closed behind him, she stripped off her gloves and removed her bonnet, then unfastened her cloak and laid it over a chair drawn up to the fire in hope that it might dry before morning. Stepping out of her half boots, she stood on first one foot and then the other while she peeled her damp stockings and garters down her legs and draped them with the cloak. She was standing with her back to the fire and her skirts held high enough to allow heat to reach her cold thighs when she heard footsteps outside the door. Hastily, she dropped the layers of cloth and spun around.

Amusement touched Nicholas's lips as his gaze lingered on the hem of her gown that was flipped up in the back. He made no comment however, not even as she batted it back into place, but closed the door behind him and moved forward with a tray balanced on his right palm. On it sat a pair of pewter pots, a squat bottle and two cups.

"Blackford was before me, it seems. He had

already convinced our landlady to make coffee for him and heat milk for Gabriel."

"I see you found the brandy, too," she said, her voice husky.

"It isn't exactly the finest cognac but should serve the purpose."

She was not quite sure what that purpose might be, but made no objection as he poured hot coffee and milk into both the cups, added a generous amount of sugar, then topped off the cups with brandy. Her cup, as she took it from him, was gratifyingly warm and she held it between her palms a long moment before sipping from it.

The brandy had bite to it, taking her breath. "Strong," she said in strangled comment.

"With good reason." He downed his in three swallows and set his cup aside, then touched her arm with its cold sleeve. "Turn around."

She met his gaze for a long moment, but saw little there except kindness and concern. If desire lurked in those dark depths, it was rigorously controlled. Revolving slowly, she put her back was to him. She drank from her cup once more, then stood staring down into it. After an instant, she felt his fingers moving with nimble precision on the buttons strung down her back. They brushed against her skin, bringing a rash of prickling goose bumps and tightness to her nipples, but if he noticed, he gave no sign. It was difficult to keep her breathing even, impossible to control the tremors that rippled over her. As her bodice loosened, she put a hand to her chest to prevent it from falling forward while she stood as still as possible, staring at the floor.

"Only a moment more," he said.

Only a moment more, and she would stand before him in her corset and pantaloons. Then he would need to loosen her corset strings before she could unhook it. "I'm sorry the button loops are so damp and stiff."

He gave a low laugh. "I seem to be all thumbs."

It didn't feel at all that way to her. He seemed quite adept, in fact. A frown creased the skin between her eyebrows. It was hardly flattering that he was so unnoticing, so unaffected. She was not quite sure what she had expected in the way of a prelude to bridal chamber initiation, but it certainly seemed something was lacking.

His hands were at her waist now, tugging at the damp strings of her corset. She drew a deep breath to tighten her abdomen then let it out involuntarily an instant later as she was freed of the whalebone constriction.

"You can handle the rest, I think," he said, his voice sounding a little odd.

She murmured her agreement and was glad when he turned away toward the bed. Hurriedly, she unhooked the front of the corset, though she was aware even so of him taking the extra quilt from the bed and draping it over his arm. He paused long enough to drag the rest of the cover to the foot of the bed, and then walked toward the fireplace while unfolding the quilt he carried. There, he stood holding it before the flames, keeping his back to her.

Juliette drank the last of her brandied coffee and set the cup on the lamp table. She skimmed from her corset and corset cover and crossed her arms over her bare breasts as she looked toward the bed, wondering if she could get beneath the covers before divesting herself of her pantaloons, shedding that last bit of modesty.

"Here," Nicholas said.

Before she could move or guess his intention, he stepped close to wrap her in the folds of the quilt he had heated. Then he bent to put one arm under her knees and the other across her back and lifted her in his arms, swinging toward the bed.

Juliette's head spun dizzily at the sudden movement while she shivered at the sudden heat against her chilled flesh. She tried to clutch his coat but her hands were trapped in the quilt's folds. She seemed bereft of speech or even sound as he strode to place her on the mattress. Reaching inside the quilt then, he skimmed his hands around her waist to find the tapes that held her pantaloons. Tugging loose their knotted bow, he stripped that last garment down her legs and whipped it away, leaving her naked within her warm cocoon.

It was done so quickly that there was no time to protest, certainly no time to stop him. She wasn't sure she would have done either in any case. He was her husband; it was his right to have her naked in his bed if that was his wish. More that that, she was grateful to him, in an odd way, for making it so simple.

The heat of the quilt seeped into her skin in a highly gratifying manner and she snuggled into it with a sense of luxuriant, almost languid ease. Small shivers still chased along her nerves, and she felt a little disoriented from the quickness with which she had downed the brandy-laced café au lait, but her embarrassed disquiet was receding, replaced by burgeoning curiosity.

What would Nicholas do next? How would they proceed in this unconventional marriage?

She had not long to find out. Nicholas turned to blow out the lamp, then began to strip off his own wet clothing. She should close her eyes, she thought, or at least veil her gaze with her lashes. Somehow, her lids would not obey her command but stayed wide open as he prepared to join her.

Coat, cravat, shirt, boots, all were flung off with quick efficiency. His pantaloons were unfastened, lowered to rest on his hip bones, then skimmed off with his unmentionables so he was left in firelight-gilded nudity. The glow of the flames licked along the muscular turning of his arms and wide shoulders, slid across the broad expanse of his chest with its narrow white wrapping of bandage, limned his hard flanks with startling fidelity as he turned toward the bed. Then it outlined him in statuesque and powerful silhouette as he climbed with pantherlike grace to its high surface and dragged up the sheet and top quilt before settling beside her.

She would have moved over to make room for him, but he would not have it. Reaching for her, instead, he gathered her close against him, tucking her head under his chin.

"Are you all right?" he asked, a quiet murmur that she felt as a warm breath in the center parting of her hair.

She gave a jerky nod but could not quite find her voice.

"It will be better soon." As if noticing the cool dampness of her high-piled tresses, he lifted an arm and began to probe the curling mass, finding and removing pins that he secreted under the pillow they were not using, uncoiling the long strands and spreading them around her.

The surface of his skin was cold, if not his hands; she could feel its chill through the layers of quilted cloth that separated them. Struggling to free one hand, she reached to touch his side, gliding her fingers around to his back and hugging him closer.

Abruptly, he was still. "Juliette…"

"You're freezing, too. You should share the heat."

Wry concern feathered his voice as he shook his head. "The trouble is that you might warm me too much."

"You mean…more than you would like?"

"More than you might be ready to accept."

An odd rashness rose inside her. It came in large part, she thought, from the knowledge that he must face Daspit soon on the dueling field with death the possible outcome. This could be the only time they would have. "And if I said that was unlikely?"

He began to rake his fingers through her hair with gentle care, smoothing the tresses that were dryer where they had been protected by her bonnet. "I would have to question if you know what you're saying."

"I know." Her voice was clear as she spread her hand, feeling the slow glide of his back muscles under her palm.

"If I…if we take this step," he said, a warning note in the deep timbre of his voice, "there will be less chance of an annulment."

"I had not thought of one."

"You're quite certain?"

"Never more so in my life."

His movements stilled. His voice when he spoke was a rough-edged and deep against her ear. "Then God must guard me from making a mistake, for from this moment you will never more be a bride of Christ but mine and mine alone."

The possessive undertone, as fierce as a vow, sent a small thrill through her. He was not as unaffected as he pretended, or as without concern. He thought to save her from the consequences of her actions tonight, but the truth was that she didn't care to be saved. She wanted to experience love with a man, to touch and be touched; she wanted to belong to Nicholas Pasquale in something more than name. She wanted everything that went with the wedding vows she had spoken, and could not bear to be denied.

"And you will be my husband," she said clearly.

He reached to slip his hand inside the quilt in which she was wrapped, gliding his spread fingers over her hip while the folds of heavy cloth rested on his shoulder. Then he lofted its weight and slid closer, melding his body to hers from chest to knees. With a wrench of hard muscles, he turned then, taking her with him so she sprawled across him in shocking contact with the heat and strutted firmness of his lower body. Once more he shifted, carrying her to her back again so they were trapped inside the warm, quilted cocoon with him looming above her, supporting his weight on his elbows with one knee between her thighs and one arm still behind her back. Long strands of her hair now coiled around his neck and over his shoulder like silken ropes holding him captive, but he seemed not to notice. He gazed down at her, his face shadowed in the faint red glow from the fire. Then his mouth curved in a slow smile edged with heated promise.

Juliette's heart beat with such hard strokes that she thought he must be able to feel it while her every breath pressed her breasts against the muscle-wrapped planes of his chest. Small tremors still shook her, though she was no longer cold but rather felt the slow rise of febrile excitement.

"You need have no fear of me," Nicholas said in low reassurance. "I won't hurt you."

"I'm not afraid, only…"

"You have heard stories of a woman's first time, perhaps? There are ways to avoid most, almost all, of the pain."

"No, no. It's just that I…I have no experience."

His voice was grave but a smile lingered in his eyes as shook his head. "A situation soon remedied."

"But you have had so many women. I may not please you."

"You please me in so many ways already that I can't think how you could fail. But you terrify me with these expectations of greatness as lover. There have not been that many ladies."

"Your repute as a Casanova—"

"Greatly exaggerated, I fear, and only because I am often abroad at night."

On errands for the Brotherhood, she thought he meant. She didn't quite believe him though she saluted his effort to relieve her mind. She lowered her lashes while brushing with one fingertip at the crisp hair that grew in the hollow of his throat. "Still, you must tell me what to do."

"Do whatever you like, *chérie*. There are no rules except to give and to take pleasure."

"That's all?"

His smile was wryly amused, perhaps at her persistence. "Well, almost all."

"You will teach me the rest?"

"It will be my honor, and my very great privilege."

She traced a path up the strong column of his neck and over the jut of his chin to the ridge of his lower lip and the smooth surface it edged. It may have been the brandy talking, but she asked then in soft anticipation, "Where do I start?"

His half-smothered exclamation was a warm breath across her knuckle. He reached to catch her hand, brushing her fingers with his lips before meshing them with his own and drawing them up to rest on the pillow beside her cheek. Slowly, holding her gaze, he lowered his head until his mouth touched hers.

He tasted of coffee and brandy and carnal intentions held in check only by determined chivalry. His movements unhurried, he tasted her, tempted her until she opened her lips to him, then he wooed her tongue to dance with his in swirling, sinuous rhythm.

It was a delicious invasion. A soft sound of wordless pleasure vibrated in her throat. Warmth rose from deep inside her, flooding her with vital heat. She surrendered to it, reveling in the sureness of her own acceptance. What she was doing seemed so right, so inevitable.

Nicholas lifted his head an instant to stare down at her. She could see herself reflected in the darkness of his eyes, along with satisfaction and something so intent that it was almost like pain.

There was nothing at all to fear.

She smiled and allowed her eyelids to drift closed while she waited. His mouth came down on hers once more and she met it, her own lips tingling, ready. Enthralled, she allowed herself to be drawn into delicate exploration of the rich inner textures and sweetness of his mouth, the velvet and satin of his tongue. The intimacy was absorbing, enticing. She savored the multiplying sensations inside her in silent wonder as she felt the expansion of her heart in her chest.

He shifted, releasing her hand, sliding his palm down over the curve of her shoulder to cup, then capture, the soft mound of her breast. His thumb glided across the sensitive peak with sure strokes, inciting it to pebbled hardness.

Currents of exquisite sensation rippled through Juliette to gather in the center of her body. She stiffened as she felt its deep internal pulsing. Nicholas made a soft sound, like a cross between a laugh and a groan, then lowered his mouth to the berrylike nipple of her swelling breast.

The grainy stroking of his tongue made her senses whirl. She slid her arm along his shoulders to his neck, holding tightly. As sensations uncurled, threatening to sweep her away, she arched, offering herself to the hot caress of his lips and tongue. And the wanton intent of that instinct sent such a rush of desire through her that she caught her breath with its strength.

Nicholas shifted again, wedging his body more closely between her thighs. She accepted more of his weight as he traced a slow path of kisses from one nipple, around its gentle mound and into the valley that rose between it and the other. Settling on the opposite peak, he suckled it with gentle adhesion. The fascinated pleasure he seemed to glean from it increased her own a hundredfold, while his position between her legs, holding them open, was gratifying in some odd way she could hardly accept, much less understand. She felt so vulnerable with the heat and hardness of him pressing against the sensitive inner surfaces of her thighs yet she had also never felt stronger. The intense need that raced in her veins was a glory she could not contain, one she wanted to share. The longing overflowed inside her, suffusing her with a yearning so achingly poignant that it might almost be taken for love.

Could that be? Had she come to love him so quickly? Was this match sanctified by the Holy Mother, a joining of souls as well as bodies and lives?

She wanted to think so, needed to in some manner she refused to acknowledge, even to herself. To grasp and hold that possibility added a rich depth of sensation to the fervor that consumed her. It allowed her to open to him, trusting, heart battering against her rib cage, as he skimmed his warm palm over her belly and downward to close his careful hold on the very center of her being.

His concentration seemed total as he probed the tender folds, his left-handed touch amazingly dexterous, sure and capable but delicate in its invasion. He soothed, testing while the heel of his hand made small circles at the apex of the mound where it rested. He reached deeper, moving his wrist in gentle abrasion and patient, almost rapt concentration.

"*Mon Dieu,*" he whispered, his breath feathering over her strutted breast, his lips brushing its sensitized surface. "You are like warm silk, so deliciously smooth. I could…"

"Could what?" she asked in ragged query as he ground to a halt, even as she threaded her fingers through his hair with feverish strokes.

"Take you here and never let you go, lie locked inside you, buried as deep as I can go in that velvety warmth, until time spins to its shabby end."

He had not stilled his infinitely gentle penetration, the cautious stretching that she sensed was necessary, yet she suspected was so seldom received. It was that care, that concern along with his words, which affected her with such gladness that her heart contracted and her body overflowed his clever fingers with hot liquid like a river breaching at a crevasse.

"Then do," she said in breathless near incoherence. "Please do."

He did as she asked, easing his way with care and the most intimate of caresses as he positioned his satinlike hardness at the hot, silken opening in the notch of her thighs. With infinite restraint and tensile strength, he eased deeper. The inner barrier, so painstakingly prepared, was reached so she felt a small sting . He breached it then with quick and beneficent ruthlessness. She gave a small cry, but it was for the sudden, plundering sensation rather than any real pain. He filled her with his throbbing length, and she felt some deep expansion as she accepted him into her melting, internal heat.

The gratification of it was so intense that she felt transfigured, incredibly alive. Her heart beat like a marching drum; tears sprang to her eyes. She wanted to cry aloud, to laugh, or both. She brushed her hands along his taut arms, wanting, needing something to hold on to to steady her world.

"Does it pain you?" he asked, his voice strained. She could feel the long length that throbbed inside of her with every beat of his heart, but he was not hurting her. She moved her head on the pillow in quick, decided negative.

"Then let me pleasure you," he replied.

"More?" Disbelief was in that single word.

A low laugh shook his chest. "I've only begun."

He was right.

With a gathering of hard swordsman muscles, he began to move in deliberate rhythm. The cadence took him deeper, brought a flush of heat to her skin, sent the blood surging through her veins. She caught her breath, spreading her hands over his chest, avoiding the linen bandage but raking her nails through the finely curling hair there before grasping handfuls of the muscular flesh just below his waist to hold tight. In a blinding instant of total accord, she found the motion he set and joined it, panting with effort, her skin prickling with incredible delight. He bent his neck, kissing her forehead, her eyes, the tip of nose before taking her mouth. There he mimicked the same sensual advance and retreat with his tongue while she invited him deeper and ever deeper.

It was primal need and startling discovery. It was endless erotic fascination. Time receded, leaving only the two of them locked in dark grandeur.

He slowed, then, entangling his legs with hers, rolled with her to bring her up on top of him again. With his callused fingers pressing into the firm flesh of her hips, he guided her for an instant then set her free. She adjusted her position, found the perfect joining. It was amazing, the sudden increase in sensation. She never wanted it to end. Her movements grew faster, more definite. He joined her, surging up to meet her, giving her the greater friction she craved. Flinging back her hair that swirled around her, she rode him to the wild tempo that pounded in her blood.

Effort made their bodies gleam with heat and moisture. Their breaths rasped in their chest. Merciless, untiring, they strained toward a goal and an end that neither truly wanted to reach. Not yet. Not yet.

Juliette could feel its approach, feel the pressure and force of it. Her muscles ached, her lungs burned but she could not quite find that final touch mark.

With a quiet exclamation, Nicholas turned with her once more, pressing her down onto the mattress. She took his deep internal invasion as he drove into her, accepted, demanded his surging control.

Perfect consummation caught them in midflight. It was a silent completion, an internal turning like a key in its lock. Shuddering with the sweet inevitability of it, she clung to him. His muscles knotted, his back arched with the internal eruption and its pulsing aftermath. He caught her to him while the glorious fury took them.

Long moments later, Nicholas eased from her and

turned to his back, drawing her into the crook of his arm with her cheek pillowed on his shoulder. Their breathing quieted and the heat of their bodies dissipated. As the coolness of the room reached them, Nicholas drew up the quilt and other covers that had somehow been dislodged, tucking the edges around her neck. She pushed a layer over his exposed shoulder, then lay still.

There were no words. What could they say?

The fire burned down to a red glow and then became gray ash, leaving the room in darkness. Nicholas finally slept, Juliette thought. She lay staring at nothing, endlessly smoothing a wrinkle in the sheet, replete but thinking of many things while listening to the even and steady beat of her new husband's gallant heart.

He was a passionate and possessive man, and a caring one. They were well-suited, so it seemed, in the bedchamber. He valued her as the center of his future home; she was convenient for his purpose, even if he could not love her. She was pleased, even thrilled, to be his wife.

Was it enough? Could she use these things to make a life for herself with him and the street boys he had collected around him?

Yet what was the point in asking? She no longer had a choice.

Not now. Surely not now.

18

Nicholas went from deepest sleep to fully awake in a single instant. He knew immediately what had roused him, a single touch, a small hand laid on the bandaging that circled his chest. Turning his head on the pillow, he smiled into the green-brown mystery of Juliette's eyes where she leaned over him, watching him in the soft morning light.

"Good morning, Madame Pasquale."

No answering smile warmed her face. "You're bleeding," she said in tones that had a remarkably accusing sound.

"Are you sure it's me?" He threw back the cover to glance over the sheet on which they lay.

"It isn't me—at least, not the worst of it." Wild rose color crept, intriguingly, from under the top sheet she held to her breasts and up her neck to ride her cheekbones. "Your bandage is soaked."

That was something of an exaggeration he saw when he lifted his arm away from his side, but still he had undoubtedly reopened the damnable slit between his armpit and his ribs. "So it is. I'm sorry that you had to sleep in my gore."

A scowl, almost wifely in nature, drew her eyebrows together. "As if that mattered! But we should see to it."

He could grow accustomed to the concern that shadowed her features, he thought. Much too easily. "We?"

"Unless you believe a doctor is required?"

"I'm sure we can manage if we sacrifice my cravat."

"Or my petticoat, though neither may be necessary. I expect our landlady has worn-out linens that may serve." She turned away as if to slide from the bed. "She's awake. I heard someone go out to the kitchen just now."

Nicholas put his hand on her arm to stop her. "I'll go. Dressing will be faster for me."

She looked as if she might argue but he didn't wait to hear it. What he thought, but did not say, was that his absence would give her time to at least don her underclothing without his presence. Much as he hated to miss that procedure, and perhaps assist in it, he had no wish to force upon her a depth of familiarity she might find uncomfortable. There would be time enough for that in the days ahead as they grew more used to each other. Besides, he had little dependence on his ability to leave her untouched long enough for her dress. He had taxed her more than he should during the night, waking her a scant hour after they had first made love and again at the dawn. The dark half circles under her eyes were a silent reproach to him.

Mrs. Clancy exclaimed over his request and offered her services as well as a pail of hot water and roll of old and soft linen sheeting. She seemed to understand perfectly, however, when he said he rather preferred the ministrations of his new bride.

And it was pleasant to sit while Juliette ran a warm cloth over his skin to remove the dried crusts of blood, also while her unbound hair trailed, tickling, over his arm and he inhaled its scent that was compounded of lavender soap, river water and her own sweet essence. Even so, it tried his self-control to the limit, given his close view of the tender curves of her breasts only half concealed by her corset cover with its lace-edged straps.

"Must you go through with this meeting with Monsieur Daspit?" she asked while rolling a strip of linen around his ribs.

"You know I cannot withdraw with honor. Besides, there is no cause."

"But you are hurt!"

"It's nothing. You must know that since you saw it." He could have reminded her that Daspit had been injured not so long ago as well, but that might curtail her lovely concern.

Her chin took on a stubborn tilt. "It looks like something to me."

"I've fenced, and fought, with worse." He tried to see her face as she bent over him, but she would not look at him.

"Not against someone who might prefer to kill you instead of merely trying for first blood."

She was wrong there, but past duels had no bearing just now. "What makes you say so?"

"I fear...I think I may have made it necessary by insisting that we go ahead with this marriage," she said as she tied a flat knot in the bandaging then retreated a step. "My mother will be confused and upset over this Gretna escape of both of her daughters. It occurs to me that she may postpone her decision over the chest until after the duel to make certain one of us has not been left a widow. All I may have done is give Monsieur Daspit a reason to...to permanently remove you."

He reached to put a finger under her chin, turning her face up so she was forced to meet his eyes. "That may be true, *chère*, but he has first to dispose of me. And I assure you I am in no hurry to give up my position as your husband."

She gave a small shake of her head. "If I had not been so sure it was for the best—"

"Then I would have been bereft."

She blinked but did not look away. "Truly? You aren't sorry? You don't regret your freedom?"

"Is this another dread possibility that you woke with this morning?"

"I suppose."

"Truly," he said in grave answer, "I am not and do not."

Her lips formed a wobbly smile that was more than he could resist. He pulled her down onto his lap and prepared to show her exactly how happy he was to be a wedded man. What more he might have done, he could say, for the door burst open at that moment and Gabriel came running toward them, crowing his delight at finding them. Blackford was close behind him, but halted in the doorway and turned his back at the first glimpse of Juliette in her state of near undress.

"A thousand pardons," he said over his shoulder, though with bright laughter threading his voice. "Intruding in a nuptial chamber is for children and fools, and I don't, unfortunately, have Gabriel's excuse."

"But you had his lead as anyone can see," Nicholas allowed with wry humor as Juliette slipped off his lap to catch the boy and return his enthusiastic hug. "Give us a moment, and we will join you for coffee and rolls in our hostess's kitchen."

"We should leave immediately afterward for the dock. I have Samson waiting with the boat, a consequence of sharing a bed with a combination kicking mule and crowing rooster in boy's form. An early start seemed best since my duties as your chief second may require more time this morning than finesse."

"You did volunteer for that honor last night, didn't you? Did I accept?"

"You were too preoccupied for it at the time."

"Then I do so now with gratitude."

"Having exhausted those who usually stand in such stead for you, I see."

"Not at all." Nicholas allowed coolness to enter his voice at the unwelcome suggestion that he might resort too often to the field of honor. "I mean, rather, to give the service its proper value."

"The question being how to calculate the worth of arranging what may be a friend's death—though I don't doubt you would do the same for me."

Nicholas frowned as he saw Juliette press her face into the curve of Gabriel's neck, perhaps to hide the drain of color from it. Blackford's mood was sometimes as difficult to follow as his high-flown speech, and was impossible to discern now with only the back of his head as a guide. The morose condemnation layered with concern seemed new, however. Or was it? Hadn't there been something of it in his attitude over the last few days? Now was not the time to address it, however, not while Juliette stood half-dressed and he in his stocking feet.

"I would consider it an honor," Nicholas said in deliberate answer, "as one of the Brotherhood as well as a friend. But for now—"

"Ah, yes, our Brotherhood."

"*For now*," Nicholas repeated, "what is required is privacy and breakfast."

"Gabriel—" Blackford began.

"He may stay," Juliette said, smiling down at the boy who clung to her while she swung him gently in her arms, turning back and forth at the waist.

"Among the chosen, yes," Blackford said as he pushed away from the door and sauntered away, disappearing down the hall so his voice floated back to him. "What it is to be an orphan."

Nicholas stared after his English friend for a long, considering moment. Then he rose to his feet and closed the door with precision.

The Englishman's sardonic mood had not improved by the time they reached the city again. Nicholas feared it might gain Blackford a duel of his own should he inflict it on the Daspit's seconds, so saw him off to his own atelier to await Daspit's seconds with some misgivings. They proved unfounded, for he returned two hours later to say that everything was arranged and the meeting would take place the following morning at the oaks on Allard's plantation. The weapons, naturally, would be swords, since the choice was Nicholas's given that he had received the challenge.

That the business had been settled so quickly indicated Daspit and his new bride had arrived back in town safely and in good time. Juliette would be glad of that much, at least.

He had left her at the Armant town house, though with great reluctance. Strangely enough, Paulette and her new husband had not been present to witness his interview with his new mother-in-law, nor his retreat from her crying and recriminations. Juliette had insisted it was best he leave under the circumstances, best that he continue his normal routine while attending to the details of his coming affair of honor. Nicholas suspected her of protecting him from the more grievous of the insults her mother might heap upon his name in her distress. Or perhaps it was only that Madame Armant might be less distraught with him in front of her. It went against the grain to leave Juliette alone, but he had allowed himself to be guided by his bride's wishes.

Somehow, there had been no mention of the marriage chest. Juliette seemed unwilling to broach the subject while her mother was so upset and he had no intention of bringing it up. Beyond consideration for her rights in the matter, it was of no moment to him if the thing was never passed to its next owner. In any case, he felt sure Paulette would force the issue soon enough.

Once at his atelier, he found the American Kerr Wallace and number of others waiting to discover if he meant to open for instruction. Accommodating them seemed easier than explaining a refusal. In addition, it seemed wise to work some of the stiffness out of his side while he had the chance.

By midafternoon news of the upcoming duel had begun to circulate, causing an additional influx of the curious; Nicholas heard whispers of it as he made his way through the crowd. Interest in his form on the fencing strip seemed stronger than usual, and he thought considerable sums of money might well be changing hands as men wagered on the outcome. Requests for special instruction were higher than usual as well. Before he knew it, the light was gone and the day had faded away into early evening.

At least there had been no comments on his hasty marriage. Or if they were made, those involved were discreet enough to do it out of his hearing.

"Shouldn't you be at home?" Blackford asked as he walked to where Nicholas stood, removing his chest pad and mask, when the room had finally cleared. "The wedding may have been unceremonious, but the usual obligations apply."

"Meaning?" Nicholas was tired and in no mood to decipher his friend's cryptic utterances.

"Protective escort for a start, then support in case the story has got about and too many lorgnettes are turned in the direction of the Armant box. In other words, husbandly duty in some arena other than the bedchamber."

"What the devil are you talking about?"

Blackford shook his head in mock sympathy. "You don't know and didn't ask. For that failure, you may find yourself sleeping alone—or not, if you hurry home at once. Some Italian diva is singing at the Theatre d'Orleans tonight, and I have it on good authority that the Armant ladies plan to attend. Daspit allowed that you have the right of escort for Juliette and her mother—"

"Did he indeed? And how did he learn of our marriage, I wonder?"

"Perhaps he paid a formal call on his new mother-in-law at last and was regaled with the story. Maybe his bride paid a visit to her sister, heard the news and passed it on. I don't know, but I am no informer."

Nicholas grimaced. "I did not intend to suggest you were. My apologies."

"As I was saying, Daspit concedes your right to escort Juliette and Madame Armant since he is obligated to appear with his own wife and his mother. As is quite proper under the circumstances, he has agreed to avoid the Armant box, keeping to his own family party for the sake of peace. My idea, for which you may thank me appropriately at a later time. But not now, if you are to go home and make ready."

Nicholas swore even as he drew his watch from his pocket by its chain. The hour was late indeed, and he could not get into dress clothes in his current state of sweat and dirt. Then another thought struck him. "Home," he said almost to himself. "That would be…"

"The Armant town house, I believe, since I saw the majority of your wardrobe being carried off in that direction earlier."

"Yes." It was the custom among the French Creoles for a bride and groom to retire after the wedding to a specially prepared bedchamber in the home of the bride, or so he had been told. There they would remain in seclusion for three days during which it was assumed they would explore all the nuances of connubial bliss while also growing used to each other's constant presence. Given the clandestine nature of their marriage, and perhaps his thoughtless return to his usual habit, it appeared the seclusion would be waived. However, he and Juliette were apparently to make their home with Madame Armant until such time as they could find a house of their own.

It struck him suddenly that Daspit and Mademoiselle Paulette would by tradition have the same requirement. What a farce it would be when his new brother-in-law and Juliette's sister followed them home from the theater after carefully avoiding them all evening. Yes, and also when he and Daspit woke in the morning and left the house together for their meeting under the oaks.

The arrangement stood to be supremely uncomfortable, Nicholas thought. He should have discussed it with Juliette, at the very least. The problem was that he had never had to consider such domestic arrangements in the past.

"I am in your debt," he said to Blackford as he reached for his coat.

"And I will remember, depend on it."

What the Englishman meant, Nicholas had no idea, nor did he remain to find out. Snatching up his hat and cane, he started toward the stairs.

"Nicholas?"

He paused, though impatient, suddenly, to be at the Moisant town house. "Yes, *mon ami?*"

"You are well enough for the meeting? You would not, *par example*, require a stand-in to fight in your stead?"

Nicholas lifted an eyebrow. "You are offering your services?"

"I may not be your equal in fame as a master, but I believe I can hold my own against Daspit."

Blackford was being modest. His skill, always of a high order, had increased during his sojourn in the city due to constant practice. He was a cerebral fighter who outmaneuvered his opponents rather than overriding them with brawn or cunning tricks. His fencing salon was well-patronized, in spite of being, rather obviously, a pastime for the well-born Englishman rather than an economic necessity. "I am sure of it. The question is why you would risk a meeting for my sake."

"Call it a whim."

"I prefer to call it friendship," Nicholas said, reaching to clasp Blackford's arm.

"Or Brotherhood?"

A dry note feathered Blackford's comment that

Nicholas might have questioned if there had been time. There was not. Instead, he gave a short laugh. "That as well, but I still must refuse. I am quite fit, I swear it."

He did not stay for more, but turned for the stairs. Still, he carried with him the brief expression caught on Blackford's face, one of doubtful, brooding concern.

At the Armant town house, he rang the bell and waited to be admitted. It was Valara who let him in and moved with him down the length of the entrance tunnel. "This is an opera night?" he asked as he strode toward the courtyard.

"*Mais oui*, Monsieur Nick."

He barely noticed that the old nurse had picked up the name given to him by the street boys. "The ladies expect to attend."

"Of a certainty. Mam'zelle Juliette has been watching for you this hour."

"I will need hot water as soon as possible."

"Mam'zelle Juliette ordered it some time past, and a tub. It was just delivered."

"For me?" Puzzlement drew his eyebrows together.

"Of course for you, since she bathed earlier. She also ordered a tray to be brought to the bedchamber, thinking you might not have stopped to eat. Nothing heavy, only rolls and cold chicken, well, and a pastry since she knows you care for it."

"The armoire at my atelier seems to have been robbed. Dare I hope the contents are here?"

"I went myself to fetch them, Monsieur Nick. I hope you don't mind. Mam'zelle Juliette thought it would be easier for you."

"Yes, excellent." It was disturbing how gratified he was at this manifold evidence of wifely consideration, particularly the pastry. He had not realized that she knew of his sweet tooth. "You will be looking after Gabriel tonight?"

She tipped her head in its white tignon. "He has been promised a piece of nougat as big as a Spanish dollar if he will eat his supper and be as good for me as for Mam'zelle Juliette."

"He must be much better."

"Oh, much. These little ones descend quickly to illness but rise quickly from it. He has entertained us all with the tale of his adventure across the river. Now, he is with Monsieur Squirrel and the others."

Amazement washed over Nicholas. "They returned, all of them?"

"Mam'zelle Juliette can persuade a crow to sing when she wishes. Besides, Madame O'Neill said to her that the way to even the hearts of young men is through their stomachs. Everyone was promised nougat."

"Before or after their baths?"

"Afterward, of course. And after they were shown their new rooms with real beds in the *garçonnière*."

Nicholas grinned and shook his head while swallowing against a sudden tightness in his throat. His

Juliette had been busy seeing to everyone's comfort today or so it seemed. What a wonder she was and in more ways than he could count. Yes, and what a strange ménage this household would be over the next few days, with the street boys, himself and Daspit added to what had been an all-female household.

His amusement faded away, leaving his features grim. "Monsieur Daspit has not arrived, has he?"

"Mam'zelle Paulette has been half the day making their bedchamber ready, but he has not come. She thinks now it will be after the opera. You know he will arrive with a hackney to collect her for tonight?"

"So I have been told." He paused. "Would you inform Madame Armant that I shall be with her shortly."

"And Mam'zelle Juliette?"

Nicholas smiled. "I will give myself the pleasure of letting her know."

Valara gave a stately nod. He thought there was satisfaction in it, though he may have been wrong.

Juliette was not in the bedchamber. Nicholas hesitated then went back out to the gallery and along it to the salon, thinking she might have gone there to wait. The room was empty. A tray set with glasses and a bottle of sherry sat on a side table, however, with the cork removed to allow the wine to breathe. He moved to pour a small glass for himself in hope of banishing some of the fatigue from his strenuous day.

As he sipped, his gaze fell on the marriage chest, which had been returned to its usual place between the front windows since the furor when Juliette had shown it to him. He paused in front of it, reaching to run a thumb along the edge of the lid, testing the wood grain.

"Nicholas, I did not hear you return—"

It was Juliette standing in the door, her gaze on his hand where it rested on the chest. She was dressed in white, the gown of angelic satin and matching cloak trimmed with swans down which he had suggested to her what seemed like an eon ago.

"*Ma chère*," he said with low pleasure vibrating in his voice. "You are breathtaking, truly incomparable."

She seemed reluctant to raise her gaze to his face for an instant. Then a smile touched her lips. "*Merci*, though the credit is yours, I believe. Well, and Madame Ferret's."

"Ours was the inspiration but you bring it to glowing life. I am honored that you chose to wear it since I had feared you didn't care for the concept at the time."

"It seemed quite proper tonight, given that I am newly married."

"Indeed. And since we are, you might, I think, call me by some diminutive. Nick, perhaps, or *cher*, or even something warmer."

"If it pleases you," she said, coloring a little, "*mon cher*."

"It pleases me, *chérie*." He might have shown her exactly how much it pleased him except it would be a shame to disarrange such artistry as her *toilette* represented, and there was no time in any case. With a rueful smile, he said, "I have much to answer for concerning my neglect today and tardiness this evening, and intend an apology in form when time allows. But for now…"

"Yes, for now you must dress. All is in readiness, I think."

"For which, I have to thank you," he said, moving forward to take her hand and carry it to his lips while smiling into her eyes. "I will attend to that as well. Later. This I swear."

The answering promise in the impish curve of her lips and slight press of her fingers was something he took with him as he strode away toward his waiting bath.

Behind the screen that protected him from drafts and accidental exposure should anyone enter, Nicholas savored the heated water in contrast to his usual cold ablutions, enjoying the comfort of it on his wounded side and the knowledge that it had been prepared especially for him. He soaped and splashed, scrubbed and rinsed, and rubbed Juliette's lavender scented soap through his hair. It gratified him in some obscure fashion to be marked with her fresh fragrance for this evening, though he thought he would buy his own Castile-made soap for future use.

He had sluiced away the lather and was on the point of rising from the tub when he heard the bed-chamber door open on the far side of the screen. He paused as he waited to see who might have entered, thinking it might be Paulette or Madame Armant in search of Juliette, for the rustle of taffeta petti-coats told him that it was a woman. To check was fairly easy since the glass covering a watercolor painting that hung above and to the left of the bathing corner made a decent reflector of the room beyond the screen. He had only to sit still and look closely.

It was Juliette, easily recognizable in her white gown as she stepped into the room then stood lis-tening for an instant as if to discover if he were still occupied in the bath. Obligingly, he dipped his cloth and squeezed it out, half hoping that she would come and check his progress. She did nothing of the kind, but turned and went out again.

Nicholas almost called out to her since he had need of another wrapping of fresh bandage. Some-thing about the quietness with which she moved deterred him while also setting off an internal warning. He sat still for a frowning instant while he turned over possibilities. The thought that she might have had something of note to tell him, something she didn't care to discuss while he bathed, finally decided him. Rising from the tub so that water poured from him in miniature waterfalls, he stepped out, dried himself quickly, and skimmed into his discarded pantaloons. An instant later, he left the bedchamber.

As he paused on the gallery, he could hear activity in the kitchen and servant's quarters below him, and also voices coming from the bedchamber of Madame Armant, or so he thought. Juliette's mother was there along with Paulette, he was almost sure. The ladies were perhaps enjoying wine and cakes or some other light refreshment to hold them until the four-hour evening performance was over. However, he did not hear Juliette's quieter tones.

Moving with silent treads, he went quickly in the direction he had heard her take, toward the salon. He slowed as he reached the French door, alerted by a flicker of movement inside the room. He stepped to put his back to the wall beside it so as to remain out of sight while still being able to see through the glass.

Juliette, a shining form in her white, was standing before the marriage chest with what appeared to be a ribbon in her hand. As he watched, she untangled it to free an ornate, rather old-fashioned key. Kneeling before the chest in a pool of silken skirts, she fitted the key into the lock of the chest and twisted it. She paused for an instant, then took a deep breath and raised the lid.

For interminable seconds, she didn't move, hardly seemed to breathe, but stood staring down into the box with wide, dark eyes. Then the air left her lungs in an abrupt rush that was audible even where Nicholas stood. Moving with great care, she closed the lid of the box, took the key in her fingers again and relocked the chest.

Nicholas narrowed his eyes as he stared at the wall on the opposite side of the courtyard from where he stood. Had Juliette's mother turned over possession of the chest? It was possible, of course. The two of them could have come to a rapport, settling the question of ownership with Paulette while he was away. Somehow, he didn't think so.

If he had to guess, he would say his bride was inspecting the chest by stealth, otherwise there would have been no need to make certain he and everyone else were occupied in their rooms. Impatience and curiosity could have gotten the best of her, and she simply could wait no longer. She might have considered that she had fulfilled the requirements for ownership, being designated as the firstborn daughter by Valara, or she could have feared that Paulette would gain ownership with a claim of being the first to marry, taking the chest away so she would never know the contents.

There was one other possibility.

She had come upon him standing in front of the chest earlier and feared that he had taken advantage of his position as her husband with free run of the house to plunder the family heirloom. Rather than trust him, or even ask him about it, she felt compelled to make sure that all was safe and in its place by looking for herself.

What had she found that left her so rigid with distress? What could have made her shut the lid at once, without touching the contents or disturbing them in any way?

She was turning toward the door. The last thing he wanted was for her to find him there. As quietly as he had followed her, he retraced his footsteps to the bedchamber and closed himself inside. There, he wrapped his own upper body in a piece of flannel he found laid ready, then made a quick job of running his straight-edge razor over his face. He skimmed out of his damp pantaloons then and donned his evening wear. Ready as he was going to be, he took up his silk top hat, cape, gloves and cane, and went back out onto the gallery.

Feminine voices still came from Madame Armant's bedchamber, and this time it was Juliette's he heard with that of her mother. Paulette had gone, he was almost sure. He had heard the arrival of a carriage and murmur of polite voices as he dressed.

The salon was empty when he reached it. Turning his head toward the marriage chest, he stared at it for half a second. Then he started toward it.

The lock, for all its ornate metal work, was a common enough type of the kind used in most household to lock away sharp knives, tea and expensive spices. He reached for the watch chain that crossed his white, shadow-striped waistcoat and took out the key to his French-made sword case. Though not quite the same, it would suffice.

Mere seconds later, he lifted the lid. Then his breath left him in short sound that held equal parts of anger and consternation.

No jewels, no gold, filled the depths. There were no bank notes or certificates of investment of any kind, nor was there any paper to show who Juliette's famous ancestress had been or that Valara's great-grandmother had ever been manumitted from slavery.

There was nothing. The chest was empty.

It was empty, and Juliette had seen him alone in the salon with it. It was empty, and he had been the last to touch it prior to her inspection. It was empty, and his bride of one night thought that he had robbed it, had taken her birthright along with her maidenhead.

Soundlessly, Nicholas lowered the lid and locked it again. He took up his belongings that he had laid aside and went in search of the ladies for whom he was to act as escort.

Juliette was cool and noticeably distant on the way to the theater. The few remarks she made were directed toward her mother. Rather than taking his arm as they walked the short distance from the town house, she relinquished that support to her parent who was more in need of it. Once inside, she did not invite him to sit beside her in the box but left him standing in the back as if he were no more than a tiresome suitor instead of her lawfully wedded husband.

Nicholas declined to notice. He was polite, urbane, consciously charming. He smiled, made graceful and sincere compliments, bowed to those he met and those who lifted a hand in greeting from the far side of the theatre. If there were others who glanced at him from the corners of their eyes while nudging their friends, he did not see them. If ladies tittered and whispered behind their fans, he was oblivious. Standing with his shoulders to the wall at the box's rear, he watched over the ladies who were now in his care with his lips set and anger burning inside him.

It was inconceivable that he should be suspected of the theft. Nothing he had done should allow such a charge. He had not been accused, no, but that made it worse. He was to be permitted no chance to defend himself, no possibility of refuting the suspicion.

He would see about that, he would indeed.

There she sat, his bride, in all her angelic white, symbol of purity, with the glow of the theater's whale-oil chandelier shining in her hair, gilding her throat and low décolletage, touching her white satin gown with flickering yellow and blue gleams. She appeared so composed, so unmoved by her supposed discovery. She seemed remote in spirit, untouched by the fever of passion or urgency of desire.

He knew better. He knew the sweet curves of her breasts that nestled beneath her bodice, the sensuous turnings of her waist and thighs. Her moist softness and the scent of her skin were engraved in his mind; her melodious moans lingered in his ears. She was a woman of deep needs and tender yearnings, responsive to the slightest touch, generous in her pleasure. There were yet reams of erotic delights he had not uncovered for her, and he would not be denied their completion.

She was his, and nothing would take her from him, not Daspit, not her mother's hysterical superstition, and not this insulting distrust that she had allowed to darken her mind. This he vowed by all he held dear.

He kept his vows.

19

Anger and anticipation ran through Nicholas's veins in equal measure during the return to the Armant town house. Impatience dogged him as well. He had never before played shepherd to an older lady of nervous disposition. The amount of accoutrement Madame Armant found necessary for her comfort—fan, comb, cushion, vinaigrette, opera glasses, shawl, cloak, wrist bouquet—was amazing. He was forced to retrieve her fan from the banquette or gutter three times and, on the third, finally thrust it into his tail coat pocket for safekeeping. He was also obliged to hear at tedious length of Monsieur Daspit's consideration in arranging for a hackney carriage to convey his mother and Paulette to and from the theater. This pointed reminder allowed no consideration of the fact that the elder Madame Daspit was a martyr to gout or that she was hastening home to oversee the family dinner she had arranged for her son and his new wife. Juliette, perhaps sensing the irritation behind his punctilious manner, gave him an apologetic smile. He was not mollified in the least.

A late supper awaited their small party on their return, one consisting of turtle soup, daub glace, sweet meats and a selection of desserts. There were no guests, not even the boys who lay sprawled in sleep on their beds as he and Juliette looked in on them. The toast drunk to their happiness and future together seemed grudging on her mother's part, a sop to convention rather than a true wish for joy in their marriage. Madame Armant could hardly wait to be done and away to her bedchamber. As a wedding supper for Juliette and himself, it did not impress. The lack of consideration for his bride or attention to her happiness annoyed Nicholas, and the proof that he was barely tolerated in the house did nothing to mend matters.

Nicholas sat playing with his wineglass after his mother-in-law had gone, watching as Juliette slowly consumed a bunch of grapes. She plucked them one by one from their stems, her lashes lowered as she passed the round, succulent fruit between her lips then delicately removed the seeds behind her napkin. The drawing sensation in his lower body became acute. He wondered if she realized what she was doing to him but could not imagine it. That obliviousness only added to his surly mood.

Finally, she was done. He got up and stepped to draw back her chair so she could rise in her full skirts. As they moved from the dining room, he put a hand at the small of her back. She gave him a quick look, but made no attempt to avoid his touch.

It was just as well. He was by no means sure what he might have done in that event.

Valara awaited them in the bedchamber. Nicholas considered dismissing her but decided against it. The old nurse had been an ally so far, and he had no wish to alienate her. Besides, he thought watching his new wife being disrobed might be almost as satisfactory as doing the job himself.

He was wrong. Merely observing the process rather than participating was a severe test of his restraint. To remain in the background long enough for a nightgown to be dropped over her head seemed impossible. The effort was likely to be wasted in any case, if he had his way. And he intended to have his way. The old fencing instructors might advise refraining from amorous activity the evening before a duel, but they had not been newly married. Nicholas, reclining in a low slipper chair with one foot propped on the large Turkish ottoman which sat in front of him, spoke without raising his voice. "Enough."

Valara looked at him then began to gather the discarded linen and say her good-nights. Leaving Juliette in her corset cover and pantaloons and her hair down around her shoulders, she went out, closing the door quietly behind her.

Nicholas met Juliette's eyes in the reflection of her dressing table mirror. Her appraisal was brief and layered with doubt. Lowering her lashes, she reached to take up her hairbrush, pulling it through the long coils of her unbound hair.

"Come here to me." His words were deep, with more of an edge of command than he had strictly intended, but he refused to soften them with smile or gesture.

She rose slowly to her feet and walked toward him. In his satisfaction at her ready acquiescence, it was an instant before he caught the militant sparkle in her eyes. Had he misjudged her? The idea was uncomfortable, and that gave him pause. Could it be he was just as glad to find fault with her? Did he prefer her untrusting since it absolved him of the need to reach the high standard she set? Possibly he wanted to bring her down to his.

He was not used to questioning his motives, nor did he spare them more than a bare instant of thought now. Instead, he reached for her as she came near, taking her hand and drawing her onto his lap.

She was all compliance and half-veiled inquiry as she sank down upon him. The way the sweet curves of her hips settled over the firmness at the juncture of his thighs was like the answer to an unvoiced need. He placed one hand at her waist with deliberate possessiveness, then threaded the fingers of his free hand through her hair, clasped the back of her head to tilt her face, then he took her mouth like a drunkard falling on new wine.

The taste of her was intoxicating with her mouth flavored by grapes and sweet woman, acceptance and desire. It melted on his tongue, mounting to his head until he groaned with their mind-spinning allure. He swept the smooth surface of her lips, the edges of her teeth, drew her small, pointed tongue into his mouth in an agony of need. He gathered her closer, unable to bring her near enough or to fill his hands with as much of her as he required.

Pressing her head to his shoulder, he released his hold and slid his hand blindly to the neckline of her corset cover. He dragged it down, freeing a breast that he caught and lifted to his mouth. The texture was so smooth yet candy-hard and sweet, so yielding yet resilient that he applied adhesion, suckling in mindless rhythm.

She caught his head, twining her fingers into his hair to hold him against her while a soft moan vibrated in her chest. The feel of her twisting against him, the weight and heat of her, was an incredible incitement.

Lunging forward with her, he seated her on the ottoman in front of him, stripped off the corset cover and pantaloons, and pressed her down with her back on its wide, tufted surface. Like a virgin sacrifice on an altar, pale white skin and rosy nipples displayed on burgundy brocade, she lay staring up at him so he saw himself reflected in the wide black pupils of her eyes. She wanted him, wanted what he was doing, was too submerged in the sensations he had created to deny him. It was what he required. It was enough. He blotted out that vision as he lowered his head to posses her lips once more.

He would be denied nothing of her, no single curve or crease. She was his and she would know it. He bracketed her breasts with his two hands, alternating his attention on their straining, tight nipples until she arched on her exotic bed with her head back and her hair streaming over the edge, offering more, offering everything.

Ruthlessly invading, he took what she presented, pressing his fingers into her while he licked a hot path down her belly and through the fine curls above her gentle mound of Venus. Where his fingers had been, he followed with his tongue, flicking the internal surfaces, pushing deep until she sobbed his name like a prayer. Finding the tiny pearl of her greatest pleasure, he suckled it in endless application while his busy, busy fingers spread her thighs wide, open to his sight and diligent plundering.

She convulsed in abrupt surrender, crying out, shuddering with the force of the release as she turned her head from side to side with the sound dying in her throat. Quickly, he opened his pantaloons and, clothed in sharp and gratifying contrast to her prostrate nakedness, freed his hot throbbing length. He positioned the tip at her wet opening, then caught her hips and pushed inside.

She cried out again, half-lifting off the ottoman, her eyes wide. He stared down at her, at their joined bodies, flesh against flesh, her flushed, swollen breasts, the nipples tightly red and moist, her lips swollen and parted with her gasping breaths, eyes vulnerable, so without defense. So completely his own.

He had never loved a woman more.

He loved her, may the good God help him.

He loved her and the feeling wrenched his heart and scoured his mind because he knew she could never match that fierce, possessive adoration, never love him in return.

Or could she?

Women were not like men, able to separate their rutting instinct from their softer emotions. He might seduce her heart as he seduced her body. He would beguile her, tempt her, force her finally to respond to him, to accept him into her heart and soul as she accepted him into her body. He would push his way inside, going deeper and deeper. He would do it again and yet again, battering down her resistance as he plunged into her now with steady, remorseless thrusts. He would make a place for himself just as he had now gained access to the deepest depths of her body by lifting her legs to rest on his arms.

It was a promise, a vow made to himself alone.

And closing his eyes, Nicholas ground his teeth, holding back while his rock-hard muscles bunched and strained at his bidding and his heart thundered in his ears, relentlessly invading her softness while she moaned, thrashing under him but taking him, absorbing his hard pounding, surrounding him with her wet heat while clasping him with drawing, internal contractions.

Abruptly he shattered, his vision splintering into bright, shimmering fragments with the intensity of the release so the oil lamp which lighted the bedchamber took on a glowing nimbus like some angelic visitation. Yet even as his body clenched, emptying in violent bursts, he knew the diffusion was caused by nothing at all except the hot rise of his unshed tears.

The dueling ground, when he reached it next morning, was drowned in fog. The mist lay in swaths on the damp ground, truncated the great oaks known as the Twin Sisters to half their height, bejeweled the hanging rags of Spanish moss with diamonds and made ghosts of the men who stood about waiting for daybreak.

Nicholas was early. This was due in part to the punctual arrival of his seconds, Blackford and Caid, in their hired hack, but also because he had been waiting for them on the banquette outside the Moisant town house. Sleep had been hard to come by during the night, and he had risen before the house servants, long before Juliette could wake and watch him go.

He had taken his goodbye kiss while she slept, unable to bear the thought of what he might see in her eyes. And he hardly knew which might have been worse, to recognize fear that he might not return or hope that he would not.

His companions were silent except for an occasional morning cough or quiet comment. That was hardly unusual; a duel was a serious affair after all. At least they made no attempt to lighten the mood with jocularity or breezy airs. As *maître d'armes* themselves, they knew better, knew the risks and the role played by lady luck which could turn the simplest meeting into the prelude to a funeral.

Daspit and his attendants arrived precisely on time. Nicholas, watching his opponent alight from their hackney, wondered briefly if he had resisted the appeal of the marriage bed and his new wife. He and his bride had reached the Armant town house late. Nicholas, lying awake, had heard no sound from their bedchamber at that hour or this morning before he set out.

Caid nodded in the direction of the Daspit party after a time. "Your adversary looks less than confident, I must say. That's the third time he's paced off the ground, kicking bits of tree limb out of his way and stamping down grass hummocks. Do you suppose he saw your young protégé yesterday afternoon, or heard what he had to say?"

"Protégé?"

"Squirrel. You know what he's been doing?"

Nicholas shook his head, afraid to hazard a guess. He had not actually spoken to the boy since their return.

"He told every man-jack who would listen that news of your injury was greatly exaggerated, that you are in fact able to lick your weight in alligators with one hand and tie rattlesnakes into ladies garters with the other."

"Déclassé as a description, but accurate," Nicholas said with a faint curving of his lips.

"I'm glad you're amused, for he has joined us, you know."

Nicholas glanced around in time to see the boy climbing down from the back of a hackney that was decanting spectators, before fading into the crowd that was beginning to gather. "Young devil. He might have killed himself hitching a ride like that."

"He cares what becomes of you, one of many with that concern. You are quite sure you're fit?"

Nicholas, still watching the boy and thinking that Squirrel probably meant to take word of the duel's outcome back to the others, barely glanced at Caid. "Not you, too?"

"Someone else had the sense to question it?"

Blackford spoke then in answer to Caid's query.

"I did, as chief second with the responsibility to put a healthy principal on the field. And still do."

"I told you—" Nicholas began.

"You did, but that was yesterday while in the grip of wedded euphoria. You appear now, if you'll forgive the observation, less hale and hearty. In fact, you look like death served up with a béchamel sauce. The only consolation is that Daspit is worse."

Anger moved along Nicholas's veins like lava flowing downhill. "I suppose you are going to offer again to take my place."

"What is this?" Caid asked, his gaze going from him to Blackford and back again.

"Our English friend thinks I need a nursemaid, not to mention replacement on the dueling strip."

"Do you?" Caid asked in his blunt way.

"I do not. My left arm may be a little stiff, but I have a spare."

"You mean to fight with your right hand."

Nicholas lifted an eyebrow. "Being handy with both isn't unheard of."

"But one is seldom as handy as the other."

Blackford set his fists at his waist. "Stubborn to a fault, you see, and with no more sense than a gosling mistaking a hawk for its mother."

"Thank you," Nicholas said, the words stiff with irony. "At least I need no noble scion awash in bombast to represent me, no son of merry England with a tongue like an adder, no—"

"Brother?"

He gave him an exasperated glare. "A vow made with crossed swords doesn't give you the right to second-guess me, much less take my place."

"What of blood right? What if I am the son of your father?"

Nicholas opened his mouth to blast the man who faced him for daring refer to his lack of birthright. Then the words Blackford had spoken turned in his mind, becoming something quite other. "What?"

"You were sired by my late father, the Marquess Derwenter. We share the same bloodline."

"Impossible. My father was a sailing man. My mother always said it."

"Oh, he had been sailing before meeting your mother, traveling aboard the yacht of his friend, the Duke of Carnhaven, while both made a covert visit to Italy during the reign of Napoleon's brother-in-law, Murat. They could not linger, being on a mission of some importance for the British government." Blackford's smile had a sardonic edge, though his eyes were brightly blue. "It doesn't change your status to learn of it now, but you may at least call yourself a noble bastard."

It was a moment before Nicholas could speak. "You…have known this all along?"

"You wonder why I haven't fallen on your neck any time these past two years, shouting hosanna? It was first necessary to be sure you were a sibling fit to claim. Then, having delayed, I thought to choose my moment."

"And this is it?"

"No doubt I could have chosen a less distracting occasion. I might have, except for the possibility of losing a brother who had become more important to my comfort than the present marquess who took over as head of the family on the death of our parent." Blackford looked at his fingernails. "A proud man, our older brother, and not at all sentimental."

"That is why you came here, from sentiment." Nicholas hardly knew what he asked for the stunned immobility in his mind. Not one brother, but two, and a heritage that stretched to the Doomsday Book most likely, even if it was on the wrong side of the blanket. Nor was he immune to the real concern which lay, like a brandied cherry buried in nougat, beneath Blackford's facile explanation.

"For fairness rather, and, let it be admitted, from curiosity and a strong need to escape the fraternal thumb. Hi ho, adventuring I went. And found it here."

Caid spoke then. "How came you to recognize Nicholas? Or learn of his existence, for that matter?"

"News of him came to light in my father's papers after he died. It seems he had intended to return to Italy and bring back your mother as a bride. That could not be allowed of course. His father, my—

our—grandfather forbade it, and arranged a more suitable wife and commanded that he take her. It was obey or be cast out of the ancestral mansion, out of society, out of the line of succession to the title. Still, my father remained attached to the memory of his continental affair, at least enough to retain a pencil sketch of your mother along with the name of the town and street where she lived—also a letter from Carnhaven, who was in Italy after Waterloo, saying there had been a child, a boy. My adventures, you realize, took me to Italy where I unearthed the birth record. The path from there was not difficult to follow."

Nicholas stared at the man who had been his friend for nearly two years and was now was so much more. A wry smile curved his mouth. "You are a romantic, *mon frère*."

Gavin Blackford inclined his head. "An inescapable failing, as it seems to run in the family."

"And because it does, because there is a family connection, I am to let you risk being killed in my stead? I think not. No, not even if it were necessary, which it is not. We will talk of this later, but for now—"

"For now, the Daspit party is ready. Yes, I see." Gavin's lips firmed, then he inclined his head and reached to pull a handkerchief of white silk from his pocket. Taking Nicholas's right wrist, he began to wrap it around the vulnerable arteries there. "But I warn you, I will hold you to this later discussion."

The sun was rising, burning tunnels through the fog, turning the eastern sky to shades of camellia pink. A blue jay called in strident warning. Gavin and Caid moved to join the others for the matching of weapons. Nicholas, left alone, breathed in the morning freshness in deep, even breaths, trying for calm.

Gavin, his brother. What did it mean? Or did it mean anything beyond an accident of love and birth? Certainly, it changed nothing. He felt different in some odd way beyond his understanding regardless, as if some missing portion of his being had been found.

He had not thought it mattered, being fatherless, that he had grown beyond caring about it long ago. It was disturbing to discover that it had been merely buried, disturbing also to realize that he cared as much for his mother's sake as for his own. She had not been deserted by choice. He wished she could have known it.

Hard on the heels of that thought tripped another just as disquieting. What would Juliette think of this new turn? Or could anything that concerned him matter to her at all?

Moments later, all was in readiness. Caid returned with the flat rosewood sword box, which held Nicholas's set of Coulaux et Cie rapiers. Nicholas unlocked it and lifted one of them from its velvet bed, hefting it in his hand where it seemed to balance as if it were a part of him. He limbered his wrist and executed a series of moves so swift that the silvery flash of them seemed to linger after he was still again. He had never been touched while wielding this blade. Perhaps whatever protective power it held would be with him this morning.

Nicholas and his two friends advanced through knee-deep swaths of fog to the fencing strip marked off with powdered chalk. Daspit moved to meet him with his seconds, while the respective physicians stayed farther back, laying out their instruments on ground cloths. Leaving their attendants on the sidelines, the two principals stepped into the long and narrow corridor of the fencing strip. From this moment, they must remain within its bounds, avoiding the marked ends since to step over them could give rise to whispers of cowardice. Nothing was more deadly than that charge to a swordsman, whether master at arms or ordinary gentleman. To be a blackguard in New Orleans was no great thing, but to be judged a coward was to be ruined for life.

When within a sword length of where Nicholas stood, Daspit swept up his blade in salute. The courtesy was answered in kind. The two of them waited, at ease.

The rules of engagement as promulgated in the *Nouveau Code du Duel* by Comte du Verger de Saint-Thomas were duly read. Daspit's chief second won the toss for position, so Nicholas moved to face what little sun there was at present. Gavin took the toss for the honor of calling the commands. He stepped forward now to the edge of the strip where he glanced from one man to the other.

It was the moment to narrow concentration, to forget conscious movements and allow instinct and learned skills to take over. Nicholas could feel the quickening beat of his heart.

"On guard!"

Sunlight glinted with blue refractions from both blades as they were brought up, meeting at the apex of their rise with a melodious chime then holding with their tips crossed. Beyond that metal arch, Nicholas met the eyes of his opponent. Daspit's expression was grim and sweat dewed his upper lip in spite of the morning coolness. His hand was steady, however; Nicholas had to give him that much.

Then the other man's gaze dropped to Nicholas's shirt front just under his left arm, the site of his injury. Had he learned of it from Paulette, or did he know because he had paid to have it dealt? Either way, the implication was that he intended to exploit it.

The honorable thing would be for Daspit to avoid that advantage. Nicholas hardly expected such selflessness. Any possible weakness was fair game when a *maître d'armes* took the field since the ultimate advantage was considered to be on the side of the professional.

The word duel originated from the Italian *duello*, which in turn came from the Latin *duellum*, an old form of *bellum*, or war, and *duo*, or two. The meaning, therefore, was two men at courteous war. It was apt, Nicholas thought. As with war, no man could tell what might happen when adversaries faced each other on the battleground of the strip. Beyond the normal hazard involved in a passage at arms, the reality of being in combat often called forth hidden attributes. Courage, that quality sometimes called "heart," could sometimes become more important than skill. With this went the question of resolve. Often the man with the greatest will to win and to live was the one who drank victory champagne with his friends.

They would see what settled this contest. Nicholas looked at Gavin and nodded to indicate that he was ready.

"Begin!"

Daspit attacked. As a stratagem, it was excellent, Nicholas acknowledged. A sudden assault sometimes carried a match since the object was to hit the adversary as soon as possible without being hit. It was not successful in this case. He was ready, and drove Daspit back with a circular parry followed by a lunge that almost ended the reprise in his favor. Daspit, desperately defending, recovered in form, however, and they settled down to the bell-like chiming of blades as they explored tactics and ruses.

Nicholas maintained the air of calm poise that had given him the name La Roche, the Rock, one often disconcerting and even irritating to his opponents with its intimation of power, or so he had been told. The aim was to make Daspit feel that his smallest error would result in retaliation so viciously swift it could not be countered. Though it might be sheer vanity, he liked to think the impression not entirely false, even when using his right hand.

Drawing back after yet another attack that achieved him nothing, Daspit spoke in frowning irony over the snick and tap of controlled thrust and parry. "I am told you took my example and wed Paulette's sister while at Gretna. I would not have thought you so anxious to put your head in parson's noose. Or have you gone through your lottery winnings already so must lay hands on the Armant treasure?"

Nicholas gave him a level look but did not relax his guard. "What makes you think money had any bearing?"

"You hardly know Mademoiselle Juliette, so can't have developed a *tendre* in that direction."

"You would say, I suppose, that it was passion which drove you to run away with Mademoiselle Paulette."

"Oh, my situation is quite different. I grow tired of counting every picayune. Then this treasure belongs to Paulette. She has been promised it all her life and sees no reason to be denied it now on an old nursemaid's say so."

"Even if what the woman says is true?" Nicholas swirled into an attack that drove Daspit back, rigorously defending, but was distracted to the point that he permitted his opponent to recover. He refused to think it might be from the awkward necessity of parrying in the opposite direction from what was usual for him.

"But is it?" Daspit said when he was able, his breath coming fast. At the same time, a puzzled expression lingered in his black eyes.

"You are suggesting that you pursued the matter as far as Gretna at the instigation of Mademoiselle Paulette?"

"Is that so hard to believe? Unlike you and her nun of a sister, there has been an understanding between us for some time."

"In fact, you love her," Nicholas said, skeptical as he thrust again.

"How could you think otherwise?"

He gave his opponent a hard stare as they moved back and forth on the strip in harder effort that clanged like a blacksmith's hammer on metal, but Daspit's manner was perfectly serious. Nor could Nicholas find reason to doubt him.

It was impossible for a man to hide his true nature on the dueling strip; it was proclaimed in his bearing, his actions and every expression that crossed his face. Daspit was a man who liked to win at all costs, but he was not without honor, not quite the unprincipled scoundrel Nicholas had expected.

After a moment, he said, "I was told that you had threatened to withdraw your suit if the treasure chest should be awarded elsewhere."

"Paulette seemed to think I might, though I never said it in so many words. Even if financial gain was my only aim, the Armant family fortune is not small and there was always her dowry."

It was a telling point. Nicholas wondered why he had not considered it before, unless it was because he had been so certain that Daspit had only the greater prize in mind. "Deny, if you can, that you paid to have me followed and killed at Tivoli Gardens."

"Killed, no. But you were altogether too formidable an adversary to risk facing without some small adjustment for fairness. Besides, you sprang a duel upon me from out of nowhere at the quadroon ball. It seemed fitting to serve you the same."

Nicholas did not bother to refute the charge. "An inch to my right, and I might have been eliminated completely."

"A mistake." Daspit's smile was grim. "The man principally hired for the job was told to strike for your arm, but his eyesight, or possibly his nerve, failed him."

"And did you, or someone hired by you, remove

the contents of the Armant treasure chest as a means of insuring fairness?"

Daspit almost let his guard down, but recovered in form. "You mean—you can't mean it's been rifled?"

"I can," Nicholas said, "and do."

"Not by me." Daspit paused. "You didn't…?"

"Not I." Nicholas, watching the other man's face, could have sworn it was the first he had heard of this turn of events. It also seemed something oddly tentative had entered Despit's swordplay, as if the certainty with which it was begun had deserted him.

"Then who?"

"That is the question."

Nicholas executed a circular riposte in answer to Daspit's halfhearted attack then swirled into an advance. "One last item, what of this challenge?"

Daspit gave a breathless laugh while executing a parry in sixte. "My *grandmère* used to tell me temper would be my downfall."

"She may have been right," Nicholas said. "But not just yet."

Hard on the words, he tossed his sword to his left hand and swept into an attack of such speed and strength that it drove Daspit back almost to his rear line. Their blades clashed, slid one against the other with a scraping shower of sparks. Nicholas stepped inside the other man's guard, pressing until their weapons ground upon each other, hilt to hilt. Then he exerted pressure and leverage, bending, binding until it seemed steel could stand no more.

Abruptly, Daspit's sword sprang free. It flashed in the sun in a hurtling arc before plunging point-down to stand like a metallic cross, quivering, in the fog-wet grass.

For long seconds, everything was quiet. Then Daspit rose slowly from his swordsman's crouch. His face was pale, his eyes wide as he stared at the blade in Nicholas's hand. He licked his lips, shook his head, then licked them again. "You did that with your left hand."

"But of course, *mon ami*. It is the hand I favor—unless circumstances forbid its use for more than a moment."

"I didn't know."

"But everyone is aware…"

"I wasn't, I swear it. I paid to have your left arm injured because it was my left that was sliced in the duel outside the quadroon ballroom, also because I would not so incapacitate you as to prevent a fair meeting between us—or so I thought. But that was not you that night, was it? The masked man I fought used his right hand."

"As to that—"

"His style was different as well—expert, yes, dangerously so—but different. I have wronged you, I think, Pasquale. Dare I hope that you will accept my apology?"

Nicholas looked down at the sword in his hand, turning it back and forth so its rich chasing caught the sunlight. "That depends," he said slowly. "That depends."

20

Juliette was alone in her bed when she awoke. She lay staring at the morning light beyond the French door while her heartbeat increased to a heavy drumming. Was the duel over already? Had Nicholas been victorious or did he lie bleeding on the ground even now? That she didn't know, was not allowed to hear the news one way or another until someone came to tell her, was so maddening that she thought she might scream with the frustration of it.

She shifted in the bed, feeling the pull of muscles she had never used before last night, never even known she possessed. The reminder brought a flush to her face while a secret smile curled around her mouth.

The Casanova of New Orleans. Now she knew why he was called so.

How extraordinary it had been—or was that only in her mind? Perhaps other marriage beds were the same but women did not speak of it for fear all young girls would rush too soon to the altar. She felt branded by Nicholas's possession yet exalted by it and enthralled at its details. There was also a modicum of pride that she had been able to sustain whatever he sought to give her, and to please him with her response.

She thought she pleased him, though she could not be sure of it. Tonight, that might be made plain. If there should be a tonight. How was she to know?

Flinging back the covers abruptly, she rose from her bed. Her morning café au lait sat cold and covered by milk skim on the bedside table, she saw. She must have been more exhausted than she knew that she had not awakened at its arrival. With a quick shake of her head, she moved to the *prie-Dieu* at the foot of the bed where she knelt with tightly closed eyes to say a prayer for Nicholas. Then she made quick use of the cool bath water left behind the screen from the night before and rang for Valara to help her dress.

Juliette needed to keep busy to prevent herself from thinking. Descending to the kitchen, she inquired after the street boys, learning that Squirrel had gone out early but all the rest had eaten and scattered into the street. Gabriel had attempted to go with them but been restrained, not without difficulty. It was Valara who had made that decision, and reaped the result, which was that Gabriel would now have nothing to do with her. He was, instead, ensconced in Paulette's room, of all places, where he leaned into the circle of her arm while she told him a story of an alligator and a rabbit that Juliette recognized as one Valara had recounted to the two of them when they were children. Neither her sister nor the boy looked up when she paused in the door, and so she went away without disturbing them. If Gabriel was some small comfort to her sister while she waited to hear from Monsieur Daspit, then that was all to the good. And if Paulette had come to care a little for Gabriel after their river crossing together, then that was even better.

While her sister was occupied, there was a matter which should be addressed, Juliette thought. She had thought to put it off until after she had spoken to Nicholas and they had agreed on a course between them, but the moment for it had not presented itself the night before. Now it seemed best to seize this time which was offered her.

Her mother was still abed, having the chocolate which was her habit rather than coffee. She sat against a bank of pillows in white linen covers edged with eyelet lace, her eyes closed and with a tray beside her on which sat a chocolate pot and cups of delicately painted porcelain. A bed jacket covered her shoulders and she wore the cap of linen and lace with hanging lappets that she preferred.

The sun was beginning to fill the courtyard outside, reflecting its bright winter light into the room. In that insistent glow, Juliette surveyed her mother, seeking to learn her mood. She saw instead a woman who was aging, her face puffy, the skin with a crepelike appearance and lines making grooves on either side of her mouth. Compassion touched her, and love. For an instant, she wondered if her mother had loved her father before he died or if there had never been more than duty and the mild fondness between them. Theirs had been an arranged marriage, she knew, but they had created several children between them. She hoped there had been more.

"*Maman?*"

Her mother stirred, opened her eyes. "My Juliette, I was just thinking of when you were a girl. You were so sweet in your communion gown and with your crown of flowers in your hair. Such a pure and precious child, really, so very reverent always. And now—"

"Now I am a married woman, *Maman*," she said to ward off anything more in that vein. "I would not disturb you for the world but must speak to you concerning the marriage chest."

"I suppose you think I should hand it over to you now that you are wed?" The tone was querulous, her mother's expression distressed. "I have been thinking about that as well, and I must tell you that I cannot consider this harum-scarum civil ceremony as a binding marriage. No, only vows spoken before a priest and blessed by the holy sacrament—"

"Please listen to me. You will think it reprehensible of me, and I do beg your pardon most sincerely, but I must tell you that I have taken the liberty of looking into the chest."

"*Chère!* You did not, tell me you did not!"

"Indeed, I must. It was my right, even if you had not yet presented the key. You were given it on the day of your wedding, you have told the tale a hundred times. It was always so, you said."

"You were not wed in the church as I was, and my mother and my grandmother before me. You had no right."

"Nevertheless, it is done. And I must tell you, *Maman*, that the chest is empty."

Her mother stared at her while her eyes widened and her mouth dropped open. Then she recovered with gasp. "Impossible! It can't be."

"I do assure you, it is. I thought…I thought perhaps you had taken the things and put them somewhere for safekeeping."

"No. No, I didn't. I wouldn't." Her voice was feathery in her throat and all color had drained from her face. "I must see…must see for myself." She began to pluck at the covers and push at her tray so the chocolate pot rocked on its base.

Juliette reached to save the pot, then picked up the tray and set it aside. "Don't upset yourself, please. There must be some explanation. Perhaps Paulette—"

"Don't say so! Your sister would never commit such a sacrilege, never!" Climbing out of bed, her mother tottered around the end, held to the post for an instant then made for the door that led out onto the gallery.

"Wait," Juliette called, stepping to the armoire and removing a wrapper, the ubiquitous Gabrielle, before running after her. She caught up with her at the door to the salon and put it around her shoulders, then helped her shrug into its sleeves. The fullness billowed around them both as her mother kept walking as if in a trance, heading toward the chest where it sat between the windows. She reached it and put out her hands, plucking at the lock while making small, moaning sounds in her throat.

"Here, allow me," Juliette murmured, and produced the key she still had in her keeping. Turning it in the lock, she threw up the lid.

The scents of old wood, old paper, dust and the ghost of some ancient perfume or powder rose around them. Whatever had caused the smells was gone, however. The chest was just as empty as when Juliette had looked the evening before.

Her mother screamed. She leaned to place her hands on the open edge of the chest and screamed again. Then she sagged to the floor like a starched petticoat left standing on its own. Juliette caught her arm, trying to hold her upright, but she was too inert, too heavy. She went down with her, kneeling at her side, chafing her hand and calling out to her.

"What is it? What have you done?" Paulette cried from the doorway. Still in her wrapper and with her hair flowing down her back, she ran toward them and dropped to her knees on the other side of their mother in a flurry of lace-edged batiste and sliding tresses. Behind her on the gallery, young Gabriel stood with his face twisted as if about to cry.

"I did nothing. It was the chest. She saw that it was empty and—"

"Empty?" Shock spread over Paulette's features. "Oh, dearest God, she will die, she will surely die. You have killed her."

If Juliette had thought Paulette had taken the contents of the chest, and the idea had certainly occurred to her, she was forced to rethink the notion. Her sister appeared almost as horrified as their mother. "That is foolish beyond permission," she said with as much force as she could manage. "I didn't take whatever was in the box. Why should I, when it was mine to see and look after."

"So you say, though I was first to be wed. And it is beyond anything strange that this treasure, safe for decades upon decades, was lost on the day it was supposed to pass to one us."

"Are you suggesting I took it? I discovered it was gone, yes, but who can say how long it's been empty."

"If it was not you, then it was the handsome devil you married. But what else could we expect when you bring such a one into the house."

"More likely, it was your Monsieur Daspit. If he could not make certain of the chest by sweeping you off for a runaway marriage, then he may have decided to take it."

"Or it could have been these hooligans you brought into the house," Paulette said bitterly. "A greater bunch of thieves and sons of thieves I never hoped to see, and why you thought it would be otherwise is beyond me."

"What is this wrangling and commotion?" Valara demanded from the gallery, her deep voice cutting across what Paulette was saying as she caught the shivering Gabriel to her for a swift hug, then ruffled his hair and gave him a small push toward the stairs. "Run down to the kitchen, *mon petit garçon*, and tell cook to give you a sweet biscuit. Paulette, cease scolding like a market woman. And Juliette, tell me at once what takes place here."

Madame Armant, as if roused by the sound of Valara's voice, moaned and tried to sit up. Her face was gray, her cap askew, and a fine line of saliva ran from the corner of her mouth.

"Oh, *Maman*," Paulette whispered.

Juliette, with a quick glance at Valara, waved a hand in the direction of the empty chest by way of explanation. Then with a grim shake of her head, she reached to take the hem of her mother's Gabrielle and wipe her face. She tried to help her to a sitting position, but her mother could aid her so little that it was near impossible. Paulette, silent, almost stricken, reached to lend her strength and together they got her up and settled in the corner of a settee.

"Are you all right, *chère Maman?*" Paulette asked as she hovered anxiously beside her. "Speak to us."

"It's the curse," her mother whispered. "I know it's the curse."

"No such thing," Valara said in bracing tones.

"Oh, but yes. I have failed in my watch over the chest."

One side of her mother's face was stiff, and it was necessary to wipe the saliva from her mouth again. Raising her eyes to exchange a look with Valara, Juliette asked, "A doctor should be sent for, yes?"

"A small stroke, I think, me," the old nurse said with a nod. Turning, she went from the room to find a maidservant to send around to the doctor's town house.

"Oh, *ma chères*," their mother said, reaching blindly for their hands, holding one in each of hers. "I am…so sorry."

Juliette smoothed the thin skin on top of her mother's hand. "Hush now, it doesn't matter."

"But it does. Must make it right, yes. I did wrong to say you might…might come home from the convent. I am being punished. You must go back. You…must."

"Oh, but *Maman*…" The protest was instinctive and from Juliette's heart.

"I should never have listened…listened to Valara. She was wrong, must have been wrong. If I had left it alone…but it must be put back as it was before. That will make everything right."

"But my marriage, *Maman*." Juliette could barely speak for the knot of pain in her throat.

"I told you. Not in the church. Annulment…dispensation…speak to the bishop. You can become a nun…nun again."

"I don't wish to be a nun."

"You must, *chère*. I swore it." Her mother's eyes were imploring, drowning in the tears that crept over her lashes. "You know I gave you to the church."

"But what of me? Don't I matter? Doesn't what I want mean anything?" It was a cry from the heart, with questions that she had asked a thousand times in the night stillness when she had been taken to the convent and shut away from her family.

"It is your destiny, *ma chère*. It is…my word, my honor."

Destiny. Honor. They were only words, but Juliette could feel them closing in on her, caging her in like prison bars. Beyond them lay all the lovely freedom she had found, all the love, the joy and the passion. All the life.

"I can't," she said, her voice breaking.

"You must," Paulette said urgently. "*Maman* swore, and her mind must be put at ease. There is no other way."

Were her mother and her sister right? Oh, but how terrible it was to force this decision upon her when she was torn by the need to know Nicholas's fate. How criminal to let her think she could escape, to let her taste the feast that was making love with him, to dream of their future, their children.

Their children. "What if I am *enceinte?*"

"The child must be given up as it would if you had strayed. There is no other choice."

No choice. To give up her child so it would never know its father as Nicholas had never known his. To give up the family that awaited her with Nicholas, the boys with their endearing ways and smiles, Squirrel so mature and solemn, and Gabriel, little Gabriel. Oh, and Nicholas in the evening, with his eyes burning with desire, and all the things he had still to teach her of love and pleasure.

Was there really no choice?

Must she really give up the man who had been sent by the Holy Mother in answer to her prayer? Must she forfeit the promise of the candle that had flared so brightly, so very brightly, in the cathedral's dim sanctity?

"No," she whispered.

"Juliette, *ma chère*—" Paulette began while her

mother stared at her as if she had never seen her before.

"No," she said more strongly. "Forgive me, *Maman*, but to swear away the life of another person as you did cannot be right since it forces them to pay for your deliverance. I am very sorry to refuse you in this, but I have made a vow as well, pledging my troth to Nicholas Pasquale. He has kept faith with me in this matter of the chest, in spite of everything, and deserves the same in return. I cannot draw back from him now, nor do I wish it. I have a husband and a family, people I care about and who need me. I must make a home for them, with or without the chest and what it may contain, and whether I am really the elder daughter or the younger. Nicholas and I will be married in the church and in the sight of God, just as we were married by the judge at Gretna, and I shall be his wife and no nun. I am a person and deserve to decide my life. This is my choice."

A step grated on the gallery at the open doorway then, Nicholas, stepping into the room, spoke with a lion's purr of satisfaction in his voice. "And I, as Juliette's husband, shall see that she is allowed it."

There was general consternation.

Juliette's mother cried out, then began to sob. Paulette, near to fainting, voice catching in her throat on a whistling gasp, looked around with eyes drowned in incipient tears. Then as another man appeared behind Nicholas, she leaped to her feet and flew to throw herself into the arms of Jean Daspit who was, miraculously, alive. Valara muttered under her breath because the two men and Paulette were blocking the door, while behind her capered Squirrel and Gabriel and all the other boys, yelling out their glee at having their M'sieur Nick restored to them. And behind them up the stairs strode Dr. Laborde, looking perplexed and disapproving and as if half inclined to think he had been called out on false pretenses.

He had not. Madame Armant was decidedly ill, and was soon put to bed with a hot brick at her feet and orders for quiet. Juliette and Paulette, with Nicholas and Daspit at their sides, gathered in the sick room along with Valara to hear what Dr. Laborde had to say. It was a stroke, mild but to be carefully watched, was his learned opinion. Valara, hearing it, cast her eyes up to ceiling and shook her head. The physician was about to administer laudanum to calm the agitation of the patient, manifesting itself now as tearful sobs and slurred speech, when Valara put out a hand to stop him.

"One moment, *Monsieur le docteur*."

"My dear woman—" the doctor began.

"I have something, me, that will do more than your nostrums to bring peace to this lady," the old nurse said with a wise nod.

"Voodoo spells and potions, I expect. I'll have none of them in my sickroom."

"Ah, no, monsieur. It is only the truth served up for all to hear. You permit that much?" The words were polite enough, but her face was stolidly challenging.

"If you must." The doctor snapped his bag closed and stepped aside, but did not put down the bottle of laudanum.

Juliette glanced at Nicholas, then put her hand on his arm in her need to make certain he was really at her side. His attention was on Valara as he covered it with his own, as if he hardly realized what he was doing. The gesture was lacking in husbandly ardor, but had to suffice for the moment. Juliette turned back to the woman who had been her mother's maid and companion before she became her children's nursemaid.

"I am not sorry for what has been done," Valara began, crossing her arms over her full chest. "I have spoken often and often these many years about Mam'zelle Juliette and how she was the firstborn, but madame, her mother, would not listen. She preferred that Mam'zelle Paulette should have first place because she was more like her in spirit, because their hearts and minds called to each other. Juliette, my Juliette, was the quiet one, the little mother, the one who did always as she was told, who smiled and was calm and older than her years. Madame said to herself that she was the perfect *petite* nun and would have it no other way. Then one last time this winter

I tried again, and perhaps Madame's conscience whispered to her. She said maybe it was so, and allowed Juliette to return home from the convent before taking her final vows. Still Madame would not speak what was in her heart, but set her an impossible task while pretending to be fair. She said the daughter who married first should be considered the older and have the family chest, knowing full well Mam'zelle Paulette was almost betrothed. She never thought Juliette would find a husband in time."

"Oh, but Valara…"

The old nursemaid ignored Juliette's protest begun in her mother's defense. "Ah, but Mam'zelle Juliette, she prayed to the Holy Mother and her prayer was answered. Monsieur Nicholas asked her to marry. All was well. But it seemed someone might steal away the chest for what was in it. The chest did not matter, but that which was inside did. It was my heritage, as well as that of all the Armant women alive today."

"Valara, you didn't…" Juliette said, as suspicion sprang up in her mind like a seedling seeking the light.

"Wait, mam'zelle, for I have not done. It is time, I think, for a tale to be told, one I heard as a girl long years ago and have never forgotten. It concerns Marie Therese, the lady who brought the chest to this place from France. She was a beautiful woman, as all women in stories are beautiful.

Many think she was an orphan because she came with others sent by the French king to be brides for men of old New Orleans. It was not so. Rather, she was the daughter of a *petit* noble in France. She had been disowned by her family, put from them in disgrace and sent far away so she need never embarrass them again. And what had she done to earn such treatment? Nothing except to lie with a man without marriage and start a baby. Oh, but that is not so bad, you say—many and many a woman has done the same. But the father of Marie Therese's child was a slave, you see, one who had come from a plantation owned by her father in the West Indies. A mulatto, he was fathered by a white overseer on a housemaid and later sent to be educated in Paris and to keep her father's accounts. When all was discovered, the mulatto went back to the islands in chains, and Marie Therese, with the chest carved by the man she loved, was sent away to marry a stranger."

Madame Armant gave a low moan, but Juliette thought it more from mortification than surprise, as if she had heard the story before and now feared its exposure. Such a secret had been the downfall of more than one family, yet Juliette could find only compassion in her heart for her ancestress, sent away from everyone and everything she knew to live in an alien land with a man who cared only that she was female. And for what, except loving unwisely?

"Poor MarieTherese," she said quietly. "She must have been a strong woman."

"Indeed, for she made the best of what she was given. The new husband was kind and not of a jealous nature. He took her into the country where she gave birth to her baby a girl. This child of Marie Therese was brought her up as a companion to the daughters she had by the man she married. And when Marie Therese died, she gave the chest with the papers that explained all these things to the first daughter by the marriage and swore her to secrecy that her past might never be revealed. And every daughter then added her secrets, the men they loved and were never allowed to marry, the men who loved them but never kissed them except on the hand, the children who were not fathered by their husbands. With the letters and diaries they wrote to calm their sorrows, they added the tokens given to them that they could not display, the fans and shawls, the rings, bracelets and faded bouquets. Treasures of the heart, you see."

Listening, Daspit sighed, then looked at Paulette and smiled. Juliette's sister shook her head. "I didn't dare tell you."

"No," Valara said with a shake of her head. "The women who kept the chest never told anyone, and in time they added their treasures and shut them away. They guarded the secrets of those who went before them until everyone thought there must be something of great worth inside. And so there was, so there was indeed, for what is more valuable than the memories of impossible dreams?"

Silence was the only answer to that question. After a moment, Valara went on again. "The time arrived when it seemed the chest might be stolen for its so great treasure. So I took the key and braved the curse to remove everything that was inside. I carried it away and kept it safe, hiding it until such time as Madame Juliette might discover that she is the woman of this generation who should and must become the keeper of these precious things."

"Oh, Valara, you might have died," Madame Armant said from her bed, the words slurred and her eyes strained and red-rimmed.

"Ah, no, madame," Valara said, while a slow smile lighted her face. "For I am the eldest daughter of the eldest daughter of the eldest daughter of Marie Therese. The tale of manumission papers in the chest was nothing more than smoke, you see, for my mother and my grandmothers were never slaves but free, always free. Your mother has been the owner of the chest, then, but I am its true keeper."

Juliette, unbearably touched by the pride and the purpose in the face of her old nurse, gave a slow shake of her head. "But you have no daughter."

Valara lifted her chin. "This is so, which is why it is necessary that the proper sister should take and hold the chest now. She and her daughters will be the keepers of the secrets of my grandmothers, as well as her own, for all the time that comes after. I am the firstborn and this is my decision. You, *chère*, are that person."

"Oh, Valara." Beside Juliette, Paulette sighed, then gave a slow nod.

"It is well," the old nursemaid said with a majestic nod of her tignon-covered head. "Some things are meant to be."

It was much later, when the day had worn away and Juliette's mother finally slept with the lines of strain gone from her face and Valara watching beside her, after the boys had all eaten and gone to their beds, after Paulette and Jean Daspit had left the house for a soirée, that Juliette went in search of Nicholas. She found him in the bedchamber that had once been hers but had become theirs in two eventful days. He lay on the bed dressed only in shirt and pantaloons and with his hands clasped behind his head. Though he had been staring at the ceiling, he turned his head as she paused in the doorway.

"Madame Pasquale," he drawled, "I was beginning to think you were avoiding your wifely duties."

She could feel the heat of the flush that rushed to her hairline. It was impossible to say whether he was serious or spoke in jest, but she tried the effect of a smile regardless. "I had things to see to, and I wished to speak to Paulette before she went out."

"Making certain she was not angry with you, I suppose, since you want all the world to be happy. And was she?"

"She is far too relieved to have Monsieur Daspit returned to her. She sends her profound gratitude to you for sparing him, by the way."

"It seemed something less than polite, to kill the husband of my sister-in-law. Besides, I believe he cares for her in his way." He paused. "Are you coming in or going out again?"

She stepped inside and closed the door behind her, then moved to take his frock coat from where it had been tossed across a chair and carry it toward the armoire. "You and Monsieur Daspit seem quite in charity with each other."

"Not unreasonable, if we are to be brothers-in-law."

"Even when he tried to have you killed?"

"You don't want him for a relative, you would rather I rid the family of him?"

She gave him a swift look. "I didn't say that!"

"Oh, *chère*, the look on your face," he said with a low laugh and quick shake of his head. "As if you had only to request it and I would oblige you."

"Wouldn't you?"

"Of course, but I know you would not ask." His warm gaze rested on her face a moment before he went on. "Your sister's betrothed explained the affair at Tivoli Gardens over the bottle of champagne we,

Daspit and myself and our seconds, broached to settle our differences and celebrate our survival. I can tell you, if you care to hear it."

"Yes, please." She smoothed the shoulder of his frock coat before hanging it away. Then she drifted toward the fire where she used the poker to stir the coals to flames.

She heard firsthand then of his involvement in the brotherhood, of Croquère's meeting with Daspit, also Nicholas's late night excursion to remonstrate at sword point with the man known as Old Cables, correcting his treatment of women like Gabriel's mother, who were unfortunate enough to come under his sway. "Daspit," he continued, "followed me to Gallatin Street where he overheard our conversation, including my threat to kill Cables. When I had gone, he visited the man on this matter himself, since it seems Gabriel's mother was his cousin."

"His cousin? But then surely…"

"If you are thinking that he should have had a care for the boy before now, he swears he knew nothing of his existence, doubted it was true up to the trip across the river in the boat. His cousin married out of the schoolroom to a man much older. She was always subject to what some call female disorders and was prescribed laudanum for it. In time, she turned to pure opium, becoming a slave to its effects. Her craving was so strong that she lost all control, went from selling her jewelry to stealing from her husband's pockets while he slept, then leaving the house for the opium dens where she lay with whatever man would pay. Finally, she ceased to come home at all, and her husband put it about that she had gone away for a rest cure. It was during this time, before she came to Gallatin Street, that Gabriel was born."

"Such a terrible thing to happen," she murmured.

"Daspit had lost track of her, but remembered her fondly and visited often with her mother who, alone of all the family, knew the truth about her last months of life and the name of the man who had led her to the drug of the poppy. Old Cables, incensed after his discussion with me, took great pleasure in telling Daspit how he had corrupted his cousin and how she had died. Daspit was so sickened by the man's tale and his gloating that he ran him through."

"Leaving you to bear the blame."

"Deliberately."

"What?" She turned to look at him, her eyes wide with disbelief. "And you let him get away with it?"

"He feared that I meant to use the scandal of his cousin to his disadvantage in my pursuit of you and the chest."

"But you didn't know of it!"

"He didn't understand that, any more than he understood why I had a care for the street boys, Gabriel among them. When I weathered the small storm of Cables's death, primarily because no one cared what became of a Gallatin Street whoremaster—forgive me, but I know no other term which fits—then Daspit thought he would surely have to meet me on the dueling field at some point. Well, or meet me again since he thought I had taken him to task for his mistreatment of his placée, to demonstrate how I could threaten his health and pretensions. He had us waylaid at Tivoli Gardens with the idea of making this future match more even. To his mind, that was imminently fair since he considered I had set upon him unfairly in that midnight duel. It was only this morning that he recognized, finally, that I had never sought to harm him."

"You might have been killed."

"A risk," Nicholas said in dry acceptance, "he was quite willing to take."

"But was his treatment of his placée, his quadroon mistress, so very terrible?"

"It depends on how you look at it. He took a mistress because it was expected, but had no funds to do it in proper style. When the woman became too grasping and expensive, he contrived to frighten her into leaving him. It's the custom to sign over to the placée the house in which a couple has lived when a man parts company with her, you know. Unfortunately, Daspit did not own the property. He preferred to appear the unfeeling monster the woman labeled him to all and sundry rather than admit he had only leased his love nest and could not afford a proper settlement."

"Such a rogue, and this is the man who has married my sister."

"A thorough one, yes." Nicholas's smile was whimsical. "Still, rogues make the best husbands, so it's said, because their wild oats have been sown and they know the value of a quiet life. It's possible Mademoiselle Paulette will be the making of him."

"Let us hope so," Juliette said, and meant it though her voice was tart.

"But what of your own rogue, my love? Did you decide that I could be fashioned into the husband you need after all?"

"As you heard, I gave my pledge and would keep it even as you have."

"Though you thought I could be a thief."

"Never," she said, her eyes widening. "I never thought so."

"You found the chest empty and kept that fact from me. Why would you do that if you didn't think me responsible?"

Now was not the time for evasion or even for pride. Juliette drew a deep, sustaining breath. "I feared you would believe I dragged you into this marriage under false pretenses."

"Gaining more wealth supposedly being my only possible reason for taking you to wife."

"Well, and as a mother for the boys."

"Neither," he said deliberately, "comes within a mile of the truth. But we were speaking as well of your grounds for taking me as your husband. What were they again, other than to be your protector with sword in hand? And instructor in the arts of the bedchamber, of course."

"You were sent to me, or so it seemed."

"Without doubt." He slid off the bed and came toward her with his pantherlike glide. "And that's all?"

"We appear well-matched."

"Excellently, and in every way that matters. Still, I ask if there is nothing more to your choice of me over the joys of your nunnery."

She watched the way he moved and the lethal charm of his crooked smile, felt the thrill of seeing him in bare feet and with no coat to mask the width of his shoulders or strength of his arms. She saw the purpose in his dark, dark eyes, the daring and the heat, and knew a kind of passionate despair.

"Your name," she said. "Pasquale, Easter, is so fitting for a former novice."

"I have a more respectable lineage now according to Blackford, though no name to go with it. Remind me to tell you of it later. For now, I ask again why you decided to take me as your husband in Gretna."

"You could have released me later," she said in a desperate bid for some vestige of dignity, "and might have if you had any respect for the traditions of the veil."

"But I have none, not where you are concerned. You are not for the church but for me, all your lovely principles, yielding ways and sweet, sweet passion. I will fight the guardians of heaven and all its archangels, sword in hand, for the honor of being your wedded husband. You are my life, my hope, and all the conscience I will ever need, and I love you beyond my ability to express, and will for all the days that are to come—and beyond them to all the days there will ever be in our narrow little world."

"Nicholas..."

He took her hand, lifted it to his lips then went to one knee before her with his effortless grace. "There will never be another woman in my heart or in my bed, this I swear on the hilt of my sword and by the Holy Mother who brought us together. And if you cannot say the same, then say nothing, but only let me love you until you no longer repine of that holiest of bridegrooms for whom you were intended and allow me to take a small corner of his place in your heart."

"I did that," she said, kneeling in her turn and carrying his hand to her cheek, "on the day you appeared before me in front of the cathedral and spoke to me as none had dared in more years than I could remember. But it was no corner of my heart you made your own but all of it. I married you for love, Nicholas Pasquale."

He gathered her up then and surged to his feet. Standing with his legs spread and the bed in front of him, he said, "We will be married again at the cathedral."

"Yes. *Maman* will insist."

"As do I." The words were strong and deep. "No tie can be too strong after this day of wondering whether you would ever be my wife again after last night."

"Last night?" She touched the pulse that throbbed in the hollow of his throat, fascinated by the deep V of skin that was usually covered by his cravat.

"I was not exactly gentle, or considerate."

"Oh. Last night. I think I look forward to being your wife in the days to come, particularly because of last night. I think, too, the Turkish ottoman must go with us when we move into our new house."

"So it shall," he said, his voice a little husky, "or I will buy you one exactly like it."

"In the meantime…"

His arms tightened around her and his voice was not quite even as he said, "In the meantime, if you don't feel that we are truly wed, then—"

"Then what?" Her gaze as she lifted it to meet his was as innocent as she could make it.

"We could wait until we have the blessing of that sacrament."

"I am your wife now," she said, grasping his shirt

collar and pulling it so his head was drawn down toward her waiting lips, "and I don't feel at all in need of things sacred to make it more acceptable."

It was on a bright and lovely Saturday not quite two weeks later that Juliette and Nicholas entered St. Louis Cathedral at the head of their bridal procession. Juliette wore creamy white brocade and a veiling of Alençon held on her hair by clusters of pink China roses. Nichols was outrageously handsome in a morning coat of blue superfine over a cream brocade vest and gray pantaloons. Behind them came Madame Armant, leaning heavily on the arm of Jean Daspit but upright and smiling. Paulette walked on her other side, and behind them came Squirrel holding Gabriel's hand, and all the other boys after them, all of them proud in their new clothes made especially for them by Nicholas's tailor and with their hair neat and slicked down with liberal amounts of Nicholas's spice-scented pomade. After the boys came Gavin Blackford, in the guise of guardian of the boy's manners though in reality as half-brother to Nicholas, and behind him trailed a multitude of aunts, uncles and cousins. In the rear walked the other sword masters, Rio, the conde de Lérida, and his Celina with their two little ones in their arms; Caid O'Neil and Lisette with little Sean Francois, the most recent addition to the circle of swordsmen, the Kentuckian Kerr Wallace and, finally, bringing up the rear with Croquère, Pépé Llulla, Gilbert Rosière and a half dozen other denizens of the Passage.

All was quiet for some moments except for the solemn intoning of the priest and smothered sniffling of Madame Armant. Then the church bell in its crumbling steeple began to ring out in clanging joy. Nicholas and Juliette, with eyes only for each other, left the church between an honor guard of small boys and under an archway of crossed swords.

And as they passed the prayer candles on their ancient, wax-and-dust-encrusted stand, the light of one taper flickered on its wick, dancing over the face of the Holy Mother nearby so her lips appeared to curve in a smile. Then it flared hot and tall on its waxen spear, leaping higher, burning brighter than all the rest.

MILLS & BOON

Historical

On sale 6th July 2007

Regency

DISHONOUR AND DESIRE

by Juliet Landon

Caterina Chester is *outraged* at the thought that she should marry! Yet Sir Chase Boston, for all his impeccable manners and charm, reveals an unexpected and undeniably exhilarating wild streak that taunts and teases her. She has kept her passionat nature tightly confined. Now it seems that this most improper husband may be the only man who can free her!

Regency

AN UNLADYLIKE OFFER

by Christine Merrill

Esme Canville's brutal father intends to marry her off – but she won't submit tamely to his decree. Instead, she'll offer herself to notorious rake Captain St John Radwell and enjoy all the freedom of a mistress! St John is intent on mending his rakish ways. He won't seduce an innocent virgin. But Esme is determined, beautiful, and very, very tempting…

Regency

THE RAKE'S REDEMPTION
by Georgina Devon

Miss Emma Stockton didn't welcome Charles Hawthorne's improper attentions. But there was something about him – and his touch – that made her shiver with pleasure. Could he change his ways to become worthy of a lady's hand in marriage?

THE ROMAN'S VIRGIN MISTRESS
by Michelle Styles

Lucius Aurelius Fortis is rich and respected. But his playboy past could come back to haunt him if he cannot resist his attraction to beautiful Silvana. And in the hot sun of Baiae their every move is watched…

MIDNIGHT MARRIAGE
by Victoria Bylin

Dr Susanna Leaf knew that Rafe was a powder keg of unpredictability and wore his secrets close. He compelled her in ways that reminded her she was a woman. And *that* – more than anything else – made him dangerous.

Medieval LORDS & LADIES

COLLECTION

VOLUME ONE
CONQUEST BRIDES
*Two tales of love and chivalry
in a time of war*

Gentle Conqueror by **Julia Byrne**

Lisette knew there was little she could do to resist
her Norman overlord – but she was determined to try.
Her delicate beauty belied her strength of character,
and her refusal to yield won Alain of Raverre's respect.
Now the courageous Norman knight would have
to battle for Lisette's heart!

Madselin's Choice by **Elizabeth Henshall**

Travelling through war-torn England, she needed a
protector. To her horror, the haughty Lady Madselin
was escorted by an arrogant, rebellious Saxon!
Edwin Elwardson's bravery and strength soon
captivated her. Yet could Madselin defy her
Norman upbringing and follow her true desire?

Available 6th July 2007

Medieval
LORDS & LADIES

COLLECTION

When courageous knights risked all to win the hand of their lady!

Volume 1: Conquest Brides – July 2007
Gentle Conqueror by Julia Byrne
Madselin's Choice by Elizabeth Henshall

Volume 2: Blackmail & Betrayal – August 2007
A Knight in Waiting by Juliet Landon
Betrayed Hearts by Elizabeth Henshall

Volume 3: War of the Roses – September 2007
Loyal Hearts by Sarah Westleigh
The Traitor's Daughter by Joanna Makepeace

6 volumes in all to collect!